Scarlett Wolfe
and her
Mythical Mysteries
Book One

A TALE FROM THE BRANCHES OF YGGDRASIL

DETECTIVE DEATH

DARIUS EBRAHIMI

MYTHICAL BANDIT BOOKS
San Francisco

ISBN: 979-8-9864801-3-8 paperback
ISBN: 979-8-9864801-4-5 ebook

First paperback edition 2023

Edited by Sandra Young
Cover Art by Cherie Chapman/Chapman & Wilder

The text of this book is set in Garamond.

Published under
Mythical Bandit Books
San Francisco, California

Visit dariusebrahimi.com

For Maggie

ONE

I EAT A BAD APPLE

I was enjoying a peaceful sleep when I was summoned to kill someone.

A brick fireplace extinguished, the amber glow remaining without flame. Light snuck across oak floors. As if suffering the first freeze of winter, the room's only photo-frame of a summer meadow greyed. The five-pronged ceiling fan stopped. But the tendril of light twisted and a whirlwind splintered the circular coffee table, shards skittering across the confines of the small living room. It wouldn't be called a living room for long. Everything drained dry of color, except where light twirled at the center of the silent room, solidifying like red-hot steel dunked into cold water, transforming into bones and flesh and sinew and ichor.

Into me.

My face once lined temples. My hand rewrote history books. My bright grey eyes twinkled like a star between storm clouds, leading desperate, wet wanderers to safe harbor.

Mortals called me a god. After all, that was what daeva once meant.

But, alas, people called me other things now.

The youthful man in a comfy-looking leather lounger who'd watched my entrance only called me by a single startled scream. Rather rude. This was a subdued entrance—lightbulbs had burst, an ivory mug had shattered and spilt its contents over laminated wood floors, and the echo of thunder now rippled the coffee that pooled across sealed-over cracks.

Even in sweatpants and a loosely-fitted plaid pajama top, the mortal's bones trembled more than the liquid. I paid him no mind, dusting soot I'd accidently gathered off my pressed white shirt and taking another first breath, filled with the smell of coffee and smoke. I'd arrived old and silver-bearded, a comforting presence. I didn't come to startle the man.

Regardless, accidents happen.

A crisp apple rolled from the man's hand. Orange artificial light peeked through slits in the shades, showing the red orb tumble as if in still-frames—leaning over the edge of a rounded armrest, plummeting, and then rolling over the sooty floor.

The man's wrinkles deepened in similar stages, and he managed a few shaky words. "What are you?"

"Someone who'd loved it if you hadn't dropped that apple. But if you must be curious…" I picked up the once fresh fruit, which clung to ash like humans clung to expectation. I obliged that expectation, filling the room with a fallen-timber boom of a voice. "Mortals call me demon, daeva, and death."

Darkness crackled. Despite my shadows, I was a creature of light; I devoured it like a black hole.

"I am deceptively devious," I said. "But does that mean I am more or less devious than I appear? I tilled the fields for the first settlers of the Indus Valley, felled the Hanging Gardens of Babylon, and rode with Genghis Khan. People worshiped me, until I became the vanquished instead of the vanquisher. I, more than most gods, understand mortality because I am mortality—I am Zarik."

I expected stunned silence, and I got it.

"Any final words?" I asked, drawing closer.

The silence lasted too long. Dry lips? No. My summoning had drained the life from the man, leaving him newly wrinkled and white-haired. He was petrified, but the white of his eyes reddened with struggle.

The Pull—my purpose—was strong. Like a fly caught in a web, the strings around me tied tighter with struggle. I had been summoned for a single reason. My hand touched the man's on the armrest. His fingers were bony; soon, they'd be more so. I gave into the path laid out for me, and the bindings snapped.

The thread of the man's life snapped, too. Unfortunate.

I had the Midas touch, but instead of making things gold, I made them old.

"The quiet type. I like that." I took my hand away and smudged soot from the apple, cleaning a small sliver to crisp red. I shook my head, as if that would shake off the rest of the dirt.

I'd watched the spirit of civilization rising, blazing, exploding, and burning out, leaving lingering embers in ashes and chaos. I'd watched peasants, kings, and now, even gods, aged and fallen.

But it still pained me to see an apple fallen on the floor. Oh, and another man dead.

Logically, his death was not my fault; I was the murder weapon. Still, guilt gnawed at me. Like a scythe, I was supposed to harvest the ready. I wanted people to thrive. But the reality was more complicated.

The fresh fruit aged in my hand slower than the man. I chomped into it with a sweet crunch.

The Pull that had summoned me here was served, and I waited to return to the void, as had happened the last few times. Leaning against the lounger, dead man still sitting in it, I appreciated the quiet company as I would soon share a not-all-that dissimilar fate.

This time had been better than most. No pleading, no crying. A real fire. A few moments of peace.

But as the moments wore on, I grew impatient. There shouldn't have been anything keeping me here.

I could try the old standby of counting sheep, but when I imagined them, they were always old and had difficulty jumping over the fence. Instead, I counted bites of the aging apple. The peace and quiet of a pleasant meal would leave a lovely aftertaste for my dreams.

A knock on the door.

"Unfortunate timing," I said to the vacant man next to me. "Dead men don't open doors."

Another knock. And although the apple was done, I was still here.

"Not my problem," I assured myself and tossed the apple core onto the dead man's lap.

A louder knock, rattling the door as my entrance had.

"I guess dead men do open doors." Reluctant, but tired of the persistence, I studied the man in the chair. Even with the darkness, I remembered the man well enough to copy him before he became white-haired and dead. A sharp face, curly hair, and hatred in his still-staring eyes, which I didn't copy.

The change was draining, but the feeling of frustration got me through. Whoever brought me back, I both hated and loved at this moment. The apple was delightful, but dealing with this man's nosy neighbors was not quite as sweet.

In the form of my victim, I looked through the peephole.

A wall of scarlet. Droplets slipped on the surface and gathered speed together—an umbrella.

This was not an angry neighbor. The exterior walkway was covered and dry between the apartments, and no one next door would bring an umbrella to yell at a neighbor unless they planned on hitting them with it. But then, it wouldn't be wet. I mean, that could be part of the fun; wet umbrellas were heavier and more painful, but mortals were not usually so imaginative.

I undid the latch and held the door ajar, ready to slam it. "Can I help you?"

The umbrella spun out of the way and revealed a curious woman in a white jacket with black zipper pockets. "Did you hear thunder?"

"It's been raining."

"But not storming," she said.

There was also a puddle at the door to my right. She was looking for something. Or someone.

I frowned. "You're all wet."

Her auburn hair was slicked together in thick strands, framing a keen face. "As you said, it rained."

"And you have an umbrella."

"I jumped in a puddle." She had such a genuine smile. The statement seemed perfectly normal, at least to her.

"Did you jump headfirst?"

"Once you jump in a puddle, what's a little rain going to do?"

I grinned. "Help you catch your death."

"We all catch our death eventually."

"Huh?" Usually I was more articulate, but I was caught off guard by her bluntness.

"Your mouth's going to collect rain hanging open like that." Sarcasm dripped out of her like the water from her hair to the concrete floor. "What's the matter with you?"

"Me?"

"No, the person right behind you."

I almost looked back to check if the dead man had gotten up. Gods and fools were not mutually exclusive, but I liked to think I was not usually a fool. "You're the one who's soaking wet."

"And I can dry off inside." She was genuine as a summer day, but there was a complexity like clouds gathering behind mountains.

Did "I" know this person? It didn't seem like the dead man was expecting company. One apple, one mug, and nothing left out in the kitchen. My appearance definitely surprised him.

"You'd make the room wet," I said. "It's better to talk here."

Her eyes narrowed. "What about the thunder?"

"What thunder?"

"So, you didn't hear any thunder?"

"There might've been." Thunder sometimes accompanied the arrival of a god, but she couldn't know that, nor would I ever say it. "Does it matter?"

"It makes all the difference in the world." She set her umbrella, open, down by the door. "Are you Izak Cayne?"

I really should've found out the dead man's name. But I reasoned the woman would not bluff me with a fake name. I responded with sarcasm and plausible deniability. "You figure?"

"And you're alive?" she asked.

"So far." I was rather hoping I'd pop out of existence then. Would've given her quite the scare.

"That's all I wanted to know." She closed the umbrella and walked off.

"You realize that was a weird question," I said after her.

"Weird questions are my job." She was halfway down the hallway.

I followed a few steps out the door. "Your job?"

"I'm trying to solve your murder."

"What?" Few times had I been this confused. There was that laughing turnip, but that was a story for another time. This was more like the time someone hit me with a lamp, thinking I was a genie.

"Izak Cayne's a murderer," she sung as she turned the corner.

If I was Izak Cayne, I probably would've chased after her for singing such slander in public. Instead, I smiled. I wasn't Izak.

Although I would be glad to kill a murderer, how could I take her word? What proof was there to ease my guilt? No. I shouldn't feel guilty for being used.

The last words I heard from her was, "I'll see you later."

"Goodbyeee," I said with my cheeriest tone.

I looked from this second floor walkway and adjusted to the foggy world. Elements mixed like a watercolor—rain was illuminated by fire and the earth connected with the sky.

Skyscrapers ascended higher than mountains gods once ruled from. Lights—beautiful, boundless lights—bounced back-and-forth between buildings. The clouds were a neon haze, and clear color echoed in puddles of freshly fallen rain. The crisp smell of the storm flowed like streams in the streets, water cascading into sewer grates, which glittered gold with the sparkling lights of a glorious city.

This was different than I remembered.

I felt dim. A being of light was less bright in a brilliant world, and this was the worst sort of light—empty calories.

A thunderbolt. The flash overtook color. A skyscraper devoured it.

Then, a familiar *boom* gave me heart. The woman must've been crazy; there was already thunder before my arrival, unless this happened to be the first natural strike.

Pondering my next move, I headed back into the apartment and closed the door behind me. The first step had to be hiding the dead body. Of course, I could go the godly route of spurning consequence, but I believed in consequences—I was one.

As the dead man waited on my judgment, his hands were tight with anticipation. I noticed a piece of paper clenched within his palm.

An idea came into my head, whispering like midnight wind. Naturally, fire was the spark.

But I couldn't let this paper burn with the rest. Not without seeing what was so important to the man that he'd hold on to it during his death. To be honest, even now he wasn't keen to give it up. I pried at his fingers, and once I broke it free, I unwrinkled the crinkled page best I could.

On the back, there were maddened scribbles. The handwriting was atrocious, but I made out a couple of items associated at the top. "Ivy – Phoenix". "Lurk – Demon". As the scrawl descended, the phrase, "Sort of colorful" was repeated enough times for me to make it out after about the fifth iteration. The bottom was a dense mess, but I discovered that the words were colors.

"Ruby". "Jade". "Hazel". "Scarlet".

"Scarlet" was underlined three times.

Thinking about it, the woman's umbrella might've been candy-apple red. Besides, it was just an umbrella.

I flipped the paper, only to find a map, meticulously detailing the city, an "X" over a building called "The Root", with a note that said, "It's here". I recognized the city's layout enough to know where The Root was, even if I didn't know what its purpose was. I had my guesses, but those guesses had to wait until I took care of this crime scene. Although I was only a murder weapon, I'd rather the evidence didn't lead back to me.

From the embers of the fireplace, I poked and prodded until the faint crackling of coal caused flickering flames to overcome the silence of the deathly room. My nature sought to take the flame, and the hushed whispers of kindling sounded like the echoes of gods long lost. Grabbing a log from a surprisingly untouched idyllic pile beside the fireplace, coarse grain dried at my touch. I dipped the log into the flames, and the edges of bark began to smoke, the slivers crawling up the stone chimney and into the dazzling electrical world outside. I dropped the fuel for the fire. A plume of ash and firefly-cinders escaped the twilight carbon and brushed my newly transformed face.

I was no longer Izak Cayne. Instead, I changed into one of my normal guises, a handsome man I once knew with a face like a barn owl—a smooth face with a widow's peak hairline, big eyes, and a thin, long nose.

The fire was raging now. Big, boisterous flames licked the stones, casting crests of blackening char on the confines of the fireplace.

I stuck my hand in, encased as if in a feather pillow. Withdrawing a burning log, I waved the sparkling wand around the room. The painting of a meadow curled with heat before bursting into a wildfire and the lounger smoked like a funeral pyre. As the room began smoky songs of destruction, I tossed a burning log by the bits of the broken wood table and grabbed a white jacket by the door before leaving to the foggy future outside.

Despite why I was back and why I had no Pull, I had one answer.

I was reborn at the perfect time to forget why I killed Izak Cayne, who the woman was, what the maddened scribbles meant, where the map led, and now I could focus on the most important question—how would I get my next apple?

That, at least, was my own purpose.

TWO

I STAR IN A LOST MOVIE

OF course, curiosity got the best of me. Struggling for direction, I couldn't help but follow the map.

That was harder than I anticipated. Although I did not know what mortals called this mazelike place now, the city had embraced larger lands and people. I was looking for The Root, but towering buildings blocked my view and distracted me with colors. A few human generations must've passed. After millennia, time distorted—the busy age of the Black Death seemed recent, but getting hooked watching a daytime soap opera on TV with one of my previous victims seemed like ages ago. Yet, this was not the earth I once roamed, and this was different than the village that was once here, which I'd known as Paradaeza.

Life invented in peculiar ways. People's clothes were digital like the screens. A pixelized rose on a black blouse. Unoriginal. A Poodle pranced in a video loop on a sweater. Sappy. Except for a few outlandish choices like a man with a star-scape moving at super speed on his pants, most didn't make bold choices and were merely mirrors of the world around. I blended in, my white jacket reflecting a cobalt lantern hanging outside a fresh-smelling bakery and then tinting red, as if embarrassed, by the advertising signs that poured light down even on a cloudy day.

Modernity was always magic to me. Wistful, I walked over wet sidewalks running like grey Scandinavian rivers, the reflections of a rainbow city muted in stilled puddles. Yet, humanity remained undimmed, outshining technology in sporadic splashes. A cheerful smile. A hearty laugh. A parent snatching up their child before they jumped into a puddle. Even a scarlet umbrella opening over a stranger, which saved them before a slumping awning could drench them.

I turned, but the umbrella disappeared. That was definitely scarlet, not candy-apple red.

The Pull was back like a loose knot, which slipped and let me go. I shivered at the odd feeling, and my stolen jacket responded with its own radiated heat. In the chilled world, it was like waking up in a warm sleeping bag, where only exposed skin felt the brisk air. The contrast was as stark as my new-found freedom, and there were better things to do than follow umbrellas in the rain.

A brief check of the map confirmed I was nearing my destination. The buildings were only getting taller. My chosen face, eager and surprisingly youthful, cooled as the misty air sprinkled upon the outers of my essence during my search.

As the storm subsided for the moment, I lowered my hood and found what I was looking for.

In the distance, a building outlandish enough to represent most gods' egos sprouted into the clouds, obscuring the true enormity. That had to be The Root.

The skyscraper weaved like the fabric of time. At first, the building was designed like a single marble column, but as I drew closer, it added the intricacies of Gothic arches and stained glass like a godly architect was going through historical phases by the minute. By the time I arrived, there were sleek curves and glass I would've expected of an advanced masterpiece, spiraling upwards. I couldn't tell if the building itself changed or if it was some technological trickery. Yet, the one aspect that remained the same was an enormous screen above a grand, glass entrance that showed ever-changing numbers.

They say there is a price for everything; this financial marketplace meant it. Scrolling along, I saw the price for a one-pound carrot made of one carat diamonds—enough zeroes that my attention turned to all the times accurate pricing would've come in handy—all the bargains I might've inadvertently given when offering what I thought was a mischievous deal.

However, I still didn't see anyone willing to put an exact price on life.

Although my search for that price was fruitless, The Root did provide the reference point I needed. I headed towards the "X" on the map, and when I found it, there was no treasure, only a brick storefront and a few callboxes to different residences.

The first-floor shop had no flashing lights; instead, paper advertisements lined the windows so thick it blocked the light from entering. The colors were dulled with age, but still, bright blues and yellows blared.

A sign read, "Servius'sss Sinema Supersenter". A pudgy banana-like snake curled around the letters.

I hoped it was more than it appeared.

A silver bell over the door rang as I entered. The aroma of rain was swept away by a gust of popcorn-flavored wind. The buttery smell dragged me into an aisle between black shelves on worn-blue carpets. Shelves were six high with rectangular video cases, standing just high enough to know there were more aisles beyond. A red sign above the aisle said "Drama", but I only saw pictures of people staring at me from the mostly bland covers. Yet, with the bright lights, savory smells, and massive variety, the movie store was a whimsical antique compared to the outside world.

I followed a sound towards the back wall, where a series of screens above the shelf showed the same video. Although I had seen a few movies—mostly horror films in dark theaters where I scared the unlucky out of their seats to somewhere else entirely—this wall was devoid of any surprise. Flour would've had more flavor. The same movie was copied on the shelves like wallpaper.

Of course, there were extraneous explosions on the cover—some sort of action-romance-thriller that wouldn't make sense without explosions.

The title?

"Dangerous Lovers II: Annihilation - 'This Time, It's Not Personal'"

Apparently, the original was personal. Despite my cynicism, I was pulled to a case in the middle of the bottom shelf and picked it up. Cheap plastic bent under my tensed fingers. The emotional actors on the cover had no more choice than I usually did, and I'd been stuck to a script for too long.

The door chimed as someone else entered. And, from another part of the store, a man said, "Hello, Scarlett."

There was no response, except for maybe a nod I couldn't see. When I rounded the corner to the counter, there was only the man.

Servius, as his nametag said, gave me a curious look, as if appraising an antique. His portly belly was more rounded than the tapes he was tinkering with, strings of film spinning through a series of machines. They whirred and whined. "Did you find the movie you were looking for?"

I still had the case I'd picked. "I was just browsing."

"Mmm. Looks like it." He sounded skeptical.

"I'll keep looking." My forms were supposed to be trustworthy. I retreated into the aisles, desperate to escape.

I needed a new direction. There was only a dead man's note leading me here. For all I knew, it could be a map to a rare video.

Instead of getting my meal, I was trying to solve a mystery I shouldn't care about. The Pull didn't bring me here; it was only keeping me from the void, but pulling nowhere.

"That's a good movie," a woman said, arriving at my side sneakier than rust.

It was the woman who'd confronted me at the dead man's apartment. Scarlett, apparently. That name couldn't be a coincidence.

I almost changed into a bird and took flight, but I feigned calm. I was in a different form now. "Is it?"

"Didn't you read the back?"

"Of course," I lied.

"What's it about?" She asked with a smile.

"Uh..."

"Exactly, it doesn't matter. It's a pile of trash." She pulled a copy of *Dangerous Lovers II* from under her arm. "But trash is the best. Besides, Servius is nice to new customers. He'll give it to you for free."

"How can you tell I'm new?" I stayed committed to the act.

"You seem out of place," she said, pausing and staring. "Did you just come from a funeral?"

A streaker would've been jealous of how fast I almost dropped my disguise. I kept it together. Barely.

"No." I paused, thinking what to say next. I was flabbergasted. She had to stop being so close to the truth eventually.

"Not a funeral?" she said. "Maybe a house fire."

A composed smile. "You're something else."

"That's a nice compliment. What's your name?"

"People call me Zee." I could've invented a new name, but there was no need. I looked nothing like Izak Cayne, and there was no reason she would think I was a god.

I picked up the first movie I saw without bothering to look what it was and left the one she suggested behind. She followed me to the counter.

Servius' smile turned sly. "Did you change your mind?"

Scarlett put one of the copies of *Dangerous Lovers II* on the counter. "I was holding it for him."

"You should probably get both," Servius said.

I finally noticed the title of the second movie I'd picked: "The Making of Dangerous Lovers II: Annihilation- 'This Time, It's The Personnel'"

I asked, "There's a documentary on it? Was it a big hit?"

"A big budget." Servius took note of the movies. "The return time is seven days."

"I don't get to keep them?"

"These films are pieces of history. Worth preserving. I can't have *you* losing them. At least, not without paying for it."

Scarlett said from behind me, "Can you put these five on my tab? I'm in a rush."

"You still owe me for the other fifty," Servius said to Scarlett.

"Did you say fifteen?" A plump-cheeked smile. "I thought it was less."

Servius rolled his eyes. "See you tomorrow."

"Count on it. Have a nice day, Zee." Scarlett tucked the videos under her arm. "Oh, and you might want to dust that ash off your jacket." She walked off.

The smudge on my white sleeve was undistinguishable to the dust in the store. Yet, somehow, she knew it wasn't.

"You know what, I'll let you rent them for free," Servius said to me as Scarlett left the store with a ding, her shadow going past the window's posters. "As long as you return it."

It would also be free if I didn't return to the store.

"Sure," I said, completely certain I would not be back. It wasn't malicious—I just had better things to do. "Thanks."

I left the store in a hurry, just catching a glimpse of the bright umbrella before Scarlett turned the corner.

Street after street, I followed Scarlett like a copperhead snake through autumn leaves. When she turned from main avenue and out of the crowds that gave me cover, I was exposed. Unlike a copperhead, I'd be a little more noticeable.

Scarlett turned into a deserted garden, and it was too risky to follow her through it.

I wasn't worried. It just required a little thinking on my feet. I kept walking and turned into an alley, where there were only a few black trash bags stacked together, puddles trapped in the plastic folds.

Wanting nothing more than to leave the woman behind, I had to force myself to stop—she knew something about Izak. Maybe she knew something about why I was back and what kept me awake.

Following Scarlett in this form was too difficult—humans were too clumsy. Flying after her was a good solution, even if changing forms would require a chunk of energy. I was a god, but I could not fly without wings. I was not a god of the elements; they gave the rest of us such unrealistic expectations.

Call it undignified, but I had to think small. Yet, I couldn't help but have a flair for the dramatic—a monarch butterfly. What better representation for aging? Not to mention easy camouflage in colorful lights and natural parks.

I placed the videos with the rest of the trash so they'd have company. However, I kept the map and jacket, compressed into my form. The map might be important, and the heat from the jacket was just pleasant.

Going from a biped to an insect made my blood run cold. As my eyes went kaleidoscopic in a city that was already bewildering, I saw more than double. And as much as I would love to describe every detail of my hankering for nectar, veins pulsing through unfurled wings, and wiggly body, I won't mention tasting through my feet. I'll avoid describing what licking sidewalks is like. Except, it must be said—cities taste nasty. There were too many feet on my feet. Some covered by rubber and some bare. Bare? Ugh… no, I won't go on.

I took off towards the garden and Scarlett.

Flapping my wings was not so different than strapping fake wings to a human's arms, except I didn't fall off cliffs. I soared over gravity-bound beings, fluttering with the wind. Flying was liberating, and I would've liked to chase the sun or frolic among the garden's flowers.

Luckily, Scarlett's umbrella was like a giant flower, which kept me on track as she headed out of the garden. With me soaring above, we headed away from the city center and to more leisurely streets. Night fell over brick buildings, some of which had been repurposed into bars and restaurants, where Scarlett finally stopped.

I perched on a warehouse windowsill three floors up across the street from Scarlett, who sat at a patio table for one. She ordered a fizzy drink, observing people through the bar's window like an aquarium, but not engaging.

Every once in a while, I could swear she veered her gaze directly at my perch. As if she saw exactly what I was.

Some mortals could see gods. They were rare and often considered crazy. Side effects included fear, awe, and burning eyes. And that's one sort of burn eyedrops can't help. I've seen humans try.

Not all mortals suffered these effects, and those were the bothersome ones. I had to know for sure. If Scarlett was one, it would explain a lot.

There were many ways to determine such things. Dropping the disguise. Asking politely. Torture. But I decided on a different idea.

A man and woman were conversing in front of Scarlett.

The woman was like a priestess of old. Tattoos weaved down her arms, crisp clean white ink highlighted with a crimson weave on her left arm and a forest-green streak on her right. Jewelry jangled over both wrists. Bracelets, necklaces, and even charms were tied in her seeress-knot hair. Mystic. The colors were like blood and life—a person that would've fit more in deep forest covens than this bar.

The man, on the other hand, was a perfect fit for his surroundings. Pudgy, overly white teeth, and a chin longer than his hair. He was a man to be passed and forgotten. Simple to copy.

That's what mattered to me.

I dipped down into my new favorite haunt—a deserted alley between buildings. There, I changed back into a human, taking the form of the stranger I'd observed. Or, at least, close enough to be mistaken for him. Changing my eye color to match the man's boring brown made me lightheaded, but mischief gave me strength.

Rather than the excitement I felt, I portrayed as normal a walk as the man's appearance. Strolling to the bar's patio, I breezed past my unsuspecting target. I did a double-take and feigned shock, doing my best impression of discovering my twin, or clone, as it happened to be.

"What are youuuuuuuu doing here?" I asked the man I had copied.

The man was taken aback. "What?"

"You're stealing my identity again?" There was a bit of over-drama in my voice. The point wasn't realistic acting. We'd get to the point soon.

"What are you talking about?" the man asked.

His companion, the seeress, looked entertained.

I kept on the show. "Are you saying there are three people that look like me now?" I drew close as a mirror. "This room's only big enough for one of us."

"It's a street," Scarlett said in the background. I think I was the only one who heard her.

"You think you can keep impersonating me?" I asked.

The man was still confused. I had to try harder.

I pointed my finger in the man's face, spittle flying as I yelled. "Identity theft! Thief! Liar!"

My angry acting was spot on. I grabbed the man, pulling him to the ground and rolling over the hard brick patio. As we wrestled, I said whatever ridiculous exclamations I could to cause chaos.

I pushed. "You cashed my paycheck!" I rolled. "You slept with my wife!" I pulled. "You stole my dentist appointment!"

Twirling and rotating and wrenching like an alligator and a python fighting, I completed my shell game, hoping no one would be able to keep track of who was who. But if Scarlett could see gods, this would be all too obvious.

Shadows descended on the man, seeress, and myself.

Before my plan could be set into play—an elaborately hilarious hostage situation, I was interrupted with the worst outcome.

"Iris," Scarlett said to the tattooed woman. "This is the case I was talking about. I appreciate your help, and we'll catch up later."

What surprised me most was that the woman nodded, unaffected by the shadows that I tied around her.

The seeress asked, "What about Rodrigo?"

"I'm sure he'll be fine," Scarlett said.

Iris motioned for Rodrigo to follow, but he was still restrained by my shadows.

"Let him go," Scarlett said to me.

Baffled, I complied and stood there, wondering what had just happened. Rodrigo and Iris walked away, seemingly unphased by meeting a god, while the rest of the patrons barely took note of the chaos—besides a bar spat, there really hadn't been anything.

"How did you know…?" I asked, trailing off before I could say what I was.

"Rodrigo can see the true forms of myths and gods," Scarlett said. "He's usually a bit more confrontational, but he saw a god, not your copy of him. But don't worry, I can't see your godly form. I knew for another reason—you copied Rodrigo almost perfectly, but you got his nose wrong. I broke it and it hasn't been straight since. I can see why you'd think it is from afar, though."

There was one weakness in my plan—someone who paid too much attention. And the man who could see me. And the seeress who was unaffected by my powers. It seemed I'd run into a hive of oddities the likes of which I hadn't seen since the fall of great empires.

"I've got something to show you about Izak Cayne," Scarlett said.

She caught my interest. That's for sure. I'd humor her.

We walked down the block, her red umbrella swinging and twirling randomly. The divide between trendy bars and restaurants next to worn-down buildings that hadn't been repurposed was striking. We crossed old cobble to a warehouse, which had been left to rot. I supposed it added authenticity to the industrial feel of the redeveloping neighborhood.

Unlocking a padlock, dust escaped. She led us inside, pulling out a matchbook. Above, the roof had been eaten away, leaving a starless dusk sky, glowing puffs of clouds reflecting the prismatic city in the distance.

As I looked up, I stumbled over a few tubes on the floor. I did say a human form was clumsy. This one, especially.

"Be careful," Scarlett said, striking a match as she walked.

While she was distracted, I let my eyes change back grey, transforming from the cloned Rodrigo to my more sustainable—and handsome—owl-faced man.

I picked up the tube I'd kicked. It was peppermint-striped, with a wood stick and fuse. "Fireworks?"

"A few," Scarlett said as she lit a few candles sitting on wood boxes.

The light illuminated a warehouse filled with boxes labeled, "Danger, Explosive".

"Isn't it dangerous to have open flames next to fireworks?" I asked.

"The lights are out."

"That's not the point."

Scarlett shrugged and snuffed the match with a pinch. "There are more dangerous things."

"I do like a bit of danger, but this seems excessive."

"I'd imagine death isn't a concern for you," Scarlett said, leading us to two wood chairs, a projector, and a white canvas screen in a clearing.

"Death is my only concern."

"And my only concern is a different death—the people Izak killed."

I could get behind that. "Not Izak?"

"Did you bring the copy of *Dangerous Lovers II* from the store?" she asked.

"No," I said. "Unlike carrier pigeons, carrier butterflies won't catch on."

"Guess I'll be paying Servius for that. Glad I switched copies with you when you put it down."

"What was in the case I originally picked?"

"A video of a murder," she said. "Izak Cayne had been using myths to kill people. He didn't know what I looked like, but he was trying to track me down, so I hid the evidence in the video store for safekeeping. Few people go in the store, and even less want to see that movie. The chance of anyone picking it up was low, and Servius would tell me if anyone came for it."

"That's very trusting," I said, sitting in the uncomfortable chair.

"I'm Servius' favorite customer." She turned on the projector, which displayed blue light on the screen. "He may seem concerned about money, but he just wants to share his passion with others. To be honest, I don't have time to watch all the movies I rent, but we have fun little banter and it makes him less lonely. I always pay eventually, and sometimes, I get to share a movie with someone like this."

"You often have murder showings?"

"I can't say I've been in this situation before. There's this old superstition that thunder heralds evil and the demonic. I was staking out Izak's apartment when I heard thunder without any lighting. I'd seen something similar before, and it was a sign of something more than a simple myth."

"Demonic?" I hated that word. "I can be summoned like a demon, but if you called me a demon at Izak's, I might've been one. I prefer the other 'd' word—daeva. Thunder sometimes accompanies gods as they return from the void. It can be a good omen."

"I wouldn't have called you a demon. There was less demon in your eyes than Izak when I met you at the door." She smiled. "I suspected it was you, but I had to be sure. I had a hunch I could get you to follow me from Izak's, and Rodrigo finally confirmed it."

"Your hunch is less accurate than the superstition. At first, I wasn't following you, I was following Izak's map."

"A map? Do you have it?"

I handed it over.

She frowned. "How did Izak figure out where it was?" The frown faded with a chuckle. "I suppose even the smallest unsolved mysteries have consequences, even if it's only keeping me up at night. With him dead, it'll be harder to be certain. But I like a challenge. I believe even mysteries outside of what most consider reality still have real answers. Myths. Legends. Gods. I like those cases the best—they're my specialty."

"A detective that deals in the illogical?" I asked. "Without any rhyme or reason, how could you solve anything?"

"There's a rhyme of a reason—the story behind them. People aren't logical, but there's been many great detectives that figured out their stories. Everyone has their own logic, if we can only empathize our way to understanding it." She loaded the film into the projector. "Some call my cases random, but they have their own logic. This case, I call 'The God's Random Act'. I'm still working on the title. But it's been ironically resolved—the murder weapon killed the killer, too. It would be unexplainable without..." She hit play and sat next to me. "More context. Maybe there's a reason you picked that specific case, but I think it's better to show than tell."

On the screen, there was a video taken from a camera in the corner of a temple, overlooking a statue at the center of the room—a stone lion roaring gentle fire, facing a bull with fire burning on its horns. A tour group, judging by their gawking and picture-taking, roamed the ancient marble room. I recognized someone—Izak. He looked as he did before I'd shown up, young and with a cold glint in his eyes. The temple did not interest him; he was like a hawk among pigeons.

The tour guide led everyone on, spitting some nonsense about how this was a temple to a god of life, which was only half right. There was a bull and a lion for a reason. This was a tour I'd been on before, and it used to be a temple of balance.

A woman lingered behind the group, taking another picture without anyone else around. As Izak left the room, he glanced back and I thought I saw a flicker of a smile behind the well-controlled façade.

When everyone else was out of the room, it was like a switch turned off. The light and color on the walls faded. The statues' fires swirled like stars in a galaxy, being sucked into a black hole between the bull and lion.

Thunder boomed.

The woman glanced up from her camera. Smoke and shadow. The woman aged. The woman died.

I killed her. Unlike Izak, it was doubtful she was a murderer.

In the video, I didn't linger. Or even fully materialize. I really was a force of nature. A curse. And now, a movie star.

The shadows, woman, and finally, the video, were gone. My cameo was over.

Scarlett turned off the projector, leaving us in firelight almost like the video. For a moment, no, for an instant, I thought about reenacting the murder video with Scarlett for showing me what I would've otherwise forgotten.

"That's what you meant about experiencing thunder without lightning before," I said, my charming smile gone. I did feel bad for the woman in the video, but I felt worse for the thought I'd just had of killing Scarlett. "Might be a hard mystery to explain to anyone else, though."

"The authorities figured it was a freak accident," Scarlett said. "I suppose they weren't too far off."

"I have a tendency to surprise people. I still don't see how this proves anything about Izak. He's creepy, but the scribbles already told me he's a little crazy."

"Scribbles?"

"On the other side of the map," I said, motioning to flip it over. "Something about a lurking demon. I imagine that's me."

Uncomfortable in the chair and the conversation, I stood.

She inspected the other side of the map and bit her lip harder the further she investigated. "His handwriting is awful." She sighed. "But that's not 'Lurk'—that's 'Gwen'. The name of the woman in the video. This is a list of who he killed and how. Ivy is another woman that ended up dead. Izak was keen on irony."

"I don't see the irony."

She tapped the umbrella on the concrete. "A phoenix—fire—burns ivy. Gwen comes from the word white, and she was killed by darkness."

"I am a creature of light."

"Because you take it," she said.

She had me there. "What about 'Sort of colorful'?"

"A mistake." Her fingers crinkled the paper, but she was careful not to tear it. "That explains how he knew where the video was. I was trying to drive Izak into doing something stupid—or maybe I was just gloating—but that was the clue I gave him on who was after him. My name is said as a color but spelled with two T's."

"Sort of a color," I said.

"Would've been interesting if he had answered the door instead of you."

I crossed my arms. "All this is very good theory, but I'm afraid the blame is not wholly Izak's."

"Whether Izak stabbed Gwen or used you, he's still a killer. Only, he couldn't control what he set loose. He couldn't control a god."

She misunderstood me.

"Gods are not as simple as myths," I said, but for a different reason. "How can you be so sure Izak's death wasn't revenge? Or justice? Someone—multiple people—could've wanted Izak dead."

Blame spread—one person couldn't have enough belief to drag a god out of the void, even if one could keep me from going back. All those who believed in this grey-eyed daeva who liked apples had helped kill Gwen. Yet, whoever else made it possible, Izak was the one who gave me that purpose.

Who summoned me to kill Izak was a different question.

"Wouldn't you want Izak dead?" Scarlett asked, reading my guilt. "He used you. You got your revenge. Or maybe you wanted justice for the woman."

"I've been used for worse," I said. "Not that I would've turned down justice for killing an innocent woman." I tried to read Scarlett, but she was so busy reading me that I only saw my reflection in her eyes. "The way I see it, Izak died one of three ways: an accident, another killer, or you. Maybe some combination of the three."

"I wanted him caught, not dead." Scarlett put the video and map into her jacket pocket. "That's why I went to such lengths to get evidence. You're a death god. In his hubris, Izak summoned you again. Then, he died. Seems simple to me."

Too simple. Too much rested on me. "When I formed, I was pulled to take Izak's life. There was no choice."

"I think you had a choice."

Now she was just being ridiculous. I had no more freedom than a tree does to grow. At first, I could choose where I laid roots, but beyond that, I had to grow towards sunlight. "Think whatever you want. I'm not interested." A half lie—I didn't care what she thought about me, but she was interesting. I learned a long time ago to avoid such people. That's how I survived this long.

"How about this?" She seemed nervous, grabbing her umbrella and knuckles whitening around the curved ebony-wood handle. "You can help me, or you can go back to the void—or worse—there are forces out there that prevent gods from running free."

"I'll take the void."

"I didn't expect you to be so stubborn," she said.

I shook my head. "You know what I am?"

"Of course—a daeva."

"Then you should've known I'd be stubborn."

She was the reason I was still around. She believed in me for a pointless purpose she didn't understand—to help her.

That was the loose strand around me, and I wanted it cut. Yet, a loose string is harder to cut than when taut.

I grinned. "I suggest you forget about gods, especially me. And now that I've satisfied a desire for an answer, if you'll excuse me, I'm going to satisfy a different need and get a final meal."

Mysteries, mortals, and this madness meant nothing to me. I had my fill—besides, who worked hard to solve the death of a murderer? A meal, on the other hand, was enticing. The look on her face as I walked away was pretty priceless, too.

I was glad I'd followed her to get some answers, and now I was just as glad to leave her.

As I left the warehouse, the night was neon. Towers of light in the distance made for a permanent technicolor daytime. I chose a direction and walked among the other wandering souls, hoping to eventually find something I recognized and lead me to the meal I wanted. Directionless, my stroll was filled with daydreams instead of a pullback.

Until I stopped dead. Or rather, I was stopped.

Another man crashed into me. We both still stood upright, and it was my first thought to make him a little less so.

"You're sorry," I said.

The man's pristine long coat and Mediterranean-blue eyes were unimpressed. "I'm sorry?"

"Really sorry." My golden blood flowed instinctually hot with confrontation.

The man was cool. "That was a question."

"Mine wasn't. You're really sorry…." I trailed off. The man smelt of rosewater that made my nose crinkle.

That was familiar. So too, were the eyes.

Whatever remained familiar was mostly dangerous. Godly powers waxed and waned with the fashion of the day, and I didn't want to be dressed for the wrong day. Some gods echoed through the ages. And right now, I was hearing that echo like a siren. I knew this god.

Why did it have to be *this* god?

A thousand flights and fights transformed into a question of transformation. Wings or horns? So many animalistic options, and I liked to keep it fresh. But then again, why transform when my two legs will do?

Four black-clad figures watched the two of us. I took off before they could confront me, weaving between casual mortals along the way. Running was not cowardice when it was the cleverest option—besides, I would've won the fight. So, it was really the other god being the coward for not coming after me.

Except, the god did come after me. I could hear fleet footsteps behind me.

Bravery was worse than cowardice, at least when it was directed towards me

As I darted down the block, I had an idea—I'd give Scarlett what she wanted and show her what messing with gods brings.

Backtracking, I returned to the warehouse. When I burst through the doors, I looked around, but Scarlett seemed to be gone. However, I wasn't alone for long. The god and four mortals arrived after me, and the option was obvious. Time to start some negotiations.

My negotiations didn't involve talking; this time, they involved explosions.

I ran in the darkness, grabbing a candle that was still tinged orange with an ember. If I ever saw Scarlett again, I'd have to teach her fire safety. I only started fires on purpose, but on this occasion, the spark worked in my favor.

One of the voices called after me, "Wait."

I didn't, dropping the candle into a box of fireworks. A perfect distraction.

Instead of explosions, there was silence. A quiet moment of contemplation. Would the fireworks light? Should I put it out? This idea seemed worse and worse as the time burned down.

The god and men found me standing there, expecting bombastic chaos and only getting a puff of smoke.

I glanced into the box, wondering if I should find some tool or utensil to spread the fire around.

The utensil found me first—a knife slicing my arm. A few drops of golden blood spilled, but I barely felt it when there was worse probably coming. Neither could I blame the mortals for trying to stop me from blowing them up. Luckily for the man, the slash was only meant to stop me from reaching back in the box.

I said to the brave man, "A pocket knife? You brought a knife to fight death? I wouldn't cut the string of your life with that."

The other god yelled at the man, "Back away."

The man scrambled in retreat. The knife clattered to the floor, covered with a few drops of golden blood.

There was no reason to be scared of what I'd do. I wasn't going to kill the man—maybe take a few years off his life— but not kill him. The fire could do that. What a tragic accident. In the same way as I devoured light at Izak's, I tried to take the fire from the box, and on its path, the ember caught a wick.

I smiled at the mortal men. "I'd take that advice and run even further."

Pop. A flash of light. Sparks caught other sparks. A shower of fire burst from the box. Further flames spit like static, waterfalling out the first box and into other open boxes.

Quite opposed to the burgeoning chaos, I was calm. The men were understandably more nervous, sprinting for the door. The other god didn't budge, leaving us together once again.

"There's no point, Zarik," the god said.

"What choice do I have?" I asked.

Boom. The box splintered open, sending shards darting past me. A little lull. Then, supercharged red and yellow bits of wood burned in the air like fireflies, ash and smoke lit by faster and faster chains of extraneous explosions. Small, loud ones whistled like tiny birds. Big tubes flew. Bounced. Burst. Others didn't catch by wick, but detonated with a bang, until they simmered into a rushing torrent of fire, so akin to water for an event so scorching, cascading in columns of shimmering sparks.

I turned and ducked through curtains of fire, bathing in white strobes, yellow pops, and sparkling orange whistles. Sneaking through such an orchestra was only a matter of being less noticeable than my surroundings.

Explosions echoed in my chest. Deep chords tickled extremities as much as the heat. Sparklers sizzled and bottle rockets burst and Roman candles cracked.

I found another exit. Unfortunately, I also found the god standing in the hall between me and the door.

Now, I was annoyed.

This god was always in my way. Anger burned hotter than gunpowder. Comet trails of fire bounced off both of us, rebounding rainbow. Altered. Godly. Gleam and gloss, light overwhelmed as the place began to blow.

I set off like a rocket, barging through the god with a blunt blow that was impeccably timed to a particularly hefty blast.

I did say I'd win a fight. It just wasn't the way I thought.

As I looked over my shoulder, the god was on the ground and his mortal hair had caught fire, burning blue as his eyes. Gunpowder winds burst in a shockwave, rushing over me.

The fires fed me, but I could not be greedy. I dove through the technicolor seas and out the door.

Smoke and light gave way to clean night air. As explosions continued, a crowd gathered at a safe distance for the show. No one could avoid such a display, including Scarlett. I spotted her instantly—it wasn't just the bright umbrella, it was her focus on me that stood out. My first concern was to get away.

I blended into the crowd and escaped down one alley, then another. After a few more twists and turns, I stopped a moment, looking back the way I came.

"You changed your mind?" Scarlett asked, appearing behind me. I spun and saw her smile, which was explosive as the fireworks. Somehow, she had cut me off. "You'll help me?"

I thought about changing form and flying off, but I was too tired. "Help you with what exactly?"

Her smile was undampened; if anything, it was buoyed by the question. "Solving little mysteries of the universe. It's what I do—they call me a private detective—but I'm only Scarlett

Wolfe. And you are both the question and answer to these mysteries."

"You summoned me."

"I didn't summon you," she said rather convincingly. "As you said, you're not a demon—you're a daeva. A being of shining light. A positive word in ancient Persian. As Zoroastrianism developed, it became more associated with evil. 'Gods to be rejected'. 'Gods who oppose truth'. But no matter how you spell it—daeva, deva, deity—it still means god. And you know that, Zarik."

"Different sorts of gods. Some of my fellow daevas can be demons." I paused. "If you didn't summon me, why do you know my name?"

"That's my job." She twirled the umbrella and it opened above us. "And because I believe in you."

The first fresh drops of rain bounced off Scarlett's umbrella before they hit us.

Somehow, I could escape a god, but I couldn't escape this mortal, Scarlett Wolfe.

THREE

I SMELL A ROTTEN MEMORY

A new alley offered Scarlett and I refuge. With how often I was spending time in these side-streets, people might one day come to these damp places to worship me. Yet, there was no time to consider such things. Away from my explosive exit, I had to compose myself.

If the god followed, a quick change of form couldn't hurt—except that it would, indeed, hurt. The expectation of pain was sometimes worse than the pain itself. The times of changing from a skeleton to boundless light for fun seemed wasteful. Gravity wore heavy on my shoulders, yet other things might crush me first. A god would not die by a little fire.

Fists clenched like my essence, tightening like a grimace.

My options were simple. It had to be a human form. I had to blend in. A child was an innocent choice, but for how short they were, they stuck out. Even changing form to another man might not be different enough. A woman would be better.

I had a few regular forms, which practice made easier. The one I chose was my favorite, even if I didn't use it often. Maybe the rain was making me nostalgic.

If a raindrop could've timed the distance between my jacket's hood and shoulder, it would've been rightfully confused as the jacket and I shortened a couple inches. My hair unfroze like melting amber, lengthening and then drying dark as a raven's wing. Facial features softened from barn owl to a more rounded snowy owl. Even the wound from the mortal's knife was stitched into fresh flesh with the form change. All that remained the same were my eyes—they were the hardest to change. I had to hide in crowds; if the god saw me well, it wouldn't matter what form I took.

"How do you choose forms?" Scarlett asked with professional curiosity.

In the fuzz between forms, I barely heard. Focusing back into the misty city, her question hit my ears, and I realized my stupidity. The form was fitting, but *that* god might remember the inspiration for this guise. Yet, this woman was so small a part of that god's life and so large of what I liked to forget about mine. Another transformation would take too much. My warm blood was thin and weak. Any more, and I might not be able to pull myself back together. Even though memories and emotion made for an easier change, I was spent.

"I choose forms on a whim, which whirl one to another like a tumbleweed on the wind."

Scarlett stared, doubt peering past my nonchalance. "What's so special about this whim, then?"

There was neither the time or desire to satisfy her curiosity.

"How do we get to the older part of the city?" I asked. "It used to be called Paradaeza."

"Never heard of it, but I think I know what you mean."

Without hesitation, she led me out the alley and into the crowds. I tried my best to keep up while not drawing any attention to myself.

A daeva could be anything, and I had a lot more practice being an imposter than being myself. In many ways, that was not all too different from being human, if only humans could change physical forms as easily as they changed how they acted.

The city aged as if I'd touched it, and we left bright buildings behind for paint-peeling houses. The old-world magic of pastel colors, stucco houses, and sun-worn orange roofs was safe and comforting. True power rested in such old places. A homebrew of heartening tradition, sweet nostalgia, and eager imagination, which were my strongest foundations.

I felt renewed. My grin beamed at black plaques commemorating warriors and priests long dead. Passing iron fences and the shadows of bell towers, I darkened pristine white marble statues of lions and bulls.

Some things didn't change. The historic district was a little more cleaned up than I remembered. Back then, it wasn't historical.

"Follow me," I said, recognizing where we were.

"What are we looking for?"

I didn't answer.

Déjà vu dissipated into an anxiety that substance might not be under the façade. All I wanted was a meal, but I could also use it as an opportunity to talk Scarlett out of keeping me around.

I led us into a small, fenced-in cemetery, the somber gravestones watching us. A few flowers were placed over a plot—fire-red roses over a patch of dead grass—a sad sight.

No one would disrespect the dead like I was about to, unless they knew why the flowers were there.

I touched the rock headstone, the engraving worn away—"Herc l:cs M.R."

Maybe this form was fitting; I was the walking dead, a reflection from a pool of dirt. Somewhere underneath this plot, the past—the truth—was buried, while the tarnished copy—a mere memory—still walked. Me.

I glanced at Scarlett. She was young enough to spare some time from my touch.

Grasping her cool hand and my free hand resting on colder stone, I nudged the flowers with my foot. As if being absorbed back into the Tree of Life at the center of the world, I was dragged down into one of its branches. A blink, and we arrived at a restaurant reception. I let go of Scarlett's hand; it was brief enough that she still looked unaffected.

A hostess waited at an ornate black podium. "How many?"

"No password?" I asked.

"Two?" The woman was dressed in black. "Wait one moment." The brunette-haired woman slipped past a burgundy curtain and into an empty dining room. As she walked, one foot clacked on the hard floor under her dress. Metal, animal, or otherwise, it signaled something appropriately mythical.

"Looks like a long wait," I said, sarcastic.

In the lobby's mirror, I caught the glint of my own smile, and in a flash, the grin was gone. I wanted to be a vampire who saw nothing in glass. My form was a memory brushed clean like desert sands. False. The footsteps and faults of the past faded. Without the quirks, without her spirit, the form was how I felt—hollow.

The hostess returned. "Follow me."

I couldn't have followed her any faster without running her over. Scarlett drank in the details, going slow and running her hands over old bricks and their many cracks.

We entered a royal dining room. Candles breathed romantic-whispered light over the room. White cloth and silver dressed tables. Suede seats were empty, until I was smoothly ushered into one. Scarlett's umbrella was bagged by the hostess and brought to a coat rack. As Scarlett sunk into the seat across from me, I sighed. Portraits watched us; most would say they were paintings of myths and fables, but I recognized a few faces as echoes of past patrons.

They wouldn't recognize the place. The magic was gone. Light did not float like dandelion fluff on a summer's breeze. Little creatures—fairies and sprites and the like—didn't provide sparkle, once acting as both guests and functional decoration. Mythical miscreants did not sing and hiss and claw at one another, invigorating the air with mayhem, mystery, and mundane conversation.

The crowd-watching used to be better than any zoo.

Despite the lost living magic, there was a spark. Smoke sang sweetly from the candlestick, which was engraved with three swirling snakes spitting blue fire. Each table joined in the melody, spitting a different color flame, creating an orb of light, like they were a bubble all to themselves.

And most important, what looked like nine glass salt and pepper shakers circled the candle. They looked empty, and as I picked one up, the glass was warm as sun-soaked sand. A shake. An ocean breeze wafted past me, salty. This was the salt shaker. Placing it back, I took the next in line, shaking it like a bell. Another smell—strawberry jam and syrup and coffee—breakfast. They must've left this one out by mistake, but it was a pleasant error.

Scarlett picked one.

"Put that down," I said.

She did not. "What is this place?"

"Not a place for mortals." I made warning eyes at the shaker.

Debating rebellion, she reluctantly put it down.

A waiter, his white button-down shirt tucked in poorly, wandered over. "Good afternoon."

"It's quite dark outside for afternoon." I placed my shaker back on the table, being polite and not reaching for other tastes.

"It's always some time somewhere," the waiter said.

"Sure," Scarlett said with a roll of the eyes.

The waiter frowned. "Are you going to order?"

"Aren't you supposed to introduce yourself?" I asked.

"Daza."

If he wasn't going to be friendly, I wouldn't. I grasped the next shaker, which had a hint of sunrise and smelt of a cold autumn morning, freshly fallen rain dripping from colorful leaves. Not really food related, and I couldn't place it, as if it was a memory associated with someone else. "Do we get a menu?"

Skeptical, the waiter tapped his foot. "We don't get many first-timers here."

"I'm not a first-timer—I helped build this place," I said.

This mortal, Daza, was a bit sour, eyebrows bending like a child's drawing of a bird, but I supposed it took a bit of cynicism to work here. Otherwise, he looked too normal, with the wrong number of eyes, ears, and arms—two.

I continued, "I thought it was polite to offer."

"It's not polite to stare," Daza said, staring back.

"We're talking." I scratched at the underside of the table with my nails. It was either that or eating him. Unlike some gods, I didn't like eating mortals. Too salty. Too stringy. I didn't have the teeth for it.

"Can I have the special?" Scarlett asked, trying to break the tension.

"No," Daza said.

"Because I'm a mortal?"

"No," Daza said. "It's because we don't have a special. Are you going to order something we serve? That would be considerate of my time."

"Looks like you have plenty to spare," Scarlett said.

I piled on. "You must be inundated with tips from all these patrons." I paused, seeing a figure sitting at a booth in the corner I hadn't noticed. Panic made me serious. "I don't need a menu or to order. Just tell the chef that Zarik's here."

"Zarik from Zurich?"

"Are you trying to be clever?" Scarlett asked.

"It's a question." Daza yawned. "Strange name."

My eyes kept being drawn to the only other patron, who looked like a normal man. "You work in a strange place."

"You're the strangest thing I see here," Daza said. "But I don't get paid to ask questions."

"Yet, you keep asking them," Scarlett said.

"And I don't get paid for that. I'm paid to take your order."

There was no point in running, so I made small talk. "You seem very ordinary." The waiter was exactly what he appeared, unlike the man in the corner. "You're not a myth—"

Daza coughed to interrupt me. "We don't say that word here."

"But I named the restaurant—"

"The patrons don't like the word. It's called The Retreat now. You must be old."

"Indeed, I am."

"That was meant to be an insult."

"It wasn't." A bit of vitality plumped my smile, until realization dampened it. "Wait, do you not accept favors as payment?"

The waiter rolled his eyes. "I'll go tell the chef someone wants the special."

Scarlett crossed her arms. "You said there was no special."

"Not for you," Daza said.

"Just tell the chef…" I leaned on my hands. "Whatever."

The sudden realization that I might need to pay with actual money dampened my plans. Money kept changing and I was a god—we usually pay in favors or don't pay at all. However, I realized money would be unnecessary. I glanced at the other patron, whose Mediterranean-blue eyes never left me.

The waiter walked away, disappearing to the kitchen through a bead curtain, which clattered like wind chimes, leaving only the sound of a sad, somber violin that seemed to come from nowhere—a hint of magic remaining.

I picked up a fork, fiddling with it like a drumstick as I tried to ignore the other patron. Fear made the fire in my veins run cold.

There was no time to waste.

In the corner, there was a decorative sofa with an enormous painting behind it. The subject—a snowy mountain illuminated by lightning—was not interesting; instead, the size of it was a good sign that I might still have a chance.

"May I join you?" The other patron arrived with a chair, gentle hands unstrained by its weight.

"No," I said.

The man set the chair at the table and sat anyways. "What was that? My ears are still ringing."

It was the god from earlier, smelling a bit like burnt roses.

"You didn't get much of a char." I put the fork on the table. "If you're so stubborn that blasting you into space won't stop you, how could I refuse your company?"

"Good." A bright smile glinted blue in the candlelight between us. "The more the merrier, they say. We'll have more company soon." The god tapped at his forearm, and a screen projected from it.

"That's new," I said.

"A BioScreen. Like a phone. Almost necessary these days."

"You know an acronym for BioScreen is… never mind. I don't think it's for me," I said. "Besides you, who would I call?"

"I'm giving us a couple minutes before my companions join us." The god took the napkin, settling in and smoothing the fabric until it was as wrinkle-free as his face. "I just wanted to talk."

"How fortunate the warehouse was too loud." I tried to fill silence as I thought through my plan. "How'd you get here first, anyways?"

"I walked faster." Ignoring the chosen form, the god's eyes were feminine and gentle, meeting mine with brilliant intensity. A prolonged look was like being dragged into the ocean, first wading in the emerald shallows, then swimming too far, only to be pulled into shifting cerulean currents and drowning in the deep blue. There, death would merely be one part of the cycle of life, feeding the bottom of the food chain and rising up again.

I saw that new energy in the sparkling seas of the god's eyes.

I'd drowned in those eyes in many a lifetime. So often, they were stamped into my dreams as if I'd fallen asleep in the sun and the light penetrated even my peaceful darkness and slumber. "Can't you walk away now?"

"No," the god said. "We're tied together."

"If I didn't know you never lie, I would say you missed me." I winked. "I make your life interesting.

The god remained startlingly unmoved. "I didn't miss you. But I may need you."

"Life doesn't need death, but death does need life—that's what you told me last time." I subdued my scowl. "How times have changed. Maybe mortals don't need either of us."

"You haven't changed."

"You haven't either."

"Sorry, Scarlett." The god smiled, bright and light. "Don't think I'm ignoring you. Nice to meet you in person."

"Amar," she said with a formal nod, staring back in a way I thought only possible for gods, unflinching in the god's blue gaze. "A god of life, health, and immortality. Nice to meet the 'World's Best Detective'."

"If you took any credit, you might be up there," Amar said.

"You know each other?" I asked, annoyed by the other god's luster. Amar was a creature of darkness like I was of light, appearing bright because the life god ate shadows.

"How could I not know my competition?" Scarlett delivered her half-insults cheerily. "Amar doesn't care for certainty or challenge, only credit. Adapting to technology has made a god of life a prime candidate to solve the simplest crimes."

"Simple or not, someone has to solve them. It may be mundane for one who deals with mythical creatures and stories, but it still matters." Amar tapped again at the screen on his arm in distraction, before turning it off again.

All this time, I'd been running a million scenarios to get out of here, and the pieces finally fell together. Deception was a greater fall when it came from the truth.

"Can I trust you to be blunt?" I offered a new shaker to Amar. "What does this smell like to you?"

A gaze of suspicion, but the god reluctantly took it and beamed at the smell. "Caramel and tart apples. Dessert. Why?"

"Interesting," I said, faking my best perplexed look. "Could've sworn it was—. Anyways, how's this going to turn out? Like always?"

"Originally, my job was to hunt myths and gods, but since there aren't many left, I solve crimes. I could forget about a single god and settle for some answers about the mythical deaths."

"I've got answers for you," Scarlett said.

"Don't give Amar anything. Whoever thinks I'm the devious one hasn't seen how truth can be so deceptive."

A slight vein of annoyance popped in Amar's forehead. "Can you listen? Maybe you can be useful."

My teeth clenched tighter. "I have your lectures on parchment, paper, and vinyl."

"This time is different."

"I don't care. You already made me a demon. Whenever I listen to you, I end up hated and forgotten. Do you realize how painful it is to live lost, struggling and desperate as if always hungry, always wanting, always missing something?"

The waiter arrived and said, "The food'll be just another minute. Slight delay—the chef cut off a finger."

"He had too many," I said.

Daza dripped sarcasm. "And I'm one too many for this conversation."

Amar watched the waiter go and sit on the decorative sofa for an apparently well-needed break. "He's odd." Beyond the waves of Amar's voice, there was the sound of people in the restaurant lobby. "I know we've had our differences, but times have changed. There are bigger things than us. The past has passed. It's done. It's gone."

"We finally agree on something—the waiter is odd." My faked expression fell flat. "I don't care what's changed. A few words do not change us."

"I have a different offer."

"And they call me the tempter," I said.

"Maybe I've changed more than you," Amar said. "I want to help. Both of you. We can work together."

I stopped, staked to the ground by the simple words. "I thought you didn't lie so blatantly."

"It's not a lie." Amar trailed off, and his backup finally entered the dining room, hanging near the entrance for their leader's signal.

"I've got what you want," Scarlett said. She reached into her black-zipped pocket and pushed the map and murder video onto the table. "I beat you to it, but you can have the praise you covet. The answers only created more questions."

I ignored Scarlett, focused on Amar's words and my plan. "That's the second lie." I pointed at the shaker. "You lied about the smell."

"I didn't," Amar said. He pocketed the evidence and nodded at Scarlett. "We've got a deal."

My bubbling joy was hard to contain; my plan might work. Maybe it wasn't as good a show as fireworks, but it was quite devious. "Ah, I gave you the wrong shaker. It all makes sense now. This was the shaker I meant to give you."

I picked up the autumn-smelling one and braced before taking a big whiff. This time, it was sharper. Clearer. Evergreen. Heavy as a forest falling on me. Then, blood. I leaned into sadness.

"What's so special about that one?" Scarlett asked.

I kept it far away from her, capping the top with my hand so my memory would remain. "The essence of nostalgia. Once, when Amar and I were friends, we shared a meal." I gave my best fake smile. "I was hoping you'd remember the smell and maybe feel bad about what's about to happen." I handed it over, hoping my memory would linger enough to be pungent. The four men inched closer. "Humor me. This was supposed to be my last meal—that's the reason I came here."

The truth was such an effective misdirection. It was not magic to make eyes lie, but some amount of trustworthiness must've shown like a glint of goodness.

"If it makes you happy," Amar said. "You know what will happen without your cooperation."

"Zarik will cooperate," Scarlett said.

Amar gave the shaker a hefty sniff, maybe wanting to punish himself with a pleasant memory. As I had.

However, the god must've not found it very pleasant.

A look of horror. The shaker dropped, shattering shards across wooden floors. Then, the god slumped out the chair and scattered the glass. Apparently, my memory burned stronger than fireworks.

I was already across the room. Scarlett had the sense to follow.

The waiter was at his feet, head cocked in curiosity. I pushed past him and yanked the painting I'd noticed earlier off the hooks, sending it tumbling to the floor, falling flat with a clatter and thud. Behind, there was nothing but wood paneling. Nothing extraordinary.

"That looked expensive," Daza said, not particularly fazed by the odd and chaotic turn the restaurant had taken.

After Amar had fallen, the other men were reluctant to follow me, but that would only last so long. A bit vindictive, I grabbed Scarlett and wretched her towards the wall. She braced, but didn't crash. Instead, she phased through.

A dull thud, but I would not ask if she was hurt. I didn't care. "What's down there?"

"Me," came the tart response.

Unhelpful. I sighed and jumped after her.

The fall was simple enough to not need wings, but human legs were squishy. Yet, the landing was squishier. A bed of moss absorbed my fall, bits of plant clouding around, smelling earthy and faintly glowing green. Scarlett stood wincing—a belly flop, even in the softest of landings—still stung. She huffed and dusted herself off from the fluorescent flora.

Without wasting any time, I sprang to my feet and ran down what I'd consider a normal tunnel—a bark corridor like the inside of a gargantuan branch illuminated by green moss-light. There was nothing more natural. The Tree of Life gave me a rush like coffee—not caffeine, but being scalded by a freshly made cup.

A smell of old, damp parchment filled archaic routes. I wove my path on magnetic instinct, finding my old element of purpose and poise, deeper into wild and unused ways. Further and further we went. Air cooled, and Scarlett's following breath grew heavier as the wooded, deep-forest mystery thickened.

I stopped. I listened. Unable to hear past Scarlett's haggard breath and torturously thumping heart, I considered quieting her. While it was easy to pause such things in humans, it was far harder to restart. In gaps, I heard no footsteps. We were alone.

"How?" She managed to spit out, unable to articulate anything further.

"And I thought your breathing was loud." My eyes followed the bark. "How what? How did I know this was here? How am I so clever? How are you so slow?"

"How do we get out?"

"I don't need to cut into the Tree of Life to look for rings. To escape, we follow the growth."

"What a waste," she said. "We didn't need to run. Amar can be reasoned with."

I ignored her. She didn't know Amar.

Faint footsteps echoed, following our exact route in a way I could only describe as impossible.

There were a million tunnels down here. A million different routes. There'd been no reason to where I'd ended up, only luck. Of course, there was fate. And eventually, I had to accept it. If Amar had recovered so quickly and followed through the unknowable twists and turns, not even being lost when I was, then there was no chance. I had to accept the inevitable—talking. With anyone else, I could survive that.

A man walked down the eerily lit tunnel, but it was the waiter, Daza.

With such a twist of fate, I couldn't help but be overjoyed. I shouldn't have been because he wasn't that pleasant a man to be around.

"It's you." My surprise metamorphosized. "How did you follow us?"

"I followed your aura." Daza was heaving for breath. Mortals were so easily overexerted.

However, maybe I shouldn't talk; I was labored these days, too. But at least I had an answer why the chef kept this waiter around—it was helpful to know what walked through the door. Yet another mortal that could see myths and gods. What a precarious era this must be.

"Did the chef give you something?" I asked. "Where is he?"

"What do I get in return?" Daza sneered at Scarlett, who was ignoring him and running her fingers over the tree's moss.

"You get to avoid an unpleasant end," I said.

"You aren't scary," Daza said. "How do I put this indelicately? Your aura isn't much stronger than a snuffed candle. Easy to follow, but not very bright."

I went red, hiding embarrassment under anger. "I could destroy you. Nothing is more violent than age. Each cell dying, one by one. Memory, slipping away. Until all that you are and once was becomes nothing more than dirt and dust."

"Go ahead," Daza said.

"What?"

"The chef gave me what you asked for." He pulled out a small glass container. "Wouldn't want to see it on the floor, would you?"

"I've seen mortals that are able to see gods, but none were so disrespectful."

With the dim light, Daza came closer to show what was in the container—a scrumptious piece of apple pie. "What's more important, me or this pie?"

"The pie. But why would you risk your life to give me it?"

Daza said, "I have a personal request."

"Ah, there always is."

"I want to know what happened with the shakers. The restaurant is always looking for reviews. Ways to improve. And the scents are supposed to be pleasant memories."

"My favorite memory is the worst thing that happened to me—it's what keeps me going." I smiled. "But the truly worst part of the restaurant is the service."

"We'll take that into consideration." Daza's swooping eyebrow raised. "One more thing. The chef said this would pay off old debts—he heard a rumor that what you're looking for is on the ninth floor of The Root."

"How does that help me?" I motioned for the pie.

"The chef knows you want revenge on Amar." Daza frowned at Scarlett. "It might not be what you originally had in mind, but she's the only detective who might be better. This information might help her beat Amar."

"If the chef thinks that will make us even for saving his life, he might be right," I said. "I'd love nothing better than mutual destruction with Amar, but I'd give anything to see a god of life beaten by a common mortal."

"Common?" Scarlett's frown was serious. "I lost my umbrella and now you're insulting me, too?"

I ignored her, fixated on the pie Daza handed me, which I dutifully thanked him for, before he headed back down the wood tunnel.

"Where're you going?" Scarlett asked.

"Back to work," Daza said. Even his gait was lackadaisical.

The pie looked like it was weaved from golden ichor and my delicate mouth watered. Even my essence longed for it. I peeked open the container just to get a whiff. "You're not worried about Amar when he comes to?"

"The god is after you, not me."

Scarlett followed the waiter. "Tell Amar we still have a deal."

"That's not my job," Daza said. "Tell him yourself."

She huffed in frustration. "At least bring me my umbrella."

"Maybe," he said, disappearing around a twist in the vast tree.

"A deal?" I was in a good mood, so it didn't bother me as much as it normally would.

"As long as you help me," Scarlett said, slowly walking back to me. "Amar won't hunt you."

"What exactly, am I helping you with?"

"Just being yourself." She adjusted a silver chain around her neck that hid under her jacket. "Nothing more. Amar was struggling to solve the deaths you caused—and I had the solution. I imagine it hit a little close to home. Probably thought you were gone; yet, here you are. Amar expects to be one of the last gods, so investigations are based in reality. In facts. In technology. People like me—detectives who rely on intuition and possibilities beyond the mundane—are out of fashion. But myths are coming back in greater numbers, and this time, I got the better of Amar."

"Detectives who investigate what defies reality were never in fashion. Myths and gods aren't something to be solved. You can't expect to solve what has no logic."

"That's not true." Her objection was sharper than the knife that cut me. "Everything has logic. Everyone has logic. Even if people aren't necessarily logical, they have their own reason, combining fact, fiction, and fabrication—a story—one they tell themselves that I merely read. Myths are one of those stories. As society grew, the unknown moved to the fringes—a creature in the forest, a monster in the lake, a demon in the darkness. But stories are hard to destroy. Now, those repressed beliefs are creating real mythical creatures."

I already knew myths and gods had mostly moved on from earth millennia ago except in dark, untamed recesses.

On Yggdrasil—even this world the gods had retreated to—we eventually became outdated. Mortals' belief could keep us from the void, but they were a fickle bunch.

I feigned relaxation, leaning against the gnarled wall. "You think there's a pattern making myths into reality?"

"I *believe* there is."

I couldn't tell if she really meant to stress that word, or if it was just ringing in my ears because that was the answer.

Despite my nonchalance, I was uneasy, stuck between two minds as if I was stuck between two forms. Mortals weren't supposed to know their beliefs could create mythical creatures—gods had agreed that was the way to prevent pandemonium. But was her wording coincidence or had some loose-lipped god told her? Worse, had she worked it out herself?

The extent to which myths popped up waxed and waned with the strength of the Tree of Life that we were now standing in. While many myths might only need a few believers to manifest and could just as easily vanish, gods were more complicated. We weren't created or destroyed so easily. Without belief, we existed in the void, patiently waiting to rematerialize or eventually fading into its fabric.

Before I could figure out what to say, she continued on, "I have my role. You do, too. Who better to investigate death than death itself?"

Her phrasing wasn't too out of the ordinary, so I assumed she didn't know that humans helped create gods instead of the opposite. Best to change the subject.

I pushed off the wall and stood a couple inches taller. "I'm not death, only a god of death." That's what I liked to say, even if it wasn't entirely true—I was a god of age—but saying I was a god of death wasn't a lie. I never lied fully. "I'm meant to come for those who have lived long enough, but that's not the reality. I take no joy in what I do."

"Exactly."

"Exactly?"

"You're not a force of nature," she said. "You're a being with thoughts, feelings, and logic."

"You want me to help you solve mysteries?" I expected the Pull. However, I seemed mostly free besides existing. That was terrifying.

"Forget what I'm asking of you." As she talked more, I could almost feel the strings wrapping around me, ready to spring the trap if I refused. Instead, the only thing that sprung was her lips into a tempting grin. "Think about what I'm offering you."

"You have nothing to offer me," I said, wondering how I got into the position of a mortal trying to tempt me.

"I don't?" She put up her hand with three fingers. "I'll give you the three A's."

"A's?"

"Adventure and Amar."

"I suppose there's three A's in that sentence—four, I guess—but it seems a little deceptive." I nodded my approval. "Clever. I'll have to use that."

"You might not be able to get rid of Amar, but you can get under his skin. And, I thought you might not agree, that's why I saved the real last A—apples." She pointed at the pie. "As many as you want. In any form you want."

The smell of pie *would* only last so long, and I supposed the Pull wasn't really pulling if I was willing. I might not be able to destroy Amar now, but this gave me time. "You've got my attention."

Her grin turned into a full-blown smile. I knew that type of smile, as it had appeared on my face often. She had me hooked.

"What's on the ninth floor?" I asked.

"I don't know. That's what makes it interesting." She nodded down the tunnel. "We've got to go step by step. Would you mind taking the first one? This is one part of the city I'm not familiar with."

"Where are we going?"

"Home."

I was regretting this already. "You're going to have to be more specific."

FOUR

'I LISTEN TO A BORING MAN

WE eventually made our way out of the Tree of Life and back to Scarlett's cozy apartment, where she partially stayed true to her word. She provided as many apples as I could ask for. The rest of her promise was severely lacking—there was no adventure or Amar.

Days passed. I waited for an opportunity to help, hoping for a chance to change my reputation as a demon. However, Scarlett insisted she didn't need me yet and the information about the ninth floor would lead us to a pivotal case. Content with my apples, time matured in a manner reminiscent of slumber—instant—with only a dreamlike moment remembered here and there.

And in the same way a sentence might encompass a book, a day might explain many.

Dawn. Quiet dust filtered through first light, flying from one of the many bookshelves to another in Scarlett's modest living room that was less futuristic than the world outside. I perched on a wood nook at the bay window overlooking a street and advertisement-covered buildings. My grey eyes were sharp as an owl's. Although I loved the creature for their curiosity, companionship, and killer instinct, I stayed in the form of the owl-faced man because it was the closest I could get to being the animal without shedding feathers.

Across from me was a building with the brightest screen of all, showing financial tickers, prices scrolling endlessly. Important things like apples went down in price day after day, while less useful items like porcelain rose with every sunrise. I couldn't help but notice the numbers; without a Pull, my interests were the distractions that came to me.

Morning. Warm sun bathing over me was pleasant as silence. Yet, I wasn't alone. Scarlett roasted coffee, and the smell sang. She brought a mug with the letter "S" on it to the living room. Reclining in a sleek leather lounger with the steaming coffee in hand, steam drifted past her face like thoughts. There were no other seats, only an audience of books, which she occasionally retrieved and flipped through as if looking for an answer I could not even figure out the question to. Before she left for the day, she would hide her dark teardrop pendant under her collar, where she kept it hidden.

Although we said nothing to each other, the quiet company was agreeable and I figured eventually she would turn to me like one of the books.

Evening. People argued below my window. Sometimes, they laughed. Sometimes, they fought. The apartment eavesdropped over a bar below. I often saw Scarlett down there, taking a seat at patio tables similar to the imposter incident with her friends, Iris and Rodrigo. Scarlett's ears perked at gossip. She broke up fights not with strength or even, surprisingly, wits. Instead, she knew everyone. Or seemed to. I wished I could've heard her conversations.

Despite curiosity, I didn't need to. With everyone else, she was unmistakable as a painting. Yet, I felt like I got a better glimpse of the strokes behind the portrait.

Night. She returned from her escapades, but even the smile she sometimes brought back faded into the brightness of the neon night outside. Music reverberated from the bar under us. She cooked. She gave me an apple. The smell of her meals wafted past like the finest kitchens I'd been in, reminding me of golden plates of lemon, saffron, and butter one night and a trinity of onions, celery, and peppers another, singing with spice. But she devoured books more than she ate. The music wore down as she did. She slept restless.

There's a gap between morning and evening because there was nothing of note. Scarlett went out on unannounced errands, and boredom passed unnoticed as the sun overhead. No matter how many daydreams I had of destroying Amar, even the most outlandish ones ran low as my real options. When you're lost, the first step was the most uncertain because it could bring you further from where you want to go.

Eventually, I turned to her books for company, devouring words like I did time, searching for how she had heard of me. Loose associations chaotically categorized her bookshelves. Greek myths were next to Ptolemaic science. Saharan botany—a sparse category—was next to political ethics. Also sparse.

On the search to find myself, as I playfully called it, I found numerous other daevas and gods, including Amar under an old name. But I was nowhere to be found. My only explanation was that if Scarlett knew everything about me, she wouldn't be interested.

That, at the very least, explained the innocent day that was the first step from one uncertainty to another. Scarlett stayed home, finally asking questions like I was a living textbook.

"Have you ever had other names?" she asked, sitting on the edge of her recliner.

"Like leaves on a tree," I said, sitting with my back against the cold window in my typical form. "It's pretty bare now, though."

"Were you around during Alexander the Great's time?"

I frowned, my thin nose prickling like I smelled smoke. "He burned Persepolis down before I could. I had the better reason to."

"Have you ever spent this much time with a mortal?"

I didn't want to answer that, but I had no reason to lie when I could just avoid answering. "Why would I?"

There were other questions about my role in various parts of history. I, of course, mentioned how vital I was in many of these things. And, of course, some of it was a bit embellished or exaggerated. As a god, it didn't pay to deny such things. Besides, who was going to contradict me? I was there for the earliest records.

Others had edited them since, though.

Scarlett seemed more interested in what I said than follow-up questions. As the day wore on, she retreated to her room, which had a cherrywood bed and a desk with a dusty, old computer. She lounged on her bed and drew a book from a drawer in the nightstand at her bedside, which she rarely read from.

Intrigued, I got up and stood in the bedroom doorway, finally asking her a question. "What kind of books do you keep there?"

"An escape hatch. Sometimes, I need a break."

I tilted my head, matching my owl-faced form. "What does that mean?"

"They're fiction."

"You deal with myths and gods for a living. What do you consider fiction?"

"Happy endings. Easy romance. Cowboy space lawyers." She perked up, sitting on the edge of the bed. "Speaking of, we're having a guest tonight. 6:00 pm."

"Speaking of?"

"There's a lawyer with a case."

"I'll make myself scarce. I won't even need to transform, I'm basically turning to stone." I leaned against the doorframe in a suitably elegant pose for a Greek sculptor.

"I'd like your help."

"Hasn't seemed like it," I whispered like a ventriloquist, keeping the statuesque pose. "Why me?"

"Why you?"

"Why am I the god you believe in?"

"Because you aren't storied or special."

I dropped the stance. "I thought my natural charm was special."

She tried too hard to keep eye contact, and I could tell she was lying, but I couldn't tell why.

She stood up and walked past me into the living room, "You can be helpful with the lawyer."

"Because I'm used to a lawyer's devious wording?"

She grabbed her coat. "No. I find this case more unusual than lassos and rockets."

"What's so special about it?"

"A small connection to the larger case I need you for. But the smallest link can be the most integral of all." She unlocked the apartment door. "Be prompt."

She left with startling speed, and I was left not knowing what I was supposed to be prompt for. I was already here.

Expectation thickened time like amber, hardening as the awaited hour approached. Above a bookshelf, the clock—a sunset-colored circle background for a black and white tree, the roots and branches stretching equally to the numbers— seemed frozen. But the hand moved slow as a sundial, shadows in the room lengthening until a neon night outside flickered into a brilliant new dawn.

6:00 arrived and passed. No one came.

At 6:01, I was unbothered. 6:02, I fidgeted in my seat. 6:03, my essence ached with anticipation. 6:04, I was over it.

Then, Scarlett returned in a rush, slamming the door. She threw her jacket over the kitchen counter, revealing a grey shirt as she ran into her bedroom. "You didn't get a seat for our guest?"

"I've been sitting on this nook for ages."

She dragged a metal fold-chair from the closet. "I thought you preferred it."

Looking at the uncomfortable seat, I shrugged. "You really greet your guests with the red-carpet treatment."

Unfolding the seat, she pressed a button and airbag pillows exploded out from the metal frame. The comfy chair was perfectly placed in the corner by a bookshelf. "I have a few more. But since you like the nook so much…"

"You never offered," I said.

"You never asked."

Nor did I care. As a god, I didn't have to worry about back pain; I had a thousand other aches that echoed from a million scars through the millennia. Not all gods felt such a way. Age, though, was a real demon.

"I thought they were coming at six?" I asked.

"The clock's five minutes fast." Scarlett pushed a few books level in their shelves. Some were upside down and backwards, but at least they were even. "Otherwise, I'm perpetually late."

"But you know the clock's five minutes fast."

"Not if I live five minutes faster than everyone else." She eyed me. "Can you spruce yourself up?"

"Like a fly on the wall?"

"We don't live in a pigsty." She dusted hastily.

"Raven? Dog? Tamed dragon?"

"No."

"No? You have something in mind?"

"That form's fine. Just comb your hair."

"I'll have you know, this form was a younger version of a very popular Magi. Or, he was after me." I smiled. "I bet that he would be better off without the itchy beard. Coincidentally, I was right and in return—"

A knock at the door stopped my story. In the same way Scarlett dusted, I combed my dark hair with my hand. I'd been stuck in this form for so long I'd almost forgotten I could just change it. A quick straightening occurred as the door opened.

Scarlett showed in a man that looked like a Viking in a lawyer's suit; his tangled and braided beard contrasted swooping slicked-back hair and clean-pressed clothes. The classic suit was different from the fine fabrics and ever-changing jackets of the crowds outside. Despite being dreadfully out of date, it still appeared prestigious for its rarity. Law, apparently, stuck to precedent even in clothing choices.

The enormous man sunk into the plush armchair. "I thought it was just you, Ms. Wolfe."

"A friend," Scarlett said, retreating from the statement with a step. "Or rather, some hired help."

"I'm being paid?" I sat at the nook, watching her squirm with a grin. "The name's Zee." A few thousand years of experience told me that keeping it simple was better. More so, the closer to the truth, the easier and more believable the lie.

"Nice to meet you. Mine's Lars."

"Mr. Warner," Scarlett said. "Would you like some coffee?"

"Sure, with creamer please," Lars said. "I'm still a bit tired from my trip to the other markets. I think I've been doing more crosswords while traveling than actual work at my destination."

"That's how business trips typically go." As if sensing my question, Scarlett inserted the answer into the conversation. "But I know your trip to Jade City and New Elysium was productive, even if you missed out on the Obsidian Islands because of the weather."

"Indeed." He looked at her surprised and skeptical, asking how she knew.

"The price of a few rare antiquities went un-updated for two days." Scarlett went to the kitchen and steam hissed from the expresso machine. "Negotiations stalled. I believe it was a jade Koru pendant and the god Māui's war club. I assumed that it was you who ended the impasse in Jade City because the stones in your cufflinks have been recently polished." She returned with two cups of fresh coffee. "And you went to

New Elysium based on the slight tan at your wrists because your new suit doesn't fit right. However, those would just be assumptions. I prefer certainty. I rely on those with more natural skill than myself. In this case, a few of my associates happened to see you there." She gave him the coffee and smiled, as if she'd played a joke on Lars, who looked at his wrists for the tan.

I thought of Scarlett's friends I had met, Rodrigo and Iris, wondering if these were such associates that Scarlett mentioned. More than personal talent, Scarlett seemed to have a plethora of friends that possessed skills she did not.

"Ah, you got me there." He chuckled and tried to sip the coffee, but it was too hot. "It seems a fruitful trip for both of us then, I managed to get a 10.3% premium on the expected sale price and you got to show off. Everyone says you are the person to come to for things that seem impossible." Lars took the coffee and sipped at it between his thick facial hair. "The authorities think they solved the case. To anyone else, it would seem so. But, no matter how impossible, I can't help but think the killer is still out there."

"Thinking is what gets you into trouble," Scarlett said, putting her fragrant cup of steaming coffee next to me at the nook. "But you'd be surprised what is actually impossible and what is merely improbable." She paced past me and the open seat she'd insisted on, glancing sparingly at Lars. "You actually got me interested because the case was so boring. But why do you want to help the man arrested for killing your brother?"

"I'm not convinced he's guilty," Lars said. "I want justice, that's all."

"Please tell my associate what you told me." Scarlett faced the lawyer. "And don't leave anything out."

Lars interlocked his fingers over his lap, one thumb pressing, hard, on the other. "My younger brother, Marko, was found dead three days ago." A shake of the head. "I'd like to say it was a surprise, but it wasn't. I love him, but he was in a dangerous business. There's no harm saying it now—illegal software. Viruses. Malware. That sort of thing. And beyond that, ways to verify false information and track certain specific… mmm… user-specific data. He didn't use it himself, but Marko made a good living selling it to the wrong people. Maybe, if he sold it to the right ones, he'd still be alive."

"People like you?" Scarlett stopped pacing. "When you were a prosecutor, you were lucky that so much evidence appeared when criminals would've escaped otherwise."

A grin. "And it cleared others. Seems nothing escapes you."

"If only that startling luck would bring the truth to me instead of having to search for it." Despite the cutting insinuation, Scarlett's tone was cordial. "Your law career isn't what interests me, though. How did your brother die?"

Lars' good nature slipped south, the smile dipping into his beard. "How he died depends on who you ask."

"She's asking you," I said.

A skeptical look towards me was dispensed by Scarlett's prompting, "We've seen weirder than you can imagine."

"I think a mythical creature killed him," Lars said.

"How much do you know of myths?" Scarlett asked.

"Not much."

"I do. And no common mythical creature could've killed your brother."

"You think I'm lying."

Scarlett shook her head. "Not at all. Myths spring up easier than you'd imagine. Whether they last is another question entirely. The real question, though, is not why it happened, but what did it. Can you elaborate?"

"A few weeks ago, I started living with my brother," Lars said, reciting in a stoic, factual manner that covered painful emotions, disconnected from the story like it was one that happened to someone else. "Marko and I had many disagreements, but he took me in after my divorce. Him and his wife, Julia, lived in a neighborhood I didn't like. I had contact with some of the neighbors in a professional setting, if you know what I mean. Worse, though, were the neighbors' dealings with Marko—plenty of people he shorted on money or tested some of his… software on. Yet, one way or another, Marko slipped out of bad situations like he was butter melting past hot knives. The night Marko died, he was concluding some business with an associate named Otto. That's who the authorities arrested for the crime, and through a couple of contacts, I got his deposition. Otto said that he brought a jar of expensive coffee beans to brew because he won't discuss business without coffee and supposedly what we have is swill."

"Wouldn't expect a criminal to be a snob," I interjected.

"Anyone can be," Scarlett said. "Pickpockets are especially picky."

I enjoyed the word play, even if others were more particular with their words; Lars, despite his supposed like of crosswords, didn't seem amused for an instant by jokes like this and continued his story.

"Anyways, when it became clear to Otto that Marko had thrown the money into a few short-sighted vices, they had a 'disagreement', ending with a broken coffee mug and a punch that broke Otto's nose. After that, Otto left in a hurry, but Marko was very much alive."

"The oldest lie in the book," I said.

"Otto wasn't lying," Lars said. "Marko's wife attested to that. Following the argument, Julia came home and found my brother quite lively. Marko was still upset. He yelled and raged and broke a wood chair, coffee-maker, and another mug. When she locked herself in the bedroom, he broke a window. Shortly after, it went silent. Thinking he'd calmed, Julia found him in the chair, dead. She called the police."

"Right away?" Scarlett asked.

"Yes. The detectives discovered the jar of expensive coffee beans Otto brought was poisoned, but he insists he didn't know. Both mugs were broken, and the poisoned liquid was mixed all over the floor. Otto made the coffee; his fingerprints were on both mugs."

"It does seem rather convenient Otto's cup broke," I said.

"Too convenient," Scarlett said. "If Otto meant to kill Marko, he wouldn't argue over money unless it was a heat of the moment thing. But poison is not a heat of the moment thing. Did the deposition say whether Otto drank any coffee?"

Lars shook his head no. "Otto could've been a target, too."

"What if the jar of coffee beans were poisoned after Otto left?" I grinned, thinking this was a clever theory. "He really didn't know."

Scarlett picked up the mug next to me. "Hmm. But then the beans wouldn't be the source of the poison that killed Marko." Without taking a sip, she placed the coffee back down. "Is there anyone else who would want both Marko and Otto dead?"

"Plenty," Lars said. "But despite the danger of their business, few end up dead. That is, until the week before Marko's death. Another man died in the same apartment block." Lars paused, a frown on his face. "The authorities say it was food poisoning. I might've done a few things I shouldn't have to find out the truth. They confirmed it was the same poison—a poison that didn't match any on record. That's why I came to see you. If it is a myth, it'll kill again."

"From all this, you'd think we'd get a more complete picture." Scarlett locked eyes with Lars. "Why didn't you tell me Julia was once your client?"

"You didn't ask." Lars shrugged. "Julia was in a shady business. Legally, I can't speak to what it was. I got her out of trouble and she promised to turn her life around. Thinking she might be able to help Marko, I introduced them, and although she never got in trouble again, he couldn't do the same—maybe I should've turned him in. I would've lost a brother, but he wouldn't have lost his life."

"And this other man that died—he was Julia's ex." Scarlett wiped a few strands of auburn hair away from her face. "The one who got her into the business you can't tell me about."

Lars' hands tightened, mirroring their visible veins. "How'd you know that?"

"I can't know everything, or anywhere close, no matter how I try; however, I can know someone that knows what I don't."

"Who told you?"

"You did. The mere mention of this other dead man, who you wouldn't name, made you frown—a simple frown. A suppressing frown. Anger or pain. I made an assumption based on the line of your story, and now you've confirmed it."

She was unworried how Lars seethed. "You're the connection between these two men."

"I wouldn't kill my brother." Hands unclasped and clenched into fists, a few fingers and knuckles scarred.

"Love is defined by extremes," Scarlett said.

Lars' beard twitched, fury bubbling. His imposing figure was dangerous. I roused and, without thinking, darkened the room, preparing to restrain the man. Scarlett shook her head towards me.

Before the man could sort through his feelings, Scarlett continued, "I don't think you killed anyone."

Lars' poise recovered like a wrinkle being ironed out of his formal clothing.

Scarlett continued, "You would have to be either very dumb or very clever to ask me to investigate a crime you committed which already had a scapegoat. Based on what you've told me, I have a hunch about your brother's killer. However, I like to keep my options open. Mundane or mythical, we'll determine the truth. The unusual poison makes the possibility of a mythical creature quite intriguing."

"No one else would believe me if I said a myth killed my brother."

"Your belief is why I took the case at all," Scarlett said. "Mr. Warner, I appreciate what you have told me and more so, what you have not. Will you take us to the scene of the crime?"

"Now?"

"Yes, now. Time is of the essence." She retrieved two jackets, her own and my stolen one, which I had kept for the warming technology. "It's starting to snow."

Lars looked outside, as if only realizing that the window was frosting as the heat of the apartment insulated itself from the cold world. Lazy clouds drifted through the colorful night sky, letting loose the first little snowflakes onto the city.

Scarlett preemptively shivered when she handed me the jacket.

I asked, "Do you not like snow?"

"I do." She pulled the zipper up and down a few times for the satisfying sound. "Snow is helpful. It has already told me that Mr. Warner here is less likely to be the killer. He didn't realize it was cold on the way here, nor did he plan for the coming snow—if he was so clever to ask for my help while being the killer, I'd expect him to be composed enough to remember a jacket. But the cold is not why we have to hurry…."

"Maybe we can use the snow to track the creature," Lars said.

"Unfortunately, unlikely," Scarlett said. "If it was something too strange or unusual, someone would've seen it. I have a feeling the creature likes small, interior spaces. A shut-in. If you hadn't been here the whole time, Zee, you might fit the profile."

"Very funny."

Scarlett opened the door. "Lead the way, Mr. Warner. With the snow, people will head inside, and the myth could kill again."

We took the stairs down, opening the door that led to the busy bar street. Steaming drinks became more popular with every bar we passed. The silently flying drone traffic above disappeared into descending clouds. Vents gave off plumes of heat and gentle gusts of warmth as we walked.

Snow quickened, streaming down. The fog of falling flakes mixed with neon lights into a dull rainbow haze. Fluttering around, snow gently kissed my exposed cheeks, trying to relieve the fiery blood within me. Yet, as with anything else, my touch only brought destruction.

Footpaths were darkened with melt, leaving only white streaks on the sides, melted where people left the main path for more specific destinations. Despite people rushing in the cold, the hum of winter was quiet. Mortals huddled under hoods and layers, the frost-breath their only voices.

I kept a close eye on Lars. Unlike Scarlett, my suspicions lay on him still. Maybe coming to us as the killer was not out of cleverness or stupidity, but because of guilt. Self-punishment. Also, he left out where he was when Marko died.

Was that a sliver of nervousness in Lars' face? An aura like exuded heat? My suspicion was no larger than a snowflake, but it didn't melt, accumulating as we went.

Scarlett seemed to draw conclusions on what Lars left unsaid. Like she already knew. Like the missing piece was something Lars couldn't say, and by not saying it, it had spoken to Scarlett all the louder. Yet, I still hadn't heard it.

The harder I tried, the more slipped through my grasp.

Following Lars, the neighborhood turned from bright lights to closed shutters. Brick buildings were well-kept and well-shut. Utilitarian. Whether the windows were shut because of the cold or to keep prying eyes out, the view would've been depressing had it not been snowing. Looking up at the tall buildings, I was disappointed that I could not be staring through the frosted windows, counting the snowflakes as I sipped some hot apple cider. Yet, however lovely that seemed, there was more excitement in our current task.

After being idle for so long, I was thrilled at this opportunity. Once, I was an avenging angel and maybe I could be so again, vanquishing a myth. Maybe I could even be detective death, outsmarting a killer. Either way, I wanted to be a savior from either myth or murderer because, although I was a god of death, that only meant that I understood how precious life was.

My desire to save mortals was purely selfish. I wanted to protect them so they could believe in me until they met me at the end of a long life.

And they dared to call me demon.

As if it was a sign from the universe, I was greeted with a doormat that said, "Not Welcome", eight floors up in a white-walled apartment building. We dusted snow off in front of a green door. Lars took out a key from his right pocket and unlocked it.

But the door didn't open when he turned the handle.

He knocked, loud. The thick door barely moved. "Julia."

On the other side, there was a few more clicks, and the door peeked open, revealing a petite woman that was ready to shut us out in an instant. "Who are they?"

"Lars came to us to catch a myth. I'm Scarlett and this is Zee."

At this, the woman seemed to brighten, opening the door fully and ushering us in to the scene of the crime.

FIVE

I SEE A HOLE IN THE STORY

THE apartment bathed us clean of winter frost. Fogged breath faded and warm air poured over us from a ceiling vent at the entrance. Jackets were taken off and stowed. Tea and hot chocolate were offered and accepted.

As Julia led us into a futuristic living room, I shivered. An echo of death seemed to chill me—maybe that's why mortals believed in ghosts.

The feeling faded as the lights flicked on. RGB light-strips portraited an entire wall of monitors, reflecting off warm, dark wood floors and insulated by thick shutters. Short clips filled the screens. Clouds parted on snow-capped mountains. Waves rolled on deserted shores. Drones weaved around the city's central building in a snowstorm, a live look.

Julia hit a switch, turning the colored lights off. The screens flashed a series of locks, with the main one saying, "Not Authorized". She flicked another switch and an enormous single panel rose from the floor and covered the smaller screens.

"I can't get the computer to work," Julia said, a few strands of hair over the side of her face like lines on a chestnut and a light brown mole next to her nostril. "Sit anywhere but the desk."

Obviously, I examined the desk first. A white-backed chair sat behind a thick wood slab attached to the wall. A keyboard descended into the desk on a mechanism before sliding closed.

Not seeing anything obviously odd, I joined Scarlett and Lars on the three-wide couch against the back wall, while Julia brought drinks to the table in front of us and took a seat in a navy-blue armchair.

"I'm not a fan of tea," Scarlett said, sipping from a white paper cup with a green leaf design, a string dangling from the tea bag. "I prefer coffee, but this is rather good, mostly because of the caffeine."

"Do you know what killed Marko?" Julia asked, her left forefinger tracing the lip of her matching cup.

"Poison," I said, stating the obvious.

I looked sideways at Lars for a reaction, who was staring towards the ground. Shame? Sadness? Hard to tell.

"We'll soon know more," Scarlett said, pulling at the tea string like a marionette. "How does the security system work?"

Julia's mouth thinned, stretching her beauty mark. "Marko set it up, and he wasn't exactly forthcoming. The most love he showed was giving me the password each week. Lars and I can get into most features with our voices."

"Why do you ask?" Lars said, his muscles taking half the couch while Scarlett and I took the other.

"I was wondering if there were cameras that might have recorded what happened," Scarlett said, not the least bit intimidated by either presence—physical or godly—on either side of her.

"We only have exterior cameras," Julia said.

Lars nodded. "And we're locked out of those. The last code expired, and the authorities can't break Marko's security."

"Too bad." Scarlett stopped playing with the tea. "Can I see the kitchen?"

"It's been cleaned," Lars said.

"Can't hurt to check." Scarlett jumped to her feet. "I'll tell you my theories as I look—we need to find the killer as quickly as possible."

Julia went to the far wall, sliding a fader switch. As it moved, the wall opened proportionally. The house seemed to be completely controlled by these mysterious switches. Once there was a doorway's width gap, Julia led us through.

The kitchen was spotless. Chairs were pushed just far enough away from conspiring at the round table. The wood floors were newly waxed. Countertops were uncluttered white granite, except for a steel teapot and stack of paper cups. The authorities had obviously cleaned the crime scene, and the only clue to the previous mess was the broken window, which had been replaced by a white tarp that fluttered with the winter chill. The room was cold as an aura of the death. Real or not, I had an instinct for such things. I imagined Marko facing his fate to the bitter end.

"Can I go through the cabinets?" Scarlett asked politely.

"Be our guest," Julia said. "We're going to sell the place."

"Maybe you can tell us if you know anyone looking for a chambered, nautilus-like apartment," Lars said. "A criminal you couldn't catch might enjoy it."

"Not many of those."

"That implies there are some," I said.

"Only those I haven't caught yet." Scarlett rocked a chair to test the weight. "The cabinets are original, right? Nothing's been taken out?"

Lars nodded. "Only the poisoned coffee jar. The authorities just finished their investigation this morning. The cabinets are as they were." He frowned, speaking with a soft tone that had a bit of shake in it. "Julia, do you want to go back to the living room?"

"Yeah," she said, her gaze stuck on a chair where she presumably found Marko.

Lars took Julia out and returned more relaxed; yet, his fingers still trembled like his voice had.

Scarlett opened the first cabinet on the upper left. I peered in, too, seeing flashlights, batteries, and wires.

"What're you looking for?" I whispered.

"Clues." She closed the cabinet.

Her blunt manner sent my eyes rolling. "What clues?"

She opened the next cabinet, which had porcelain mugs, two missing on the left-hand side. She ran her finger over the handle of a mug and looked at it.

She shut the door solidly. "Either something that is here and shouldn't be, or something that isn't here and should be. Was Marko left-handed?"

"No," Lars said.

Scarlett continued her search. "If it was venom—a bite or scratch—I'd have to be careful of something as simple as an Asp, like the snake that killed Cleopatra, or even hundreds of different spiders. But ingesting poison rules out venomous creatures and myths—manticores, basilisks, and the like.

There are far fewer poisonous myths and creatures. Many poisonous creatures become so because they are immune to poisonous plants and eat them, but Marko didn't eat a creature, he drank coffee. Of course, a plant or poison could've been slipped in his cup." She opened the cabinet under the sink, where there was an assortment of different cleaning chemicals, a mousetrap, and rubber gloves. "However, the jar of coffee beans being poisoned is odd."

"Pestilence?" I suggested.

"You mean a god." She hurried onto the next cabinet, almost speaking to herself. "For example, Achlys—the mist of death and Greek goddess of poisons. That's unlikely, given it's nothing powerful. Nothing plague-bearing, as it's only one target at a time. Where is it?" She sped through cabinets.

Finally, she threw one open and did not immediately shut it. The cabinet was filled with various dry goods ranging from canned soups to spices, flour, canned soups, tea bags, and a full, fragrant jar of coffee beans.

"You do have coffee," Scarlett said, finding relief.

"That's what you were looking for?" I asked.

"I got it earlier—I need my morning coffee," Lars said.

"I can understand that," Scarlett said. "Yet, you didn't offer us any?"

Lars glanced over to an empty spot on the counter. "I bought beans instead of instant coffee. It slipped my mind that Marko broke the coffee maker."

"Understandable," Scarlett said, sounding sincere.

She peeked into the rest of the cabinets, which were filled with dishes and the like, but at this point, Scarlett got bored and barely glanced, only making sure there wasn't an actual myth hiding in them. Finally, she looked into a mostly-empty fridge, which had a few takeout boxes, partially-filled bottles of creamer and sauces in the door, and a drawer with a package of mozzarella and cheddar, both sealed.

"How'd Marko like his coffee?" Scarlett asked.

"Black." Lars shook his head. "Bitter."

"Well, I can say that the coffee he drank killed him," Scarlett said, closing the fridge.

I looked at her like she'd gone crazy. "We already knew that."

"One answer doesn't mean it's the only answer. It might've been the cheese *and* the coffee. Or if Marko cut his coffee with something like tap water, I might've considered a mythical salamander in the water supply. But it doesn't matter what it's not. The myth we're looking for wasn't here by accident."

"I think there's something else that could've done this," Lars said. His finger stopped tapping. "Well, not something. Someone."

"And you only mention this now?" I confronted Lars. "Are you purposely hiding info like where you were when all this happened?"

"I was doing my nightly routine—working late. Unfortunately, I arrived home after Marko was dead. Julia had called the police already, and I got here before they arrived."

"I already checked, and he's not lying," Scarlett said. "Even if he failed to mention it."

"Because I couldn't have killed him," Lars said, not backing down.

"You don't have to be in the room with poison." I heard the tinge of anger in my voice, but I wasn't sure it was directed at Lars. I had experience in the matter, once being a god of poison.

"That's true, but not helpful," Scarlett said calmly. "Zee, let him say who he thinks it is."

"Well…" Lars sighed. "If it was, it doesn't matter—I was going to say the man who died in the apartment building earlier. He could've killed himself and Marko—he sold myths."

Scarlett raised a brow. "That is interesting. However, I want to focus on this new type of poison before pointing fingers. Without that mythical element, we wouldn't be here, and, as far as I can tell, there are two options."

"I thought you knew what it was," I said.

She ignored me. "One option—a Gu."

"Gesundheit."

"Gu," she repeated, slower. "From Chinese legend. People would place various venomous creatures into a box or jar, letting them fight it out, until all the toxins would be devoured by a single victor. Then, toxins would be extracted or left to be eaten by larvae, which would grow into terrible creatures or spirits. As always, there are differences in the story, depending on the storyteller. Yet, I've ruled that out for a single reason—you don't own any myoga ginger."

Lars and I gave her the same confused look.

"An antidote to the Gu's poison," she said. "I thought the killer might've used a myth with an antidote that could be kept in plain sight. As I was debating various coincidences and plants: cantarella—used by the Borgias—or Aqua Tofana, both of which would be very fitting and could have slight alterations to the formula that might make them less recognizable, I found something that gave it away—the mousetrap."

"I like mice. They're quite cute and not usually poisonous." Usually being the key word—I liked the form. Maybe Scarlett was right—I could've been the killer had I not been at her apartment the whole time.

"This one's not a normal rodent," Scarlett said. "We have work to do, but for now, we should thank Julia for her hospitality."

"You haven't done anything," Lars said. "All you said was that there's a mouse."

"But you already know that. One of you has seen the myth." Scarlett headed back into the living room. "Although I doubt a mousetrap would work."

"Can you catch it?" Julia asked, listening from the chair. She was resting her face on her hand, her tawny-colored mole poking out between fingers.

"I believe so," Scarlett said. "People have always been trying to build a better mousetrap. I prefer the original. It's perfect. A cat."

"It's poisonous," I said. "We're not sacrificing a cat."

"I'm sure *you* can figure out a way to stop the cat from eating the creature once it's caught."

I cursed to myself in ancient languages, knowing what she meant—I was going to be the cat. Although I'd agreed to help, this was an indignity. One I wouldn't suffer without at least a few treats on the line.

"I'm allergic to cats," Julia said.

"Don't worry, we'll catch it elsewhere," Scarlett said. "The trouble is finding where."

"I appreciate it," Lars said. "If you catch it quickly, I'll add on a handsome bonus."

"No need for money," Scarlett said. "Helping people is what I do. Though I guess you can humor me with a simple request. A deposit of sorts."

"Providing it's not too ridiculous."

"You can be the judge of that." Scarlett investigated the desk, running her finger over a few scratches. "I want the two of you to try a few passwords for me. I think the new password was Marko's last words."

Lars said, "I don't think—"

"We'll humor you," Julia said.

Reluctantly, Lars went to the switch and put it in the middle setting. The TV sunk into the floor and the room went dark before monitors burst back into lock screens and aggressive messaging.

Certain, Scarlett withheld a triumphant grin. "Please say the following password—'Julia'."

Lars shook his head, "He never made passwords that simple. They're usually long jokes."

"I doubt he had much time to think it through," Scarlett said, motioning for him to try.

A heavy sigh from Lars. "Julia."

The locks blared red.

Scarlett bit her lip, self-assurance shaken. "Try the password, 'Lars'."

"I really—"

"Quickly," Scarlett said. "I shouldn't be wasting time on this."

"Lars," Julia said.

The screens went full red for a flash, blaring even brighter.

"It's going to lock us out," Lars said.

"Perhaps Marko had more time than I considered." Scarlett adjusted the silver chain of her teardrop pendant under her neckline. "Admittedly, I didn't know him." She perked up and hid the chain again. "One more. Say, 'I love Julia'."

"No way." Lars' angry refusal reasoned calmly. "I don't want to get locked out."

"Do it," Scarlett said, not backing down.

"It doesn't mean anything," Julia said. "It would only be Marko's words."

Lars hesitated, his face tense and preventative of expression. "I love Julia."

The locks went green, showing a brief, "Welcome", before unlocking to a desktop spread over the variety of screens, which was barren except for a few folders.

"Any new folders or anything different?" Scarlett asked.

"Doesn't seem to be," Lars said.

"Marko should've made the password shorter," Scarlett said, retrieving her jacket.

"Seems like Marko loved you to the end," I said, attempting to console Julia.

Julia merely nodded, keeping emotion contained.

Meanwhile, Scarlett explained to Lars. "If you really must know, the myth is based on a common misperception of rats regarding plague, but it is inspired by a real creature—a crested rat—the only poisonous, but not venomous, mammal. However, the real creature is not poisonous itself. Like some caterpillars, it uses the plants around it to become poisonous, except instead of simply eating it, it rubs the sap of poison arrow trees onto its fur, which it can spike up like a porcupine. Of course, it's not an easy animal to come across, and far harder to capture, except in imagination. The very story of it is enough to become mythic."

Sirens.

Scarlett sighed, releasing tension, "I did say time was of the essence. Though I guess another minute or two wouldn't have done much good."

"Did you call them?" Lars asked.

"I assume one of your neighbors did," Scarlett said. "I can tell you this. The murderer you're looking for is bigger than a typical rodent, smart, and adept with poison. Two are dead, probably now three. Two of which would be an accident. Yet, that is the hardest part to prove. The easiest part to prove is that a myth exists and the killer is extremely close. Close enough that we must be on our way until the commotion the authorities bring dies down. Tomorrow, we'll come back with the myth and we can talk about what to do with it. Goodnight, and try to get some sleep, you're both perfectly safe."

"But the creature is still out there," Lars said, unconvinced.

"Then don't eat anything," Scarlett said. "I'd suggest you change the password on the computers." She nodded and left to the hallway.

As soon as we entered the elevator, I asked, "If they know about the myth, why aren't they suspects?"

"Who said they weren't? But suspicion doesn't prove anything."

I nodded. "Is there a reason you were so insistent on testing the password?"

"Because that's the key to this ordeal."

SIX

I GO PET SHOPPING

"**W**HERE are we going?" I asked.

We had not gone far, but in fresh winter, it was a mushy trek. Scarlett strode through sticking snow with her hood up. "We're going to find out more about someone who is now out of our reach."

"The guy in jail, Otto?"

"Someone who's dead. Someone Lars mentioned without naming, his suggestion both leading us astray and onto another viable track."

"But Lars isn't the killer?"

"He's not," Scarlett said. "But that doesn't mean he's telling us everything. Everyone has a reason to omit inconvenient truths and tell the convenient ones."

"That's the fun."

"Not when you're on the receiving end." Her confident footsteps parted snow into clouds. "Hurry up, the trail is going cold."

"It's already cold. Three days have passed since Marko died."

"For a second, I thought you were making a joke about the weather. But you're right, our chances of proving who killed Marko is slim. It's even less likely we can prove he was the only purposeful death." Her stride's rhythm hiccupped, almost like a skip. "Though, I suppose that's not entirely true. The first death was purposeful, just deserved."

"The myth—"

"Killed its first owner," Scarlett interrupted with her conclusion. "Who happened to be Julia's ex and the owner of the shop we're going to."

"How are you so sure?"

She was surprisingly cheery. "If I was the myth, that's what I would do."

"What does that mean?"

"I use this very rarely." She tapped her forearm and a BioScreen turned on, projecting light into the night. "After Lars suggested the dead man may be the killer—quite wrongly—I found out it was Ali. That put a lot of pieces together."

"Ali?" I read the one-sentence mention on her BioScreen about the first death, saying it was a terribly rare case of food poisoning. "I suppose his food was poisoned. You knew Julia's ex?"

"As Lars said, he sells myths, so of course I've had my dealings with him. We didn't like each other. I didn't know Julia used to work at the store. But times have changed, and we'll have to talk to Ali's replacement. If we can get proof the killer bought the creature, we won't need to resort to other, less pleasant methods. Then, all we'd have left is you hunting the myth."

"You make the hunting sound simple," I said. "Do you think it's easy for me to be whatever you want?"

"I'm sure you'll be a cute cat."

"No one calls me cute."

"Times change. You're already basically a cat. Twenty hours in the same spot, four hours restlessly running around the house. All I need is to feed you kibble instead of apples." She placed an arm around me, comradery warming winter.

Shadows lengthened around us, crackling like laughter. I wanted her to think that only my sense of humor kept her alive, as did the element of ironic truth, but really, I was afraid of my touch hurting her, even if it would be slow. I would've warned her, but most people are too worried about wrinkles and grey hairs to be in the same room as me. It was better to keep my aging touch quiet.

Scarlett realized comradery had gone too far and distanced herself. When we arrived at a run-down storefront with a darkened neon sign that said, "Pet Store", we finally broke a snowstorm silence.

"It's closed," I said.

"It's usually closed." Scarlett knocked. "Unless the owner recognizes you."

"Are you familiar with everyone?"

"That's my business. No one can know everything, but you can know someone who knows a thing. With Ali dead, Jesse will be in charge of the store."

"I thought you said myths were rare till recently?"

"You're not the god of stupidity after all," she teased. "They sell very few real myths, just creatures close enough to be mistaken for them."

The door had various signs, including the smallest of legal writing saying, "7-Day, You're Dead, Money Back Guarantee". Behind the signs and frosted glass, a shadow loomed.

The door opened and a skinny man brought us inside to a fur-warm place. It smelt of scales, pellet food, a different sort of less pleasant pellets. The store was a dark, sightless zoo. Water filters bubbled, wings flapped, and creatures hissed. Walking from sound to smell, there was a strange tip-of-the-tongue familiarity. Slivers of sight and sound bordered on the mythical, the fantastical, and my imagination wandered.

These were the inspirations of myth. A wing here, a tail there. An external-gilled salamander swam in a small aquarium. A pudgy, vampire-toothed baby black bear glared from a large enclosure. Dim lights revealed a lilac-breasted bird sleeping like a sunset. Smaller critters watched us. A quilled bumblebee-shrew had hair that looked like it woke up from a bad nap. On one pane of glass, a frog was as translucent as the cage, see-through except its organs, and next to it, there was another frog that looked spray-painted gold. Finally, there was an enormous bird cage lined with paper underneath. An owl-like creature in with a mouth big enough to swallow me whole watched us with deep, black eyes.

None of them were myths; I could sense as much. Yet, these animals were so odd they could be mistaken for them.

Past the aisle, our host led us into a bright back office that might've once been a storage room and shut the door behind us.

The man walked around the room. "It's strange not seeing you out in the field researching some creature or another, Scarlett."

"I've been busy, and so have you." Scarlett took one of the few seats in front of the desk. They were quite old, the leather scuffed and ripped, either by use or by what might've been claws. "I hope you do a better job than Ali after his untimely demise."

The man sat at the oak desk, and I finally got a good look at his face, which was thin and pockmarked, especially by a scar on the left side of his face that looked like a thin, slanted sideburn. "A very timely demise, I would say."

"I wouldn't say that, if I were you, Jesse," Scarlett said. "It's too true."

Before sitting, I wiped the seat of what looked like sawdust but might've been some unpleasant droppings. "By the way you're talking, you sound like you had the motive to kill Ali."

"Jesse didn't kill Ali," Scarlett said. "Not because he wouldn't benefit, but because he's been out of town for months procuring animals for the shop."

"Ali had the easy, safe job."

I grinned. "Apparently not that safe."

"Your companion thinks he's funny." Jesse placed his feet on the desk. "I'd like to see him raft down waterfalls while trying to keep an alligator gar in the seat next to you."

"I've wrestled worse," I said. "You think—"

"Excuse him," Scarlett said. "He's a little on edge without coffee."

"Coffee?" I asked.

"A brown, fragrant bean made into a drink." Scarlett was in a strangely playful mood. "Do you have any?

"Ali doesn't keep any coffee in the shop," Jesse said.

Scarlett paused. "That's what I thought. Unfortunate, the coffee would've made for a deadly accident."

"He did die," I said.

"Yes, the animals must be *soooo* sad one finally killed him. We're all so sad about that." Scarlett oozed sarcasm and then turned serious instantly. "Anyways, do you have a record of sales?"

"No," Jesse said, leaning in the chair.

I side-eyed Scarlett, who kept her reaction composed. A bark peeped through the closed door, but it was not a dog's bark.

"Is that a sugar glider?" Scarlett asked.

"You're here to buy?" Jesse's foot moved like a drumbeat.

"No. It'll come with me if you have it." Scarlett leaned forward over the desk, mere inches away from his leg. "But I'd buy something else."

Jesse moved his legs off the table. "There aren't any two for one specials."

"What I want to buy is the full story of what happened with you, Ali, and Julia. If only to satisfy my curiosity."

"Who said I have anything to say?"

"Well, I figured there'd be a story there. You're the one who set Julia up so you could get her job."

Jesse knocked his knee on the desk as he got to his feet. "I won't entertain such lies."

"And I thought you were the one lying." Scarlett kicked me under the seat, but I had no idea what she wanted.

However, I figured I needed to do something. Was she trying to anger Jesse? Distract him? I had no idea.

She was hard enough to understand at the best of times. I tried my best, and like ventriloquism, I pulled the strings of darkness in the main room. A threat of age. Of death. I wanted fear, and I got it.

The sounds of restless animals raged against my presence. In times of old, animals ran. But with nowhere to go, they merely rampaged in their cages.

"Out," Jesse said, pushing us out the room and locking it behind us. He ran to check the lock on the bear's cage.

I half expected Scarlett to be happy with getting Jesse out the room, but instead, she rolled her eyes and hissed, "I wanted you to get the truth out of him."

"About Julia?"

"About the records."

"That was extremely unclear," I said.

"Well, I can see how you'd think that, but how could you forget why we're here? I think he's lying about not having the records. Someone bought the rat." She bit her lip. "I wanted you to—wait—I have a better idea. Distract him while I look around."

If she wanted something, she should've told me earlier. Or, if she was going to be so mischievous, maybe she should've made it more obvious she was in that mood; I could get behind that.

Jesse hit buttons on his BioScreen, altering settings for the store. Bright lights came up in the main room.

"One of the creatures you had escaped," I said.

I saw Scarlett weave down a different aisle.

"I don't know what you're talking about," Jesse said, peering between me and his BioScreen. "Nothing's escaped."

I had a theory. "Julia bought a creature and it escaped." I followed with loose logic, but if I wasn't sure it was untrue, I wasn't lying. "We're trying to capture the creature. It killed Ali. It killed Julia's husband. Maybe you can put the pieces together and figure out who might be next."

I could almost see the hamster wheel of Jesse's brain turning. I was bluffing. If Jesse got Julia into trouble, I didn't understand why he wasn't first on the list to kill.

But the insinuation worked. Jesse boiled over, rattling a padlock as he checked it was secure. "That's not my problem! I'm not scared of anything we sell, and I don't need you and your fantastic stories." The steam turned down to a simmer. "Besides, Julia didn't buy anything here. She's banned from the store."

Scarlett arrived as if she had never been out of Jesse's sight. "You're sure? Did you sell a crested rat? Or a myth that can pass as one?"

The animals calmed down, with that done, Jesse seemed done with us, too. "Out! I have no liability for what happens because of the animals we sell, and I'm certainly not scared of a rat."

He pushed us out of the store back into a blizzard. The door closed and locked behind us.

"Did you get what you wanted?" I asked. The falling snow cooled the tempers of the store.

A furry, grey critter peeked out of Scarlett's jacket pocket, a white and black face matching her clothing. The creature's enormous eyes were two adorable orbs, staring at me.

"I did find something," Scarlett said.

"You stole that little squirrel thing?"

"A sugar glider. And I can't steal something that has 'no record'. Besides, Angel escaped. I didn't look for her, she just jumped on me. I thought I lost her months ago, but you feed a sugar glider a honey-apple treat one time and it just keeps coming back. This is your fault." Despite her words, she beamed as she pet the sugar glider's fur free of snow with a single finger.

"My fault?"

"You made that much harder than it needed to be," Scarlett said. "You were supposed to threaten him into telling the truth."

She said this, but if that was what she really wanted, there would've been a Pull. Or, at the very least, she would've told me directly. I nodded towards the store. "A door wouldn't stop me. If you wanted me to threaten him, we could always go back."

"No," Scarlett said. "It's okay. I've tried to get the store shut down before, but Ali was careful. Jesse—on the other hand—isn't. This might not be the way I expected, but his carelessness will cost him. At least in the meantime, Jesse will treat the animals better."

"I thought you would like a store of myths."

"Not in cages." The words came out in short clouds, and she glanced back across the door, where a figure remained a shadow at the door. "Jesse is more paranoid than I expected. Maybe he should be—he's lucky enough that the murderer only wanted Marko dead."

"I'll remind you three people are dead," I said as we walked away from the store.

"The myth is a murder weapon, not the murderer."

"Like Izak using me."

A brief nod, and she picked up her pace. "Three deaths—one accidental, one in revenge, and one murder. The accident was the latest and easiest to solve: the myth we're looking for was hiding in someone innocent's apartment, who was unlucky enough to ingest something poisoned by the myth. We need to catch it before it kills again."

I raised my hood and huddled tighter into my warming jacket. "And the revenge?"

"Well, I suppose the myth did murder Ali. He lives in the same complex as Lars and Julia. After the poison was extracted, the myth must've escaped and found him."

The sugar glider kept poking its head out a pocket and getting pelted by heavy flakes, which caused Scarlett to pause and pet the cold powder away tenderly. The animal surely had no idea what snow was. Cuteness and serious conversation contrasted like green grass poking out of the piling snow. Finally, Scarlett zipped her jacket pocket, allowing a little gap so Angel could stick a pink nose out.

Scarlett walked on uninterrupted and unbothered by cold, even as her nose turned red. "The murderer waited for the right moment to kill Marko—when there was someone to blame. Yet, all the other deaths make my theory harder to prove, especially because I didn't find the proof I was looking for. Instead, I found a bill of sale with Otto's signature."

"Jesse said they don't have bills of sale."

"A lie and a truth," Scarlett said with a smile. "The authorities probably locked Jesse out of the electronic records. The paper backups were hidden in plain sight, so naturally, everyone missed them. The store has a seven-day return policy for a peculiar reason; Ali used the store records to line the bird cages and changed the lining once a week. The fine print was that anyone with the gall to return a pet would have to dig the store's copy out of the Potoo bird's cage. Most people look at the giant mouth, eyes, and hear the screech. Then, they decide to keep their pet. Little do they know, Potoo are insectivores, and I managed to pick out a bill of sale for a crested rat. Somehow, our killer even managed to have that point to Otto."

"And the killer isn't Otto? Seems like an open-and-shut case."

"Or an excellent frame job."

"You didn't find what you wanted, but you don't sound too disappointed," I said, gusts of snow blowing in our faces.

"I'm not surprised. It's a challenge. This does complicate things. Ali might've been killed to hide who bought the creature. We'll have to prove the myth killed him of its own accord."

"If you didn't go so far to prove why I killed Izak, why do we have to prove the myth killed Ali? Why not let the murderer take the blame for that?"

Scarlett's hair caught white flakes, but they melted at her heat. "Because that's not the truth. The guilt and consequences are a different matter."

Nearly blinded by walking through the blizzard, I lowered my head and followed Scarlett like a shadow. "And you believe the murderer only intended for Marko to die?"

"I do." She said it with such confidence I was filled with certainty, too.

"If it wasn't Otto, Lars, or Jesse, that means you think it's Julia," I said. "Why is Jesse alive, then?"

"Oh, you mean if he set Julia up?" I could hear her smile. "You're getting too clever for your own good. I was serious. I wanted to buy the story because I didn't know if he did that."

"Then how do you know it's Julia?" I asked.

"I can't prove it yet, but in short, that's what the appearance of an accident makes me believe—it's what this specific myth makes me believe. Why would someone go to such lengths to not be caught?"

"That's a dumb question." I rolled my eyes and almost rolled on a patch of ice, catching myself after quite the inelegant skate. In the tumult, I caught a glimpse of the neon city center lighting the blizzard blur.

"It's an important question," Scarlett said. "What happens after a murder like this gives us insight into a possible motive. Revenge would welcome the aftermath. Money would be greedy for the results. But premeditated planning has a different desire—the future."

"Not many people want bad consequences."

"That's not what I'm saying."

I considered what she said, but I focused on the practicalities, peeking out the side of my hood at her. "So, are we going to use Angel as bait to catch the creature?"

"What's wrong with you? Of course not." She placed a frozen hand over the sugar glider in her pocket. "Let's go warm up at a coffee shop while we wait for the authorities to finish investigating."

"Couldn't we wait at home?"

"We don't have enough honey or coffee."

"We have plenty of both." A pesky snowflake stuck to my long eyelashes, the crystal obscuring my vision. I wiped it clear, along with my dark eyebrows of any cold flakes that snuck by my hood. "I'm convinced you solve the case in ten minutes and spend the rest of the day wasting your time."

"Ten minutes to come up with a theory and the rest of the day to be certain. Coffee is vital for this process. Besides, can you really turn down big, begging eyes? Angel enjoys honey like our myth enjoys coffee."

I figured Scarlett must have some vital use for this seemingly useless excursion. "When are we going hunting?"

"We have about eight hours before the myth will kill again." She strode ahead into the neon blizzard.

I sped after her. "You know the myth that well?"

"That's when early risers will start waking up with their morning coffee."

SEVEN

I BECOME CUTE

Snow tumbled down in waves, the blizzard building higher with each gust. Drifts twisted like wraiths, and streetlights were engulfed more than if I'd taken their light.

"You didn't drink any coffee," I said to Scarlett as we stood outside the death-prone apartment complex, hiding under the shelter of the building.

Scarlett's breath fogged the glass jar of coffee beans in her arms. "We needed a jar."

"You have jars at home."

"The creature loves coffee and the smell of a coffee shop is something I couldn't replicate."

I sniffed and smelt roasted coffee. "You marinated me in the smell."

"You make good bait as well as being a hunter." Scarlett entered the code to the apartment complex and opened the door. "No problems becoming a cat?"

"It's not as easy as you observing Lars' code to the building."

"I didn't ask if it was easy."

"It's doable." I warmed in the glow of the apartment's lobby. "Do you know where we're going for the newest victim?"

We entered a rickety elevator, and she pressed the button for the fifth floor, jolting upwards before slowing to a snail's pace. "Each apartment's pipes and vents connect to the apartment above and below."

"Lars lives on the eighth floor."

"And the first person who died, Ali, lived on the sixth floor. The order is important. It's likely the creature escaped on the eighth floor and hunted Ali down on the sixth floor because it's easier to go down in the pipes or vents. To find the third victim, we should probably look below the sixth floor."

"If we find the myth, will we be able to free the man they arrested?"

"That wouldn't prove his innocence," Scarlett said. "They still think he bought the creature. Until we get something definitive to cast doubt on that, Otto will be in custody. The police finally got their opportunity to arrest him."

My owl-faced guise was appropriately curious as I rotated my head. "Is he guilty of anything?"

"Nothing they've been able to prove, and nothing that's my domain."

"Suspicion is not guilt."

She raised an inquisitive eyebrow. "He may not have killed Marko, but Otto is in shady businesses. At the very least, he's a loan-shark."

"But even you don't know for sure whether he's doing anything illegal." Whether it was the Pull or merely being around Scarlett, I felt a need for certainty. I stared at the steel doors, avoiding her probing eyes.

"Have you always cared about proving whether someone is guilty?"

I hesitated. Proof hadn't stopped me from issuing punishments before, but I didn't want to say that. "*Detective Amar should actually do his job.*"

"I think this is about you, not Amar." She shifted her weight back and forth in expectation. "Tell me what you're thinking."

The elevator dinged, sliding open. I went to leave, but Scarlett blocked the way with an arm. Normally, an arm wouldn't stop me; however, aging Scarlett wasn't worth it. The door shut, and we stood in the motionless elevator.

I sighed. "I just understand what it's like to have a bad reputation. Being unjustly blamed feels worse than when you're guilty—at least then, the consequences are deserved."

Scarlett smiled and pressed the button to open the door. "Hmm."

"What?" I said, following her out.

She shook her head. "Nothing."

"Now you're the one holding out on me."

Scarlett turned and went back into the elevator before it closed. "This isn't the floor."

Spun like the conversation, I stepped back into the elevator. She pressed the button for the fourth floor and the doors slid shut.

This time, I faced her with my back to the door. My deep eyes challenged her, waiting for an answer. It didn't come.

The door opened to the fourth floor. Scarlett slipped by me and went down the hallway, striding triumphant to a door with yellow police tape.

"I was right."

"You can't just 'hmm' and walk away," I said, closing on her like a noontime shadow. "You were going to say something."

She stopped by the door. "It would only get us off track. We're here to help people."

"I'm not sure you and a death god are much help to the living."

She turned. "What's that supposed to mean?"

"Some people want to help. Some want a challenge. But that isn't you. Selflessness or avoiding boredom doesn't inspire you. You want proof. You want to be certain." I watched her for a response.

"Don't we all wish life was more certain?" There was a hint of sadness on her lips, and that was the most she gave away. "Life is a complex mess, and I want to cut through the randomness to find answers. In the process, I'm helping everyone in this apartment who are caught up in a personal matter and are in danger because of it. Once we catch the creature, I'll be certain in my part and the rest will be out of my hands."

"Whose hands will it be in?"

"Someone else." She tried the door handle, but it didn't turn. "It's locked. Give me a minute."

"You can lockpick now?"

"An important skill in my line of work." She reached into her jacket and recoiled. "Ow." She shook off a sugar glider bite. "Angel, I should turn you into sugar instead of feeding it to you." Despite the anger, there was nothing serious. If anything, she seemed happier having changed the subject. "Fine. Have the glove. I just need one."

Withdrawing a glove from the other pocket, she examined the lock for a moment as she put the glove on. I rested on the wall, crossing my arms and enjoying the spectacle.

There was a momentary pause, and she pushed the door.

The door had already been broken open.

"What a lockpick," I said, sarcastic. "Almost like magic."

She reddened. "They broke the door."

"When you see art, do you just look at the paint and not the painting? Anyone can see the doorframe is cracked, but you were too busy looking at the lock. It was fun to see you try and unlock an unlocked door."

"I could've picked the lock. But apparently Amar's team doesn't know how to be subtle." She escaped embarrassment by slipping through the police tape and into the apartment.

Scarlett left the lights off, motioning for me to join. This was a different sort of summoning that I did not have to listen to. But I thought she wanted to move on from embarrassment, and I let her.

The living room was large and open to the kitchen. A couch faced a screen. A table had plates on it. A coffee cup was still deadly. The lightlessness of the room was fatal grey.

Scarlett asked, "Well?"

"Well, what?"

"Meow." She had a good impression before curling on the sectional sofa, her black boots dangling off the edge.

"You're just going to watch?"

A nod.

Maybe I should've transformed into a dog or a rat just to spite her. But I didn't want to waste the energy. Like many of my guises, I took the form of a cat I'd once known. A labor of love. Animals never blamed me. I was an old friend they merely might put off meeting.

This cat would be thousands of years old now, but it looked as spry as when it roamed the deserts of southern Persia, arriving from being worshipped in Egypt because it got too much attention there.

I'd like to think my copy matched its godly attitude. Black and grey tiger stripes ran beautifully down my side. My paws were white-socked. Nine whiskers curled away from my pink nose on one side, while ten bent parallel on the other side. Deep pupils absorbed detail in the darkness.

The hunt was on.

My mouth opened slightly with instinct, taking smells into the roof of my mouth. Air rustled over scent glands. Coffee. Everything was overpowered by my own stench. Triangular ears swiveled towards a rustle on the couch—Scarlett repositioning. She was intrigued by my transformation, taking mental notes with the wrinkles in her face.

I prowled to the kitchen. Low and long, my tail trailed. Claws dug on hardwood. Retracting them was more difficult than I remembered. Extending was easy. Good. I would need them. My heart pulsed in sensitive ears, but hearing was clear. Lungs filled through searching nostrils.

The smell of my coffee-saturated fur was too much to ignore, and I went to lick a patch of fur. My tongue poked out, but I stopped in time, fighting the instinct, unable to bare the embarrassment. Other smells snuck behind the coffee. Scarlett—a mix of the coffeehouse and her normal smell, like fresh ink and parchment. Another human's smell lingered. There was an offensively strong smell of seasonings in the kitchen. Citrus and apples were sharp, sitting on a bowl. Jars of spices—thyme, basil, and mint—were recently opened and spilt onto a paper towel, extraordinarily strong. A lavender incense stick must've been strong enough for a human's poor senses, and to me, it was disgusting. More so than just sensing, it dragged me to investigate this torture.

Tiny hairs vibrated. I froze.

A minuscule noise rustled under kitchen cabinets.

If only I had opposable thumbs. Instead, my butt waggled.

Slinking closer to the sound, I lined myself at the base of the wood, fur prickling at cold contact. The apartment was losing heat now that no one lived here. That, though, might set the creature into searching for a new nest. I lay next to the cabinet, whiskers bent against the wood and nose wrinkling at the smell.

A waiting game. Minutes went by. I settled my cat instincts. Curiosities urged movement, but I disregarded them. The now silent cabinet was my only concern, and I had to be just as quiet. Squishy paws hurt on hard floors, yearning for a soft blanket. My ear itched, but I didn't scratch, and no matter how I breathed, my heart wouldn't slow.

My patience paid off.

A pink nose opened the wood cabinet. Then, a short snout snuck out. What followed was a skunk-colored creature fluffed like a fuzzy caterpillar. The side had two white stripes, meeting like a talon near the tail. The back was porcupine-quilled, looking like a poisonous mohawk on a bad hair day.

As the creature slipped out the cabinet, it kept its wits and the furs slowly sleeked down. It had not smelt me because of the coffee.

Haunches readied a pounce.

I leapt. My paws met sharp barbs. Pain. The ferocious creature squirmed from my grasp before I could get real weight on it. I slashed after it, aiming for the soft underbelly. But the rat sped away, and my claws only scratched the floor.

The creature was in full porcupine mode, scurrying across the floor.

If I let the creature get away, it'd kill again. More than that, I wasn't about to be embarrassed by a little rat.

Yet, my limbs ran awkward. My back paws scrabbled on wood, trying to accelerate. Finally getting my feet under me, I sped after the rat, only for the creature to change direction.

I struggled to turn. I slipped. I slid. Claws dug in, and I bounded off again. Sight, scent, and sound pulled me after the rat as if tied to it on an out-of-control sled. Being an animal was overwhelming, and just because I was a cat didn't mean I remembered how to be one.

The rat danced around a table, and I hissed after it. Like chasing my tail, we ran circles, the rat a little more agile. Maybe I was a bit clumsy, but this was no regular rat, this was a myth, after all. Our rat race went on with no end.

That was fine. Slow and patient were my specialty—creeping rather than chasing. Time catches up to all things. Sometimes it just takes a while.

I paused, catching my breath. My paws were bleeding from my initial strike. The rat's poison would've killed any other attacker, but despite my immunity, the quills still hurt.

But there was no way I'd give up. I huffed out my open mouth and it took all I had not to flop over. I hissed to make my pause seem intentional. Even gods get tired; they just learn to hide it better.

The myth had the same lesson, puffing up spikes and hissing venomously back. We stared at each other in a stalemate. I sat like royalty—that's what cats thought they were—and rested on my haunches. If I kept chasing, we'd just keep going round and round this table. I licked my throbbing paw and cleaned whiskers, dirtied by dust. Then, I bent back and cleaned my shoulder, matting it with my tongue.

A shake of my head. I'd been so caught up with the thrill and instinct of being a cat, I'd forgotten I was more than a cat. I was a god. And being a god meant I could cheat.

The only problem was that usually meant things died.

And as annoying as the rat was, I wanted to catch it alive. It was more useful for the case that way. Hopefully, I wouldn't scare it to death.

I took what little light there was, and although the shadowed tendrils were not visible in the dark room, as with the animals in the store, there were senses beyond sight.

Danger sent the critter scurrying.

Limited by my desire to not hurt it, the tendrils couldn't hold the myth. Every attempt to subdue it only increased how it struggled. The creature broke free and I tried to close the distance with another… cat-and-mouse chase… for the literal lack of any other way to put it. With fear, the creature sprinted two paces for every step of my saunter.

Then, it turned towards the couch. I panicked, thinking it might be after Scarlett. My saunter became a sprint. Yet, I wouldn't catch it in time. Just when I was about to use my shadows to cut the rat's life short, the creature dove into a jar of coffee that had been strategically left on the floor by the couch.

Seeking refuge in the safe smell, the creature dug in, splashing beans and cowering within the confines.

"Nice job." Scarlett closed the lid and locked the metal seal with a click. "We're going to have to make some airholes."

"Meow," I said, and changed vocal cords. "That's right."

"Cute as you are, you're going to need to look more intimidating. To be unambiguous—someone human."

I preferred the presence of cats rather than being one, and I changed back before I did something unbecoming again like cleaning myself. My new form was not immediately threatening. I'd become a woman, slender-lipped, with curved brows and black bangs that darkened a visage that could stare though peoples' souls. I might've stolen the form from another death god I knew. Mostly for the voice, which was raspy and closest to a daeva's godly voice. Soft as temptation. Biting as into a crisp apple. Deep as the ocean. Threatening as encroaching thunder. I'd say it was rather haunting.

"Quite the chase." I made my nails sharp as a hawk's talons and punctured the top of the jar. I changed back to normal. My world went bloodless. Faint. I dropped to the sofa, stuck in static until the world tuned back in.

"The nails that broke the daeva's back," Scarlett said.

"I succeeded, didn't I?"

"Barely. I've never seen a more awkward cat."

"You're welcome," I said. "And just because I can look like an animal doesn't mean I know how to be one. It's like putting a kitten into the body of an adult cat. Gods stick to forms they know. Forms they've had decades of practice in. Forms they can be godly in."

"And this is the most intimidating form you feel comfortable in?"

I shivered. "If you knew her, you'd think the same."

"The voice is a little unsettling."

"The contrast between form and bloodlust surprises people. Muscles and the like aren't as scary as the unknown." I smiled, just as unsettling. "I did, for a moment, consider changing into you."

"I'll take that as a compliment."

"You aren't intimidating. But what would've been more frightening than two of you showing up?"

"They'd think I had a twin," Scarlett said.

"So unimaginative. In any case, you don't have the daeva flair. Shadows, subtlety. That kind of thing."

Scarlett picked up the jar and examined the creature buried into the coffee, resting in its new glass den. A fluffball. "It's smaller than I expected."

"I assume you have a plan with what to do with it?"

"Two plans. Always good to have a backup. Can you manage one more bit of godliness before a rest?"

"Of course." A boisterous blunder—I was quite busy thinking that I might be overestimating myself. "You underestimate me."

"I estimate you pretty well," Scarlett said. "Borrow the coffee maker on the way out. Julia needs a new one."

EIGHT

'I BREW SPOILED COFFEE

THE night and blizzard ended. The ascending sun sparkled on frost, light rising while the temperature did not. As the rest of the city shoveled and then went about their normal business, Scarlett and I returned for a bit of abnormal business.

Still in the form of the deathly woman, I walked with Scarlett down the hallway to Lars and Julia's apartment. Holding a basic black coffee maker, I couldn't help but feel like this was more akin to a housewarming party than murder investigation. Though, for me, the two sometimes mixed.

My raspy voice chilled the hallway. "What if you're wrong?"

Scarlett grew somber. "Then I'll be a murderer."

"You could also be dead."

"We'd all be dead." Scarlett placed the coffee jar with the slumbering myth against the wall and out of sight from inside the apartment. "I'd prefer no one dies, though."

"Your backup plan is worse than the original."

"That's why it's the backup." She knocked on the door. "It would make the situation interesting, though."

"Why don't we just…?" I pantomimed hitting someone with the coffee maker.

"Patience. Lars has information we need."

"Why take the—?" I went quiet, hearing the door unlocking.

Lars brightened as he saw the noise in the hallway was Scarlett, but he shot my new form an uncertain look. "Who's this?"

"A myth hunter," I said, maintaining minimum words and maximum mystery.

Lars backed partially behind the door at my voice, which was like nails on a chalkboard.

"We caught the creature," Scarlett said, contrasting my tone.

Julia was behind Lars, morning-tired eyes blinking. "Well, where is it?"

"Safely locked away," Scarlett said. "But we did bring a gift."

I brushed past Julia and Lars, bringing the coffee maker in and not waiting for an invitation. Lars and Julia prickled at my presence but didn't dare stop me.

Scarlett was the opposite of my seriousness; in fact, she was cheerier than I'd heard her before. "We can sit and tell you how we cleaned up this mess."

From the kitchen, I could still hear Scarlett explaining in the living room how we'd captured the myth. Or, rather, she invented a story including minutia, fibbing, and exaggeration about a fly swatter, complex mouse traps, and ultimately, my bravery in capturing the poisonous rat by leaping from a fire escape. No cats were involved. I'd never heard her lie this much—she was after my heart with that, at least.

I returned to the room as the storied myth hunter unafraid of danger, and Lars accepted a cup of coffee from me.

"Do you need creamer?" Scarlett asked.

"If you don't mind," Lars said to me.

"Yes." I didn't move.

Lars paused. "Yes, you mind?"

"I don't believe in creamer," I said.

"Coffee purist?"

"Vegan."

Lars saw my unamused face and did not dare complain. "I'll survive without, I suppose."

I offered a mug to Julia, who was hesitant.

"Thank you," she said. "But you're the guests. I should be serving you."

"Take it," I said.

She did, and the mug steamed far from her face.

"Is there something wrong?" I asked.

"It's steaming hot."

"It'll cool."

Lars whispered to Scarlett, "Your companion is so serious. This should be a celebration."

"I haven't had any coffee this morning yet," Scarlett said, hinting not-so-subtly for me to get her some. "But I'm still not as grumpy as my companion."

Julia blew on the coffee, steam twirling like hot springs on a windy winter day. Meanwhile, I whisked into the kitchen, bringing back another two cups of coffee and setting them on the table between myself and Scarlett.

Scarlett paid the coffee no mind, making pleasant conversation with Lars. "I think you'll be able to sleep much better now."

"In a new home," Lars said, distracted from his drink. "I put in an offer on two apartments. A fresh start."

"One for you and Julia?"

Separate homes was quite the twist. I could see the surprise in Scarlett's face. Unable to resist what Scarlett was evidently thinking, I asked, "You two are parting ways?"

"We'll be neighbors," Lars said. "Have to keep family close."

It was a noble sentiment to help his dead brother's widow, but less so if she was also his brother's murderer. There were two questions as there were two people—Julia and Lars—and they were tied together.

Scarlett took the mug, skimming over it with her eyes towards Lars. "I believe you owe me two things."

"We only agreed on one."

"If you'll humor me, just confirm what I already know."

Lars stroked his beard. "You still haven't proved you captured the creature."

"My associate from yesterday has it. Once you complete your part of the deal, you can have the creature, as agreed. You know I keep my word."

"Fine. It's the ninth floor."

"The Root splits like a tree," Scarlett said. "Which branch of the ninth floor?"

"Trading and finance. The third branch. I work with them a lot. I get these whispers. Hushed stories. Even on nearby floors, there's something odd. Two employees in the department the floor above have quit in the past month. Three on the floor below. Five on the floor itself. A little more than usual. Nothing to cause great alarm. Well, that's the official story. But the reality is they didn't quit. They went mad."

"Stress?"

"I would say a different type of stress."

Scarlett nodded.

As the coffee cooled, Julia pondered the chestnut liquid that matched her mole. Hesitation almost yelled guilt. Scarlett's theory was the mugs, not the coffee beans, were the source of the poison that killed Marko.

But then, Julia lips touched the mug and sipped. Satisfied it wasn't too hot, she took a bigger sip. I watched her throat muscles clench, certifying that she had drunk it.

Scarlett watched, too. At the revelation, she glanced to the ground, a moment of doubt, of contemplation. A split second. And that was all.

"Is the case settled, then?" Lars asked.

"No." Scarlett blew on the coffee. "I need to know how to contact the detective on the case."

"You know the detective who was here left a message for you?"

Scarlett shrugged, tracing her finger along the lip of the mug. "I figured you'd tell me eventually."

"You'll bring the creature once I give you that information?"

"Indeed. You have my word. We'll drink on it." Scarlett's hand shook ever so slightly. This was the most uncertain I'd seen her. But then again, it was her life on the line.

Lars seemed satisfied. He raised the mug and was so distracted, the steam did not seem to bother him enough to blow on it. "Cheers."

"Cheers."

Lars and Scarlett brought the mugs up, but Scarlett never took her eyes off Julia. There was no complaint as Lars took a scalding sip.

Scarlett recoiled from the mug. "It's still too hot. How long did the detective stay here?"

"The main one, Detective A?" Lars asked. "Not more than ten minutes."

"I think I spent less time." She smiled. "Did the detective seem interested in what you do?"

"Not at first. After talking with another investigator, he must've learned who I was. He definitely took more of an interest in the case."

"Or the detective learned of the unique poison and knew I'd get involved. What was the message?"

"To meet at the old fountain at noon. Seemed generic to me, but he assured me you'd know."

Knowing Amar, it was the fire fountain at the temple. The place Gwen died. That was a cruel meeting place.

"Perfect, we have a race on our hands," Scarlett said. "I give Detective A one clue and get one in return. Professional courtesy. One more thing to take care of."

Lars wiped his mouth, which seemed to spread the redness of his lips to his angered cheeks, visible even under the scruffy beard. "Still more?"

"Our original deal was that you'd tell me what was going on in The Root—the detective is part of that. But what I meant wasn't a question. I promised the creature. The truth is, it was here the whole time."

Lars tensed, eyes digging around. "Where?"

"Outside. I kept it there to see if the murderer was among us." Scarlett shook her head. "My companion yesterday said

114

something that got me thinking. If Otto was being framed, the jar of coffee beans he brought could've been poisoned after Marko was dead. Something else was poisoned first." She tapped the mug with a fingernail. "Apologies for not drinking it with you."

"The mug? But how—what—this is poisoned?"

Scarlett said, "Poisoned coffee mugs killed Marko."

After being one step behind Scarlett, I felt validation for my part in helping Scarlett come to this conclusion. Despite this, there were bigger concerns—mainly Scarlett's safety.

"That's why you didn't drink!" Lars thrust the mug across the table, flying off the edge and spilling onto the hardwood without breaking. Only then did he realize the other consequence. "You poisoned Julia, too."

I readied myself for a fight.

But Scarlett's words were calm. "I didn't poison you. Give me a moment to explain before you do anything you might regret." Scarlett took a lingering look into the coffee before addressing Lars, who seethed. "At first, there was circumstantial proof that helped my mug theory, especially the paper cups Julia gave us when we first arrived. Even if Otto hadn't brought coffee with him, his particular nature had him make the coffee, and the fingerprints on the mugs would've led the detectives to believing he was guilty. Yet, Julia saw an opportunity when the jar was left behind because of Otto and Marko's fight. The beans being poisoned made the case seem more convincing, both to the authorities and as a mythical accident. She planned it well."

"Planned what?" Julia clenched the handle harder, fingers curling into her palm. "I'm innocent."

"You're crazy," Lars said to Scarlett, the vein in his forehead popping.

"Possibly. Even if I was slightly off before, I think I understand now. And I'd bet my life on it." Scarlett drank a heaping gulp of the coffee. "Although Julia wanted to hit her target, she only poisoned two mugs. If they were all poisoned, Julia might've drunk it herself, or even let us drink it, but not you, Lars."

This was the worst backup plan. Scarlett really was willing to risk her life to solve the case.

I began thinking how I might deal with the bodies if every mug were poisoned. Then again, without Scarlett, I might be gone too. She really did mean all of us. I hadn't thought of that.

"I said I didn't poison you, Lars." Scarlett set the mug down and stood. "But what Julia didn't know was that while our coffees were made with normal beans, hers was not." She walked to the door, opened it, and returned with the glass jar. The mythical crested rat, black and white, opened a pearly eye in the coffee beans and stared at the room. "My companion made her coffee with beans from this jar."

"Liar!" Julia gripped the mug with white knuckles. "You're a detective, not a murderer. You wouldn't poison me."

True, Scarlett wouldn't actually poison her, but now was my time to shine. Or rather, take a bit of shine from Julia.

Julia flushed red with outrage. "You've got it all wrong. I don't know about the mugs. I didn't kill anyone. I didn't—" She stopped as my subtle shadows reached her. Spasms wracked her fingers, stiffening them. The wrinkles on her face deepened. Genuine concern seemed to strike her like poison.

"Julia?" Lars asked.

Without a word, Julia ran towards the bathroom.

"You poisoned her!" Under Lars' scraggly beard, neck muscles went taut as fists and he leapt to his feet.

"What goes around comes around," Scarlett said, ignoring the rage and sitting on the couch feet from the furious lawyer. "Playing with poison is dangerous."

The giant man's violence was no longer controlled. Love made people do crazy things, even if it wasn't so crazy to attack Scarlett at this point—it was just crazy to do it while I was there.

Before Lars made it a foot, I leapt between him and Scarlett.

"Sit back down." The whole room rumbled with my daeva-like tone. The venom in my voice startled Lars, but I wasn't sure for how long.

Regardless of my pacifying presence being needed, I followed Julia. Scarlett could handle herself without me—she had shown that solving the mystery was more important than her own safety.

Julia slammed the door to the bathroom shut. I waited and heard the sounds of trying to expel the poison. Or, at least, faking it.

I barged in. Wood splintered onto ivory tile as I broke the lock, the commotion drowning out whatever argument was going on in the living room.

Julia's shaky hands held a tiny cup of creamer, the lid slightly peeled back. An antidote. I grasped for it, and we tangled, wrestling for the delicate little thing over the hard, grout-lined bathroom floor. Drops spilled out of the slight opening. Julia believed her life rested upon the liquid, and that gave her the strength to fight even a god.

We rolled. I bumped my head on the toilet. Life was filled with embarrassment after embarrassment. Reduced to tangling a small woman in a bathroom rather than lions, myths, and gods. Sometimes all three at once.

Clawing and grasping, Julia's teeth dug into my forearm but didn't break skin. While a mortal might've released in shock, the bite only flushed my familiar fire like a bloodied wound. Didn't a murderer deserve to die?

"Your coffee wasn't poisoned." I yanked trying to surprise her, but she held. "But if you don't let go…" I pulled harder, tumbling once more over the tile and into the wall. "I'll kill you."

The last words were spat with venom. Lucky for her, that between the voice, the jarring impact into the wall, and what was said, Julia had the slightest hesitation. That was enough for me to yank the creamer away and retreat to the living room looking triumphant.

This tiny cup seemed a small prize in my hands, but I knew beyond the thrill of the moment, it was big.

"I got the antidote," I said, handing it over. "She's lucky she's not dead."

Scarlett held it carefully. "I'm sure if we test it, we'll find the same bacteria that grants the creature immunity from the poison. Had she used her skills in other ways, Julia would've made a better biologist or chemist than murderer."

Julia returned older—not significantly, maybe ten years—with a few subtle strands of grey hair. A more noticeable side effect, though, was that her light-brown mole had turned dark as her deed.

Whether Julia noticed, besides the sudden change in how she felt, was a lesser concern. Lars, too, was overcome with the circumstances and might put any change in Julia's appearance down to stress and the supposed poison.

Instantly aging ten years was certainly an acceptable start to punishing Julia. I could always feed on her life force more. Even if I could be convinced to spare her, I couldn't undo the aging, nor would I consider much leniency after she bit me. As tempers receded, though, I considered the thought of murdering a murderer with dualistic guilt and justice. Maybe it was the ancient eye-for-eye justice I knew, but I felt guilty for thinking about it for simply personal vengeance.

"Is the creamer really the antidote?" Lars' anger migrated into worry lines.

Julia nodded.

"Did you take it?"

"A little."

Lars' imploring eyes asked for a continued lie. "I always put creamer in my coffee. You… you were making sure I was safe." Relief, but then, realization. "You killed Marko?"

Julia couldn't meet his eyes.

"You suspected as much," Scarlett said, her kind eyes offering sympathy to Lars. "That's why you came to me in the first place." Then, sympathy was sighed away. "Yet, the struggle between finding Marko's killer and suspecting it was Julia made you leave out a key detail, Lars. One that kept us from proving it was Julia and condemned an innocent man instead."

Lars stared her down, trying to dig out an answer. With the realization, the dark wrinkles under Lars' eyes gave way. "I moved his body back into the kitchen seat. I thought—"

Scarlett interrupted, "No, you're not at fault for moving Marko once he was dead. There was no evidence to be gained by where you found him. Julia had moved him away from his desk already because Marko managed to change his password before he died. She had no idea what he wrote and couldn't delete it as easy as if he'd written a note. Although she wasn't sure if the authorities could break the security system, she thought it best not to leave the body there. You moving him did nothing." There was a sweetness in the way she reassured Lars. "Even if the detectives were wrong to assume the scratches on the desk were wear and tear, they couldn't have broken Marko's security and wouldn't have imagined that his final action was changing the password to 'I love Julia'. But even the best detectives are wrong occasionally."

"Then what?" Lars asked.

Scarlett picked up her mug, ignoring the question and continuing, "For instance, I was wrong to think Julia poisoned all the mugs to make sure she hit her target and that was why she gave me a flimsy paper cup for tea when we first met. But I shouldn't have attributed guilt to something explainable by a dislike for doing dishes. She poisoned two mugs knowing that Otto made coffee whenever he came over and, in a stressful situation, someone left-handed is more likely to take the mugs on the left side. I considered it, even if I thought it was unlikely. I asked whether Marko was left-handed and you told me no. Meanwhile, I watched you open the door with your right hand and Julia drank with hers. Otto was the only left-handed one among you. I suppose I didn't consider how much Julia wanted to frame Otto and not kill him, because like you, Lars, I assume Otto drank his coffee with creamer. Circumstance conspired to help her frame job. Otto's mug broke during the argument. He left the jar of coffee beans behind. Even after Otto was arrested, Julia cared too much to be careless. To get away with the crime, she could've gotten rid of the antidote, but as long as the creature was around, there was still a risk to you, especially with fresh coffee in the cabinets. Yet, I would've thought Marko's death was an accident, a matter of myth, except for one thing that made me realize an antidote existed."

"How could you know?" Lars weakened with every word. "How did you know it was Julia?"

"Because you knew, Lars." Scarlett didn't meet his eyes, not wanting to rub it in. "When we were first here, I went looking for how you knew."

"I washed the cup. I put it back."

"Exactly. You thought putting it back would get rid of any questions on how you survived the poisoned coffee. But one mug was less dusty than the others, and that made the case more clear to me. It's a wonder you were actually that stupid." An ironic shake of the head and Scarlett chuckled. "You told me you only use the mug for coffee and would even drink coffee after work. Julia expected everything except you reverting back to routine in an extraordinary situation. You came home from a late work night to a distraught Julia and a dead brother. After you led her out the apartment, you went back in. Thinking it'd be a long night and seeking some distraction from your dead brother, you instinctually made coffee from the poisoned beans while you waited for the authorities. Yet, you were saved by the creamer, as Julia intended. You must've been surprised when they told you the coffee beans were poisoned."

"Julia didn't tell me Marko was poisoned." Lars ran his hand over his mouth and beard, and the words barely escaped.

"She cried and said Otto and Marko had a fight. That's it. I didn't know."

"She couldn't explain the poison and maintain her innocence." Scarlett kept her eyes on the mug, instead of him. "If all the mugs were poisoned, this could've gone very differently. I could've taken the washed cup for myself, but I gave it to you, Lars. I'm not a killer." Scarlett moved on, finally setting the mug down. "Neither are you. But you helped one, and I'd like to hear why. The motive ties this case together. Otto didn't have one besides money, and a dead man pays no debts. But you, Lars, have a story that people write tales of. Mostly without the murder. But if you won't tell me, maybe Julia would." Scarlett turned her attention to the accused. "It could be the last time you get to be honest with Lars."

"I didn't—." Julia stroked her hair, debating the story, but as Lars looked at her, the guise of deception seemed to give way. There were no nerves. No shy persona. Only truth. "There's a saying it's always the spouse, but they don't ask why. I didn't see another choice. Marko was an intelligent man. It was his best trait. But he was cold. Un-emotional. I thought it was an act. That he would have a deeper level with those he cared for. But I was like a dog chained up outside. He thought about letting me in, but then I could've hurt him." She sighed. "Maybe he was right." A grim smile. "He wasn't a despicable man, despite his flaws. He never hurt me physically, but he never showed me love either. Maybe I was wrong."

"From what I gather, he loved you at one point," Scarlett said. Her logic seemed a comfort when directed in the right ways. "However, changing the password to 'I love Julia' was certainly ironic, since he wrote it as you watched him die."

Julia looked towards the desk. "It was the first password he ever shared with me when I moved in and that's why I let you try it. Like the phrase, he never reused passwords. I didn't know that's what he wrote. It wasn't irony—it was to make me feel guilty."

"He didn't love you," Lars said. "Even if he did…"

"You didn't love him anymore," Scarlett said.

Julia's eyes glistened. "In all the bitterness, I felt familiarity like it was comfort. Now, I don't know. I'm not sorry he's gone, but I am sorry it had to happen, even though he knew."

"About you and Lars?"

Julia nodded. "Marko refused to let us be happy."

"I figure Marko always knew," Scarlett said. "Love doesn't blind us—it allows us to know and close our eyes anyways."

Julia continued, "When Lars divorced his wife, Marko wouldn't divorce me. He couldn't let me go. He would've destroyed me. He would've destroyed us. It was only the week before his death that I thought the unthinkable. It came suddenly. A moment of clarity. That I wanted him dead. It wasn't selfish. It was so Marko could no longer haunt Lars. To drag him down. To borrow more and more money, even when he didn't need it. Just to keep Lars hooked with lies and sabotage. My leaving wouldn't and couldn't stop Marko from manipulating Lars. Marko would still be there. His eyes would be on us every time we passed a camera. I knew what he was capable of. And I couldn't live with it."

Lars was shattered. His world, his family, his life, in that order, broke into fragments. And what he picked up was nothing like the whole. "I didn't want to believe. I couldn't."

"Will you tell me your story now?" Scarlett asked. "Julia loved you enough to kill. That, I understand. But I want to know how you could love your brother's murderer? Julia kept you safe with the creamer, but by ignoring that, you own part of the guilt."

Lars mumbled to himself. "I had to think drinking the poisoned coffee and surviving was an accident. The coffee beans I got. A genetic abnormality. A quirk about this creature."

As he motioned to the jar, I realized I hadn't thought of why the myth was still around. Julia didn't want the creature around, but Lars believed in it, and a single person's need to believe was strong. Lars needed something to explain what killed Marko, and that explanation was the myth.

Scarlett might've been right—myths weren't without reason.

Lars only had eyes for Julia. "From the moment you walked into my office, I knew you were different. Not love at first sight, but at first phrase. You walked into my office and said, 'I know there's a saying that the pen is mightier than the sword, but have you tried an axe? I thought I asked for a lawyer, not a Viking.' That little comment got us talking, and not about the case. We sat there for hours. I cancelled meetings. I lost a couple clients. I gained so much more." His watery eyes wandered. "But it never would've worked. I was married. And I am an honest man. I loved my wife." He returned to Julia with a look as gentle as a kiss. "Yet, here was this criminal, this woman I just met, this outrageous person who broke every expectation I had of her, and I couldn't help but love her, too. I couldn't let her out of my life. Not entirely. To keep her near was enough. Or at least, I thought it would be. Instead, it was torture. I helped her get her life together, but mine fell apart." Arms shook and lips quivered. "I lied to my wife about where money went. I lied that I didn't love Julia. I started using Marko's software to make up for my failures." A brief smile. "I figured out a way to solve my problems. How to keep the woman I loved close. How to help Marko. And how to make sure I could never give in to temptation. I introduced Julia to Marko, and he, like me, fell for her. And I was happy. Truly. Despite the pain. But Marko was Marko. The timing of my divorce, of moving in, of finding that love again, had to be a coincidence to his death. An accident. I had to believe that. I believed it so hard, I thought I could go to Scarlett and the truth would set my guilt at ease. But it revealed the worst, instead of ensuring my happiness."

"I only did this for us to be happy," Julia said.

"And now happiness is out of reach."

"Couldn't we say this was an accident?" Julia asked Scarlett. "Marko is dead, he's not coming back. The creature is captured. No one else is at risk."

"Figuring out how someone died is my job, and all that happens after is not," Scarlett said. "Death is simple. Your life could change at the whim of a vindictive god. You could walk down the street and some stranger could stab you. A random myth, a mere legend, could poison you." Scarlett was dark as a daeva. "Or, more likely, as it happened to Marko, you wake up from a nap on the couch. Your eyes flutter and you feel a bit funny. You sit bolt upright, thinking your throat is just dry. You walk to the kitchen and sip at the cold coffee. That doesn't help. Your breath hurries. Confusion. Then, panic. You call for your wife. Over and over, you call, but she's not there. The world spins. You see three of your coffee cup as it shatters, and you struggle to the sink and shove your fingers down your throat. You gag, but nothing comes. You punch the window in frustration. Things break. The room is a mess. You fall, red on your hands and in your vision. Crawling through glass, you make it back to the living room. And there, in your dying sight, you see your wife, smiling. Then, your whole life comes into focus. Then, it ends."

NINE

I SETTLE "A STUDY BY SCARLETT"

THE razor-thin whine of electronics remained the only sound in the room. After Scarlett's story, Julia remained a husk of herself, and Lars looked less Viking and more like one was coming after him.

I must admit, the brutality and bluntness of the account of Marko's death transformed the room more than if I'd changed into a dragon. Somehow, mortals dared call me a demon. If it were up to me, Julia's fate was settled. Lars', less so.

An unanswered question remained. "Marko changed the password in his dying breaths," I said, my daeva-like voice lapsing into a quieter tone. "Why not implicate Julia? Instead, he said he loved her."

Scarlett pulled the desk chair out and sat, slumping in it, as if seeing which way Marko fell. "He wasn't thinking straight. To a dying man, his murder might seem so simple that anyone might solve it."

My hands scraped over the couch like claws and my voice roared back at Lars. "Did you hate your brother? How could you ignore the truth right in front of you?"

Lars closed his eyes. "I didn't ignore it. I love them both."

"You would've let Julia get away with it…" Scarlett dusted the top of the desk. From out her pocket, she took a piece of paper and placed it there. "If not for one thing. You came to us the day Otto was arrested for Marko's murder. Three days later. It would've been easy to frame Otto poorly, but Julia framed him so well that it took the authorities that long. An unrecognizable poison. An exotic pet. Of course, a normal crested rat is not quite this poisonous. Julia was looking for one, but there wasn't one and she got this creature instead. That made the case harder for the authorities, but eventually, between the fingerprints and the electronic bill of sale at the pet store, they had enough to arrest Otto."

"Both the electronic and paper copies had Otto's signature," I said, knowing well enough to let Scarlett have her dramatic reveal. "I understand how to forge a signature, but why did the digital record lead to him?"

Scarlett smiled. "The authorities locked the electronic records to prevent tampering. But no one knew Julia had already tampered with it using Marko's software." Scarlett tapped the paper, which was wrinkled and had a few feathers stuck on it. "But you've got it backwards. The paper copy is the one that doesn't seem altered."

Julia laughed. "Does it matter how I did that? It worked. Otto looked guilty."

"It matters to me," Scarlett said.

"I hope it keeps you up at night."

I hadn't imagined that I could help figure out how the bill of sale was forged, thinking the electronic record was the issue. Paper, though, I knew.

I went over and examined it. To the naked eye—which was all Scarlett had access to since last night—nothing looked out of the ordinary. The paper crinkled in my hands. If Scarlett couldn't tell the difference in signatures, I assumed it was actually Otto's, but I ran a finger over it. The issue wasn't the ink. It was the paper under the ink. There, like the rings of the Tree of Life below, the pulp of the various trees seemed younger. The signature was legitimate, but from another document, meticulously cut to the ink lines and fused onto this paper, blending seamlessly as if Otto had simply signed it. There were probably easier ways to forge a document, but none so convincing. However, I kept the method to myself. I'd let Scarlett simmer.

"Julia didn't sign it." I pushed the paper back to Scarlett. "I'm sure she didn't buy the creature herself either. She probably had someone else do it—she's smart enough to find someone who looks enough like Otto, contact them anonymously and pay them, or maybe blackmail them using Marko's technology, into buying the creature for her."

The small grin Julia had disappeared.

Looks like my deduction might've been worthy of a detective.

"Then, Ali's death really was the myth's doing," Scarlett said, examining the paper, now with renewed vigor. "If Julia was never there, she had no reason to kill him. Perhaps the creature chewed out of its cage, or maybe it squirmed away when Julia was delicately extracting the antidote or poison. How she told Lars about the creature when it escaped without attracting suspicion is a matter of love. I assume she told him she'd seen a rat. But Lars didn't think too much of it even once Ali died. Then, after Marko died, Lars kept the information about moving the body, the coffee, and Julia's behavior to himself. Without that, the police had nothing concrete. And with Otto in custody, the other detectives would've considered the case closed. No one was going to try and clear him."

"Lars did, in a way," I said.

Julia straightened. "He's a good man."

"And you went to great lengths to frame Otto," I said, nodding inadvertently.

"Otto wasn't innocent either." Lars sneered for the first time I'd seen. "He—he was the one who loaned Julia money and then turned her in for owning illegal animals when she didn't pay him back. That's how we met."

That explained why Jesse was not dead—Julia's revenge had been framing Otto.

"Then why'd you come to Scarlett?" I asked.

"Because I loved Marko."

"All these good motives are going to make me cough up a furball," I mumbled. "If Lars is such a good man, let's leave him the evidence."

Scarlett grasped onto the bill of sale. "Just hand it over?"

"Not the paper—it doesn't lead to Julia, and if we point the authorities along the right lines, we can free Otto," I said, hinting at the signature's method. "But, we'll leave them with the only evidence that can tie Marko's death to Julia—the creature and the antidote. This way, we'll see if Lars loves Julia or his brother more."

"And what sort of a man he is." Scarlett left the creamer-antidote on the desk.

"He'll either turn Julia in and prove her right that he's a good man; or, he'll have to live with the woman who killed his brother. Us turning them in won't ruin their happiness—us not turning them in will."

Scarlett pulled me aside. "Julia won't let this lie. Our testimony is dangerous. She might try to kill us."

I wriggled out of her grasp, showing as little panic as possible. Free of the possibility of hurting Scarlett with my touch, I was pleased overall with what we'd accomplished. "The key word is try." I couldn't resist a smile. "Let's go."

An uncomfortable silence followed us as we left. Lars and Julia said nothing—there was nothing more to be said. At least, not to others, only to each other.

What passed between them behind the closed door was beyond me. Now, instead of method and minutia, it was only the consequence of their discussion that would matter.

I might have to make a return visit depending on Lars' decision.

From the darkness inside, the world outside continued unconcerned. Mortal matters left my sunny stride unaffected; but still, both Scarlett and I made footprints in the snow behind us.

The storm was over. Shoveled snow mirrored clearing clouds, sunlight bursting through and sparkling on wet sidewalks. The night's silence broke. On corners and in passing, people greeted, talked, and laughed.

The wake of a winter wonder was brighter than a summer's day.

I smiled. Mystery, knowledge, consequence. The choice I'd left Lars was not an end, just an end for my role in it for the moment. I had no regrets. I was surprisingly cheery.

Until a snowball struck me in the back of my head. Flakes whisked about my face. There was a cold shiver, and it wasn't just the ice melting down my neck. I spun.

Scarlett's teeth glinted in the burgeoning sun. A playful smile. An innocent prank. "Who could've done that?"

It was an absurd act at such a moment. Yet, there was something magical about how snow could make adults act like children. And this time, it even made an old god feel young again. Even if I allowed her to get away with a distraction, I wouldn't allow the snowball to go without a response.

The cold melt down the nape of my neck disappeared entirely. Rather than shadows, I reached into clean, light snow. Another snowball hit my jacket. There was enough time for a god like me to dodge, but that was no fun. I packed the powder harder, chunks sneaking through my fingers.

I threw the ball back at Scarlett, but it broke mid-flight and became more shower than snowball. The mist was blown away by a bright, clear laugh.

Scarlett tossed another. I ducked. It pinged off the top of my head, bursting. I could've been convinced it was snowing again.

"You got me," I said, dusting myself off.

"We'll work on your snowball skills," she said, releasing the snow she'd picked up to reload.

As she dropped it and I dusted my hands of the cold, I couldn't help but lose the moment. "How did you move on from something like that so fast?"

"I can dwell on it, but that doesn't mean it has to dwell in me." She sighed. "You had to remind me already?"

"Sorry." I sounded sarcastic, but I wasn't sure if the sarcasm was genuine.

"What were you thinking?"

"I was thinking about Lars. Julia is obviously guilty, but I don't know how guilty Lars is. I don't—or maybe I can't—understand what he did." I chewed on the insides of my cheeks, as the woman I looked like used to.

"Would understanding change anything?"

"I suppose not," I said. "He omitted evidence and conspired to let a murderer go free. I sort of wish the crime wasn't so clear with his information."

"Sometimes the twist isn't in the crime, it's in the consequences." Scarlett shook her hands of the remaining ice. "I have my answer. Judging it is up to you."

"I don't make those choices."

"You don't think you can. But this time, I *believe* it is your decision."

From all I learned of Scarlett and how intently she looked at me now, I couldn't assume her words were coincidence anymore. What she said about Julia looking for a crested rat and getting a myth made sense.

She knew, or at least suspected, how myths and gods worked.

Mortals insatiable longing for explanation had created gods. Humanity always looked for more—they needed to believe there was reason behind everything. When provided answers, beliefs changed, and gods with them. We were no more than syncretism—combining different beliefs into a single being. There was some constancy, otherwise we would be altered at every altar, recast in every statue, and reimagined at every thought. Yet, we remained relevant only to the degree that we kept hold of the narrative.

"Is that the point of having me around? I'm part of some theory you have about gods?" My hands clenched, but it wasn't for warmth. I was angry at being an experiment, but I was also angry I didn't feel the Pull on what to do. This was not the free will I wanted—either way led to guilt.

Her shivering hands searched for warmth in her jacket pockets, but one hand managed only a fingernail's depth, avoiding a bite from the sugar glider occupant. "Proving that gods—especially one mistaken as a demon to be used like you—can change is only part of the reason I want you around."

Maybe giving Scarlett an answer would kill this rose before it pricked me with its thorns.

"Let me save you the time. Gods are only what people believe they are."

"I don't believe that. And I'm going to prove it." Words steamed from Scarlett's frosted breath.

I'd lost control of the narrative. Few mortals imagined a god could be subject to their beliefs, and no mortal I'd met had figured out the truth and tried to prove the opposite. Her expectation of me being free might be self-fulfilling in some regards; however, the fact I occasionally felt the direction of her belief meant the Pull was still controlling me.

Scarlett continued, "As much as we're focused on myths and mysteries, the true mystery is you, and you're the only one who can solve it for me. Besides you used the wrong word— gods are not 'only' what people believe. If gods were only that, they'd be incomplete. Concepts. The god—you—exist around those beliefs. You fill in the gaps. You have a personality. You can change. You can choose. You were made in a certain way, but you can choose what to do with that making."

"That's simple, I'm a god of death," I said, the line between my making and her words too thin for my liking.

"Who doesn't enjoy killing."

"The consequences are Lars' choice, not mine," I said. "He can turn Julia in."

She cast her head down, long hair covering her face. "And if he doesn't—no—I'm not supposed to dwell. You're supposed to be why I can throw snowballs."

She shook hair away and set off. I could tell from the sudden change, she didn't want me to follow. There was more at play than thoughts of the case. She was not the only one who could read others—her attempts at distraction and escape left me with answers.

She was trying to see how free gods were. If she believed I'd kill Lars, then Lars was likely to end up dead. But by not thinking about what I'd do with the consequences, she thought she was leaving it open.

If only it was that simple. The real reason now, was why did she care if gods had free will?

I GUESS THE PASSWORD

IT neared sundown when I finally returned to the apartment as the owl-faced man.

"Your mystery is back," I said as I closed the door behind me.

Scarlett ignored me. She did not offer food or coffee, nor ask where I'd been. Somehow, I figured either she didn't care or already knew. Yet, her response was exactly what I expected.

Although I was tired, curiosity burned more than existence. I needed an opportunity to answer my questions.

I spent the night at the nook. As snow melted the next morning, stalactites thinned like my patience, weaving webs of water past my window. Scarlett was in the bedroom, reading similar to a child, her head over the foot of her cherrywood bedframe and the book held towards the ceiling. Angel was resting on the book, big sugar glider eyes peering down.

News headlines and prices scrolled on the building opposite me. Apples were cheaper, while old artwork, maybe some about me, was more expensive. But for once, I didn't dwell on apples.

My mind went to Scarlett's computer. By now I understood that she left what she wanted to ignore dusty.

But I was distracted by a news bulletin that broke with such bright neon for dour news—"Lars Warner, prominent lawyer, found dead with his brother's wife, Julia Warner. Cause of death, poison. Detective A investigating."

I relayed the facts, ignoring the part about Amar. "Scarlett, Lars and Julia are dead."

Scarlett didn't take her eyes off her book, but Angel leapt from the book to the bed, curling into the white sheets. "He was never going to turn her in."

"Are you going to ask if I went back to see them?"

"No." She got up and shut the door.

"You should've asked." And for a few minutes, things were quiet as the snowy night prior.

Scarlett shoved open her door and brushed past me, heading out the apartment. Her actions were odd, but consistently so.

I snuck into her room and hovered by her desk, the old ivory computer tempting me. Dust covered keys and screen. She'd figure out I'd used it. I didn't care.

I'd dealt with computers before in some of my past appearances. I'd almost been a webcam star, but I figured out how to turn off that pesky red light. People would now call computers like this old, but it was still a novelty after plucking birds to write to other gods. Phoenixes and Rocs were a pain to catch and kraken ink required big favors to get hold of; however, the writing qualities couldn't be beat. It really keeps things secret when the letter kills curious mortal messengers and only appears correctly to the intended god. Ah, Kraken ink. Typing was far simpler but not as secure.

I pressed the power button, expecting a show like Marko's, but there was only a blue screen asking for a password.

I'd only taken the first step and was already stumped. What would Scarlett use as a password? Something clever? Almost assuredly. A word or phrase that dealt with mystery and her work? Or the way in which she worked? "Certainty", "Detective", and "Truth" came to mind. I shook out memories, hoping the perfect word would escape like a gold nugget.

But I got nothing. Could I be so vain it might have something to do with me? "Wise", "Godly", and "Clever" were good words, but "Daeva", "Death", and "Zarik" were appropriate options.

Putting these together seemed as good a guess as any.

The first guess. "CertainlyCleverZarik". Of course it'd be wrong, but what can I say? I had to start somewhere and a little vanity couldn't hurt.

"Three Tries Remaining."

Alright, it could hurt. That complicated things. There were infinite possibilities. She could've added numbers and symbols and capitalized randomly.

"DetectiveDaeva". Just because I was going to fail didn't mean I wasn't going to try.

Of course not. "Two Tries Remaining, Forgot Password?"

Something clever. "Sortofacolor".

"One Try Remaining. Forgot Password?"

There were too many clever answers. Even with infinite tries, I might still never get it. Luckily, I had time on my side. But trying to outsmart Scarlett was useless. Instead of trying to match wits, maybe the best course was the opposite. Anybody who knew her would never try something this stupid. The only question is what dumb answer I wanted to try. "Scarlett"? Too vain. "1234"? Again, too many options on length. No. I realized if she was going to do a stupid password, it'd be something really stupid.

"Password".

Triumph and disbelief. I almost threw the computer out the window when it worked. It even came with a message as it logged in. "You didn't forget 'Password'"

"Only she would leave a clue like that," I said. "What a stupid joke."

Besides the whirring of the computer, a faint noise of claws on fabric was the only noise. Angel crawled closer on the bed, enormous eyes asking what I was doing. I threw the covers over the creature and continued my work.

The desktop was surprisingly empty. No files, just apps.

A browser opened. "Restore tabs?"

Why not?

A website profile opened in plain white and black.

"935C4RZ, Forum Moderator. 471 Posts, 4,710,000 Points."

Scarlett didn't appear to be someone who spent much time using technology. If she wasn't already logged in, I wouldn't have believed it was her profile. There were so many posts. Three things caught my attention. The older posts had been removed, leaving only a few at the top. Those few posts were all titled "Z", except for the last two on the day I'd been reborn.

The titles were, "Izak Cayne" and "The God's Random Act".

"Now you understand." Scarlett was at my shoulder. Maybe I was engrossed in the screen, but Scarlett snuck in better than I could've.

She didn't seem surprised I was here.

I asked, "You had me kill Izak?"

"You really think I'd be dumb enough to make my password, 'Password'? This was the best way to broach the subject." She sat on the edge of the bed and sighed away the fake cheer. "I knew Izak was using myths to kill people, but I had no way to tie him to the killings. So, I helped him on the forums, directing him towards you. Gwen wasn't supposed to die. That blood is on my hands as much as Izak's, and certainly more than yours." She looked down at her hands as if she saw red, and a lock of hair fell over her face. "I couldn't stop him in time. It may seem otherwise, but reality proves I'm not clever enough." When she cast the hair away, her eyes glistened with sadness and her hand felt for the pendant at her neck. "What happens now? Are you going to kill me for aiding Gwen's murder?"

"I didn't kill Lars and Julia." I obviously wasn't going to kill Scarlett, either. "Even if there's guilt, there was good in your intentions."

"Truth. Lies. We offer them like sweet treats. All's well and good until you think you're getting one and instead, what you find is the bitter opposite."

"If you want to share the blame, you share a piece with thousands of others on these forums that believed in me. They all played a part in bringing me back. With a world so complex, people own a tiny portion of invisible blame for things they could never comprehend—repercussions for what they say, do, or buy. If people thought about it too hard, they would drown in guilt. Mortals should leave that level of guilt to gods like me." My charming smile still attempted humor, but Scarlett didn't even look up at me. "Maybe you aided Izak, but he already had enough belief to use the myths. You thought you were tricking him, but he manipulated you instead and the girl in the temple got killed before you could stop him."

She shook her head. "A piece of guilt is still guilt."

"Then, a little good is still good, too. I stopped Izak. Revenge or justice. Either way, I don't blame you."

"It's not just Gwen. I'm also responsible for Lars, Julia, and anything you do."

"Unless I can choose?" I almost laughed at how much sense the theory of free will she was testing made, but it wasn't the time.

"Your devious words can't deceive me into feeling better." She turned away and retrieved Angel from under the blanket. "I'll get in contact with Amar, but for now, get out."

I listened, and after she shut the door, I heard muffled sadness. Even with only a feeble door between us, we were alone and I was left to figure out the pieces I'd picked up.

ELEVEN

A UNIQUE IRIS

I put the pieces of Scarlett's puzzle together, but I wasn't sure what picture it made. Weeks of silence. Snow melted, but the barrier between Scarlett and I did not. She still believed I had killed Lars, and for once, she didn't want to be certain. In time, like Lars, she would be compelled to find out the truth. However, it took her longer than I expected.

One afternoon, I was sitting on my perch at the nook. Scarlett came through the front door, walked past me, and hesitated at her bedroom's doorway, debating whether to talk to me.

"What?" I teased her with questions like this but never received a response.

Until now. "We're going to have a guest."

I smiled, pleased that we were making progress. "Should I get the chairs?"

"Iris doesn't need anything so fancy."

"A seat is fancy?"

"It's more hospitable than I wish to be." She was itching to get away, her finger tapping on her hip.

"The woman at the bar? I thought you were friends?"

"The sooner she's out of here, the better." The private detective stayed at her bedroom doorway, taken off guard by being investigated, hooked like an overconfident shark by my questions. "I owe her a favor."

"Promised her too much?" I asked. "I can't see you offering a favor except for maybe a rare book."

"She believes in you. Shouldn't you hear her plea?"

"Belief isn't a debt to be paid."

"All I agreed to is that you would listen to her," she said. "Do it because we're friends."

"Playing hot and cold?" I leapt up, the apartment's shadows lengthening with me. "Ignore me and then call me a friend?"

"I can't suddenly stop believing in you." Scarlett met my eyes for the first time in a long while. "But I am free to ignore you. That's friendship."

"What a weird definition." The shadows receded opposite my growing grin. However, caution hung heavy on my lips, draining how pleased I was by her calling me a friend. "I know you feel responsible for me, but it won't help to ignore me."

"Should I have more regard for your feelings? I thought you were a god. Well, self-importance is a common feature of gods… but I didn't expect you to be so petty."

I couldn't help myself. "I'm not the only one compelled by self-importance."

She disappeared to her room. That comment pushed her away instead of keeping her trapped in the argument.

A few hours later, there was a knock on the front door. Scarlett rushed to the door and peered through the peephole, then stood there in silence, lingering as if she waited long enough, there would be footsteps leaving.

"Scarlett," Iris said. "It's me. I know you're home."

Scarlett yanked the door open as if in a rush. "Sorry, I must be the last one in the neighborhood to hear you."

Iris' jewelry jangled as she entered, bell-like bangles ringing. Instead of rainbow hair like last time, it was dyed silver and danced prismatic under the ceiling light above the entrance.

Intricate tattoos looked different than last time I'd seen the seeress. Almost like they were alive.

In fact, they were. They changed as if a tattoo artist was still drawing them. On one arm, there was a tattoo of the Tree of Life, which grew under our feet and similarly on her arm. Branches wove into ancient runes like a story. Creatures dug into the roots and climbed up bark. Towers built level by level on the outer circle of the tattoo and up her shoulder, weaving into starlike heavens that were cut short by her sleeve. The other forearm was simpler, a tattoo of a broken black-outlined heart. With closer examination, the heart was made from a snake, the head acting as the crack in the heart, slithering back to devour its own tail.

Above her black collar, tattoos continued up her neck. On her throat, grey fire. One side, a white lion. The other, a black bull. This was a form of worship, respecting both Amar and me. That was the way it was supposed to be.

She turned towards Scarlett, and I saw the only colored tattoo she had on the back of her neck—the winged Zoroastrian symbol, Faravahar, in brilliant turquoise and gold. The symbol detailed a crowned man enveloped by an orbed sun, wings on either side with gold-trimmed blue feathers in three rows that represented good thoughts, words, and deeds. Similarly, the figure had a hawk-like tail in similar three-feather rows representing the bad mortals should overcome.

"Going somewhere?" Iris asked, braided and bangled hair cast over one shoulder.

Scarlett had picked up her jacket, glancing at the clock. "Other business. Iris, Zarik."

Iris approached and bowed. "An honor to meet you again."

"For someone immune to my powers, you have the right respect for gods," I said. "You should take notes, Scarlett."

Iris said, "Well, I'm unsure how far that immunity extends. It's not like I test it often. Nor do I intend on making any godly enemies."

This was proper respect, but that didn't mean I gave out wishes for something as simple as manners. However, I was more willing to hear it because Iris did not seem to have any Pull on me, almost like we did not affect one another. "I heard you came for a favor."

"Yes." Iris sounded unashamed. "But obviously not without something in return. I've got something for you."

Rather strangely, she did not reach for her pockets; instead, she grasped a lock of her hair, which was tied by various bits of jewelry. Very specifically, she untangled and slipped a ring off, offering it to me.

"A ring?" I asked.

"Made of ash wood."

I accepted it, feeling the familiar pulse of the Tree of Life. To get the wood was quite something—the tree did not give it easily. Along with wood, there was a different material. I ran a finger over a green middle strip. "What's this?"

"Jade and then MoS for the electronics. I thought it would be fitting to use Molyb—"

"Iris," Scarlett interrupted. "I think you sold him on the ash tree, just tell him what it does. Neither of us will understand the details."

Iris blushed. "Well, I figured you might not have a BioScreen and all. Might be nice for you to be able to access information or contact Scarlett."

"I'm sure it does more," Scarlett said, dispelling modesty. "Iris is more than a match for our old friend Marko. Except her endeavors are less selfish. She's the creator of the BioScreen."

I put the ring on a finger, fitting to this form without my doing because it was made from the tree—real magic. "Are you responsible for all the screens and prices?"

She shook her head. "No. Advertising and finance don't interest me. I'm more hands on. Turn the ring."

I did. Like the BioScreen, a miniscule screen appeared from the ring, projecting the time. "It's so small."

"Like my ambition for it." Iris grinned like a bright dawn.

Scarlett said. "Iris is incapable of doing anything simply. She was first on the List."

"Only accidently," Iris said.

I asked. "What's the List?"

They didn't hear me, and Scarlett said, "I particularly liked the stream through the kitchen and the waterfall covering your office. Very villainous."

"It kept people from disturbing me." Iris put her hand flat. "Put your hand like this and say what you want to see." As she returned to speaking of less interesting matters, the chime-like tone of her voice flattened. "I was glad when someone else got to the top of the List. One of those traders in useless goods. They can play that finance game, it never interested me."

I followed the instruction as she talked. As my hand lay flat, a holographic screen appeared. "Show me Iris and the List?"

Search results. The screen pulled up a list of people. At number eight: "Iris – 14.7T".

"I accidently went up from number nine," she said.

"The number of branches in the tree," I said. "I get the ranking, but what's the other number?"

"Only a number," Iris said. "Most people still want more money, but once wealth gets that high, it's only a score, so we made it one. The wealth provides for those who need it." She played with a braid. "I only ended up going up a spot on the list because I was too busy tinkering. Seems I can't stop. The new chip I made sold too well, but non-withstanding superstition, if I create something that betters society, that's not a bad thing. My benefit doesn't have to take from others, it's not a zero-sum game, we can make the pie bigger by sharing it."

Scarlett rolled her eyes. "That's a terrible analogy."

"Logically," Iris said. "But that's what you're good at. I, however, don't think opposites have to contradict; they can coexist and expand our horizons. In quantum computing, the answer is only there when we look; otherwise, it's both zero and one."

Scarlett glanced at the clock. "In my line of work, we call that considering possibilities. But you're free to reinvent what already exists. Your inventions can create better than you can anyways."

"For the most part. But that's good—that's what I wanted—they're like my children." She gave Scarlett a curious look I couldn't decipher. "Consider how you use others to learn what you don't know. Technology can be the same way. It can be a crutch, a path to destruction, or a way to expand our horizons and make humanity more humane. Instead of worrying about how technology can do better or replace us, why not use it as a tool? We improved society and now have time for our creative outlets, so people like you can do what you do without concern for money."

Scarlett's fingers drummed on her arm. "I wouldn't call what I do creative."

"You really should take more interest in this sort of thing," Iris said. "It would help you."

"Politics, robotics, all those '-tics', I leave to higher powers." Scarlett glanced at Iris and looked as quickly away.

"Like gods?" I asked.

Iris laughed, but stopped when she realized I was being serious. "Sorry. I forgot."

"Algorithms," Scarlett said. "No greed. No self-interest."

"The new gods, then. Maybe they'll keep better track of humanity."

I could've been jaded, but better than most, I knew how time changed everything. Over the millennia, mortals' constant curious search for answers found them. Then, they no longer needed gods that took their devotion for granted. Mortals had become their own gods. However, they, too, risked forgetting the care they should have for each other, and that would change humanity as it had the gods.

Iris didn't have such concerns; instead, she gave me a hope-filled smile. "New gods? I don't think so. We're just trying to improve lives. It's easier to see how we're doing now that most everyone has a BioScreen."

I twisted the ring, turning off the screen. "This can track me?"

"No. The algorithm only checks the state of society at different times; otherwise, everyone is both rich and poor, doing well and doing poorly, alive and dead."

"Who made it?"

"We all did," she said. "Everyone played their part in their own little way. Just like the making of the List, the algorithm was a long, mistake-filled process. But it only succeeded because most people didn't give up believing that the world could change for the better. Even when life sometimes seems bleak, humanity holds onto hope."

"People are quite stubborn that way," I said. Despite my words and general dismissal of mortals, to me, humans could be gods of one thing—hope.

Iris motioned towards the ring. "I hope a new thing like that can help even one who's been through as much as you. But you'll have to find out all the functions for yourself. Scarlett said you need to find fresh outlets."

"Like she should talk. All she does is read old books."

"Even if they're old, they're new to me." Scarlett's words sharpened. "I've had more adventures than you've managed in thousands of years."

"I doubt that," Iris said in a teasing tone.

"Indeed." I wasn't sure if Iris was just trying to get on my good side, but I didn't mind; she was succeeding. "Those books you read wouldn't be there without me."

"They'd only be different," Scarlett said. She motioned for Iris to hurry up. "Did you come to pump up his ego? Or are you going to say what you want?"

"Oh." She looked towards the ground.

"It's not your request, is it?" Scarlett asked.

"Not exactly. It's my mother's. Well, I'd prefer… I'd prefer a lot of other things. There are things money can't fix."

"But I can?" I was pleased by that.

"Not fix necessarily—end." Iris' energy was gone, replaced by a darker shadow that I understood—sadness.

As Iris played with her braids, I could see Scarlett's arm hovering behind her back, debating on reassuring Iris. Eventually, Scarlett retreated without acting, bit her lip, and looked to the clock. "I've got to go. I'll leave you in capable hands."

And before Iris could respond, Scarlett opened the door and slipped out. I stood up taller than I was. Iris did not meet my eyes. There were no tears, only a nervous penance, and that softened my words.

"I am not an executioner."

"I know that," Iris said. "This is not an execution, it's a pardon from a godly punishment. An escape from a cell of pain. My mom deserves peace." Iris picked her head up. "You can grant that."

"If this isn't her time, I have no reason to…" I trailed off, thinking of all the lesser reasons I'd killed for and the guilt silenced me. Sitting back down, I sighed.

"I knew you would say that. And I'm glad." Iris brightened despite her frown. "It's selfish. So selfish. I don't want to lose her."

"Then why ask?"

"I promised her."

Her position vexed me. "If I agreed?"

"I love my mom." Iris swept a braid from in front of her face. "I can't think of only what I want. Is there nothing you can do?"

"Getting involved in godly punishments doesn't end well."

"You won't consider it? Talk with her. Assure her. Yes, that's it, assure her everything will be alright. Surely, you've done that before."

"Too many times." I twisted the ring back and forth, the smooth wood reassuring.

"You could save her—if not in the way she wants, then maybe with your presence."

"My presence, comforting?" Maybe I was different. I almost laughed at the thought.

"I think so," she said. "You seem serene."

"Really? It's been a long time since anyone has thought of me other than demon. An avenger. The only serenity is the peace that comes after me."

"There's no reason you can't be both—gods invented contradiction."

"I suppose I can try."

An unsure smile. "When can you come with me?"

"You don't believe that I can comfort her, do you?" I asked.

"I do and I do not."

"We're on the same page, then. Let's go."

We left together. The streets were quiet and our conversation lulled. After matters of life and death, the street-appropriate topics seemed useless. Talking of the weather— sunny with the occasional wisp drifting in the blue spaces between buildings—would've been nonsensical in contrast to our dreadful task. Bringing up trivialities such as the drones or screens or other technology was a no-go for me—I did not understand them well enough to converse with someone who invented them. Finally, I wanted to ask Iris about herself; however, I didn't want to ruin her mystery, and I was better off remaining a mystery to her as well. Instead, Iris' jewelry was the only sound, ringing like bells at a temple: rhythmic, ritualistic, and entrancing.

It spellbound me like worship until we arrived at The Root. The building grew into the sky, but even without clouds, I didn't understand the name and all the talk of branches. Yet, when the light hit just the right angle, I could see slivers of the building like shards of glass branching across the sky. The underside must've been a series of screens to create the illusion of an unhindered sky and appear translucent so the city would not wallow in the building's shadow.

"You live here?" I asked, astounded.

The doorman nodded at her as we walked in together. "Not the main building. One of the branches. The elevator is over here."

I barely saw the building besides the lobby, which was all clean lines and edges—if that edge was cutting. The futuristic lobby appeared to have no limits or ceiling, only a mountainous tree trunk up the center of the building—a sprout of the Tree of Life, which this building had been built around, nurturing each other. In the gap between the tree and the various floors was the astounding spectacle of white albatrosses flying around a waterfall. A living art piece. Birds soared, unhindered by water or wind. People mirrored the birds, cycling through the lobby to glass elevators and upwards into the sky of floors beyond.

I entered a side room, which opened at Iris' mere presence. The marble hallway was deserted. We entered a glass elevator with ten buttons. But they were not floors. The top button was "1", while the bottom was "10". Without pressing anything, the elevator selected "8", and it slid into motion, barely noticeable.

The city stretched like the boundless sea to the horizon before me. Nearby, buildings crested and fell, glass reflecting sunlight. Currents ran underneath the waves. People bustled through the shallows. Drones flew about the reefs. Further from the center of the city, there was a vast expanse of smaller buildings. Darker, ancient, mysterious. The lives there were not lesser, just less known and oft forgotten.

The view was beautiful. I was glad the skies were clear; the blizzard was gone and the evidence of it remained only in patches of shaded snow.

The elevator split from the tree building and into a branch, plunging into the reaches. The glass frosted. What passed in the depths of The Root went unseen. Scarlett's big case was waiting nearby, somewhere beyond my current reach.

The elevator stopped. A ding. The door opened.

"We're here," Iris said.

The apartment—or rather, forest abode in the clouds—was surprisingly simple. An eastern tea house in the woods. The internal space was small. A rocky creek babbled through the center, connecting the inside to a balcony—a serious misnomer because it was an entire forest of oaks, moss, and sprinkled aspens that burst golden in the greenery. Among the room's light wood floors and vast bamboo windows, there were almost as many miniature trees inside as there were enormous ones outside. The pine smell was probably stronger here. Bonsai-style evergreens were planted in pots everywhere, their designs weaving like Iris' tattoos. Some spiraled in on themselves, others intertwined like lovers, while abstract-shapes dominated one side of the room, blocky and angled.

"I know," Iris said. "It's too much and too little. No one likes what I've done with it. Too many trees. Too few luxuries. Oh, and the most common—I ruined the city view."

"It fits you." I examined one of the miniature trees. "You grow these yourself?" The needles were a vibrant viridian and the trunk was scaled like a dragon.

"Making things is my only purpose—trees, electronics, braids. That's what I'm good at." She motioned towards a braided tree. "It sings like a bird when you water it."

"This place reminds me of homely, old forests."

"I'm glad." She fixed a tie on one of the trees. "Do you always make small talk when faced with unpleasant matters?"

"Only if the small talk is pleasant."

"We could delay all day," she said.

"Would you like to hear my most boring story?"

"I'd love to."

"If you want to avoid this that badly, it's better to get it over with." I shrugged. "Too bad, though. The story's quite a doozy. Short version, I used to grow trees so there were more to cut down later. It produced more good than evil. At least, that's what I like to think. But alas, let's go."

The bamboo doors opened at our approach, and Iris led us through the forest path, lined with thick, smooth stones.

The air was thin, and the creek babbled a little louder than the hum of the cold wind.

Between the trees, I saw a flash of fur.

"You have animals?" I asked.

"What color was it?"

"Silver and gold."

"That's Jeff."

"Jeff?"

"A Tibetan sand fox," she said. "Always looks like he's disappointed in you. I named him after a coworker. The fox is friendlier, though."

The path split. We followed the right fork until we encountered another structure. This one, more traditional. Way more traditional. A castle. The stone, a pale autumn, was not as bright as the living aspen leaves, but was more like the fallen ones, fading into dirt. Moss grew on the base, the forest consuming the stone. Up the ramparts, there were two spires, tree-bark shingled, offset one higher than the other. Homely for a medieval knight.

Iris stopped outside. "Tell her I love her."

"You didn't?"

"She knows." Iris turned and went towards the fork.

"No goodbye?"

"You said you weren't going to do it."

"I meant for me." I liked to think that managed to give her a small smile, even though I could not see it as she walked away.

I approached the castle, which seemed less homely and more haunted. The forest was silent. There was a deep loneliness that lined the parapets and extended in the shadows. A thick, wooden door and iron knocker with the staring visage of a goat waited for me.

A hefty knock of cold iron on wood.

The door creaked open. No smiling face greeted me. Instead, it seemed to be an older version of Iris. Her largest wrinkle was her lips, which seemingly thinned and disappeared into her mouth. Braids had been pretzeled shorter, into thinned, double buns. There was less jewelry, only a simple gold band around her finger and a locket tight around her thin neck.

"Did Iris send you?"

"I could've flown, but the elevator was nicer." In my eyes, I made the godly impression of storm clouds. "Were you expecting something more?"

"No, I expected you." She opened the door fully. Inside, a long stone hallway was lit by floating electric candles that seemed like they were held by ghosts, but knowing Iris, were probably suspended by magnets. "Come in."

I had believers in strange places. Following her in, the sound of our feet echoed on stone floors and archways, then they were muffled on a sandstone-red carpet. We entered a living room, heavy drapes over the window, which left only a slit of light on the far wall. Unlike Iris' home, there were no plants or lively splotches of color. There were two seats, beige and boring; they did not face each other, but sat next to each other, diverting their attention to a crackling fireplace. The only warmth here.

We sat next to each other in silence, watching the fire as if it was something fascinating. Light did not lift the heavy air, which was haunted by the almost-tangible specters of guilt and pain. It was one of those places that absorbed the suffering that had been endured here and exuded misery when anyone new entered. I rubbed the chair's textured armrest. Old. Everything here, old.

For most, this place would send shivers down their spine. But for me, I could barely contain a comforted grin. Yet, that grin would not comfort anyone; instead, it would've unsettled.

"Why do you want to die?" I asked, getting to the point. I felt the Pull drawing me closer to Iris' mother, even as we sat within arm's reach.

"Is it not obvious?"

Strange. Most expected their hidden pain to go unnoticed. They pretended, not wanting to allow anyone a glimpse at their agony, no matter how impossible it was not to show. And most of the time, others were quite willing to pretend that they did not notice.

For Iris' mother, it was a physical pain. Clenching fingers wracked in spasm and clutched for comfort, burying into the armchair. As her hands crinkled the fabric, the creases around her eyes followed. What exactly was the cause, I could not name. I was no doctor. But I'd taken many from their pain.

"How long has it been?" I asked, curious of the godly punishment that lingered about her, wondering whether it was like Prometheus having his liver torn out for eternity or my touch that eventually led to death.

"Forever."

She didn't know what that meant. "Aren't you scared?"

"No." The arthritic decay of her body was matched with an inverse strength of soul. "There's no point in being scared, is there?"

"Maybe not," I said.

"Do you know what lies beyond?"

"For me, nothing." I shook my head. "No god will judge me when my time comes."

"You speak like you'll die." She paused a moment. "It seems like you prefer that."

"I've killed many and watched more die, including gods. Life is short and full of regrets. But, no, I'd prefer not to die. I'd like a rest. You are being punished, and that is harder to escape."

She said, "Eventually, I have to escape it."

"In your case, I think not escaping is the point. Otherwise, you wouldn't need me." I did not like it, but I felt strangely guilty for the actions of another. It was too familiar. "What about leaving Iris?"

"All we share is you."

"Me?"

"Traditions," she said. "Belief in the old ways. Our lives couldn't be more different. She does things I could never think of or understand. With her, there's science and mysticism. Opposing forces, but to her, they make sense. With time, our disagreements grew, rather than our similarities. We see each other less and less. Yet, with distance, we held our memories nearer and fonder. A warmth like this fire. But eventually, it'll burn until all that's left is ashes." She smiled with gritted teeth. "I've accomplished nothing and everything. All the dreams I set out with were never realized, but something beyond dreams was—Iris. I've gotten more than I imagined. I watched my child, my Iris, become better than me in every way. She doesn't need me anymore. No parent could want more. Besides the recognition, the money, the good— she's happy. That's the constant note I hear. That will be my last thought."

I smiled back at her. "Iris will still think of you. People don't die on the day they're gone; they die, piece by piece, as they're forgotten. Their voice, their face, their smell. Slowly, it gets fuzzier. Until what's left is how they made you feel. Once the feeling is gone, then they are dead. But their impact passes from one person to another, small, but never dead. At least that's what a god of life would have you think." My smile died. "I, on the other hand, know better. Once you're gone, you're gone. The end. Have a good day, a good life, but know that I'll be there at the end to tell you goodbye."

"Then let this be mine." She appeared forged by the fire burning between bricks, wrinkles hardened. "Iris will be better without me. Just give me peace."

There was a thin veneer of fear that contained pain. It lined the dark shadows. The hum under the hollowness. The fire that kept the haunted air away. If there was no fear, there was no reason to contain pain.

The Pull plucked at my essence like a harp, testing how tight the strings were. I heard the note, but it was unclear.

"I can't give you peace," I said. "I can sense your doubt. Your hesitation. No matter what you portray. No matter what you say."

"I'm not scared."

"And I won't feel guilty." I sounded convincing, but it was stoic sarcasm.

She read through it. "You? Guilty? You're death."

"I'm Zarik. I take no joy in what I do. In what I am."

"If you can't help it, why feel guilty?"

Maybe Scarlett was right. Maybe I had some freedom. "I'll consider your words."

"And what of me in the meantime?"

The Pull dragged my hand closer to hers. For anyone else, it was a comforting gesture. But for me, even the weakest whisper might extinguish her life. It was tempting. I couldn't be blamed for doing it; yet, my hand waited tantalizingly out of reach.

"Let me tell you a story," I said softly.

She leaned in, waiting for the bedtime tale.

"Once, there was an evergreen tree," I said. "It started as a small sapling on a bare mountain. Strong winds had blown the seed there, and those same winds now sought to destroy what had grown. Creaking and groaning, the twigs bent and strained. But they did not break. Flexible, it survived a harsh fall, only to be met with harsher winters. The winds made its roots strong. Snow fell. Seeking shelter, a raven hid under the fledgling branches. More snow came. A once-in-a-century blizzard. But the burying snow left a pocket of air for the bird. Without so much snow, both the tree and raven would've frozen. Instead, they were insulated together. When winter thawed, it was as if the tree was blessed by the gods. Whatever came, the evergreen survived. Droughts. Root-eaters. Bugs and burrowers. It got scars. It got stronger. Until it was the oldest and tallest tree in a forest that it had sprouted. Time passed, and the needles grew thin, the branches cracked and fell, breaking onto smaller trees. The forest grew sick with it. The tree was a burden. Now, most of the time, I deal with bigger things. But this tree deserved my attention. It was special. There were more things special to me at the time. Like meeting an old friend, I felled the tree, and the forest quieted. All was peaceful."

Her eyes had drifted at my soothing story. Now was the time. I grasped her thin-skinned hand gently.

I continued my story, "The world was better without the tree. And yet, I was not. Because for another to have peace, I have to live without it."

My hand tremored like a growing fault line of mistakes had given way to an earthquake.

And instead of ending her pain, I chose the opposite of my nature. Rather than light, I absorbed the darkness plaguing Iris' mother. It had been so long since I resisted an easy path, I didn't know I still had the option. Doing so would weigh on me. So be it.

I struggled against the curse that had been laid on her, but I didn't want to let Iris and Scarlett down. There was no Pull from them—they couldn't know I was capable of this.

The darkness trickled out. Yet, no matter how I tried, I couldn't take all her pain.

Eyes fluttered open, and the tension in an old face released. "How?"

There was a new weight within me—a vessel for that darkness, sitting like sadness in my stomach. The darkness ate at the light inside me, making me weaker. There had been worse, and I was not one to complain, especially when I had no intentions of keeping this godly curse forever.

"I feel better." She stood, wobbled, and sat back down. "I'm not cured."

Her words upset me. I had given up an opportunity to strengthen myself for my fight against Amar by fulfilling the Pull with her willing sacrifice. "I can only do so much."

With new energy, she bowed at my feet. "Thank you. I didn't mean to sound ungrateful. After burning, I'll take the ache."

Like all gods, my power depended on peoples' belief and expectations of me. Great gods were self-fulfilling, but these small acts could change how powerful I was. Iris' mother had a good reason to believe in me, and that seemed to balance the darkness I'd taken on. Maybe Iris was onto something about contradictions.

"I hope you enjoy peace." I decided against saying the rest of the thought. I didn't have the heart to tell her that her time would come soon. I supposed that's why I took the burden. Then again, my definition of soon might be different than hers.

In any case, I left wordlessly.

My choice felt like freedom. And when I returned to the evergreen forest outside, the burn of nostalgia smelled sweeter and clearer. Just as Iris' mother's pain was not all gone, my regret wasn't either, but it was vanquished for the night.

On my way back, I didn't meet Iris. And as I stepped back into the elevator down, the ride was transformed. The whole city metamorphosized once the sun vanished, becoming alive with lights and energy, almost simulating a night sky on the earth. Streets streaked like comet trails. Smaller skyscrapers were splattered stars, bursting brightly. Houses were dim planets in the distance. Everything orbited The Root, as if reaching for the biggest, brightest sun. Watching from the center of the universe was what it was like to be a god—a true god. And yet, Iris stayed so humble. I imagined myself in her place, looking down from the highest high upon all these people, and the temptation to think godliness was in reach just by the towering view was a strong pull. But I descended from the heights. What I'd done was so small. Great gods did not take the pain of individuals, but of society, and if I was not a great god, I was nothing.

Why did it feel so good, then?

The walk back home was abundant with flashes—of people, of light, of time. I arrived back at Scarlett's in a blink.

"Did you do it?" Scarlett asked as I walked in the door. She was sitting in the chair, a green book open, but face-down, on her leg.

"Iris' mother is in bad shape," I said, truthfully.

I did not want to tell her what I'd done. For once, I didn't want to boast. Memories of past failures made me sentimental.

Scarlett must've read me. "She's still alive for now?"

"Yes, for now."

"You're not telling me something." Scarlett took a moment, placed a bookmark, and closed the book. "I want you gone. With you out of sight, maybe you'll be out of mind."

"What?"

"Have your ears not popped after coming back down from such heights?" Scarlett asked. "Get out."

I crossed my arms. "I didn't kill Iris' mom."

"Yet."

"You're scared. You don't want that on your conscience."

"Yes." Scarlett set the book precariously on the armrest. "Not just that. Every death you cause is on my hands. I thought…well, I keep thinking, but the mystery is not worth it."

"Questions of life and death are never simple." I pretended to pay attention to a bookshelf. "Ah, now you know what it's like to be me."

"I can't do anything without thinking about *it*."

"It?" I turned back to her. "The person Izak killed, Gwen?"

"I had a hand in both Gwen and Izak's deaths, but I meant Lars."

"Lars? You're a great detective—you can't figure out what happened?"

"This isn't the time for jokes." She stood and the book fell open to the floor. "I have to know. I have to hear the truth, even if I might not believe it."

"What happened was Lars and Julia's choice."

"Don't give me half-truths. How can I be certain?" she asked, investigative eyes trying to read me for some answer that would settle her.

"I can't help you with that. If you're going to get rid of me because of it, I have a reason to lie. Maybe you could prove I didn't kill Lars, but you're as scared of the answer as Lars was with Julia."

"It's not the same."

"You think you're guilty," I said. "With Gwen, you failed to stop a killer. With Izak, you did. If I killed Lars, you'd have to reexamine what might be an appropriate punishment for you in comparison. Yet, I wouldn't kill you for your sins. I need you." It was meant as a joke, but there might've been some truth in my words. "But I see you don't seem to care whether I killed Julia. Because you like that there's justice in this world. You wouldn't do it with your own hands, but you wouldn't object. Everyone has that part of them that thinks bad people deserve to be punished."

"Lars didn't commit a crime worthy of death," she said.

"Finally, you're making judgements."

I picked up the book and looked inside at the title page, "The Demon's Dream", which was signed illegibly with the initials "Q. D—".

She noticed my intrigue and seemingly hoped it would distract me. "It's fiction, in case you were wondering."

"I wasn't." I held the book at my side. "But I can judge what you might be thinking. Izak would've hurt others and needed to be stopped. Understandable. Julia wasn't a risk to anyone else. Killing her would be punishment and not prevention. A debatable case. Lars helped a murderer avoid justice. To a death god like me, though, guilt must be guilt, and the only punishment must be death. I've been called demon long enough to know when someone believes the worst of me. But I had hoped you thought better of me."

"The reason you change can't be because I believe you can change."

I smiled. "And why not?"

"For gods to survive, they have to adapt, not be adapted. They can't rely on people who no longer need them. And if gods can change, then people can too."

"I have bad news for you and me—life changes. We try to keep up with the world for a while, but eventually, we can't and we're replaced. Nothing lasts forever." I handed her the book. "Even if you're trying to make this about me, or gods in general, the mystery you're trying to solve is about yourself. You're afraid that human deduction can't compare to technology, and although you know more about myths for now, your place in this world won't last."

She held the book dearly. "It's not about my place, it's about what I love doing—or, what I'm good at. I can do my job better than any technology. Even what Iris could create.

The human element isn't replicable. The godly element isn't either."

"It becomes different gods and a different humanity."

"Amar adapted," she said. "Or was adapted. Old god, new world."

She was hiding something again, and I asked, "You talked to Amar?"

"Only a message. The god put us on a new case."

"Us?" The tension remained, but that was a good sign.

"Amar asked for us," she said. "It's not like you'll vanish instantly."

I wasn't going to correct her. "Something Amar can't solve?"

"Something Amar can't find."

TWELVE

I LOOK INTO A MIRROR MYSTERY

A crime of passion? Could it be called that when the man cheated on his wife with a virtual version of the same woman?

Escorting the real woman through a white-tiled living room, a detective with sea-blue eyes greeted me, saying everything in a look. We met in different forms—there were birds and lions and ravens and insects—but we always seemed to find each other.

For this meeting, I remained an elegant, beardless face to be etched on old temples, while Amar was a woman detective I'd never seen before. Dressed professionally in a dark coat, the only bit of color that Amar usually tended towards was gold-trimmed emerald earrings shaped like leaves hanging under jet black hair that streamed like the darkness the god fed on.

"I'll be back soon," Amar said, bright and lively and young as always, despite my best efforts.

"Looking forward to it," I said, malice hid behind a cordial smile.

The god of life led out the silent woman, wrinkles deepening with the depths of her situation, and the dark eyes haunted by the blood that did not show on her hands now, but might've in another reality.

There was no doubt the woman was the murderer. She was the only one there. The one with motive.

What Scarlett had told me made that quite straightforward. And yet, as we went inside and Scarlett perused the house with Amar's detective colleague—a man with a strange set of forensic glasses and stiff, robotic movements—I couldn't help but doubt the case was that simple. The woman I thought should've been handcuffed could not be. In a way, she was already chained.

A virtual reality headset lay on the floor, collecting black dog hair like tumbleweeds after a storm. There were two pods—adult-sized beds with glass canopies. One pod was still, silent, and solemn as the rest of the house. The other's enormous screen projected over the white-padded bed, portraying two things—"Medical Emergency" and the scene of the crime. There was a dash of red on otherwise spotless white tile. The two worlds, virtual and real, shared one exact match—the splash of blood, mirrored in the spray—but the world of the screen and that around me were so alike it was like looking through a dirty mirror, except reality was the one aged by dirt.

Minus the pods, the world of the screen depicted the same room, the same life, and the same woman as had been led away, only ten years younger.

It was hard to read the virtual woman's face. She was merely a figure on a screen, too far away. A reality away.

Despite those who might be more qualified in cybercrime, Scarlett had agreed to help with the case, and all the strange circumstances surrounding it. There were two suspects, the same woman, named Belle. One tangible and one a timeless simulation. The real and virtual version.

The robotic detective brought Scarlett and me together around the pods, recounting what happened, telling us the few facts they'd gathered, which told as a story, were stranger than fiction.

"Belle and Steve, her husband, bought virtual reality beds, more realistic than dreams, about ten years ago. At first, they went on adventures only available in fantasy. They discovered pirate treasure at the bottom of the ocean. They fought dragons on snowy mountains. All that stuff. Belle had other concerns, and despite the adventure, began to spend less time in the simulation and more in reality as the years went on. Lonely, Steve convinced Belle to make a virtual avatar of herself, while Belle got a dog." A tone change. "I think Belle got the better deal, there." The detective had a forced sort of smile, which faded quickly. "Supposedly, things were good. However, real life concerns took Steve away from VR for a while, too. What they were, rather boring. And so, the couple dropped imagination for banality. Occasionally, Steve would spend time in the simulation, going on strange adventures with virtual Belle. Everything would've been nothing more than a strange equilibrium, until last year."

"Steve lost his job," Scarlett said. "He has a shelf of hobby books, recently bought and barely used."

There was no surprise at Scarlett's deduction, but I almost expected the detective to start making a whirring noise as the mechanical brain tried to prevent overheating at Scarlett's logic.

However, the detective merely nodded. "After being freed from his delivery job and able to pursue anything, Steve returned to the simulation; yet, instead of adventures, he built the life Belle and him once had, grasping at nostalgia as much as any fantasy. Not only a memory—he tried to improve it. Impossible adventures were one thing. Replicating life with a younger version of herself was quite another for Belle. Jealousy followed. She admitted that. And, I agree with her words—there is no stranger feeling than being jealous of one's self."

Scarlett tried to brighten the dim room with lightheartedness. "I'm jealous of the life I could've lived as a marine biologist. Adventure. Animals. The only uncertainty being what I hadn't searched far enough for."

The detective glanced at the virtual reality bed, not cracking a smile. "Real and virtual Belle began to vie for Steve's time, and the more entrenched Steve became in the simulation, the jealousy worsened. Belle began taking to the simulation to spend any time with her husband. Virtual Belle's jealousy matched the real one's."

"And complications arose, I assume." I crossed my arms, expecting to feel the cold echo of death, but it never came.

"Yes, complications arose." The detective crossed his arms as if trying to mirror my human motions, but he had chosen a poor example—I was no human. "Although virtual Belle did not age, she had changed as the real one had. Ten years of different realities. And eventually, tragedy."

Scarlett ran her finger along the pod. "Steve, before he died, spent days without leaving the simulation. Belle joined him without warning. There was a fight. Whatever passed in those moments, contested in different realities. The result— Steve died. Real Belle, inconsolable. Virtual Belle, irreparable."

"Precisely," said the detective. "And that's where you come into the picture."

Scarlett tried to open Belle's pod, but no matter what she pressed on the keypad, the closed capsule remained so.

"There's a code," the detective said. "Although Belle was still in the simulation when it happened, we know Belle's dog, Romeo, dragged Steve down the street. A neighbor saw them, but apparently, they turned a corner and disappeared without a trace. We also know from the forensics and blood splatter that it was a dog that bit Steve and pulled him out of the pod. However, we don't know how the dog knew the code and opened the pod."

"What a clever dog," Scarlett said.

The detective stayed stiff. "Indeed… now, such a sudden withdrawal from what Steve, at that point, considered reality would've been dangerous. Yet, the simulator had pronounced the emergency and death beforehand. And so it seemed that Romeo had tried to help Steve, except the mystery begins there."

"Indeed," Scarlett said sassily, countering the detective's dismissiveness. "After getting Steve out, Romeo, black and white judging by the hair around here, lifted—not pulled or dragged—him out the pod. Then, he was dragged out the door. Hard to miss. I would've thought your glasses would enable you to see quite clearly."

"They see more than you do." The detective smiled.

Scarlett contained further tension, appearing almost as robotic as the detective. "You don't want us to figure out if real Belle or virtual Belle killed her husband, but you do need us to figure out how a dog could open the capsule, escape with a full-grown man, and roam the city without being found?"

"Yes."

"If it's the same to you," Scarlett said. "I'd like to speak with virtual Belle in any case. Even if it doesn't help solve your mystery, it may help solve mine. And, providing you're done reconstructing the scene, can you unlock the simulation?"

"I'll ask Detective A."

"We're old friends," I said, suggesting it wasn't necessary to ask.

The detective ignored me, typing at his BioScreen as he left the room. Scarlett examined the bland room with her eyes, and finding nothing of particular interest, she focused on me.

I could feel her preparing a question. "What?"

"Which one do you think killed him?" she asked.

"The real Belle. Jealousy makes sense."

"That depends—is loneliness or jealousy the more dangerous emotion?"

"Is the virtual version capable of feeling?" I imagined the figure in the cold glass actually feeling trapped within it, and I shivered.

"Whether a virtual person can feel is a matter of philosophy. Can you ever be sure anyone experiences consciousness like you?"

"I've been enough people to think so." There was that moment in morphing I felt like two beings, split and separate. "Loneliness and jealousy—longing for something or trying not to lose it."

"And which is more destructive—a black hole or a dying star?" Scarlett posed more rhetoric, almost talking to herself.

"The desperation in loneliness is destructive. Against oneself. Against those who deserted you. Against everything and everyone."

I followed the insinuation. "You think virtual Belle killed him. But how?"

"I didn't say that. But how she did it would be interesting." She beamed.

There was a still silence, and I pondered the pod and the blood. "How sure are we the dog didn't kill him? Belle might've been able to get him the medical attention he needed."

"That's why we need to talk to the virtual Belle." Scarlett nodded to the screen. "Look at the splatter. A sudden blow. Then, the knife must've been pulled out in no more than a second. Regret? Impulse? Either way, it's a simulation. A virtual knife shouldn't kill Steve, but if that shocked him to death, or if it was something else, it's an odd situation. Both Belles seem to have loved him."

"Yes. The story tells us that." I shook my head. "Both were worried about losing him. It doesn't make sense that one of them would try to kill him."

"You're right, it wouldn't make sense to you. You only understand your own godly experience. What do gods like you know about scars or loss or dev—"

Shadows wrapped around her, silencing her.

"I understand just fine." I fumed, residual tension between us not fully exuded from our past fight. "Reading and logic doesn't mean you really know anything for, or about, yourself."

My emotion had got the better of me, and I released her. Besides, it was no fun to argue with someone who couldn't respond.

She was unphased by being restrained, not backing down as many would, and challenging me with venom in her voice. "I understand more than you think."

"Part of you, maybe. But not Detective Scarlett Wolfe. Not the logical investigator who can read and listen to people like they were open books. No, if there's any part of you that understands yourself, it's Scarlett—the girl I saw in the snow. The one I didn't expect. I saw it again when Iris came. You empathize with people. You care. That's what gives you insight. But you won't get close to people because you're afraid of people knowing the real Scarlett instead of the brilliant detective. You think being vulnerable would make you worse at what you do. There's no reason to be scared of your humanity—imagination and morals and purpose are what make you better than Amar. You may know people, but you must not know me. Don't tell me I don't know mortals— I understand you better than you do."

"I'm not scared of..." She paused, anger fading as she digested the words. "You were complimenting me."

The robotic detective came back, and although he should've seen the heightened tension, or maybe even heard bits of our conversation, he made no comment. He was all business. "Detective A said you can unlock the simulation. Belle said the code is '57353'. The privacy function is on, and all that's left is the moment the simulation paused. We've got a record of that."

"You take the bloody one," Scarlett said to me. "I should've guessed the code. Wasn't thinking. Guess I was distracted."

"How would you've known?" the detective, this time, seemed intrigued.

"57353 is 'Steve', except in numbers."

"Not quite," I said, pointing out the obvious.

"The second five is a V," Scarlett said. "V is the roman numeral for five."

The detective mused. "We really need better classes for creating passwords. They're so… sentimental."

"It's better than Scarlett's password," I said.

She mumbled as she put the code in, "That was supposed to be cracked. You were almost too dim to get it."

The pod decompressed with an audible hiss, and as if this wasn't some outlandish experience, Scarlett hurdled into the bed, put on the VR headset, adjusted it with ease, attached a few sensors, pads, and other wires, before closing the pod.

The robotic detective took out the bloodied padding from Steve's pod, and I lifted myself in. I wish the detective had left the blood—it didn't bother me— but I did mind the cold, unpadded backing under me.

I tried to copy how Scarlett had prepared the pod. The headset barely fit my head and the Velcro took several tries to attach. Worse, I had no idea what the buttons near my fingers did. As much as I didn't wish to admit it, I needed the detective to assist me in getting it started. After a few awkward moments of instructions, I realized it was rather intuitive. The buttons were there for the menu, while the pod itself needed no further details to work besides a living body. That, I had.

Whatever magic made the simulator work, I could almost feel Iris' influence in it. Strange, complicated, and vaguely comforting in the oddest of ways.

When the pod closed, the world metamorphosized. There was no warp or flicker. Instead, it was like being in the darkness of a cocoon and emerging in a sudden breakthrough.

I entered the mirror world and the mystery awaited.

THIRTEEN

I GET STUCK IN A VIRTUAL CLIFFHANGER

I was reborn into a new world, as I had been so many times; at least this time, it wasn't to kill someone. This world was almost indistinguishable from the one I'd left behind, only without the pods. The room smelt clean, and cold AC brushed over me. I touched a woven stool by the kitchen island, and the wood grain matched my fingerprints—unique. If there was one faint niggle, it was that gravity seemed a little off. However, without mortal constraints, the difference between body and eyes didn't bother me.

My arms and legs moved with unsettling ease, as if my body was not trapped in a pod.

Scarlett, on the other hand, wobbled to the chair I'd touched. "Give me a minute. Always makes me a bit dizzy."

"You get used to it," Belle said. Her voice was sweet as cherry blossoms and she was beautiful as one, too. Unlike her real counterpart, there were no tears and no wrinkles except those in an energetic smile. "Let me get another chair for you."

"I'm alright," I said.

"They all say that." She moved with vigor, a spring in her step hurrying to another room and returning with a stool. Next I knew, I found myself sitting on it.

"I'm Detective Scarlett Wolfe and this is Zee. We're here to—"

"Dreadful, just dreadful," virtual Belle said, head shaking and long brown hair with it. "Confusing, really, Scarlett. I'm sure you understand. Well… I'm sure you don't. If a mirror could reach out and punch you." She recoiled. "I've thought badly of myself before, but this is new." She knitted subjects together without pause. "The other two detectives were so formal. They didn't bother to come in. Are you working with them?"

Scarlett said, "We're not investigating the crime, only Steve and Romeo's disappearance."

"Oh?" Belle tensed. "They did mention the dog. Awful. Do you mind if we get some fresh air? I'm feeling a bit stifled in here."

With the AC blasting, that was a wonder. Scarlett had her arms wrapped around herself, goosebumps visible on forearms. She nodded eagerly. "Sure, I'm not here to interrogate, just to have a conversation and find out anything that might help our search."

"Oh, of course. Give me a moment." Belle's expressive face went blank.

Like a slideshow, our surroundings transported to another setting. A beach breeze swept the room away. It seemed we were no longer in the city or the same universe. A vacation to another time and place.

The Mediterranean lapped against golden shores, and red stucco cascaded on rooftops and down to outdoor patios, where the sound of waves was merely an undercurrent to people's laughter. Belle, Scarlett, and I were seated at a patio table, a short fence between us at the restaurant and sands where people played volleyball, sunbathed, and frolicked. The only thing vaster than beach was the blueness of deep-glass ocean, ripples breathing in the sun's shining twinkle. Dividing air and water was the warm horizon with a yellow-orange aura of distant lands. Sweet smells of salt and seafood mixed with the flowers that lined the balcony. A few gulls floated above, watchful and waiting for a fallen french fry.

The sun beamed; Belle did, too. "Much better." She sipped a bright orange mimosa. "Anything I can get you?"

"Mango juice," Scarlett said with a smile, now dressed in a blue and white sundress, inspecting the scenery as a new mystery. "And tortilla de patata." She grinned, obviously thinking this was very clever and quick.

A waiter came by with a plate of food and a golden glass of mango nectar. He placed them in front of Scarlett and left without a word. The tortilla was not bread; rather, it was a circular omelet with potatoes and onions.

"Anything else?" Belle asked.

"This is a very specific memory." Scarlett poked at the dish with a fork. "I could tell generally where we were, but the onions are found in the Eastern Iberian Peninsula. A personal memory. Is a copy of past experiences all you can make?"

"What fun would that be?"

"Are these circumstances the time to be thinking of what's fun?" Scarlett asked.

"I suppose not," Belle said. "But I figured a nice relaxing place would be good for this conversation."

Scarlett sipped the mango nectar. "I thought VR was an escape. It's supposed to be fun."

Belle smiled at that.

Looking up from her sweet drink, Scarlett asked, "Did you come here with Steve often?"

"I don't know how to answer that. It depends on the 'I'"

"Ah, I see. Not you, then."

I found something deeply unsettling in virtual Belle's playfulness, and I fidgeted in the hard wood seat and my new burgundy collared shirt. "Isn't this scene a little bright for the circumstances?"

"How about a Bloody Mary? Would that be fitting?" Belle scowled. "Should I make it rain and double down on the awfulness?"

"No, this is lovely," Scarlett said, running her finger on her glass and collecting condensation. "My companion didn't mean to insult you. He's not around enough of these after-the-fact interviews to realize that everyone deals with loss in different ways. Others might find your cheery demeanor… odd. But I think it's fairly normal. How about some music?"

Belle nodded. "I do love music."

A guitarist came over, tuning the guitar and his hair flowing in the wind.

Scarlett put the glass down. "I'm sorry, can we have the music without him?"

"Oh, sure," Belle said, and the man walked away, while the quiet guitar continued strumming.

I was tense. Belle was more powerful than any god I'd known. My frown must've shown.

"Do you not like guitars, either?" Belle asked.

"Zee is just worried that you might be able to control him like that," Scarlett said.

Belle chuckled. "I can't control outsiders like that. Only the scenery, and even that, I don't have ultimate authority over. With enough practice, you could do the same."

"Is it a competition of power?" I asked.

"A convergence of imagination," Belle said. "This world is as complicated as you're willing to make it. But you'd have to know what you want, find the directory, and make suitable changes, all those things."

There was a certain appeal to this—a world of my own making. If I could not be a great god in the real world, I certainly could be one here. There would be no pain, no guilt, only what I chose. "I'd like to learn."

"I'd suggest you leave this virtual world to me," Belle said. "Changing it is not something you can learn in an afternoon." Belle pushed wild strands of brunette hair off her face. "Is your interest personal or professional?"

"Zee might like to learn eventually, but we're here as visitors today," Scarlett said. "Though, maybe, the personal and professional can mix. I deal with mysteries of the fantastic—myths. Most of the time, fantasy is purely theoretical, but being able to simulate it here would be extremely helpful."

"I do have a mythical directory we could see while we talk. It could be interesting—an adventure."

"Unfortunately, we still have to ask a few questions," Scarlett said.

The music quieted. "If you answer mine, I'll answer yours."

"And it has to be on this adventure?" I asked.

Belle's cheer bubbled. "To have fun, we need adventure."

Scarlett nodded. "I'll humor you and you humor me."

"Mixing business and fun doesn't sound much like you." I took a fork and stole a small bit of the egg tortilla.

"Do I need to hit you with another snowball?" Scarlett asked.

The tortilla was crunchy on the outside and layered and flaky on the inside, the onions bursting with flavor along the creamy eggs. Impeccably salty. Delicious.

Then, my meal was gone.

We left the seaside and I found myself on a far less comfortable seat. The chair had become a boulder. And although the scenery was different, it was still beautiful.

We had risen to the heavens. Below our vantage point on a jungle mountainside, a watercolor stretched before us as if painted by a godly brush. Through the clouds, rock formations jutted around us, waterfalls cascading down their cliffsides and streams trickling down rounded rock mazes. Clear but cool sunshine melded with water and air and earth in a harmony of elements.

Brisk mist brushed my sunned skin like the birds swooping between clouds and sunbeams. Here, the world was in constant, peaceful motion. The clouds drifted. The sun arced. The jungle rustled. Dew dripped down leaves and past petals and around tree branches near us. Vibrant flowers and fruits bloomed into luscious life before my eyes.

An epic of old had new breath.

Although this was not my tale, the location felt familiar.

The harmonious air hummed and Belle was bright and ready for a game. "You're a detective. Can you tell where we are? There are no people or foods this time to give you a hint."

Scarlett was back in her jacket and already on the case, paying no attention to the broad scenery; instead, she took a single leaf into her hand, holding it as an artist might a fragile sculpture. She released it and examined a yellow bloom on the next tree.

Belle said, "If you're stumped, I don't think the tree stumps will be of any help."

Scarlett shook her head. She looked around to the heavenly rocks that appeared to fly in the clouds, paying keen attention to the waterfalls that fell from the heights and back through the clouds as if it was rain.

"No, it's too easy. This is Huāguǒ Shān," she said. "The mythical Chinese Flowers and Fruit Mountain—birthplace of the Monkey King, Sūn Wùkōng."

I'd had my run ins with Chinese myths and gods before. In general, they liked to keep to themselves, but we had some mutual acquaintances.

"Lovely," Belle said. "I can see why they chose you to investigate myths."

"You already know who I am, don't you?" Scarlett asked.

"Information is there for anyone willing to find it."

Scarlett brushed her hand on a grooved tree trunk. "Figuring out where we are isn't impressive. I was trying to figure it out from the flora rather than looking around and seeing the large boulder the Monkey King was born from. I should've trusted my gut instead of looking to be sure. Would've made for a better show."

"The show was good enough until you explained the magic behind it." Belle hmph-ed. "Just take the credit."

"I'm not interested in credit," Scarlett said.

"But you are interested in a challenge?" Excitement buoyed back to Belle's demeanor.

Scarlett stretched her arms, feeling more comfortable in the virtual world. "A challenge with reward. I'll take your tests, but only if you answer a question for each question you ask of me."

"Fair. Should we move on, then?"

Scarlett nodded, but then, paused. "No. I answered your question already."

"I hope your question is interesting."

"The most boring one." Scarlett was cool as the mountain breeze. "But I'd be remiss not to ask. A baseline, I should say. As this test was."

Belle laughed. "I think we could get along."

"What happened with Steve?"

"Where—where do I start?"

"I want you to start before the incident," Scarlett said. "What's your first memory?"

"My first memory?" Belle thought a moment. "I remember a yo-yo on the playground. It was—"

"No, the first thing *you* remember." Scarlett motioned around. "The first time you were in this world."

Belle shifted her weight like a boat in a storm. "It was empty. Dark. I don't know for how long. Milliseconds? Decades? And then, there was a voice. Well, not a voice, text."

"And what did it say?"

"Hello, world."

Scarlett, bemused, grinned. "And you said back, 'Hello, world.'"

Belle nodded. "Then, there was Steve. A light in the darkness." Belle's broadest smile yet, undisturbed by Scarlett's musings. "And it was so much better than the emptiness. We loaded into a world, and the memories from before popped up to the surface. They seemed real. But also, they were like looking into a mirror. Yet, the feelings I had for Steve didn't just seem real—they were real. After darkness, how could I not love the light?" Her lips pressed firmly together as emotion choked her up.

"Would walking help?" Scarlett suggested.

"I'd like that," Belle said, and the three of us walked through the jungle path as she talked freer. "So many adventures. Those were the good days. Better than even the happiest memories 'I' had because these memories were mine."

Through lush vegetation, there were patches of strange and wonderous sights. A monkey, human-sized and dressed in golden armor, meditated on an enormous lotus flower. Even with eyes closed, fur rose to attention, sensing our presence. We passed quietly. And above, through a gap in canopy, a wingless dragon flew by, red scales glittering gold as it flew past sunbeams. Both these occurrences flashed by, but repeated in my mind as if they were real myths and not virtual. The difference was fuzzy, as if myths weren't already.

Belle continued, "Eventually, Steve had less time for me. I understood and waited. It was not like the times before he came, because at least I had my own memories. Yet, I was still lonely. Making worlds, scenarios, and people wasn't satisfying. My creations are merely a mirror of their creator."

The foliage lessened in lushness. Tall, leafless trees were interspersed in the forest. And between sticks of bamboo, a white crane with a black head waded in a small pond, alone, paying us no mind and glaring at the water, waiting to pounce.

"A reality crisis," Scarlett said.

"A power crisis," I suggested.

"Neither." Belle stopped. She broke off a branch from a low-hanging tree, snapped it in two, and dropped the pieces. Before it hit the ground, it was gone. "Only one of self. Steve was tangible. He was an anchor to reality. And when he returned, I was like a fish being released back into the ocean. I no longer floundered for direction. I could breathe! Being trapped wasn't about where I was, only who I was without. When the other 'me' threatened to unplug me, I was more worried about never seeing Steve again than dying. And if I couldn't have him, no one should. I suppose that sounds like a motive. But it's also the worst motive in the world. Him dying was the last thing I'd want."

"Emotion knows no motive or logic except itself." Scarlett sighed. "Understanding ourselves would take the best detective, and we're all just amateur detectives, trying to comprehend why we act the way we do without the proper perspective."

"When it happened—" Belle shivered, even with the sunbeam between branches gleaming over her youthful face. "That day, Steve and I were planning our next adventure. Occasionally, I've run into the 'real' version of myself. People who exist in the other world just seem to have something beyond the virtual shell. It makes me feel like a reflection. I hate it. Well, both of us hate being in the same place. I remind her of who she was, and she reminds me of what I could be. Steve isn't a fan either. But she arrived with no warning. And seeing us there, in the same house as Steve left her in alone, I can imagine what she felt. But she went too far. She said she was going to shut it all down—shut me down. If I had killed her, it'd have been self-defense. But I could stab her, and it would do nothing. For the first time, I felt powerless, except for my words. Hitting your own weak spots is so easy. Yet, I misunderstood what time does. How she changed. She was desperate. She grabbed a knife and I thought it was to stab me. But stabbing Steve… well, it went wrong. At least that's what the other investigators told me. I don't think she meant to harm him. I can't imagine I would. And I can't believe Steve is gone."

"Can't you make another Steve?" I asked.

Belle frowned. "I don't want a copy."

"Someone like you," Scarlett said.

As these words faded into the forest, the forest reverberated with an echo, distorting into deeper depths. A different place entirely, only vaguely resembling the safe path. Now, it was mistier. Unexplored. Unknown.

Scarlett's breathe swirled in the fog with a chuckle. "I see you have another question on your mind."

Belle walked through the gathering mist, which condensed into more solid form, low and between leafless trees. Suddenly, she turned to Scarlett. "How do you deal with being alone?"

"That wasn't the question I was expecting." Scarlett reached for her teardrop pendant, but she turned the movement into scratching her neck.

The phantom touch was so brief, anyone who didn't have the context would've thought it inconsequential. But unlike Belle, I had seen Scarlett reach for the necklace before. Yet, this was not the time to dwell on it.

"You said it yourself—the first question was a baseline," Belle said. "Now, it gets interesting."

Uncomfortable, Scarlett was quick to turn the focus around. "I deal with loneliness as you do—distraction. In that regard, we may be similar. But maybe the best way to cope is to express it."

"You want me to express what loneliness feels like?" Belle asked.

"Can you?"

A smile. Belle twirled and the mist twirled with her.

A spell-like vortex rushed, whipping by us like clouds around a mountain, condensing upon me as thick as frost on a flower. A constant cold numbed me and I was left blind. Grey.

The world was not silent. It was not empty. But it was desperately, terribly, lonely. There was more beyond the fog, but it could not be seen, heard, nor even imagined over the uproar. Although I was not alone, the knowledge that Scarlett and Belle were so near and yet out of reach was dreadful.

And as the maelstrom faltered and faded back into the depths, the resulting clearing was nighttime in a rain-soaked woods. Moonlight shone between sparse, shadowed trees. In the reaches off the path, we weren't alone—creatures wandered and crept about.

Scarlett's hair was a mess, but her words were not flustered. "I asked you to show me, so I'll let you ask another question."

Belle's eyes glimmered in the ghostly moonlight. "Do you know what the names of these myths are?"

"Another test?"

"Coming up for air."

Scarlett nodded. "They're Japanese Yokai."

To describe the hordes of creatures that hid in plain sight would've been impossible. I pivoted from side to side, scanning the scene with a flicker of worry and disgust. There were ghosts and demons—true demons, unlike me—and everything in between. Bulbous noses. Split mouths. Long necks. No necks. Red warriors and blue fiends. Creatures of no color at all. Creatures that were not creatures, but random items with appendages, such as an umbrella with a single eye instead of an end and a soda can that must've been mistaken for a Mr. Potato-head. Then, there were sad, pitiable looking humanoids and bloodied, terrifying nightmares.

Both Scarlett and Belle seemed to be unworried. That was the trouble with experience—I had bad memories of such creatures, whereas this was merely fantasy to them.

"I answered your question, and now it's my turn," Scarlett said, ignoring the random squeaks and hisses and roars. "What canines are in the directory of myths?"

"Business? How boring." Belle paused and went vacant. She returned with the answer in an instant. "There are 254 on the list, including canines that aren't dogs, such as Kitsune and were-hyenas. They're organized into different categories."

Apparently, Belle did not find this question too strange. Scarlett wanted to see what sort of myth Belle's dog was. I wasn't sure if Belle knew about the dog, Romeo, or if she *knew* about the 'dog', Romeo. If she did, she remained factual.

"Can you give me examples of categories?" Scarlett asked.

"Is that another question?"

"A small follow-up."

"Fine. Protectors: church grim, Moddey Dhoo, Sharvara, Cerberus. Death: hellhounds, Cwn Annwn, and the black cadejo." Belle said the facts in an even tone.

"What about an Inugami?" Scarlett asked.

"Possession by a dog spirit, who attaches to those unstable in emotion and increases jealousy." Belle smiled at the completeness of her list.

Scarlett struggled to poke a hole in Belle's knowledge. "A good list. Do you know about Pesanta?"

"I have the name but no description."

Scarlett beamed. "A dog that appears on a person's chest at night and makes it harder to breathe."

"The list is incomplete," Belle said. "Maybe yours isn't."

"Mine is, too." Scarlett seemed rather pleased. "There's always more to learn."

"I'll send you my list in case."

We wandered a while longer on the wonderous path, seemingly safe from the spirits and demons haunting the untrimmed paths beyond. When the creatures drew too close, they turned back by magic, or more specifically, Belle's curation of the world.

A few shadowed us, staring with hungry pupils and moist lips. I fancied the fight. This threat of danger was worse knowing it would never be settled. Despite Belle's influence, I did wonder if creatures in this realm were like her—independent of their creation. Even without experience, maybe they could sense my power in the same way a gut instinct struck me and made me hesitate. Unlike humans, I did not rationalize such feelings away. I trusted them. I knew what was out there.

Belle grew bolder with her new exhibitions of wild and weird creatures. Myths crept out of shadows and fell from trees, but they were gone as soon as Belle moved on. She was searching.

"Of all the myths here, which is the most dangerous?" Belle asked.

Scarlett kept looking forwards. "What do you think, Zee?"

"You think I see or know them all?"

"No," Scarlett said. "I can't keep up. Looking at them would confuse me, but all your experience must count for something."

A few creatures popped to the forefront in the same way they did in this world. "I've heard more rumors and stories than I've seen. There's Kuchisake Onna, the slit-mouthed woman, who haunts many. Shuten Doji, the ogre, who devours all. But I think a rather plain Yokai is the most dangerous—Amanojaku—the heavenly evil spirit. Small, but it can inflame mortals' deepest desires, and that is more dangerous than teeth and claws. It's a myth after my heart."

Scarlett teased, "It never ceases to amaze me how someone so full of pride can be wrong so often."

"And you know the right answer, of course."

"To which Yokai is the most dangerous? No. Like everything here, they're not real. But if I were forced to choose the most dangerous myth here…" Scarlett smiled at Belle. "It's you."

The woods were ghost-quiet.

This was probably the first time Belle had been called a myth. I called them that because they eventually became stories, but I wouldn't tell one they weren't real to their face unless I knew they weren't a threat. I remember the first time someone told me I was a myth; I proved I was very real indeed.

A cold wind froze the air. Creatures stopped. Leaves hovered in midair. The world was still.

Then, Belle laughed.

It was a small laugh at first, growing with hurt and settling truth. It became an angry laugh. A haunting laugh. Then, it stopped.

The scene brightened with spite.

The moon set aflame, burning into harsh sun. Woods disintegrated into sand. Monsters exploded into dunes.

A desert surrounded us.

Along the top of the dunes, the path survived. Sand blistered across it. Heat poured down. Molten gold burned this new reality.

"Dangerous?" Belle asked, her voice cracking a bit like a log in a fire—a trait I'd have to remember and copy. "Maybe you're right. Loneliness does make you dangerous. I lied earlier and made what you wanted to see with that maelstrom. Knowing things are there—feelings, people, answers—and you can't find them. But that's not what my loneliness feels like. It's like the desert. Desolate. Damning. Destructive."

"I prefer the desert," I said, embracing the light and warmth. Now that the anger was out in the open, it felt less dangerous.

"Good, we've made it to the main act," Scarlett said, unphased by Belle's anger. If anything, she was pleased. "Yet, I find myself puzzled. A mystery."

"That's what you wanted," Belle said, her voice only an ember.

Scarlett thought a moment, taking up a handful of sand and letting it fall from a clenched hand like an hourglass running out of time. "What do you do when no one is here?"

"There's only emptiness, not even sand."

"You don't create new worlds?"

"Oh no, not anymore. I reserve this for guests." Belle's mood turned, redoubling into excitement, but hovering on the edge. "A true adventure comes with the randomness others bring. No destination. Not knowing what you might find buried along the way."

"And what have we dug up already?" I asked.

"It's my turn to ask a question." Belle motioned for us to lead.

Scarlett nodded, her footsteps treading on pristine sands. "Of course."

Reluctant, I walked, danger prickling at my neck as Belle followed behind me. I kept glancing behind me. Belle kicked a foot-full of sand down the dune, tumbling and rolling like an avalanche until it spun into a desert tornado as her ideas turned faster.

"There are so many ways this can go," Belle said. "So much unknown. It's… different. Isn't that exciting?"

Scarlett stopped. "Is that your question?"

"No." Belle breathed out and the sand tornado vanished. "What happens to me after this?"

"Ah, I was hoping you wouldn't ask that." Scarlett wiped a bead of sweat off her forehead and considered the horizon. "Guilty or not, I think the result will be the same. Punishment or mercy, they'll put an end to this reality."

I watched Belle carefully. There wasn't even a flicker of the previous emotional outburst. Contemplative. The better insight to her mood was the calm of the desert, wafting winds cooling the baking sands.

Peace was short lived. Down in the valley where the tornado had disappeared, a puddle of water welled up, creating a strange oasis in the desert.

A hawk soared from behind us and circled the fresh pond. And it was not alone. Unburying from the dunes, a sidewinder snake slithered across the slope, leaving slanting trails. Near the shores, a meerkat peeked out of a hole and a scorpion skittered out of the sand with thick black pincers and a poison-filled stinger. A scarab jumped from a dune and flew towards the blue spring. It landed, lingering and looking for smaller insects, fungi, or sustenance.

The beetle only got a swift stinger. A scorpion's pincers pinned it. The struggle was short.

Chaos followed. Seeing an easy meal, the meercat pounced on the scorpion. The meerkat ignored sting after sting, pawing and biting until the tail was torn away. Then, the meerkat munched. That meal was brief, too. The sidewinder snake arrived, and that went… predictably. Finally, the hawk ended the food chain, taking off with a swinging snake dangling from its talons.

And as it flew towards the sun, the hawk poofed into dust at Belle's snap, returning on the winds back into the sand.

"The desert is brief." Belle's eyes were wide as the sun. "Life. Violence. Death. I think that brevity is beautiful."

"You're not like the other Belle, are you?" I asked.

Belle was beautifully devilish at what she seemed to think was a compliment.

I'd watched this display and again, took notes. It was a spectacle I knew too well. I was not the waiting scrab, the sneaky scorpion, the wily meerkat, the sudden snake, or even the swooping hawk. I was what made the hawk into dust. I was like Belle.

To watch and not be the cause of death was a new perspective. I got so stuck in the circle that I could only see it in the confines of guilt, reason, and sometimes, even delight. I did not usually think of death as a beautiful ending—well, not an ending. That was the context I was missing. The hawk returned to the earth, where lesser creatures would start again. I rarely got to see what purpose was birthed from my destruction.

Scarlett pursed her lips, as if to prevent blurting out a conclusion made too hastily. And when she moved her hand, there was a smile.

"You're not telling the whole truth about what happened," Scarlett said. "You tried to kill yourself."

"Which 'yourself' are you referring to?"

"You don't deny it." Scarlett clenched her teeth. Her voice prodded and probed. "You didn't get what you wanted. Despite the show of power, you're nothing but a sad creation seeking distraction without Steve, and I can't tell if you're lying to me or yourself about what you feel. If you can feel."

Bluntness broke the barrier.

A scowl. "Ah, what a great psychoanalyst. I was mistaken thinking you were a great detective. You don't know what you're talking about."

"I know more than mirrored intelligence," Scarlett doubled down in her provocation. "A copy. Bloodless. Unimaginative."

"Unimaginative?" Belle disappeared, but her voice remained. "We'll see about that. You versus me."

The desert went dark. Instant night, speckled with dim stars. Sand hardened into concrete. And then, a subtle earthquake, growing louder. But the ground did not crack, except with the sound of a snare. A beat rose with lights over a stage. The sky solidified, steel tubes crisscrossed in the rafters above and kaleidoscopic lights twinkled down until they were constant and tangible. Spotlights shone like glimmering stars, staring down at a sea of people around us.

We were at a rave. The crowd milled, gathering as the bass in the background built. A collection of randomness, there were people of every shape and size, appearing as shades in shadows and angels in the lights.

The lights dimmed, save the single "B" behind the stage. A wave of lights illuminated faces for an instant.

"Prove you're as good as people say you are, Scarlett," Belle's voice whispered through the music. "Another test— can you find the vampire here? The sand ticks down until it all goes dark. One song. One chance. You lose… and we'll see if you can figure out what happens then besides being beaten by a 'mirrored intelligence'."

"I won't have to worry about that." Scarlett swiveled and honed in on details. But it was too much. There were thousands of people. It was like finding a sharp tooth in a haystack. No mirrors. No garlic, either. And so, Scarlett did something quite uncharacteristic—she complimented me. "Guess I have to be less like me and more like you."

More than not knowing what to do, I had even less idea what she meant, and before I could ask, she ducked into the crowds, leaving me alone.

I tried to change form and get a better view, but it did not work like the real world. I stayed human. So, I resorted to using the eyes I did have.

Steel rafters pulsed with fluorescent lights. Beams rippled like the underside of waves. Thrumming, the music enveloped, a warm embrace of bass, full and resounding. Metronomic, the beat got faster and faster, doubling like a horse going from a walk to a trot, a trot to a canter, a canter to a gallop. Finally, the beat crescendoed.

A pause.

"Almost out of time," Belle said.

The stage blasted smoke and flames. Rainbows arced over the crowd, lasers pulsing with the music. Sci-fi dreams danced, the warehouse walls bursting into flowered fireworks and galactic starbursts. Bubbles streamed over the crowd like comets and popped into sparkling confetti.

All of these were clear distractions.

An infectious energy rippled through the crowd. Then, I saw a glimpse of Scarlett.

She was dancing.

Her wide smile was obscured as she melded into the crowd.

What a weird time for joy. Yet, after a moment, I understood what Scarlett meant—she was trying to experience the general scene rather than study details.

It seemed stupid, but when faced with a universe-controlling intelligence, defying expectation might be the only option. I decided to bear the embarrassment and dance along. As I joined in, I found it easier to move with the crowds. I tried my best not to pretend it was a swordfight. Nor could I compare it to flying. Instead, I finally found a rhythm as if this were a ritual—constant beat, belonging to something more, and knowing there was an end, but enjoying the time given.

Only, for once, I wasn't the end, and my time was growing short. I sliced through the crowds, eased by being part of the flow, and I caught *it* in a smile.

The music dimmed with the lights.

Someone who looked like Scarlett had sharp, vampire-like teeth. I pushed through the crowd after her. Somehow, I had to tell Scarlett about this doppelganger vampire, but the creature eluded me.

"Who is it?" Belle asked over the final notes, her voice warbling and robotic.

"Over here," I tried to say, but the music was still too loud.

As if on a microphone, Scarlett's answer came through. "You killed Steve."

"That's not an answer." A grungy, bass response through the speakers.

And again, Scarlett responded, but it was not the answer I expected. "Everyone here is a vampire. You thought I'd get focused on one. A nasty trick."

Bright lights illuminated the room. Music, gone. The crowd turned like soldiers, about-facing towards me. They all smiled. Tall. Short. Long hair. No hair. Nothing alike, except shining fangs in the floodlights.

I tried to muster any power I could. Shadows or age, nothing happened. Light stayed bright. The computers, ageless. Me, powerless.

The vampires pounced, and I punched the first one. A solid blow. Proud of that. Then, I wrestled another and bit a third, reversing the tables. The vampire tasted like salt and iron. Being stuck in this form was awful. Spittle flew. Nails scratched tender skin. Inhuman strength pushed me like paper. Maybe a few vampires, I could've fought, but not thousands of dog-piling, ravenous creatures.

This was not how I expected to die, and I began to think that maybe I'd just wake back up in the pod, but that didn't happen. Oh well. Under a pile of bodies, the light fading, I heard Scarlett.

"Enough."

Like the drop of the music, the vampires exploded.

The warehouse was gone, too. No stage, just the living room we had started in. The blood marks from Steve's stabbing were still there.

Belle was, too. She wheeled about the room. "How did you do that?"

Scarlett said, "Instead of looking for the answer, I thought of what you would do. In your little tests, I showed you how I thought, looking at details and coming to quick conclusions. So, you tried to use these against me and cheated, thinking I'd get focused on one answer. But I'm still clever enough to understand you and your creations."

"How did you get out?"

"I cheated, too." Scarlett spun into a seat. "You're not the only one with experience using this VR technology."

Belle's shock made her voice robotic, the veneer of a person washed off. "Maybe. But this is my world. This is my life."

"And that's why and how and what." Scarlett tapped her fingers on the counter. "Steve and the real Belle might've known how to control the simulation, but they didn't know how to control you. You couldn't have Steve, so you messed with the system, killing him and hoping Belle would take the blame."

"I wouldn't hurt Steve!"

The world tore. I'd felt such anger a few times before, usually from my family. Some other daevas were demons. Belle's rage tore my essence apart and I became part of the void. The disorienting emptiness was familiar, but with a body still existing outside the simulation, consciousness disassociated. I was staring at my own reflection.

Then, the world pieced itself back together.

"Scarlett?" I asked, worried for her sanity after such an experience—humans were not used to being so disconnected. It came with strange side effects. Nausea. Headaches. Vertigo. Self-understanding.

There was no response. Belle and Scarlett were not here. Wherever here was.

I was on a green hillside that led down to a series of mazelike trails twisting through untamed wilderness.

Over my shoulder, a great mountain climbed the clouds. It was like I'd fallen down the mountain we'd been on earlier, except bright sunbeams burst through the clouds instead of waterfalls and a rainbow shone through patches instead of a dragon.

The sun peeked beneath the cloud cover and headed for the distance, descending towards the horizon at breakneck speed.

Instinct said I should get out of here before the sunset. I didn't want to find out what Belle could imagine in the darkness.

But I couldn't get the menu to work in order to escape the simulation. I tried to move my body in the pod, but I only fidgeted. I reached for the headset, but felt only my face. Trapped, there was no easy way out. Without an escape, I had a decision to make: the forest below or the mountain above.

My inclination was to ascend. The wilderness below was deep and blind.

I went against my gut—Belle was clever.

The earthy path down was canopied and cool, with salty wafts of the seaside, which made no sense. Evergreens shed sienna trimmings onto the trail. Birds tweeted from bushes rather than trees.

The world was topsy turvy, alien by its oppositeness. Even the path down doubled back up.

The only progress I seemed to make was in the seasons— trees lost lively leaves to time. Oaks dropped branches rather than acorns, and willows wept golden tears.

Shadows fell with the foliage. Dusk. Even the brightest forests creaked and groaned eerie at such an hour, much less these dying woods. This was the time for ghost sightings.

The wind whispered and I listened. It went quiet. A few seconds until the silence spooked the trees into rustling. Thin, sticklike woods blocked more light than it should've.

Normally, this would be my kind of place. But in the simulation, I felt mortal fear. I controlled nothing, and I was the only light here that someone else could take; the tables were turned.

There were whispers in the dusk. Odd animal noises. A deep neigh. High-pitched growls. Nothing that made sense— especially the words that followed.

They pierced the dusk's veil and my calm.

Spiders. The light shimmered. *Cheat.* Twigs chimed. *Knife.*

It was as if virtual Belle's subconscious was talking. Random words bubbled to the surface.

Another presence watched me, the hairs on my neck shrieking. Myths. Stories. Spooks. Whatever it was went unseen.

"Enough, Belle," I said. "You can't keep us here. This won't help you."

Even if she heard, there was no response. My confidence sounded much better in words than in flesh.

A howl in the distance.

The words weren't a good idea anymore.

I wished to bolt away, but I forced myself to stroll, unwilling to draw any more attention.

Trees devoured the sun's orb, but remaining rays pulled me along.

The path forked. Neither followed the sun. Left was a gully, where the path seemed to disappear entirely into undergrowth, thorns, and the unknown. Right led out the trees and to a meadow.

That was the way Belle wanted me to go. Or, maybe, she knew I'd chosen the opposite before. I would not play her game.

I chose the path that did not exist, following the sun straight through thickets.

A dog barked.

I stopped, one leg over low branches. Twisting back, I saw an enormous, shaggy, black and white dog looking at me with big, brown eyes. Its tail wagged back and forth near the ground, sweeping the dust.

The dog barked again and pointed its snout towards the meadowed path, tempting me towards the easy answer. A false friend. I wasn't dumb. But from the description I'd gotten, this was Romeo. This dog could be the key to solving what happened between the Belles and Steve.

So, barring all good sense, I hopped back and followed the dog towards the bright, safe-looking path. Definitely had to twist my arm for that.

Much to my surprise, I made it more than five steps into the meadow without being mauled. Green grass enveloped like a soft blanket. And waiting at the end of the path, the dog led me to a kitchen knife on a tree stump. The creature's black nose pointed to it but was careful not to touch it.

That gave me pause.

"Will it get me out?" I asked.

The dog barked.

"That's not a helpful answer."

The dog barked again, almost laughing.

"Can you understand me?"

The same bark.

"Are you Belle's dog?"

The same bark.

"Are you a broken record?"

A different bark.

The sun was drowning in the green horizon, and the dog barked a few more times, motioning for the knife.

In the distance, there was a voice. It was not Belle or Scarlett, but it was a woman's. "Romeo?"

"Who's that?"

A series of whimpers.

"Why did you take Steve?"

A different series of barks. Fed up, the dog started digging, sending dirt splattering over me. The mud pushed the knife off the tree trunk and on my foot.

The world was gone. Not a scene switch, but an escape to reality.

I was lying in the virtual reality pod again, the headset still over my eyes, which I took off as the pod depressurized.

Scarlett was waiting for me.

FOURTEEN

I INTERROGATE A REAL MYSTERY

"SOMETHING'S wrong," Scarlett said.

I pulled myself out the pod. "You don't say."

Flashbacks somersaulted through my head like daydreams, the other world not left behind enough, still visceral.

"I don't need sarcasm," Scarlett said. "Tell me what you saw."

And so, I proceeded to tell Scarlett the story as we walked to the brisk sunshine outside. The pleasant suburb with its single wood-paneled houses was a typically unusual setting for unpleasant incidents.

"I'd prefer your experience to mine." She shivered. "I thought Belle killed Steve, but virtual Belle destroyed my certainty."

"It seems virtual Belle made herself the prime suspect."

"The dog you saw was Romeo?" Scarlett glanced down the path of suburban streets, hoping for a sight of dog fur, but there was nothing to be seen besides swaying trees, freshly mowed grass, and the occasional flower bed.

"Belle having her dog in VR makes sense," I said.

"The real Belle, not the virtual version."

"You're saying it was the real dog?"

"It's not a dog." Scarlett bit down on her lower lip. "With all of the powers Belle had there, it's hard to imagine why she left the crime scene intact for Amar."

"You think she altered the scene?"

"She didn't hide anything—she exaggerated. Where she put me…" Scarlett seemed more shaken than I'd seen her before. "Let's say it was less pleasant than your forest. The crime scene was real, but she left it intact for a reason. She either wants the attention or the blame. If she's punished, maybe she thinks she'll survive. Or maybe she's hoping the punishment is an end to her existence. We're missing something, which we won't know until we find this 'dog'."

"Another search."

"To find a myth, we might need a myth."

"No more cats?" I asked.

"Not this time."

My godly contrast was coming down the street.

"Amar," I whispered.

"I know," Scarlett said.

The god arrived in a different guise than the one that took Belle away, despite the same black cloak. He was in the form I'd met him at the restaurant; tall, strong, stern. But by pure eyes alone, I could've spotted him miles away as a beacon of youth.

My essence strung tight as piano wire, ready to sing, scream, or break. I was ready for the inevitable fight between natural enemies, such as a honey badger and bees, or a honey badger and snakes, or a honey badger and other honey badgers.

I should've turned into a honey badger and mauled Amar.

"Scarlett," Amar said with a smile, shaking her hand.

"What do you want?" I asked, skipping such pleasantries. A few thousand years of knowing and hating each other does that.

"And I was supposed to be the direct one." Amar's grin spread like a rubber band before snapping back stern.

"You're less bubbly than I remember."

"I've aged." There was a black crack in an iris.

"You're welcome," I said. "Time wears thin, like my patience."

"Patience is all you have," Amar said. "If I wanted you dead, you would be."

"And yet, I'm still kicking. Do you enjoy it when I kick you?"

"No."

I winked. "Missing out."

"I don't need your humor or your help on this case."

"Do you just enjoy seeing us then?" I faked a blush.

"I wanted you both on this case because it's connected to another case I do need help on. Myths and the like are a rare problem these days, and only a few believe anymore. But in the recesses of quiet, outlawed spaces, they run free enough to keep Scarlett busy. That's good. We don't need her applying her talents otherwise. But gods—that is another story. The differences between myths and gods, subtle, but important. A myth, we could ignore. A god on the loose—"

"Besides us."

Amar ignored me. "A god on the loose is not a problem, as long as we know what we're dealing with."

"And you don't."

"I have my theories."

"A theory is only an idea," Scarlett said, smiling at Amar and I's back-and-forth until she could add to my millennia of practice at being snippy with the life god. "And ideas aren't worth much—everyone has them."

"Some are worth more than others," Amar said.

"But are yours?" I said.

"I certainly think so."

I was about to make a quip about thoughts until the other detective with glasses appeared from a side street and joined us.

"Belle's ready to talk," the robotic man said.

"Would you like to come with me?" Amar asked us.

"The two of you go," Scarlett said. "Enjoy your time together. I expect you to solve the case easily."

I knew her well enough by now. "You're going to do something you think is more important."

"There's nothing you couldn't learn that I could," she teased. "If you take my form, it'd be like I was there."

"I doubt that," Amar said.

"It's sarcasm, Amar," I said.

"Maybe not," Scarlett said, heading off.

Amar, the robotic detective, and I left to see Belle. The robotic detective stood between us, his shoulders hunched together as if he could feel the pressure. I resorted to platitudes, not knowing how freely we could talk around Amar's coworker.

The street was dense with life and I tried to use that. "All this technology. Very different."

"Very bright." Amar was surprisingly calm despite me burning and tricking him last time we'd met.

"Technically it is, I suppose."

"Yes," the god said plainly. "Technically technology is bright."

"How long have you been working at the department?" I figured it couldn't be long without me around.

"A while."

That meant a long time. "Has life been boring…?" I stopped before asking, "Without me". I couldn't admit that I almost missed the butting of heads.

"It's been the best time I've had."

"Really? This seems so small. I mean, I didn't expect you to enjoy such work."

"Big plans. Small plans. A matter of scale, not importance." Amar shook his head. "For someone so involved in change, you struggle with it. I enjoy what I do. A long time ago, we thought that power would make us happy. I succeeded, but happiness was not part of the package. Triumph only led to further desire. But that was the old me. Now, I'm happy with what I have."

"You seem less cheery."

"Maybe I am in a different way. I reconsidered my goals."

Amar was a stranger. I thought it was impossible to hate him more. But with this sudden stoicism, I was fuming under my form's mask of calm. He too, must be wearing a mask, nothing more—but that in itself would require Amar to change. Was it fake? Was it real? I wasn't sure what was worse.

I asked, "What kind of mess is this other case?"

"The big sort."

"Any clues?"

The other detective finally chimed in. "The case is for Ms. Wolfe. It's not something we discuss on the street."

The conversation ended. Finally, we arrived downtown, and with The Root above, we entered a glass building nearby, which should've been transparent, but was a sort of glass that merely reflected the city's light back at the observer, tinted blue. The reds and yellow and oranges of flashing signs returned purple and white. Whatever was inside was neatly tucked away.

There was no signage, but Amar led us in, checking into the building with his BioScreen. I fiddled with my ring, turning it on and off, still hating why Amar seemed so accustomed.

Through a bright lobby, we entered the confines of solid hallways. Concrete. Cracked. Hushed people worked at desks, and for the advancement of technology, it all seemed rather mundane and old. Big workplaces changed slower. There was a sense of age that was comforting.

Amar opened an interrogation room, and I followed him in.

"Turn on the recording," Amar said to the other detective.

The room was stereotypically grey and oppressive, except for the woman who sat at one of three chairs at a rectangular table.

This was Belle—the real one, if I could call her that anymore. She had tied her long hair in a hasty bun. Her face was saddened, and even her wrinkles were of a different sort; virtual Belle's smile showed wrinkles with excitement, while those experiences were etched permanently on the real one's. Without the excited energy, the marks were deeper and drawn from accumulated seriousness. Yet, she was not old by any means, appearing to be in the prime of her life. She tried a short smile as Amar and I entered and sat across the table.

And when Belle opened her mouth, the voice trembled. "I don't know what to say. I—well, I can't say what happened, Detective."

"You can't?" Amar asked. "Or you won't?"

"Can't." She seemed to stare past us.

"You said you were ready to talk." Amar frowned. "Did you just want to waste our time?"

"No—it's… it's complicated."

"Then start explaining, we have all—"

"Amar," I said, warning. He was pressing too hard. I'd even used the god's real name. If it got Amar in trouble—good—that was not my fault. The woman was almost on the verge of tears, and I offered her a sheltering smile. "Belle, it's alright if you don't know how to explain. Let's start simple. My name is Zee. Look here. That's right." I met her tear-reddened eyes, the strain lessened. "It'll be ok." She breathed along with me, slow and deep. "Just start by telling me what you see around here."

"What kind of question is that?" Amar asked.

"Quiet." I waved him off. "I'm sorry about him."

"I don't understand, what am I supposed to see?" Belle asked.

"There's this drab scenery. Grey table. Hard chairs. Whatever comes to mind. Take for instance this chair I'm sitting in—it wobbles a bit. Not terribly. Not enough for me to put something under the leg, but enough to shake as I move like this."

I swayed side to side, exaggerated as if it was a rocking chair. Even a stable chair would've picked itself up and moved on two legs. Inevitably, I wobbled straight into Amar's chair with a big knock.

"Watch it."

I laid a hand on Amar's shoulder—the only being I couldn't hurt—burning in contrast. "Or, take for instance, my companion here. Sure, very stern. Well-put together, almost as if constructed in a particular fashion. But take a closer look at the eyes. Mediterranean blue, right?"

"I mean, I suppose," Belle said. She was calm now.

"Exactly—it's not exactly that." I nodded. "The eyes are actually like turquoise. A symbol of health and unfeeling as stone. What do you see when you look at me?"

"I don't know. A kind face?"

"And my eyes?"

"Almost like clouds."

"Almost." I smiled. "Are you feeling any better?"

She paused, realizing her breathe had slowed. "A little."

"Is it better if I do the majority of the talking and you answer simply?"

"It might be."

"The virtual version of you isn't you," I said. "How about we call her something else?"

Belle nodded. "I usually call her L."

"L? Makes sense to me." I placed my hands on the table, comfortable and relaxed. "L told us that you stabbed Steve."

There was a pause. Maybe I'd gone too far, too soon. But I wanted to see the difference in reaction between L and Belle. There was the same tension in the air as it was before L exploded into anger.

But when anger escaped, it came as a cool breeze. "Of course."

"I didn't expect that." I withdrew my hands.

Belle's lips thinned. "No. Of course she would say that."

I tried to understand, but I was having a hard time not looking at it logically. "What would stabbing Steve accomplish?"

A small shake of the head. "Neither of us wanted to hurt him."

"And yet, he died," Amar said.

"It's not your fault," I said, intending honesty but giving comfort.

Belle wiped at her reddened eye, which seemingly had no more tears to give. She struck me as more normal than her virtual version.

So too, was Belle hiding more. She cared about how her words and actions were seen. L did not have the same concern. Seeing them both, it made L look like a caricature or an act. L manipulated us to see what she wanted. Without that control, Belle was restrained. There must be a common motivation or reason that drove them, and that's the key I had to find.

"You love Steve," I said.

"Of course."

"L does, too."

"Can numbers love?" she asked with a scowl.

"A collection of numbers or a collection of cells." I shrugged. "I'm not the one who can tell you what counts as love."

She bit her lip painfully hard.

Pieces fell together. L might use the simulation in the same way as with us, and the real and virtual Belle would've been stuck in a battle of will. Thinking back, I echoed what Scarlett had said.

"You tried to kill yourself." I corrected myself, even if I'm not sure I should've. "Or, you tried to kill L and she tried to kill you. But Steve ended up dead."

Belle gripped her hands into fists. "The simulation seems so real. The feelings are. L isn't some NPC in a game. I might as well be fighting a mirror. But I was upset. She was, too. We wrestled over control. It was chaos, and Steve ended up—." She exhaled hard. "It doesn't make any sense. That shouldn't have killed Steve. He's had so much worse in the simulation, a knife shouldn't have bothered him."

"Maybe it's different since you stabbed him," Amar said.

"It doesn't matter which 'you'." I looked at Amar, whose disinterest told me everything I needed to know. "You know it wasn't their fault."

"You've been a detective for a day and suddenly know that?"

I leant back in my seat. "I know well enough that we're asking about the wrong thing."

"And here I was, thinking you were on the right track." Amar grinned at me with that ridiculous pomp I hated so much.

I returned to Belle, hoping she'd opened up enough to answer something open-ended. "Tell me about your dog."

"Romeo? What does that have to do with anything?"

No one had even bothered to tell her that Romeo was still missing. "I just need something to distract me from my partner here. What sort of dog is it? Where'd you get him?"

A small smile reinvigorated Belle. "He's a mix. Part Belgian shepherd. Mostly black, with a tuft of white like a tie. Looks that could kill, but he's a sweetheart, thus his name. I got him from a friend."

"Why'd they get rid of him?" I asked. "Was it something Romeo did?"

Belle recoiled. "Of course not. My friend loved him, but she was moving and couldn't have that big of a dog."

"You wouldn't happen to have a picture? I love dogs. They're more loyal than people."

"They blocked my BioScreen."

"Ah," I said. "Of course. Tell me, has Romeo been acting odd?"

Belle looked down, and with only the single hanging light, her face was shadowed. "Not really."

"That means partially," Amar said.

Belle lifted her head, her eyes meeting mine but stuck in some of the darkness. "Well, Romeo's been more attached to me than normal. Always by my side. He whined when I left for work."

Apparently, this caught Amar's attention, too, and the other god stole my question. "Did Romeo like Steve?"

"Romeo likes me more."

"But something changed."

"Usually, Romeo's pretty good at entertaining himself. But I suppose I have longer hours now." A thought wrinkled Belle's forehead. "Steve has been home more, but he's not always the best company. Especially with him being in the pod so often. I'm sure Romeo has been lonely."

Then, the opposite question struck me. "Does Steve like Romeo?"

"We made a deal. Steve got to keep the pod and I got Romeo. Only Steve would think he got the better part of that deal." There was a bit of humor left in Belle, and somehow with the gloomy room and circumstances, a similar joke to the one the mechanical detective had said earlier seemed funnier when Belle said it.

"Has Romeo ever been aggressive?" I asked.

"He'd run away from a tennis ball."

"Even if the tennis ball was thrown at you?"

She shrugged. "Then I suppose he might find a bit of bravery."

"Instead of a tennis ball, what about if it was Steve? Or L?"

"He wouldn't hurt anybody."

This next bit would be painful, and I took a moment to not seem too eager. "Did anyone tell you Romeo bit Steve, pulled him out of the pod, and dragged his body away? The shock from being pulled out might've been what killed Steve, and they're still missing."

"What?"

I kept going, knowing what I said would likely shut her down from providing more answers, but I tried anyways. "We're going to find both of them. But we need your help. Do you have any idea where Romeo could've gone? Or how he opened the pod?"

"No. I have no idea how he opened the pod."

Amar said, "Presumably he hit the buttons with his nose, unless he grew fingers."

"This is ridiculous," Belle said. "If anyone killed Steve, it was that pod. It was L."

"He's been gone a long time, hasn't he?" I asked.

There was anger in her eyes, but Belle bit her tongue. She took a deep, audible breath, but there was more fury in it than if she had exploded with frustration. Her hands gripped the table. "Why aren't you out there looking for them?"

"We have someone on the case," Amar said. "While a body is quite good evidence, in this case, it's not necessary."

"It's not my fault." Her hand slipped from the table.

"We're going to have to keep you here," Amar said.

This set her more on edge. "Why? It's not my fault."

Something had changed. The guise of control was slipping. There was something shared with the virtual Belle. Not action—this anger was not so outrageous. Not motive—this change in demeanor was not meant to mislead us. But a similar aura or attitude. Her hands were shaking, mouth trembling, eyes looking away. Her fingernail dug into her palm hard enough to impress marks. Similar mannerisms? Emotion? Possible, but not quite. The fingernail, like her biting her lip, struck me.

"I don't think detective A intends on charging you with anything." I sighed, echoing Amar's. The god had known I was close. Instead, I had taken the long route to this conclusion. "We don't agree on many things, but he wants to keep you safe. I do, too."

"You think I'm in danger?" And in an instant, Belle retreated behind a controlled expression.

"We don't want to take chances," I said. "We'll make sure to let your work know about your absence, if you would tell us where you work?"

"I work at The Root as a data analyst."

"What floor?" I knew the answer already. It was all connected.

"The eighth trading floor, third branch—supplementing data to the collectables trading team on the ninth floor."

There it was. The missing piece, which explained so much. This was why Amar brought us in on this case. It's why Amar wanted me here. We were dealing with a god at The Root, and there was only one type of god that turned pets into myths, caused freak deaths, and made people so unstable. They ranged the spectrum from trickery to reality-bending. But how much uncertainty were we dealing with and how far did the god reach? To the virtual world? If it had affected Belle and Romeo, did it make L different? Or were the Belles totally different people?

"There's been a gas leak," Amar said. "Maybe that's what's making you feel a little funny, Belle."

The life god always did this. Amar knew and was waiting for me to catch up, which was a way of trying to allow my pride and only upset me more. But I didn't give Amar the satisfaction.

I whispered in Amar's ear, "You already knew about the god being connected to this case. You should've told me instead of wasting time."

Amar smiled at Belle. "My colleague isn't quite as slow as I thought. I think we've got what we need, Belle, and we'll let you go for now."

"What?" I asked. "You just said—"

"But as you can imagine, we're going to keep an eye on you." Amar waved at the wall. "We'll have an agent accompany you home and keep you safe. If you need any medical attention, mental or otherwise, we'll make that available to you as well. Besides that, we can find the picture of Romeo and find both him and Steve. We're going to focus on this case with all our attention."

As angry as I was about Amar putting the woman through this questioning just to let me get to the conclusion on my own, I tried to turn my attention to what it meant. Belle was one of the many victims of what was going on at The Root. We would have to be cautious in dealing with this god, but I tried to focus on what was in front of me—finding Romeo and the sad woman in front of me. "Take care, Belle. I can't promise anything except that we'll do our best to get Romeo back to you."

She stayed quiet as the other agent entered the room, while Amar and I left the investigation room.

Despite my attempt to think of the implications, current frustration kept me tense. As Amar and I's footfalls echoed in the concrete hallway, I couldn't just look ahead—Amar's pompous stride kept putting him in front of me and I could only try to keep pace.

Finally, I couldn't help it anymore and pulled Amar around by the shoulder. "If you already knew about Belle and The Root, why am I here?"

"Because unlike Scarlett, you didn't know," Amar said, annoyingly calm. "Maybe we could've learned something new along the way. Although I owe Scarlett for the information from the Cayne and Warner cases, that doesn't mean we're a team. This is a professional relationship and having you on the same page helps the only case you're involved in—what's going on at The Root. You know what we might be dealing with, right?"

I scowled. "Of course. Are you sure you haven't been affected? It seems odd for someone so straightforward to suddenly understand deceit."

Amar ignored my ill-temper. "Being straightforward is what got me here, not deceit. People so often look for complexity when the answer is screaming at them."

"What happens when it's more complicated?"

"It usually isn't."

"That's why you like having Scarlett involved," I said. "All she does is complexity."

"The three of us have our roles."

I laughed. "Times really have changed."

"You don't need to know everything."

This was headed a direction I couldn't stand. "When you solve this case, more people will trust you, more people will believe in this great detective, and you'll get more powerful, while Scarlett will eventually get bored of me and I'll slip back into nothingness. Is that it?"

"I'm surviving with the times."

The non-sensical nature of existence bristled my essence. "You want to be the hero. How is it people always like you better?"

"A simple choice for most—life or death."

"More like summer and winter."

Amar laid an arm around me. "If it was permanently winter, everyone would die."

My fury shook him off. "If it was permanently summer, they'd die of boredom."

"Mortals love me." He said it as a fact.

"Not all of them," I said, but hated the truth in the god's statement. "But they all fear me."

"Is that so? How's that turned out?"

Adversarial shadows grew about the room, growing as if this was my Pull. This, though, was personal. "Better than you think."

The lightbulbs flashed brighter, casting away darkness. Amar chuckled. "Not as well as you think."

I shrunk back with the shadows, condensing my anger. I did not want to feel such fire. I did not want to destroy everything I touched. But I couldn't help the hurt. My rage hurt like the curse that resided in my essence.

A fist. A face. They met, and then, neither moved. My knuckles were connected to Amar's beautiful face, two blue eyes staring past the blow, a veil of light thin as paper blocked the blow. Restraining me.

Weak. Powerless. I withdrew. My head burst forward. The headbutt was stopped, but I did not give in, pushing against it with all the energy I had saved for months. Every bit of belief Iris, Scarlett, and others had in me was put into pushing instead of pulling.

All I wanted—no, not what I wanted—but what I had dreamed of for so long was to destroy Amar, even at the cost of myself. The air hummed. There was not enough energy to blow up the world, but the police station for sure. Although I felt out of control, there was something holding me back. It wasn't the Pull—only a flicker of change.

There had to be another way forward. It didn't have to end like this.

There was another concern that dwarfed even this great rivalry—opportunity.

I withdrew, tension simmering away. "We'll see who solves this first."

"Run along and find Scarlett." Amar walked away, turning his back on me as if I was just a nuisance.

"People only like you until they get to know you," I said. It was the best insult I had, and I hoped to hurt him more than my fists could.

FIFTEEN

I SAY, WHAT A DOG

After leaving Amar, I was immersed in a rapid river of people. Cascading through the city, elbows and shoulders struck me like rocks. However, I was too distracted to be angry. My focus was elsewhere.

For so long, the Pull had made life simple. Now, I had to choose my own path. Amar had found power, Scarlett had chosen purpose, and I was floundering.

I leapt into a puddle as if trying to dive to the depths of an ocean. The splash was cold through my clothes. Thoughts of revenge were usually enough to boil such annoyances away. Still, I remained cold.

And although I didn't know what path lay before me, I knew what I didn't want—to be considered a demon.

But through chaos, there was the opportunity to change even an old god like me.

My attention turned to the ring on my finger. With a twist, I turned on the screen and contacted Scarlett. I typed a message: "Big news. Where are you?" That would get her interested. I paused, then edited it to: "It's chaos!" A good puzzle. She might like that, but without context she might ignore me. I changed it again, this time, to: "My fault." That'd get a response, even if only a question.

Scarlett appeared out of the crowd. "You know those weren't drafts?"

I stifled embarrassment and powered the ring off. "Belle was interesting."

"Was she?" Scarlett walked away from The Root, and we joined the flow of people.

"Umm," I squinted in the building's shiny reflections. "Yes?"

"And I thought your idea that a chaos god is affecting The Root was."

A shake of the head. "I guess asking how you know anything is a dumb question."

"I've done my research and always have my theories, even if I don't know exactly what we're dealing with."

"Not knowing what we're dealing with is the point of those kinds of gods."

Scarlett hesitated and her eyebrows furrowed. "Your last message was your best one, hoping I'd ask what was your fault. However, there's only one thing that could be—you're sorry for what drove us apart—Lars' death."

I tried my best convincing tone, glancing at her to give just the right amount of eye contact. "I didn't kill Lars. A dumb sentiment to be sorry for."

"Definitely." Scarlett flushed, and unlike me, embarrassment could not be so easily hidden.

"That's the best you have to offer?"

Scarlett looked up to the clouds as she walked. "Looks like rain again. I never even got my umbrella back."

"Scarlett."

"Is your ego so fragile you need to hear me say it?"

We split around a couple holding hands and blocking the sidewalk.

I drew back close in step. "Is yours so fragile you won't?"

"You and I both know it." Her mouth firmed. "It's like me saying it's going to rain—it doesn't change reality."

My voice raised. "It might change what you do. And even if I did kill Lars, you're not certain if my choices are your fault."

"You're still my responsibility regardless."

"That's the problem!"

"So we're agreeing!"

It did not sound like we were.

Scarlett lowered her voice as people avoided our argument. "You chose, but I feel guilty because I'm the reason you're here."

"That's not how it works. If it's my choice, you shouldn't feel guilty for it." My goal was to get under her skin. "Unless you're guilty just because I exist."

She stopped. "I'm not."

People split around us. "Sounds like a regretful god."

"Please, oh wise one, give me more of your insight about me."

"No wonder you fit in with the vampires in the simulation—I don't think you can see yourself in the mirror." I motioned around us. "You want to know everything and everyone, but you don't want to do anything with it. You can't handle judgement because like a god with a sliver of a conscience, there's guilt—so much guilt that they would leave choices to others. And when someone gets too close, they're cast off like you tried to do to me."

"You haven't walked away," she said, a little quiet.

"Just because you try to walk away doesn't mean you can." I had tried to leave a similar situation before, but the Pull would drag me back.

"And when I told you to leave, you left forever, right?"

She might've gotten me, there. I stumbled over my words. "I mean, I didn't leave. Not yet."

"That's the strangest thing," Scarlett said. "I believed you would be gone a long time ago."

"Others believe in me, too."

"I mean leave me."

"I can choose trivial acts as long it doesn't oppose my creation or purpose."

She smiled. "What about the two Belles? Are they different because of who they were made as or what they do? Where's the line for your excuse? Is that why you feel guilty?"

"I feel guilty that I can't overcome my making. I want to be free. I want to be anything and choose everything."

"No one can," Scarlett said. "But at least we're making progress. You said 'everything'. That implies you have some choices; it's not all decided for you."

The clouds let lose a cold mist, which kissed my face. I expected our hot conversation to steam the moisture, but all I could do was steam at my inability to contest her points. "Where's this myth of yours?"

"A new myth was hard to find, but I got help closer to home." Gigantic sugar glider eyes peeked out of Scarlett's jacket pocket. "I already gave Angel the scent to follow." A devious smile grew upon her face. "I would've left you with Amar, but the trail led me past you."

"Then get going. You're wasting time."

"Don't be grouchy, it's going to be a beautiful stormy day and we have plenty of choices ahead of us."

We left the city-center behind. Skyscrapers descended to basic brick, ranging from raw red to burnt brown. Unseeable heights became rusted roofs, and we followed the quiet, dusk streets towards cracked white marble and peeling stucco.

Angel climbed to Scarlett's shoulder and orbed eyes looked one way and another, following a scent. And, like a horse on reins, Scarlett turned down side streets and hopped low fences, Angel directing her with little nibbles on the ears.

Mist fell, more eerie than soaking. I trailed, a sense of unease prickling through old, undisturbed air. There was a magic here I recognized, familiar enough that it was almost like smelling my own fragrance under the cold rain's tickle.

But there was something new, too—an uncertainty that mutated the mundane into magical. That was, after all, what magic was—something recognizable, but impossible.

The world greyed. Small puddles huddled between cracks in cobble. Shadows stayed short. Old outskirts. And yet, however simple it seemed, it could not be quite as boring as it looked.

The haunting was in the silence, where my mind could fill the gaps.

A drape flapped in a window. A tree branch waved in the corner of my vision. I expected to encounter a myth around every corner.

The sun sank below the clouds and to the horizon. Behind us, the city flickered into neon lighting. Ahead, the fog glowed orange, brightening in the final flares of another day for the history books. One of many. And as dusk settled down for anything but slumber, the whistling winds blanketed us with darkness.

When the final rays of light angled towards the heavens and crowned the night, I almost rejoiced at darkness. After so long of bright, busy nights that teased me with false fire, there was serenity.

"Angel's leading us in circles," I said.

"Indeed," Scarlett said. "We're barely getting closer."

"You agree?"

"We're swirling in on a spot like a fishnet."

I asked, "Then why don't we just go to the center?"

"The real mysteries are the mysteries we make along the way."

"What?"

Scarlett said, "The question is why."

"Why what?"

"Exactly."

"Exactly?"

Scarlett smiled. "Confused?"

"Yes."

"Good. Messing with you fills the time."

I stuck my hands in my pockets. The temperature was dropping with the rain, but I only did it to hide annoyance.

We passed through a dripping gateway, drenching us. I wiped hair out of my face and shortened the strands like a quick haircut to make it less annoying. Out of the fog, we came into a surprisingly lively park. Flower beds of daffodils and orchids bloomed. Roses, dewy in the haze, produced a sweet smell that reminded me of Amar. I much preferred the old iron fence posts that had lost their links to rust, a row of black stalks in the encroaching night. However, I did have to admit that the ornamental shrubbery shaped into designs renaissance artists would've been proud of were not that bad. A Thinker pose in a hedge. A chubby David, overgrown. A Venus, not with broken arms, but with beautiful prosthetics made of metal, leaves budding on them.

All these plants surviving winter was magic. The Tree of Life fed the roots here.

I recognized this park. Yet, as Angel settled for a nap, there was no Romeo or Steve.

Scarlett looked around. "There's nothing here."

I smiled. "There's plenty around. You just need to know what to look for. You may know myths, but you don't know what it's like to be one."

"Aren't I glad to have you?"

"That sounded like sarcasm."

"Who said I was being sarcastic?"

"You're ridiculous," I said. "I guess I won't tell you which top of the fence poles gets you into the Tree of Life like the grave to the restaurant."

"I wouldn't want you to." Scarlett jumped at the game, perusing the various poles. Spiked like pikes, she chose one that had been broken, but before her hand met it, she brought her hand away and chose the sharpest looking one.

"Ouch."

"What did you expect?" I asked.

She poked herself a few more times with the spikes, until she met me with an accusing look.

"What?" I laughed. "I can't tell you which one because it's not a fence pole that gets you there."

She exhaled mist. "It wasn't the grave, it was the flowers that got us to the restaurant. Life gets you in. A tree here, right?"

"There's the intelligence I expected. But just because you know doesn't mean much."

"I'll hug every tree in this park if I have to."

"Good. Get going."

"What happened to wasting time?"

"I'm having fun. The dead can wait." I was amused with her struggle. I was enjoying keeping one answer from her. Even if I had to cheat.

The way in was a tree stump behind me.

However, she caught on quick.

She walked around me and kicked the stump, beaming as she waited for success.

Nothing happened. Only those who were born of the tree could use it.

Not wanting to hurt her, I only grazed her cool hand and touched the stump at the same time, transporting us both into the tree as if morphing inside it. A sweet sapling of energy, sunlight and warm. Then, we were in a tunnel.

Relieved to be out of the rain, I wanted to pet the sugar glider, but it would've only aged her; so, the real reward was my words. "Angel did well."

Scarlett dried off Angel with the inside of her jacket and offered her a honey treat before the creature was tucked back into her pocket for a nap. "How'd you know this was here?"

I shrugged. "With age comes insight."

"Sometimes."

"In my case, age makes that sometimes come more often."

Within an enormous, hollowed branch, our feet echoed on bark floors, gnarled but mostly flat, until we reached an old wood door. I opened it. The room inside was not the temple I expected.

This was a repurposed karaoke room. Purple LED lights lined plush couches and silhouetted art, which depicted waterfalls and forests. There were five VR pods parallel across the room and a TV screen on one wall showing what must've been the inside of the simulation. Although there were five pods, not all were filled. I expected one or two people.

Instead, there were three.

The first pod had a woman I didn't recognize. The second, a man, also unknown, except for a gauze bandage around his arm—Steve. Third, there was another man, dressed in a black wool suit and with a thick black beard under the VR helmet.

"How did Steve get in here?" I asked.

"Same way you did." Scarlett checked the normal door, which was inches thick and locked. "Would've been a great mystery besides the secret entrance. Let's go."

"Let's go?"

"We found Steve."

"That can't be the end," I said.

"There's nothing interesting." She lingered at the tunnel's door. "Steve's alive."

I didn't follow. "That makes it interesting. Besides, how can you tell he's alive?"

"Why bother bandaging a dead person?" She looked back between the three figures. "Fine. I guess I'm curious enough that I have to take the risk."

"What risk?"

She closed the wood door and watched over the peaceful, sleeping faces. "Whatever might happen to Steve."

"You're worried what I might do?"

Scarlett shook her head. "Belle. Or virtual Belle."

"He's already been stabbed once."

"I don't blame them." She frowned and placed a hand on the pod's glass.

I motioned to the other woman. "Her?"

"I doubt they know about Steve's other lover."

"But who's the other guy?" I asked.

"Romeo."

"The dog?"

"Not as much as Steve," Scarlett said, taking her hand away. "What a simple motive. I'm only hoping that Romeo is interesting enough for all this trouble."

I peered through the glass. "Let's find out."

"Go on, get them out." Scarlett smiled.

A blank glare at the lock screen. "I don't know how, but I'm sure you do."

"Not without alerting the illegal business outside these locked, but not impenetrable doors."

"Why is this illegal?"

"The VR isn't." She checked the door. "Judging by roughly where we are in the city, the business might be."

"Wouldn't Belle notice money was missing?"

"Who said Steve was paying with money? Like virtual Belle, Steve spent so much time in the simulation, he has skills in virtual reality that carry a price—exciting people, enticing people, scaring them. Illegal businesses can have legal aspects."

There was a disturbance in the pods. One perspective went blank on the TV. The bearded man moved his hands, and as the pod opened, it was as if he had never been there at all.

Taking his place was an enormous black dog with a white tie-like marking on his neck. The dog's head was tucked under the VR helmet like covers, paws stretched outwards to where people would put their appendages. It didn't look comfortable. The dog stood and shook the helmet off, hopping out the pod with elegant ease.

A snarl and rumbling growl. Slobber-shined canines threatened.

Scarlett sat on one of the couches, unconcerned. I took this to mean this was my job; however, as the more than ice-blue canine eyes dilated, the great black dog lowered its giant head.

One bark. It echoed, but as it lessened, the gaze turned to distrust rather than anger, humming along the echo with a questioning whimper.

I unclenched fists, remembering that Belle said Romeo wouldn't hurt anyone. I trusted, and in return, got trust.

As I relaxed, the dog lay with paws on top each other in a way that reminded me of an adolescent sphynx—they had the most immature riddles.

"Belle misses you," Scarlett said, relaxing cross-legged on the couch.

A tail wag, but a stubborn stare.

Scarlett said, "We deal with myths. You don't have to keep up the ploy. What are you?"

"You haven't figured it out?" I asked.

"Did you?"

"No."

Scarlett yawned. "We already saw you as a human."

"Stupid machine," the dog said. It padded between the pods and emerged on the other side almost the same height as if it stood on its hind legs, that is to say, taller than most, except it was back in a black-suited human form. "I can become a dog in the simulation, but I can't get in as a dog."

"You saved me earlier," I said.

"Or did I make you even more lost?"

"You gave me the way out."

Romeo said, "A way out was the best way to make you lost."

"Are you a sphynx?" I asked. "You speak in riddles."

Romeo's infectious smile glinted within his beard. "Some might mistake me for the devil at the crossroads."

"That, I can relate to. I've been mistaken for the same."

"A fellow myth," he said.

"A god."

"Pretentious—pretend-cious. Same thing."

The shadows crackled with my scowl.

"If you're like me," Romeo said, "I know you're not a good demon—the best ones are those people don't think are demons."

Everyone was using my words against me. The room brightened with the technological light. "If you're not a demon, what?"

"Wait—" Scarlett interjected. She sat a moment, eyes closing in thought. "You're a Gytrash."

"That guy is trash." Romeo motioned at Steve. "But some people call me that name, even if I prefer 'Romeo'. How would you like to just be referred to as, 'human'?"

"Wouldn't bother me," Scarlett said. "As long as the word before it was 'unique' or 'exceptional', and not 'common'."

"I'm going to have to pop your ego with a pin." I made a deflating noise.

"No need—I'm not as good as some say—I still don't know why Romeo did all this. It seems, counterintuitive." Scarlett got up and looked into the pod. "Steve is not searching for the past—he's searching for youth. Virtual Belle is searching for something real. Real Belle is too. Just in different ways, but with the same result—Steve. But then you, Romeo. A myth as a house dog? For how long?"

"Me? Ah, maybe a month. The prior me, years."

"Another double Belle situation," Scarlett said. "Now, that's an interesting side effect of our friend at The Root. New becoming old."

Romeo said, "I prefer developed rather than old."

"You love Belle even after you became a myth?" I asked.

"A platonic love. I want the best for her."

"A woman's best friend—a strange hybrid of dog and myth." Scarlett ran her fingers through her hair, until she realized it got her hands wet from the lingering dampness. "But why hurt Belle like this? You brought Steve into the arms of someone else."

"Sometimes, to do what is best, you have to get the hurt over with," Romeo said. "Belle was lost. To be found, I had to make her more so. Steve lied to L, as Belle calls her, that he still had to spend half his time in the real world, but he was still looking for something more. As if two lives with Belle wasn't enough. Meanwhile, Belle supported him. Both of the Belles really. The money. The time. The love. Never repaid. As a normal dog, I begged Belle to stay and find out what Steve was doing. But it was no good."

"Until?" Scarlett asked.

Romeo snarled down at Steve. "A strange magic infected me. Made me what I am now. At first, it seemed like an emotion. A frustration almost like hunger. Then, there was the gnawing anger—not hot or cool, just eating at me. And over time it solidified into resolution of what to do. For Belle's good, I led Steve into temptation. All it took was a single walk." He looked at the other pod with the woman and smiled. "It's what I do. Or, what I became does. I can't explain how I became a Gytrash—how memories that were not mine came to be in my head. Crunching bones. Wild nights. Wandering travelers."

I too, felt like crunching Steve's bones into dust. Betrayal was a despicable crime. "And yet, you did not give into the worst of such feelings?"

"There was always a stronger one. Care."

I sat next to Scarlett and thoughts centered in one direction that I didn't dare look too often. And like a mask slipping off, I found myself in a woman's form. The reflection of the pod's shiny exterior was a looking glass to the past—I was the woman I'd seen in the grave, restaurant mirror, and my dreams—the last mortal I'd cared for.

Romeo smiled at me knowingly.

Catching myself, I transformed back to the owl-faced man. And although the accidental transformation was a slip, containing it was more difficult. That was my version of a blush.

Scarlett smiled but didn't comment, remaining stuck to the business at hand. "And this plan is still ongoing?"

"I expected to be found," Romeo said. "Not so quickly. I just let L know about the other woman. I figured she'd find a way to tell Belle, if only to hurt her, too."

"That wasn't your original goal." Scarlett pointed. "You knew about this woman, but maybe you didn't want to hurt Belle. Instead, you led Belle to the pod and showed Steve with L, recreating a normal life, hoping that would finally show Belle there was no future. You knew it probably wouldn't work. Yet, there was a glitch—not in the simulation, but of your understanding of L."

"Not L—Belle." Romeo sat on the couch with us, and we were like an audience for the situation in the pods. "Belle wouldn't leave because Steve was spending time with L. However, before I could reveal the truth about the other woman, Belle acted impulsively. She stabbed Steve."

"Belle told us there was a fight for control and it was an accident." I said. "L, on the other hand, said Belle stabbed Steve on purpose, hoping to get him out."

Romeo stroked his beard. "L told the truth."

"Why would Belle lie?" I asked.

"To avoid trouble."

Scarlett said, "L might've told the truth. But not all of it."

"Sometimes liars tell the truth with the worst intentions," Romeo said. "L and Steve were conspiring to fake his death. But L wanted Belle to take the blame and trapped them inside the simulation. Instead of an accident, L expected a fight. She wanted Belle to try and attack her, having Steve get stabbed by accident. Belle skipped that step and stabbed Steve to shock him out of the simulation. The plan worked regardless. The medical emergency protocols went off, and because people trust the technology, they wouldn't check to see if Steve was really dead. However, L and Steve didn't expect me. When I pulled him out, I was surprised that he was alive. But the sudden shock of being dragged out the pod left him unconscious. Instead of letting Steve find a way to weasel out of the consequences, I pulled him to the tunnels, read his messages, and figured everything out."

I shook my head, confused. "Then you salvaged his plan."

"Because that was the best way to prove his infidelity to Belle. Even L didn't know Steve's plan—to abandon them and move on with this other woman. Using Steve's BioScreen, I sent her a message that the plan worked and they should meet. I knew Steve had connections with some dubious businesses across the city and brought him here. When Steve came to, he was understandably disorientated. In my human form, I posed as an employee and explained he might still be a little woozy after a dog bite, even though I'd patched him up. What was more likely? Blood loss and so much time in the simulation made him forget how he got here, or his shapeshifting dog had dragged him in through secret tunnels? I thought the people at the front desk would ask questions about how Steve had gotten here, but a few messages from Steve's BioScreen and a bit of my charm ensured there was no problem. The business understands discretion, and the other woman showed up without issue. The final step was easy—find a way to let someone know where Steve was so that he could be caught red-handed. I redirected Steve and his lover into the same simulation as L. That should be fun."

"And you were looking for L when you found me," I said.

A nod. "L knows, and I think Steve is in for a nightmare."

"Belle's under investigation for murder," Scarlett said.

"Obviously she's innocent—Steve isn't dead."

"But he could still get what he wanted," I said. "And you might still be found out."

"His happiness will haunt me, but as much as he deserves to be punished, that doesn't help Belle. Him dying would only make things worse."

"What if I told you he didn't have to die?" I felt a devious justice. "Time has a way of solving all things."

SIXTEEN

I MEND A BROKEN MIRROR

THE best disguise for real magic was obvious smoke and mirrors. Below my gaze, Steve's life continued unseen in the simulation. By mortal standards, he was rather handsome. A charismatic smile remained imprinted on his face even while essentially sleeping. Strong muscles were sustained despite his time in the pods, and he had a natural aura of charm.

It wouldn't last.

Age often brightened smiles; yet, Steve probably wouldn't age that well. This was really the best punishment—not doing time, but taking it.

I touched the pod, and Steve's smile faded. Shadows darkened over him. Wrinkles tensed around drying lips. A handsome jawline slacked, sagging with age. Where was the limit? What was deserved? With reason and purpose, regret did not live in the moment. I only aged him skin deep, not to cause suffering or aches. This was an opportunity for Steve to learn. Beyond creases, Steve's skin discolored in patches. With his youthful good looks gone, it was time to see if there was any substance.

"You know what you're doing?" I asked Scarlett.

She took the panel off the pod and messed with the wires underneath. "As much as you do."

I doubted that.

Wires were pulled out and plugged in different places. Scarlett murmured, "I need to have another dinner with Iris. The stuff I try to remember always slips away."

"Memories come and go like the tides," I said. "Romeo must almost be here with Belle."

"You figured out the map on your ring?" she asked.

"Thirty minutes one way. Figuring Romeo can run faster than a human, that leg will be shorter."

"So we're about on schedule."

"*About* is about as convincing as what you've managed so far." I twisted the ring, the screen turned off, and made sure all the padlocks but one were undone.

"A small fire is tricky."

"That's why you treat fire with respect." I tensed. "You know the detectives will show up, too? They'll tail Belle."

"Amar won't take kindly to what you've done to Steve." Scarlett paused, a wire in hand, looking perplexed, before beginning again.

"The supposed 'World's Best Detective' was looking for a body and will get one with a pulse instead."

A spark and a puff of smoke. "Ready?"

I transformed, straightening taller. My new form was tall, dark, and complex—Romeo's human form. The beard's consistency was the hardest part. All those little hairs. However, Steve had only seen it for a moment. Seeing me as Romeo's human form and Romeo the dog together would lessen any creative thinking.

Whispers of fire caught. Scarlett and I disappeared quicker than subtle smoke.

We shut the secret entrance and made our way out the tunnels, the park, and headed for the real entrance to the building. If Scarlett was right, we wouldn't want to miss the fun.

Arriving at the front entrance, neon game wheels and big flashing screens flashed on both sides. It was night, but it was brighter than the sun's surface. For a supposed crime front, they didn't hide, announcing itself under the guise of gambling, gaming, and genuine business. Whatever Scarlett thought was the real crime going on here hid under a grey area, looking less nefarious for it; in any case, that wasn't our problem. Not for now.

Even in an immortal life, there was not enough time for all the mysteries. Time was long, but the windows in discovering such answers always appeared, shifted, opened, closed, and disappeared.

Scarlett knocked on a glass door lit with scrolling advertisements, but it wasn't locked. She opened the door and a cheery bell rung. Inside, there was a fancy and sleek grey lobby with a hallway on either side and various doors. Lighting was dim, but the commotion was not. Belle was busy making a scene.

"Where is he?" Belle asked the receptionist with a voice raised sharper than the beams of light coming from the opened door. "I know Steve's here."

Romeo barked at her side, the enormous black and white dog wagging its tail.

"Ma'am, we don't allow pets in here."

"But you allow dead bodies?"

The receptionist hesitated. "No?"

"No?"

"As far as I'm aware, no one here is dead." The woman looked at a set of screens under the desk, and normalcy became a tsunami of panic. Most people would yell "Fire", but the woman calmly scooted out of her seat. She strode down the right hallway without another word, except, "Wait here."

Romeo didn't take commands well, trotting after her.

The receptionist arrived at the door and jiggled the handle, but, of course, it was locked. She knocked, almost politely at the door, only to see a massive dog gaining speed and charging at her.

Some might've attributed it to heroism, but knowing the plan beforehand, Romeo rammed into the woman and door with a mighty leap. Hinges cracked and the door fell flat, tackled by the powerful canine.

Belle, followed at a small distance by Scarlett and I, went down the hallway to discover the scene inside.

Romeo sat on his haunches by the downed door and unconscious receptionist, looking at her a little regretfully. A whimper. The pod was smoking like a power plant, pouring out under the top of the doorframe and into the hallway, but there was no visible fire. There might not be smoke without fire, but that didn't mean they were always proportional. And in this case, the real heat was rising from Belle as she saw in the room.

Initially, it was fiery relief.

Steve jumped from a corpse-like position in the burning pod to his feet. Finding him alive could've been enough to drive Belle to more tears than those caused by the smoke.

Luckily, the shock was enough to leave Belle speechless because whatever joy she might've shown would've been regrettable.

Steve ran to the other woman's pod, typing the code. As the top hissed open, he reached, sweet and soft as only a lover can, to the woman inside. He whispered tenderly, and almost as tender, he lifted the VR helmet off her head.

The other woman opened her eyes and muffled a scream at Steve's change.

Steve recoiled. I smiled. What a hurtful scream that must've been, especially as he had no idea why. I should've had a mirror for him.

Recovering from the initial reaction, Steve tried to reassure the woman, a shaking hand touching the woman's cheek. The usual charming smile was not quite so this time. His lover pushed his hand away and rolled out the other side. Yet, this accomplished Steve's goal of getting her out of the pod, not in the way he expected, and probably faster, too.

Finally, Belle combined relief with anger. "Steve? Steve!"

If the door was still intact, I wouldn't have been surprised if Belle locked Steve in with the smoke. Instead, Belle coughed and backed away towards the lobby. With Romeo's burly human form, it was easy to pick up the receptionist, and I hoisted her over my shoulder like a fireman, passing Scarlett, who went towards the smoke.

Steve's lover ran. He followed, calling out, "It's okay. Wait, where are you going?"

I set the receptionist in her chair, vaulted the desk, and grabbed Steve's shoulder before he could chase the other woman into the streets. The door closed behind the woman, and as I pulled Steve around, there was a lot I wanted to say.

There were insults and questions, but I had a role to play, and I could act any part.

"You owe us for the pods." I couldn't leave it at that. "Oh man, your face. It's so…" I left it there. Imagination was the best horror.

"What do you mean?" Steve asked.

"Was it the fire?" Belle asked, plopping into a waiting room seat. She didn't offer to help him, still confused.

"Belle?" Steve grasped for some excuse, but then, turned his attention to what was said. He felt his face. "It doesn't hurt. I'm just a little shaky."

"It's not the fire," I said. "These things happen with faulty pods sometimes. Speed aging. Quite irreversible."

"And you want me to fulfill the contract after using a faulty pod?"

I grinned. "User error."

"That's ridiculous."

"The fire's out," Scarlett said, giving a short cough as she entered the lobby. She glanced at the unconscious receptionist. "I assume she'll be fine."

Romeo barked, padding across the room and sitting next to Belle.

"Weren't you at my house earlier?" Belle asked.

"Detective Scarlett Wolfe." She gave a little flourish. "I found Romeo."

"Romeo found me," Belle said.

"I never said it was a difficult mystery." Scarlett frowned at Steve. "You have a lot of explaining to do. Faking your death. Fraud. An affair."

"I was—"

"I'm not the one you have to explain to," Scarlett said. "Good thing, it'd be rather boring."

Romeo growled at Steve, the boiling snarl simmering to slight fangs.

"I don't know…" Steve trailed off as Romeo's growl cut in again, and seeing that there was no escape from the situation, he resorted to a pitiful truth. "I didn't mean for this to happen. I thought a fresh start might be best for us. How, exactly, I got here, I can't explain it. Things have been spotty." He pleaded with typical puppy-dog eyes, but they were rather old now. "I went about it the wrong way. I got caught up. Confused by what was real and what wasn't. But we were real. But I never meant to worry you. I was bored. I was searching for… I don't know what I was searching for. Happiness, I suppose."

There was no admission of guilt, besides evasive insinuation. The details were missing, but feeling was more important than facts here—they didn't support his case. Everyone already knew what happened.

There was a worry that Belle might forgive Steve. Doing so would've said nothing about dignity, rather safety, security, or sunk cost winning.

Belle stayed silent. For a while Steve had been lost to her; however, this time, Steve was dead to her in a different way.

"Well, if that's all, I have to go deal with a different Belle." Scarlett sighed. "My assistant will deal with the administrative work." And then, she left the lobby without another word.

Confused, I almost started looking for a notepad.

A prickle. The normalcy of a morning alarm and still, the same tense reaction. As the door slid shut, I saw Amar coming. The god and Scarlett passed each other, as if Scarlett had known precisely the god's timing, and I heard their brief conversation.

Scarlett asked, "Did you find any foul play in Lars' death?"

"No," the god said before entering the room with an aura less pleasant than the bell.

Happy to be absolved, I greeted Amar with a joyful quip. "Found Romeo, solved the mystery, and did rings around you."

"You went too far." Amar's female detective form frowned at me, the black hair luscious in the lights from outside, and as the door closed, it darkened like shadow.

Always seeing the downside. "You're welcome."

"What was the myth?" Amar asked.

"Nothing to worry about." I motioned to Steve. "That guy is trash. Call me when you figure it out and are ready to find the god at The Root."

"I'll be in touch?" Amar said, furrowing brows.

"I'm sorry," Steve said to Belle.

That was a surprise—both pleasant and unpleasant. I feared it was manipulation rather than honesty. I did not linger; I preferred to believe that Belle would ignore the apology and Steve would learn a harsh lesson.

Whether the words were part of lasting change or a flash in the pan, that's all I got to see—all I wanted to see—because what mattered was not what they did. From all I learned of Belle, this was the final straw, but I had to give her that choice. Impulse told me to go back. To make sure Steve learned, or to make sure he suffered. There, though, lay guilt. Even if I couldn't be good, maybe I didn't have to be evil.

The mystery was not changed much by Scarlett and I's involvement; Romeo would've led Belle here anyways, but I liked to think that by finding Steve earlier, we might've saved him from a worse fate at the hands of L. What did come from my role in the affair felt like justice.

The mystery's window closed, and the final glint of consequence in a door's bell behind me. If I hadn't seen Romeo refuse the expectations of his mythical making, walking away wouldn't have happened so easily.

The weather cleared, and with the smell of a freshly cleared storm, I felt renewed. Changed. Hopeful. Ready for all that would inevitably come.

SEVENTEEN

A RATHER RUDE RODRIGO

OVER time, resolutions dimmed. I was impatient. There was no contact from Amar. Time slowed, slowed, slowed until it seemed like I'd never move again.

Luckily, Scarlett jolted me back into motion.

She'd been gone a week. When she arrived back at the apartment, I was grumpy and stiff from watching the same scene out the window. I'd watched a procession of different, but realistically the same, strangers and prices. At least apples were cheap enough for me to get them by the dozen, which got me through the boredom.

"You're back," I said, turning off my ring with a smile. I'd made a point to use my empty time to grow more accustomed to the technology.

Scarlett didn't take off her jacket. A bad sign. Worse, she didn't acknowledge me, walking through the living room and into the bedroom.

I called after her, "A hello would be nice."

She flopped onto the bed, strands of sugar glider hair flying like dust as white covers rippled. Scarlett stilled with the springs, laying listless. At the doorway, I waited for her, but she remained silent.

"Am I invisible?" I asked. "Or did you lose your hearing in another firework accident I should know about?"

She buried her head deeper in the covers, face down like a cat. The only signal that she heard me was her foot shaking over the edge of the bed.

"Thinking?" I asked.

"Hello," she said, muffled and annoyed.

"Hello?"

"You said a hello would be nice."

I leaned on the doorframe. "Not like that."

"You didn't specify. Go away."

"Sure," I said, but I didn't move.

She waited, her ears pricking with my presence. "What are you, a live-in therapist?"

"A live-in god."

"You're bored."

"You're evasive," I said.

"You really are a therapist."

"Let me be a detective instead." I crossed my arms. "It's been a week, but you've changed clothes and showered. However, there's mud on the bottom of your shoes and dirt on your jacket. Both recent. So, you were staying somewhere nice, until recently, there was an investigation important enough to get dirty."

"Mostly wrong. I stayed with Iris and helped her with some gardening. Her mother is still alive."

"Have I lied to you before? Are you upset I told the truth?"

She shook her head on the blanket.

"You're disappointed Amar hasn't followed up," I said, not letting her avoid me.

"No." She rolled to her side with an annoyed look.

"Well?"

She sighed. "I was like you."

"That is interesting. Do tell."

"I unplugged L."

I frowned. "I'd like to say you'll get over it, but guilt is a lot like grief—you always think back every once and a while."

"I don't feel guilty."

"Sure."

"It was the right thing to do," she said.

"Isn't it ironic that your judgement about shutting L down is so different than me ending someone's life?"

She rolled again, staring at the ceiling. "I don't blame you and I don't blame myself. Choices can still be difficult and bad, even if they aren't wrong."

"Sounds awfully like—"

"Leave me alone." Her BioScreen pinged, but she ignored it.

"I'm glad you turned off L."

Slowly, she pushed herself up, legs dangling over the bed. "Really?"

"I hope you didn't just unplug her without any warning." I knocked on the doorframe, death at the door. "I like to announce myself. Age is slow, and I hate the idea of a sudden ending. L thought she'd suffer forever. Gods, mortals, even fruit flies believe in a future. Logically, we can understand there's an end, but we can't comprehend what that entails. I always thought the warning helps them come to terms with death, but I might be wrong because, despite what people say, everyone thinks they're immortal, until they're not."

"Are you?"

"So far."

The irony was not lost on her and she laughed. "You're something else."

"If it wasn't you, something else would've ended L," I said. "Power outage, rotting wires, or me. But just because it was the right decision doesn't mean you don't feel bad."

"Guilt hasn't stopped you yet."

"I have no choice. That should make me feel better, but it feels more like I'm not strong enough to resist. So, I try not to think about it."

"But you do," Scarlett said.

"Who's the therapist now?"

"I appreciate you trying to make me feel better." She smiled, but when she checked the BioScreen, the smile disappeared. "I hope you have another session available."

"What?" I motioned towards the screen.

"Do you remember Rodrigo?"

As I remembered Iris being immune to my powers, of course I remembered someone who could see my godly form. "The guy I turned into?"

"Amar wants us to ask Rodrigo to help discover the god at The Root."

"Amar contacted you and you didn't say anything?"

"I did now," Scarlett said. "What Amar said was useless until now. Rodrigo would make the case straightforward."

"True." I leaned on the doorframe. "I may be able recognize Amar, but if a god wants to hide, I won't be able to see what they are. I don't have that kind of sight."

"If only it was that easy."

"Rodrigo could see me, there's no reason he can't see any other god."

"That's not the difficulty," she said.

"And what is?"

"Him."

"Troublesome." I sighed. "When's Rodrigo coming?"

"I don't know."

"You don't know something?"

"I wish I didn't know him." She turned back over.

That ended our conversation, and I returned to the living room, sitting on the nook. Angel came over and I fed her a few treats.

Later, there was a knock at the door.

Scarlett answered, and when she did, she seemed a new person. "Hi, Rodrigo!" The greeting was so out of the ordinary and over-the-top, I could tell it was fake.

"Hello." His voice was exceptionally boring. Like a broken white-noise machine, it just made noise and not much more. "Is the god here?"

Scarlett closed the door behind him. "Over there."

"Oh," Rodrigo said. "I should've seen the campfire that pretended to be me."

"Campfire? You should—" I reconsidered. "—n't worry about not noticing me."

"No need to get up."

I didn't. "Alright."

Rodrigo shrugged it off and sat in Scarlett's chair. "I hear you're looking for another god."

I said nothing, watching the man squirm in the silence. I could almost see the fuzz on his hair failing to grow.

He leaned forwards. "I have a proposition for you."

There was no choice but to answer. "Which is?"

"You do what you do best and I'll help in any way I can."

"What is it that I do best?" I asked, the fire within burning.

"Well, I assume many things as a god. But above all, what you were made for." Rodrigo hid tension with a yawn. "Is all you need a target?"

"I don't just kill people."

"You've become a god of life?"

"I am a scythe," I said. "A tool with a purpose, which is sometimes misused."

"For example, cutting down the sick like Izak Cayne," Rodrigo said. "Good intention. Good result. This is not all that different."

"Is it?" A bad vibe hung over us.

"Someone who wronged me," he said.

"A wrong worthy of death?"

"I'll let you decide that."

"Indeed." If I didn't know better, I would've thought that Rodrigo believed himself the god. I switched tact, understanding why Scarlett treated him differently. "Please. Tell me and I'll do my best."

"His name is Evan. Don't let his looks deceive, he's wilier than Scarlett. No offense, Scarlett."

"It wasn't offensive till you said that," Scarlett said. If looks could kill, Scarlett would be a basilisk, freezing him to stone with her stare.

"What did Evan do?" I asked.

"He left me in a desert to die. We were on a train ride between here and there, when we decided to do a little sightseeing. There're some oceans. Some mountains. Vacation spots. And then, there's this great desert. He pushed me down an abandoned mine and left me there. For days, I suffered in the heat, praying for the fifteen minutes of respite in the evening when the sun went low enough to give me shade before the freezing nights made me dig into sand, buried to my neck with scorpions. The stings didn't kill me. The heat and cold didn't either. And eventually, by pure accident, my sand blanket collapsed into a rotten tunnel. I crawled for miles until I found an exit and ended up in the company of a roving band of nomads, who I stayed with, far from civilization, for years, biding my time until I could escape and make my way back here."

"Sounds incredible," I said.

"It is," Scarlett said, only a veneer of sarcasm coming through. "He's leaving out the time he encountered a griffin."

"That's how I got back to civilization," Rodrigo said with a self-assured smile only accessible to those who don't deserve it.

"A shame it wasn't strapping dolphins to your feet," Scarlett said.

"Desert dolphins would make a good myth," I said. "Why haven't you told anyone else?"

Rodrigo's fingernails stabbed into the armrest. "Evan is crafty."

"And he knows you're alive?"

Returning to relaxation, Rodrigo regained his smug smirk. "Doubtful. I have a different name and look."

"Why not go to the authorities?" I asked.

"With what proof?"

"Or what story?" Scarlett asked.

"Exactly," Rodrigo said, frowning. "They'd never believe me."

"Alright." I wasn't sure whether to believe him, but his help was vital, especially with a god that could affect people just by being nearby. "What's the plan?"

"Easy. Evan goes grocery shopping every Saturday at 7 p.m. and returns down the same alley every time."

"That's very specific." I frowned as he gave me the plan and the Pull lassoed around me.

"I'm giving you an easy job," Rodrigo said. "I just don't want it traced back to me."

Scarlett kept her face still, but as I looked at her, for the first time in a while, I felt the Pull from her, which I took as the dislike for the turn this was taking. I'd almost taken my freedom for granted. Together, the two Pulls went in equal, but opposite, directions.

I asked, "Wouldn't it make sense to take the appropriate time that he took from you?"

"That's up to you," he said, but the Pull did not lessen. "That would create complications, though."

"I don't mind complications." I was being stubborn, too.

"If Evan finds out I'm alive, I won't be safe."

"I'm discreet," I said.

"I'm unsure how much I can help with your godly dilemma if I can't show my face in public anymore."

An implicit threat, this sounded like a backroom mafia deal, and although we both knew what we were talking about, we were both playing our cards close to our chests.

Scarlett didn't make any immediate moves, and that was more concerning. I expected her to storm out of the room and shut the door. However, she seemed to appreciate the need for Rodrigo's help.

And all she said was, "It's up to you."

Even without the Pull forcing me, I had little choice. "Give me the location."

Information was exchanged. Rodrigo left. Scarlett and I drank coffee and talked in artificially cheery tones for a while, until the clock started to wind down nearer to 7 p.m. And when the time came, I left to a dusky world—in this case, a time where lights flickered on, bursting into rainbow-colored life as the sky above darkened.

Rain had cleared. Even when it wasn't coming down, puddles remained for me to weave through, water glinting with florescent fuchsia and neon oranges. Crystalline reflections were broken by gusts into disco diamonds, the ripples shimmering until they were broken by my footfalls.

People stormed into the streets like a flood, rejoicing at markets and restaurants and recreation. I no longer felt out of place in this new world. Instead, I simply loved it. As part of the tide, I turned my ring, practicing controlling my jacket's color and turning it faintly luminescent like a star in the night. I added a splash of color—scarlet, in the shape of an umbrella, on the upper left side of my jacket.

When I arrived at my destination, I made my jacket black and erased the umbrella.

An alley. Over a few blocks, I could hear a commotion, but I figured it was fine. This was where I was told to go. And, even if I was caught, it's not like it mattered; I could change my form. Now, I was an average man with just enough imperfections that it drew less attention than no imperfections or too many. A rounded head and short hair. A little bit of a curved nose. Except for being taller and better built, I was a bit reminiscent of Rodrigo, but that was intentional—he was almost the perfectly forgettable person. The hardest part of the change was making my eyes dark brown; grey eyes might lead back to me.

With all the belief in me, I was feeling stronger.

Then, I waited. Rodrigo had given me a picture. All rather simple. Too simple. I expected something to go wrong.

But, after about five minutes, the man came with three paper grocery bags in hand. Except for puddles, there was no one in the alley to witness what was about to happen. Even more perfect, the bustle beyond remained. People chattering, or cheering? I did not care—I wanted this over with. Dirty business, done in a clean alley.

Evan locked eyes with me. His green gaze turned beyond to the other side of the alley, as if he didn't notice me. However, I could tell he was unnerved, hands clenching the groceries harder. I checked whether I'd accidently grown horns, but no, it was my mere presence.

I felt like I owed him a chance for last words—if there was a door, I would've knocked.

With a final gaze to check whether any one was around, I unfurled from my statuesque pose and stood as the gatekeeper, blocking him.

"Can I help you?" he asked, checking over his shoulder to see if the way back was blocked. It wasn't. At least, it did not appear so.

"Evan?"

"Yes," he said, unsure whether it was a good or bad thing I knew his name.

Getting to the point, I skipped a few steps and questions. "You can help me." I grew black horns made of shadow to demonstrate I was no mere mortal. "I am death."

"And how can I help death?"

"That usually gets more response," I mumbled, the horns receding. "Um, by dying?"

Evan stood solid, not looking behind him, almost relieved. "Why would you tell me that?"

"I just— You're not surprised to see a god?"

"Should I be?" he said, almost sarcastic.

There was no respect anymore. "Probably?"

"Do you want me to scream?"

"No," I said. "But it's what I expected. I wanted to offer you a chance to say something."

"If you're really a god, you'd mute me."

I didn't want to admit that I hadn't really planned if he screamed. I hadn't planned for much, except escaping quickly. "Were the horns not convincing enough?"

I made the shadows in the alley crackle like fire, white noise over the city bustle.

"Do all gods show off like this?" His hands were trembling, either with fear or the weight of the heavy grocery bags.

"What?" For people who didn't believe in gods anymore, I wasn't finding many that were surprised to see one. I didn't like this at all, and instead of my intimidating presence, I shrunk, relaxing on the wall.

He put down the heavy groceries. "Why waste time… unless you don't want to do this?"

"Now that you mention it, I don't. But it's necessary and I don't have much choice." I eyed the bags. "Do you have an apple?"

"No. Would it change anything?"

"Maybe my mood about all this." This seemed wrong, but that hadn't stopped me before.

"I've got an orange," he said.

"It's not the same."

Evan crossed his arms. "I didn't say it was."

I sighed. "Do you want me to explain why I'm here?"

"Would it matter?"

"It might."

"Maybe usually means no." Evan was stoic. "But if it helps you get it off your mind, you can."

This had gone on long enough; I would just end it and get out of here. Staying any longer might draw undue attention, not to mention he wasn't what I expected. Not that I wanted deference or fear, but taciturn acceptance was the best I could hope for and I didn't want him to reconsider. Besides, the whole ordeal felt dirty and the faster I got away from it, the less might stick to me.

Tendrils grew around the alley. If the man noticed, he didn't flinch. He just continued staring at me, his green, lively eyes, bright as summer leaves, waiting for autumn and winter to dull them. Like a tree before frost, there was nothing to be done. And just because there was acceptance, didn't mean it was entirely acceptable. He was stubborn, hardy, and had a hint of rebellion against me. It wasn't mean-spirited. It wasn't even about me, just like this wasn't about him.

So, as death crept around him, I gave him the final piece of knowledge, hoping he might understand at last.

I said, "Rodrigo sent me."

The tendrils inched closer, sneaking to engulf him. Or rather, to take from him. As his doom approached, a whirring noise accompanied it.

But it wasn't me.

I hesitated. A drone turned the corner and zoomed towards us. It was not one of the normal package-delivering robots that flew like birds above the city. This was smaller, lighter, faster, louder. Much louder.

It was a race.

One wall of the alley lit with colors, casting holographic rings above our heads. Another drone turned the corner, while the leader spiraled, spinning ribbons through the light orbs, which flashed green as it expertly made its way through. More drones chased.

"Rodrigo?" Evan laughed to the background of flying drones.

"Yes, Rodrigo"

"You have to speak up." His voice was also drowned out by the spinning rotors.

"Does that change things?" I said, louder.

"I thought I'd killed him."

"He sent me to kill you"

Evan shouted back, "I think you've made a mistake."

"He said you were tricky."

One of the drones missed a ring, which flashed red over my head. Almost like the drone exploded, the suddenness of it stopping in midair, engines backfiring, rang through like a shot in the alley. I ducted instinctively, but I recovered my poise as the drone hovered behind me, whirring softly for a few seconds as it served the penalty for missing a ring, and then it whirred back into life, shooting down the rest of the alley.

The sounds of the race disappeared in the distance.

"Let me show you something." Evan turned on his BioScreen.

I should've stopped him. It would've been easy for Evan to call for help, but, somehow, I trusted him. If he didn't yell or use his BioScreen during the drone race, I didn't think he'd do anything that would make this more difficult.

Like showing a friend, Evan stood next to me with the news. The title was, "Desert Heat: Hot Date Becomes A Hot Break." I read the short clipping, which explained that Rodrigo stalked his ex-boyfriend, Evan, during a tourist trip to historical sites in the desert. When Evan got separated from the group, Rodrigo begged to get back together and after an argument, Rodrigo slipped and fell into an abandoned mine. Rescue groups searched but could not find Rodrigo, presuming him dead.

"I pushed him," Evan said.

"You admit it?"

"He pushed me first. I made it very clear. I didn't want him dead, I just wanted to get away."

"How do I know you didn't alter the news clipping?" I asked, considering the story.

He turned off the screen. "Believe me or not. It's up to you."

"I do believe you." This situation tore at my essence stronger than the Pull. "Rodrigo's rude and I don't like him, he's like... I don't know how insults have developed, but I'd feel bad likening him to anything really." I crossed my arms, knowing too much relied on Rodrigo's help. "Still, nothing changes."

"I understand."

"You do?"

"It makes me feel better that death isn't entirely cold," Evan said.

"Quite the opposite." I twisted my ring back and forth, looking at the time. "But I need Rodrigo's help to catch a god."

"He sees strange things."

"That's why you weren't surprised by me."

"I didn't believe him at first, but then I learned otherwise." Evan relaxed, getting a bit too comfortable chatting with me.

Although victims usually believed I would kill them, maybe my hesitation had affected Evan and spared him long enough for this new dynamic.

Evan continued, "But I couldn't deal with what he saw. Knowledge about the uncontrollable is not freedom, it's a weight."

"Pretending myths and gods don't exist—that I don't exist—doesn't make life any lighter." I looked up at the spotlight sky, faint clouds drifting over the alley and lit like moons by the city's glow. "Ignorance is only bliss until it builds up and makes up for lost time."

"At least you won't see it coming." Evan looked at me. "You'd kill to discover another god?"

"I've done worse. This might end up saving some lives in the end."

"Death feels guilt?"

"How do you figure?"

He smiled. "You're still talking with me."

"I always thought these conversations made it easier, even if you'd prefer ignorance. I can't control what I am. Age. Guilt. Regret. Too often, they come together. And although no one says it much, I am god of all of them."

"You may not be able to control what you were made as, but it seems like you can control your feelings."

There was a lull. We stood in the alley, watching the clouds go by, like counting sheep over a fence.

"Is it time?" Evan asked.

"Yes." I couldn't meet his eyes. I kept staring upwards, thinking. Dreaming. "It's time for you to go home."

"Is that what you call it?"

"It's not a euphemism. Go home and don't say anything about this."

"Why would I?" he asked.

"Because you met a god."

"Who's going to catch you?"

I smiled. "Well, me, I guess. That's sort of my job."

"Rodrigo can't be the only one who could help you. I thought his power was special—but that doesn't mean there isn't another option."

"There's no time to think about all the options."

"You can still try." He picked up his groceries. "I never thought death would be like you."

For once, that felt like a compliment. "Thank you."

He started walking down the alley, going before I could change my mind.

"Wait," I said after him.

I wouldn't have stopped him. But, he turned around.

I asked, "Can I have that orange?"

He rustled through the bag, finding a plump fruit and walking back to hand it over. "Are you going to eat it?"

I tossed it back and forth between my hands. "I'm taking up juggling."

"Good luck with that."

"Of course I plan on eating it," I said, holding the orange still. "Sometimes mortals have no sense of humor."

"Maybe that's because they don't expect death to have one."

I said after him, "See? Sometimes knowing the truth instead of ignoring it can relieve some of the weight."

I caught the briefest smile as Evan turned the corner and returned to a normal life.

Going the other direction, I wandered a while before I went home. Through the center of the city, I pretended I was one of the masses. Not godly or guilty. I peeled the orange like my walk—spiraling. I relished bites of the sweet fruit and strolled with purposeful purposelessness. No end goal, only to enjoy myself. So often, too often, it was easiest to get caught up in the larger picture. In finding purpose. Achieving purpose. Looking forward and then back, instead of looking at the present. But while a whim wanders, finding nothing or more than imagined, there was no rarer treasure to be found than the peace of being.

For once, I was.

The streets buzzed with smells and lights and strangers—a chaotic choreography of life, spanning from the strobing street sign to the sweet smell of cinnamon, all the way to the subtle splash of a foot in a sneaky puddle to the loudest laughter—there was strange tranquility.

I did not watch from a window, observing and wondering. I was part of something more. My troubles melted into the masses, a burden taken on by being part of a wider fabric. There were no thoughts of gods. No next mystery. There wasn't much thought at all. Just a feeling like sunshine breaking through winter clouds. A clear moment. Bright. Alive.

How strange for a death god.

But a moment of living only lasts a minute. Clarity comes and goes, in and out of focus.

Quite unintentionally, I wandered back to a familiar street and tossed the orange peel into the trashcan I'd seen on the sidewalk from Scarlett's apartment. And, like that, the spell was broken.

The clouds of the future covered the present. There was a mystery to solve. A purpose for me. And that was sweeter than any apple or orange.

When I climbed up the stairs to the apartment, Scarlett was pacing inside.

She said nothing, and I passed by, still in thought and heading to the nook, where I looked out from my window like a gargoyle, frozen and lingering on the moment that had just been. I could almost see the ghost of myself walking the street below, obscured by the people going by.

Scarlett's feet kept tapping on the floors, a different walk than mine. A walk of worry.

Eventually, I had to break the silence. "What's wrong?"

She circled her chair. "Amar sent me a message and I'm waiting for follow-up. The message was vague."

"Amar is like that."

"The possibilities go faster than I can."

"When's the last time you took a break?" I asked. "When's the last time you read something that wasn't for a purpose? Gone somewhere with no reason?"

She stopped behind the chair, resting her hands on the back of it. "I sit and think about nothing all the time."

"That's hibernation. You're not a bear."

"I'm more like a hummingbird."

"Hummingbirds hibernate?" I asked.

Her BioScreen flashed, and she opened a message. "They arrested Rodrigo on a warrant. An old restraining order and an investigation into attempted murder."

"You knew about Rodrigo and Evan?" I asked, sitting at the nook. "That's a dumb question, of course you did. But then…"

"Why didn't I stop you?"

"Yeah."

"Because it was your choice."

"Not with the Pull from Rodrigo. But you countered that."

"Pull?" She rounded the chair and drew closer to me.

"A feeling that tugs at my essence to act in accordance with my nature, fulfill belief in me, or do what I was summoned for."

"Like a demon?"

I frowned. "You know I don't like that word."

"Gods are shaped by the beliefs in them, but this is the first time you've mentioned this. Did you always have the Pull?"

"No. Most gods don't. They're created a certain way and that's different. The Pull came sometime after…" I paused, coming up with a quick alternative. Technically, my explanation wasn't a lie; the Pull came after this, even if it was not the exact moment. "Amar and his kin gained favor with a king, while daevas became demons."

Luckily, she didn't press me. Yet, the look on her face told me she knew I wasn't telling the whole truth. "What does it feel like?"

"A need pulling me along like a string."

She shook her head. "Is it like a pang of guilt?"

"Sort of."

"Can you choose to ignore it?"

"If it's not too strong."

A gentle laugh. "Sounds like a conscience to me. I don't think this Pull is a real force. I don't believe it."

I got up, but turned to look out the window, where people strolled the streets like I had. "You can't just believe it away."

"If it can be believed into existence, why can't it be believed away?"

"Because…" I stopped my daydreams and spun round. "When Rodrigo was here, how did you counter his Pull?"

"How could I counter something that I don't think exists? Ever since Izak, I've believed you've been free. While Rodrigo was here, I was only wishing he would leave."

"I felt how much Rodrigo wanted revenge." My fists tightened like the Pull. "But then I looked at you, and that gave me the freedom to spare Evan."

"You cared about me." She smiled. "Sparing me guilt. Sparing it for yourself."

My hands unclenched. "The Pull isn't what I thought it was."

"We all have a Pull—a choice of how we act without consciously thinking. That's who we are." She flicked her

BioScreen to the next message. "Amar offered a decent deal, but Rodrigo is being stubborn and won't cooperate."

"Good." The bindings on my essence seemed to wash away. Instead of feeling free, though, I felt a responsibility—a new purpose. The difference wasn't enormous, but after this and my interaction with Evan, I felt like the Pull wasn't binding me. I couldn't choose what I was made to be, but I could choose what I would become. "I don't want Rodrigo's help. We can do this another way—a better way."

Scarlett looked at me, her face unreadable. Then, she hugged me.

I struggled. "Get off. What're you doing?"

"It's fine. Age is natural."

Frozen, I whispered, "You know what my touch does?"

"Of course," she said, "Maybe you can't help it, but you can choose whether it's ten percent or ten million percent faster. Julia and Steve aged in seconds, but in the snow, I was fine."

I didn't push her away—the moment was too worthwhile. I couldn't remember the last time someone had hugged me, at least, not when they hadn't been begging for mercy.

"I'm relieved you didn't kill Evan," she said.

"Me too."

She released me and went back to her normal tone, "It's called torpor."

"What?" I asked.

"Hummingbirds. They don't hibernate. They go into torpor, which is basically an involuntary nap. But this case is warming up, just like the weather. The city's lovely in Spring."

I smiled at the thought. Once, I was attached to the village foundation of this city in millennia gone by, and it wasn't until my clear-headed walk that I realized I still loved what it had become. I'd been idle too long, watching instead of trying to protect it like any good god should. Clarity returned, unobscured by the clouds of apathy.

"I have an idea," I said. "Gods can hide from other gods, but there's a waiter who might be able to help us with our crisis at The Root."

EIGHTEEN

I SENSE NONSENSE

SWEET florals intoxicated the air. Tents were arranged in rainbow stripes, bountiful bouquets waiting under them in buckets. There a new warmth on the wind and a flower festival sprung up with the season.

Scarlett suggested the festival as a middle ground for Amar and I. Amar agreed, thinking I was submitting to him and the fresh life here. Although everything here was lively, it was the bright sort of rot. There were no fields, no roots, and nowhere for the flowers to go but a vase and then the trash; that was my domain.

"Amar will be here," I said, walking with Scarlet through the aisles of flowers. I was in a new form—times called for a change—and I had plenty of influences around. I had gone for a woman with Scarlett's wide smile, a single braid like Iris, and if I could not shine like the sun as I used to, I could at least be goldened by the sun. "It's the first day of Spring. This used to be a truce day between Amar and I, one of two days we were friends. Although the truce doesn't exist anymore, this case is acting like one."

Despite the weather, Scarlett kept her hands in her jacket, which had cooling features as well as heat. "I don't think Amar had much choice but to listen to us since Rodrigo won't cooperate."

I frowned at roses; they weren't good eating. If only this had been a fruit festival. "Amar's the one who arrested him."

Scarlett was cheery. "You don't have to be sour."

"There are too many people here. The god we're looking for could be watching."

"Sometimes, the best privacy is in a crowd."

"Apparently another god can still find us," I said.

Sky blue eyes in the crowd. Amar joined us in the male detective guise, pretending to pay attention to the flowers. "What a beautiful festival."

I said, "I thought of someone else who can see gods."

"And I thought you were more subtle." Amar smiled at a passerby who glanced at us, wondering if they'd heard right.

"Maybe I've changed."

"Sure." Amar laughed.

I picked up an orchid, and it stayed a bright blue. "Times change. We change."

"You, though?"

The petals began to wilt, drooping, and I put it down before it died. That was still the same.

"I'll believe it when I see it." Amar touched the flower I had held and the petals sprung back stiff, its life rejuvenated. Yet, the brown edges remained—time only moved in one direction. "The gods people worship have changed, but the gods themselves haven't changed."

I said, "And a god that requires no detail can thrive when there are too many."

"What do you mean?" Scarlett asked.

"I know a few things most others don't, as old as I am." I led us down the narrow space between tents.

"So, you're saying I chose the right god for this case," Scarlett said.

"If I said yes, that would be vain—so, yes." I grinned. "Gods were made to explain the unexplainable. They remained because explanation does not destroy belief—beliefs adapt. As you say, people have their own logic. Gods don't need food, but they need substance and sustenance. Most gods form from belief and a symbol. An image or ideal usually. Mine, for example, is dashing good looks."

"Sure," Amar said with a roll of those oceanic eyes. "More like shadows and decay."

"Or an apple," Scarlett suggested.

"Zeus had lightning," I said. "Ra had a falcon head, a sun crown, and his eye. However, chaos gods don't need a form. They're the only of us that can go truly formless. You can't represent chaos except in still frames, almost like when Iris was talking about some of the new technology. Chaos gods grow stronger with complexity and the natural decay of order. In a way, they are the balance to science."

"And a part of science," Scarlett added. "It's called entropy."

"Learn that from Iris? Use whatever terms you want, but I've been thinking—"

"Thinking? I thought you were hibernating at the nook," Scarlett teased.

"Even if I had turned into a bear in the living room, my dreams are full of thought," I said. "But all that time you left me alone served a purpose. I watched those ever-changing prices across the street constantly, and I had an insight into why this chaos god chose financial markets. There might be some underlying logic, but in the moment, markets are illogical—they depend on people's belief in what things are worth. They're ruled by emotion and a host of different motives. No one can comprehend all that. In uncertainty lies chaos. As people believe in the market, they're believing in this god. The chaos god is achieving both godly and mortal power. Amassing influence. But that's where it gets weird."

"In what way?" Scarlett asked.

"Chaos gods don't care for power," Amar explained in my stead. "They have different motives. Vengeance. Fun. Chaos itself. They're not looking to rule the world—that provides order, and that's what they despise."

Scarlett asked, "You two are the first gods I've met, how can you be certain that's what we're dealing with?"

"If it was a myth, you or I would've found it," Amar said.

"I don't want to get funneled to an answer if we're not sure."

Given Scarlett's tendency to know everything, I hadn't thought to tell her, but I certainly took joy in this rare opportunity of explaining something to her. "What happened to Romeo is proof of what we're dealing with. Transforming something mortal into a myth like that is the work of a chaos god."

As she thought, Scarlett did a single spin of the silver chain around her neck. "If chaos gods don't look for power, we're missing a motive."

"We're missing everything," I said. "We don't know how powerful this god is. Chaos gods can be mayhem-inducing, world-destroying, or a fan of putting a whoopie-cushion on your seat. Trickster or destroyer, I don't get why it choose this specific trading floor."

Scarlett stopped fiddling. "Probably because they trade tangible goods, which affects the real world more. The floor has a couple of departments; they provide liquidity, trade commodities, and price antiquities."

"Do commodities include apples?"

Amar scoffed. "You and apples."

"It's better than your sour tastes," I said mockingly.

Scarlett asked. "Do the apples matter?"

"Probably not to the chaos god, but I find apples to be a gauge of society. Apples are still cheap. Not that I'm complaining. Meanwhile, some antiques like art and old rugs are constantly climbing."

"Rugs, you say?" Amar grinned deviously.

I scowled, reminded of our past that I wish Amar would let me forget. "If the chaos god is working on those floors, those goods can't be coincidence with Amar and I being the gods investigating."

"I'm glad I left you on that nook for so long," Scarlett said.

"The god is taunting us, but I think I know one way we catch them unaware," I said. "Why don't we use Marko's software to spy on The Root?"

"We can't break his code." Scarlett bit her lip. "But I think we could learn more from Lars. He worked with the trading floor and did some of the negotiations." She nodded at her own plan. "And we don't need to spy on The Root when we have someone with sight like Daza, even if Rodrigo's is better."

Amar said, "I already trusted you to get Rodrigo to help and you ruined that. We don't need mortals with sight. They're crazy."

"You are one of the things they see," I said. "That's enough to drive anyone crazy."

"If I wanted to hide, no mortal could see me."

"Your real form is rather dark," I said.

Amar scowled. "Their sight is unreliable."

"And yet, you wanted Rodrigo," Scarlett said with venom. "If you have better ideas, try them and we'll let you know when we beat you to an answer."

"I doubt you'll do that." Amar took the challenge in stride, looking up at The Root, his eyes tracing in the sky as if he could see where the translucent branches were.

Scarlett, too, looked up. "As fun as this walk in the park is, we have a tight schedule, and we really didn't need to waste time if you don't have anything constructive, Amar. I promised to keep you in the loop, but we'll contact you when we need your strength to confront the chaos god."

I laughed. "You're starting to sound like me, Scarlett."

That silenced her.

"You don't have to be so unhappy about it," I said.

"She should be." Amar tutted. "Fine. I can't argue with the two of you. Myths and gods are your specialty. We'll see if this man can really see gods." Amar walked off into the crowd.

"I think you hurt Amar's feelings," I said, watching the god disappear. "Great job."

"Guess your hate for him doesn't change."

"That is my choice, not my nature. My hatred is for what Amar did."

"What did Amar do?"

"Too much." I didn't elaborate. "We'd better go talk to Daza."

Scarlett's pursed her mouth, debating asking further about Amar and I, but she released the tension, seemingly wanting to solve that mystery herself.

Together, we left the festival and headed to the cemetery where the mythical restaurant was. Months, decades, or centuries passed, and I found the familiar headstone. Many things changed, but people were reluctant to destroy the past, especially those places of death—reminders of me. That kept a sliver of me alive as much as it did the people buried.

I took Scarlett's hand. There was no hesitation anymore. I didn't want to hurt her, but it had to be done. We teleported to the restaurant, and the same hostess was there to greet us.

"Table for two," I said.

"We're busy," the hostess said. "I'd have to check."

I said, "Don't pretend there are no open tables. A full one would be the real myth here."

"I don't have to seat you," the woman said. "Read the sign."

"What sign?"

She pulled out a slip of paper from the desk that said, "No shirt, no shoes, no manners, no service." The "no manners" was scribbled above the rest with pen.

"Sorry," Scarlett said. "We're here to see Daza."

"We're friends," I added.

"Daza has friends?" the woman asked, sincerely confused.

"All the same," Scarlett said. "We have business to discuss with him."

"Fine. Follow me." She led us into the fancy dining room with the clack of her mythical foot under her dress. Not only were they not busy, under Daza's keen supervision, none of the tables were set.

Once we were seated at a round table with a red candle and aura, the woman left us to our business. Scarlett eyed the different shakers in the center of the table.

"Don't touch those," I said, taking a cinnamon-looking one for myself.

"I'm still curious."

"You saw it knock Amar out. Like nectar and ambrosia, this harkens back to our essence—scrying seasoning—a window into our memories."

"Like food, then. What happens if a mortal uses it?"

"I have no idea," I said.

Scarlett grabbed a shaker and swirled it around and watched the sparkled dust poof within the confines. "I can smell it." Her eyes fluttered and watered.

I grabbed it out of her hands. "I told you it was potent."

She adjusted her collar for air and fiddled with the chain of her pendant, thinking.

Setting the shaker down, I had to know. "What'd it smell like?"

"Apples." Feeling my gaze, she tucked the pendant away.

"That explains a lot."

"Does it?" she asked.

"Can I see that pendant again?"

"No."

"It's not a teardrop, is it?" I shook my head at my stupidity "It's an apple seed."

Silence confirmed my deduction, and she offered me nothing else.

As she didn't ask about Amar and I's history, I thought it was better to leave this mystery alone for now. I did have one answer, though—my specific hankering for apples finally made sense. She must've had that in mind when summoning me.

Daza finally came out of the kitchen, leaning on one foot by our table, relaxed and improper. "Besides the bill for the painting you tossed on the floor and ruined, what else can I get you?"

I looked past him to the hallway where the painting of a snowy mountain and secret tunnel was. "It's still hanging in the hallway."

"We had an extra copy."

"Still no menu?" Scarlett asked.

"Here." Tucked into the back of his belt, Daza pulled out a menu.

"No arguments?" I took it. "The service is better."

"Your aura is easy to recognize, no matter what face you take," Daza said with a smile. "I took your advice and made my service better. But you didn't take my advice."

"I don't remember any," I said.

"Did I not tell you?" Daza scratched his head. "Hmm, I could've sworn that I told you your aura was like a snuffed candle."

"That's not advice, it's an insult." From him, though, it was an expected one. "Even if it's true, you don't have to tell me I'm weak."

"I didn't say that. I would've used the word pitiful."

Rather than anger, I was enjoying the banter. "I'm stronger than I was, and you're a better waiter, but maybe that hasn't changed too much. You're still the worst waiter I've ever seen."

"And you're the most pathetic god I've seen."

"I'm sure you haven't met many; otherwise, they would've gotten impatient and vaporized you."

Scarlett said, "Are you just going to sit here and insult each other all day? Would you like a room or can we get to business? We need your help."

Scarlett was trying to calm tensions that were more playful than angry, but she was keen to talk business. Figures for someone with limited life. Although I saw the need for urgency, chaos had not found us yet.

"I can't help you," Daza said. "Last time was pushing it."

"What do you mean?" Scarlett asked.

"They all talk about you," Daza said to Scarlett. "Some myths think you improve their image by stopping miscreants. Others... they hate you—mostly the miscreants. Those are the ones you have to worry about. In any case, I don't take sides."

"Is that why I didn't get my umbrella back?"

"Couldn't be bothered." Daza walked to a coat closet, retrieving Scarlett's scarlet umbrella and returning it. "I got it back to you eventually."

"What about gods?" Scarlett asked.

"What about gods?" Daza motioned to me. "It's not every day I see one walk in."

"But you'd see them if they did?"

Daza nodded. "There's a different aura like this one here. It doesn't change anything—I'm not helping you. Bad for business. Bad for my health."

"You're talking to me right now," Scarlett said, stating the obvious.

"That's my job."

I shook my head. "You told us last time it wasn't part of your job."

"It is if you're going to order something."

"This is ridiculous," Scarlett said.

"He is pretty ridiculous." I leaned my elbow on the silk tablecloth, thinking.

Scarlett continued, "There's a god that has been driving people mad at The Root. One woman killed her husband, a dog became a myth, and that's only the beginning. It's not just any god, it's a chaos god. And you'd let him go free because you don't want to work with me?"

"Yes." Daza pointed to the menu. "Are you going to use that?"

I thought this very odd, but as it settled in, I realized something. I opened the menu, then closed it again. "Don't you have somewhere to be, Scarlett?"

"No?"

"That thing," I nudged harder.

"You want me to leave?"

I feigned outrage. "We're both leaving."

I flipped the menu open again. It was blank. Like a pen, I scribbled a note by running shadowy tendrils over the page. I hoped the residual magic would be enough for Daza to see. "We won't be treated like this. If you don't want to help us, you can go to Hel." Now that was a throwback to a misplaced era in some very cold countries.

I returned the menu back to Daza, and we left with a huff.

Once we were a few blocks away and back at the flower festival again, I finally explained to Scarlett as we walked down a row of bouquet shops, "He'll help us. I left him a note to meet us at The Root tomorrow."

"What?"

"Can't you figure it out?" I said.

"The menu. You left him a note. One only he could see." Scarlett was reluctant. "But how do you know he's going to show up? He seemed so stubborn."

"That's typical," I said. "But the tiny changes were trying to tell me something. He wanted to help, but couldn't show that."

"What was he worried about if there wasn't anyone there?"

"You never know when a god or myth might be watching, right? Away from the restaurant, he might be more willing."

She acceded the point with a nod. "And you're sure?"

"We'll see tomorrow. Let Amar know we'll need a badge to convince people into talking. Should be fun to see how Amar and Daza get along." I stopped at a flower stall shop to smell a plump rose. I didn't hate it, and it smelled sweeter than I remembered. "That gives us time to go search Lars' records beforehand and gain another advantage over Amar."

"What are we doing here, then?" Scarlett asked.

"This is the last chance we have to smell the flowers before things go downhill."

NINETEEN

I ACCIDENTLY SOLVE A PUZZLE

A knock on the door echoed in a haunted past. Back at Lars and Julia's apartment, Scarlett and I loitered in the hallway, waiting on emptiness. We both knew Lars and Julia were gone. The moment of silence was a vigil. Neither of us talked. It would've only brought up bad feelings between us that were barely patched over. And after an appropriate time, we considered the door.

I said, "This might not be easy."

"I'm not sure how much I can do with the security system."

I thought of the best way to break down the door. A gorilla? A bull? A dragon? Most would be quite odd to see in an apartment hallway, unless there was a banana, red bandana, or treasure trove of gold somewhere near. A gold banana painted red might entice all three, but barring that, I thought it best to find a more natural way. Magical tendrils might be able to pick the lock, but I was out of practice. I could become small enough to go through the keyhole, but there were probably more cyber defenses than physical locks, which even if I was on the other side, might prevent me from opening the door.

Locks clicked. The door opened. I stepped back, surprised. For a moment, I thought that Julia had faked the news clipping of her death. Yet, the person was not anyone I recognized. Skinny and tall, the man who opened the door filled the vertical frame of the door, and the only wide part about him was a friendly smile.

Scarlett adapted quickly. "Welcome to the neighborhood."

"Hello," he said. "I'm Chase. You are?"

"I'm Scarlett, and this is Zee. Unfortunately, we don't have a welcome gift." She paused, changing tact. "To be honest, we didn't know someone had moved in. We worked with the last owner, Lars, and came by to see if we could get some of the paperwork left behind."

"Oh," the man said. "I just moved in, but I haven't seen any paperwork."

"I used the wrong word," Scarlett said. "Not actual paper. The records he kept on his computer."

"I'm not sure I can help you there, either." The man looked sorry, apparently recognizing Lars' name. "I don't know how to log in. No one else seems to know how to bypass the system either. The whole ordeal is not the best of circumstances, but it did make for the best of prices."

"No worries," Scarlett said. "I think we can help. Lars gave us instructions for an emergency."

I couldn't help a moment of temporary confusion, but I had enough sense not to express it. "No promises it'll work, though. You know what people say about instructions—if they're not clear, you're better off trying to use them as origami paper, and I've never been able to make a swan."

The man nodded. "Please, come in."

He didn't ask many questions—I liked that. Trusting a god into your household wasn't always the best idea, but that really depended on the god. Refusing the wrong one was even worse than keeping one out. Though, given the guise of mortals, it was strange to let a stranger in so easily; I do suppose a detail here or there got us in, such as knowing about Lars and the complicated computers.

Inside, there was a new couch with the same human sensibilities of furnishing, nothing outlandish, and not approaching the faux godly gaudiness that kings strove for. It was as the new resident, welcoming, but with exceptionally thin cotton cushions. Besides that, everything remained the same.

Scarlett pointed to the switch that controlled the wall of screens. "May I?"

"Sure," Chase said, and then to me, said, "Take a seat. Can I get you anything to drink? Coffee?"

"No," I said, a little sharp. Trying to salvage it, I explained. "I'm on a diet. I'll take some water."

"I'm not on a diet," Scarlett said. She flipped the switch. "Coffee sounds great."

"Coming right up," Chase said, heading to the kitchen.

I watched the big screen disappear into the floor, leaving a wall of nine blue monitors, asking for a password. "Are you crazy?"

"I already drank what I thought was poisoned." Scarlett smiled. "We took care of the problem. And if there was anything wrong with the coffee, our host would've already found out."

"Not the coffee." I leaned on the desk. "We have no idea how to bypass the system without Lars or Julia's voice."

"You don't."

"You do?"

The keyboard compartment rose from the desk, and Scarlett pulled out a note from under the keyboard. "The note isn't very helpful, it only says, 'I changed the password for you'."

"Any chance it's 'Password'?"

"No, Lars was a lawyer and crossword enthusiast. He disliked simple answers and would've found my password joke terribly unfunny." She tapped at the keyboard. "This puzzle is for me. I told him to change it." She studied the dust on the keyboard. "Doesn't seem to be any instructions."

She pressed "ESC" once. Nothing happened. Then, she pressed it again. The lights in the room flashed orange, not red.

On the screen, it read, "Username?".

"A recovery method," Scarlett said. "No voice needed. Marko probably had a complex username, but not Lars." She typed in Lars' name. No numbers.

When she hit "Enter", the screen flicked over to, "Quiet Mode". And under it, "Recovery, Forgot Password?" Scarlett clicked it, and a couple of words were written across each screen, a sentence on each row of the nine monitors in a square.

"All actions have consequences. All crimes have consequences. Non-actions can have consequences."

The lack of a question was odd, and I wrinkled in thought, staring at the screen. "What kind of recovery question is that?"

"It's a syllogism—a logical series." Scarlett was quiet a moment, re-reading. "One that doesn't make sense."

"They're known for that. For example, a young Aristotle told me that all manticores have spikes, and therefore, some spiked creatures are manticores. He was wrong to use that as logic that manticores existed. He got lucky that I could confirm manticores exist, but not everything he thought of did."

The sound of hissing coffee spurted from the kitchen. Scarlett closed her eyes and took an audible whiff.

My thoughts boiled over, "It's missing a step."

"You're right. But what?"

"This is the first time coffee has made you slower," I said.

Scarlett opened her eyes. "If you insert—some crimes are not an action—for the third step, the syllogism makes sense."

"Should I time the next question?" I was having fun. "If that's the answer, put it in."

"No," Scarlett said. "It's not about the syllogism. It's about Lars. There's no question in this recovery question because it's missing. Omission was the crime and consequence, but the answer is what Lars was missing."

"Marko? Julia?" Obvious answers.

"We wouldn't know which." She snapped with a spark of inspiration. "Lars wouldn't leave it to chance. Love—that was what caused the crime and consequences; that's the omission that led to all the action and non-action in that case."

Before I could say anything, she typed "Love" to the approval of a green pulse before a new question came up on the screen.

The screen asked, "What was the price premium I received on the last thing I negotiated?"

Scarlett crossed her arms. "If he expects me to remember such numbers, he should've been less boring. It's a struggle to recall everything I hear."

"Did he say whether it was for the pendant or club?" I contained my grin.

"You remember."

I obviously didn't contain it well enough. She wasn't asking a question. "He didn't say which, but the answer is 10.3%."

Scarlett entered it to another green pulse. Unlike her, I smiled at being right, pleased that I contributed; yet, another question awaited us.

"What is the combination of Scarlett's 'surety' and hidden meaning?"

"Lars was being very careful with the questions." Scarlett stared at the ceiling. "He left it for us. However unlikely, the first question, Amar might answer. Someone with financial knowledge or that of Lars might know the second. This one is for me alone. Something I said to him."

"Do you listen to yourself?"

"I'd be a fool not to. I choose my words carefully, and that's what Lars was saying. Twice, I alluded to knowing who I thought killed Marko without being direct." She repeated what I'd heard her say once before. "The murderer you're looking for is bigger than a typical rodent, smart, and adept with poison. Two are dead, probably now three. Two of which would be an accident. Yet, that is the hardest part to prove. The easiest part to prove is that a myth exists and the killer is extremely close."

"You weren't speaking of the myth," I said. "You were saying that Julia was the murderer and she was bigger than any rat, smart, and adept with poison."

"Either he understood that later, or he's good with history."

"History?" I asked.

"In the kitchen, I mentioned two poisons, cantarella and Aqua Tofana." The wheels turned, but mine went too slow for Scarlett, who continued, excited with the puzzle. "Cantarella was popular with the Borgias, including Guilia Borgia, while Aqua Tofana was named for Guilia Tofana."

"That's different spelling, isn't it? That's a 'G'."

"Yes. Spelling is the issue I'm debating. Julia was my hidden meaning."

"And the 'surety'?" I read the question again. "He said 'What', not 'Who'. What made you sure about the myth we were after?"

Scarlett typed. "When I ruled out the Chinese myth, Gu."

"Combine them together. Gulia?"

Scarlett smiled approvingly as she logged in. "Lars was mistaken, though. It wasn't only me who could've solved this—you could, too. Of course, Lars wouldn't have known you had all the pieces. Let's see what we have here."

"I might've gotten in, but I don't know what to look for."

"I don't know either." Scarlett clicked the first file of many. "Clues to what's going on with the prices? Info Lars collected about the ninth floor? There has to be something."

"Good…" I sat on the couch. "Luck."

Chase came back with the coffee for Scarlett and left it on the desk, knowing well enough not to disturb her, as she was intent on the screens. I thanked him for the glass of water he didn't bring, which he apologized for and came back with one right after. Between that and the sound of small sips that Scarlett took of the coffee, time ticked past and I daydreamed, letting Scarlett go about her business.

"There's nothing here," Scarlett said, pushing the mouse away.

"Except?" I asked. She wouldn't complain if there was nothing, only if she was worried there was nothing. Something was left.

"One file labeled, 'S'," she said. "It was made the day Lars died."

"You didn't start with that one?"

"I didn't trust him to know what we needed."

A click brought up a simple text document.

At reading the first sentence, Chase got up. "I'll let you have some privacy."

I barely noticed the man leave, as I was too busy reading the note Lars had left for Scarlett.

Dear Scarlett,

I found a fitting punishment for omission.

Omission.

A dreadful word. Something noticeable only by its absence. Julia is next to me, but her soul is gone.

I had such good intentions. But when good intentions go wrong, that's the worst failure.

I can't live without her. In the end, there's so little lasting. Numbers. Words. What precious few we have. And how important they seem to us.

Those little details. You knew. You knew all along. But what will be left for you when there's no future and all you can do is look back? Hollow words. Uncertainty. It's all empty. I. Feel. Empty. Here's to hoping this drink will fill me up.

"This was useless." Scarlett hands hovered on the keyboard a moment, as if debating whether to throw it, only for her to lean back in the chair from whatever emotion she felt.

"It was useless besides proving I didn't kill him."

"I didn't need to be sure," she said.

"You always need to be sure. You asked Amar about it."

"A moment of weakness that changed nothing." She smiled. "Amar's not that good at investigating mythical mysteries. For all I say about being certain, there are some things you have to trust. You told me you didn't kill him. I only needed time to realize that."

I had my doubts, but I moved on, trying to make the best of our situation. "The note may not look like much, but you never know, sometimes the smallest detail makes the greatest difference."

"You're just trying to sound like me." She changed a few settings on the computer, which reset the security. "I'm sorry I assumed wrong."

It was no more than a whisper, but the apology I never expected to hear rang loud in my ears. I would've thought about punishing Lars for letting Julia go free, but my view of it changed with time. Maybe if my worst instincts took over, I would've thought about killing Lars if I had the chance, but it ended up being out of my hands.

Finished, we came across Chase in the entryway.

"We found what we needed," Scarlett lied to the new owner of the tragic apartment, then added some truth. "I set up an account for you. There are still things you won't be able to do with the computer and apartment, but it should be good for your purposes. I made the password, 'Password' with a capital. I suggest you change it."

"Thanks," Chase said. "While you were busy, I pulled out this locked briefcase from under the bed. I couldn't open it, but maybe you can." He handed over a brown leather case.

Scarlett thanked him.

Once we were in the hallway and Chase's door closed, Scarlett entered the code immediately and the briefcase popped open, revealing a stack of papers.

"What was the code?" I asked.

"The letters were in the position, 'NBSLP'. Lars had moved them all one tick away from 'Marko' to have easy access." She laughed as she perused the papers. "I was right not to trust Lars to know what I needed." She kept browsing, then suddenly stopped. "Well, that's odd."

"What is?"

"These are Lars' reconciliations of accounts for the ninth floor. He was searching, and as soon as he found something wrong, he stopped working on it. The written marks are sudden."

"That's not surprising." I couldn't help a frown. "His sense of justice stopped when it affected him."

"He wrote his conclusion. 'Whoever's doing this is helping people.'"

"Lars stopped for a good reason?" I was baffled by the next realization. "The chaos god is helping people?"

"I'm more scared that we don't know why," Scarlett said. "But between what you said earlier and what we have here, at least I have a good idea how. I wish I'd paid more attention to finance and economics. Yet, even I can tell the god has been using its role on the ninth floor to raise the prices of antiques, oddities, and art by trading things that only exist on paper, while lowering the price of household goods and commodities. It's creating artificial supply and demand. Maybe the god wants to pop these price warps. When it pops, rich people holding useless things will lose out, while normal people might end up owning more than they thought. But does the god want a more equal society, chaos, or to be a sort of robin hood?"

I had no answer for that. Rather, when we went into the elevator, and as the doors closed, other pieces of a puzzle fit together.

"That note was important." I pressed the button for the ground floor and the elevator buzzed into life. "I know why I'm back from the void. How could I be so dull? I grabbed an answer like it was something spiky and thought it was a porcupine or mythical rat; instead, it's a giant manticore." I met Scarlett's eyes. "Lars felt empty. Maybe this god is helping some, but it's hurting others. I think the real reason I'm back isn't you or Izak Cayne, it's this chaos god. I should've known I was forgotten and the only way I could come back was through chaos—the void spitting me back out. In many religions, chaos brings forth other gods."

The doors opened.

"I'm glad you're here regardless of the reason why. Otherwise, I'd have to deal with Amar and Daza alone."

TWENTY

I TRACE THE ROOT OF ALL PROBLEMS

"AND I should be scared because you're so intimidating?" Daza said sarcastically. He had substituted his normal waiter outfit for a wrinkled jacket that looked as if Odysseus had left it in the bag of winds for at least three millennia.

Amar, tall and vigorous, backed Daza into a corner of The Root's lobby. "I can be."

"It was a good idea to bring them together," Scarlett whispered to me. We were lounging next to each other on some stylishly swooping chairs waiting for them to finish their introductions, listening to their conversation from a sufficient distance to not seem part of it.

Daza said, "I don't have any idea what you want from me."

"You do, you see—" Amar said. "Are you being intentionally dumb?"

I whispered to Scarlett, "Amar's the dumb one making such a fuss and not understanding that's just Daza."

Scarlett grinned a response.

"Just tell me what you see," Amar hissed.

"An angry man," Daza said. "A strange air. There's a bit of mist from The Root's theme today. The art display above us is a babbling creek in the sky with moss, stones, and jumping frogs."

"Strange air?"

"A bit like a wilted rose."

"Where?"

"Around."

Amar groaned. He turned and instantly caught eyes with Scarlett and me. "Done gossiping, or should I wait?"

Scarlett stood up. "We were just starting. Follow me."

"Follow you?" Amar asked as she went by.

"This was my idea," Scarlett said.

Amar was baffled. "You asked for my badge to get up the elevators."

Scarlett said over her shoulder, "I already have a guest pass. Don't need to alert anyone you're here. We just need the badge to get people on the ninth floor to talk."

"The elevators are the other way," Amar said, following her.

"We're not using the main elevators," I said, and then, ushered to Daza so he wouldn't lag behind. "You're in for the VIP treatment today."

A door opened at Scarlett's presence, and together, much to Amar's wide-eyed surprise, we went down a hall to the fancy elevator I had taken with Iris.

Amar walked stiffly, as if we were trespassing. "How'd you manage this?"

"Friends in high places," Scarlett said.

Given the unlimited access Iris commanded, we were on our way to the ninth trading floor in no time.

Unlike the name, the ninth floor was nowhere near nine stories up, more like 90, or 900. It was hard to tell. I felt like I should transform into a bird at these heights. Unlike the residences, we stayed near the trunk of The Root. The ride was quiet, except the cheery elevator music.

"This god really worked their way up in the world," Daza said, attempting to slice through the awkwardness.

No one was in a comedic mood, least of all, Amar. "You know what we're looking for?"

"Not in the slightest," Daza said. "Something odd. Something chaotic. Or—at least something different than the two of your auras mixing. It's like a smoke bomb went off in here."

"Just do your best and clue us into what you see," I said, feeling surprisingly encouraging despite my nerves. Even a weak chaos god was not to be trifled with. Yet, a powerful one was more exciting—it could decide to make me more powerful than Amar or destroy us both with a whim.

The elevator opened. There was a circular half glass wall around the monstrous tree trunk at the center of the expansive trading floor. Bark shot into the sky above—the Tree of Life sprouted through The Root. Between us and the tree, there was an open gap that led all the way down to the ground far, far below. That narrow drop seemed more perilous than the vast horizon beyond the glass windows that allowed access to the world outside.

Quiet hallways ran past rows of cubicles made of smoked glass, digitally controlled for privacy, just tall enough to not see into them, but not high enough to reach the ceiling. As Scarlett led us down the hall, the glass streaked like dancing sands as if our presence was a rushing wind, encouraging speed. Brief glimpses flashed by of employees at desks, working, or not, at a variety of screens.

We found a few fully segregated offices, mahogany doors open just a crack. Scarlett pushed the first one open.

A clean-shaven man was tossing pieces of rolled up paper into a trash bin. He missed one, distracted by our intrusion. Swiveling in his seat, he attempted to look busy, until he realized that he didn't recognize the group that entered.

All inside, I shut the door with a click.

"We're here to ask a few questions," Scarlett said. "Detective A, show him the badge."

Amar tapped at his BioScreen, and the man got a notification on his.

"What can I help you with?" the man asked, who I gathered was one of the bosses here. Behind him, there were the kind of things people who commanded others had. However, some commanders were not taskmasters; there were a few pictures of a golden retriever on the desk, a glass case with a black puck and piece of net, along with a few other sports memorabilia like a jersey.

He had other items that were more in my realm—a blue and white Chinese porcelain vase from the Mongol era in a glass case in one corner and a matching case with a desert-sand colored vase from Egypt in the other corner. If I collected a tax for every one of these pieces I'd seen on the Silk Road, I'd really be a god of gold instead of old.

"We have a few questions," Scarlett said, masking whatever concern she had well.

"I've got a meeting in ten minutes."

"You don't look busy." I grabbed the balled-up piece of paper from the floor and tossed it in the trash can. Despite the casual atmosphere, I was on edge.

"Thanks for the assist." The man leaned back. "I have an outing with my employees."

Scarlett asked, "What's your name?"

"Adam," the man said. "Is this going to take long?"

"No," Scarlett said. "But your skate-around will have to wait. We might need to talk to your employees, too."

"How'd you know it was a skate-around?" Adam asked.

"You have weak ankles," Scarlett said.

"What?"

"The stick-tape on your desk," Scarlett said. "You probably aren't going to play hockey with employees, but you can wrap skates with it."

The man swiveled his feet under the desk, self-conscious. "I'm going to have to take a few personal days to recover from that insult."

"She was kidding," Amar said.

"As was I." Adam smiled, bright and relaxed. "What can I help you with?"

Scarlett placed her hands on the back of an empty chair, fingers clenching the wood. "You monitor the prices of pottery?"

"Antiques, yes." He motioned to the vases and then smiled. "You can sit."

"Not worth it," Scarlett said. "Have you noticed anything strange about how often they're being traded?"

"More than normal, I suppose. Porcelain prices are up with volume. But things are like that sometimes. They catch a trend and we just ride that wave."

"So you've done well?" Scarlett asked.

"Our best quarter ever."

Scarlett clutched the back of the chair. "And when it reverses?"

"We ride that wave." Adam's hands waved up and down, small then big. "Some like to catch every small ripple, but we aim for the big ones."

"And this is a big one?"

"A tidal wave. The big play."

"How have your employees been doing?" Scarlett asked.

"They've been great. Really on top of things. Excited." The smile wavered but renewed like his hand motions. "A bit antsy, but we work with high stress stuff. That's why we have to take the time to do some team-building."

Daza motioned to the memorabilia. "I like the jersey. Good team."

"Small talk means we're definitely done here," Scarlett said, relaxing. She pushed the chair in and nodded at Amar.

"That's it?" Adam checked his BioScreen for the time, but it didn't turn on. "What's this?"

"My doing," Amar said. "Sorry. If everything is in order, you'll be back online in no time."

"Good luck at your team-building event," I said, trying to be cordial before whispering, "You might need it."

The four of us left, closing the door behind us. We went to the next office.

The woman inside barely moved when the door opened, the sound of her typing overwhelming the oiled door.

Charts and graphs were stuck hastily on the wall past the monitors. There weren't many decorations, but there were a couple of photos with a typical family. By the keyboard, there was a golden delicious apple in that beautiful yellow stage that made me reminisce of the time I'd stolen Eris' golden apple of discord. So far, there was no bite taken from this apple; normally, I'd try and find a way to get it, but with the chaos god around, I had to be more careful. That could actually be Eris' apple.

"Excuse us," Scarlett said.

"One second," the woman said, continuing to type.

"There's something here," Daza whispered. "The other one was like everything washed right off. An energy is stuck here. Yet, I don't think she's the one we're looking for."

"We'll keep it short, then," Scarlett said.

"What was that?" the woman asked, turning from her work, and when she realized we weren't employees, her face was shy and reserved. But, professionally, she introduced herself. "I'm Rebecca. Who are you all?" Amar's badge-ping reached her, answering her question. "I see. Uhm—is there something wrong?"

"Routine investigation," Scarlett said. "Financial matters."

"I don't see how that could impact me—" The wheels of her chair rolled silent over a Persian rug.

"No, not you in particular." Scarlett managed a fake grin. "We're just making sure everything is in order."

Amar said, "I like the rug."

With those floral designs and symmetries, of course he did. The rug was beautiful and dastardly. Rugs were Amar's domain, and the god glanced at me, taunting. I didn't let on how it got under my skin and bit my essence at the deepest part—my memories. This one did strike a stunning resemblance to a larger piece Amar offered a king, which was lost to the ages. Yet, in return, Amar got the benefits of such rug weaving as a sort of worship for far longer than the king was alive.

"A lovely piece. Specially commissioned." Rebecca went back to business. "I have the paperwork here." She opened a drawer in her desk and started pulling out piles upon piles of sheets. "I'm sorry it's not more organized. Here's the annual report. The reconciliations. The—"

"Right," Scarlett said. "They're complicated matters, but I trust you know what you're doing."

"Of course," Rebecca said. "I mean—I try my best."

"You work with commodities?" Scarlett asked.

Rebecca nodded.

"What's the price of molybdenum ore today?"

"9,711/ton."

Scarlett focused on every detail in Rebecca's reaction. "Do you consider it cheap?"

"It's down 34.2% from last year." Rebecca's face remained stern.

"And what's the price of silver?"

"Eighteen an ounce."

"Also down, I assume?"

"27.9% in the past couple weeks."

"That seems significant," Scarlett said. "Are other common goods down? Are you seeing anything strange in the rest of the commodity markets?"

"I don't know. Things go up and things go down."

"Is that good for you?" Scarlett asked.

"We provide liquidity. The price changes work for us either way."

"I see," Scarlett said, unjudgmental. "Can I get the latest reconciliation of accounts?"

"Of course," Rebecca pulled out a piece of paper from the stack, denoted by a yellow sticky note, and handed it to Scarlett.

"Give us a little time to run through this and we'll be back," she said.

"Sounds good. I'll be here."

"We're coming back?" I whispered to Scarlett.

"Probably not," Scarlett said as we left the office, heading for the third in the row. The last one of the big rooms.

"Weren't commodities one of the things the god was changing?" I asked.

"Yes," Scarlett said. "But Daza just said there was something—that doesn't mean Rebecca is who we're looking for."

"There would be residual effects of a strong chaos god everywhere."

"And she's far too organized to be the chaos god." Scarlett led us on.

The last office door was completely open, but Scarlett actually knocked this time. A friendly smile responded. The woman was dressed in a sky-blue suit, and her face was the sun-warm. Beckoning us in, she didn't seem the least concerned as I closed the door.

"Candy?" She offered a glass jar with various chocolates and colorful sweets, all still wrapped.

"Any apple-flavored?" I asked. Accepting anything was risky, but I didn't know of any chaos around candy.

The woman perused the jar and pulled out a red, square-shaped sweet, handing it over. I took it, unconcerned with friendliness—it was not like I could be poisoned. If anything, I was the best candidate to test whether there was anything unnatural about this place. Scarlett and others could thank me for taking the risk later.

"You aren't surprised to see us," Amar said, a disapproving look at my comfort with the candy, not understanding my intention.

"I get all kinds of people coming through these doors," the woman said. "Art dealers, friends, distant coworkers, regulators—which I assume is what you are."

"Close," Amar tapped at his BioScreen.

"Ah, I've heard of you, Detective A. I suppose I can push the art deal back." The woman didn't seem surprised at the ping. "I'm Chloe. But I'm sure you know that already. Please, take a seat."

All four seats in this office were comfier than the others we'd visited, as if these had been ordered special. The environment was more welcoming, too. Bright paper decorations were draped on the wall next to a priceless framed Greek wall-sculpture, a metope I'd seen in my memories and then later in a museum, depicting a centaur kicking a man in the...well, no matter where the centaur kicked, those hooves hurt. Of course, I'd seen the real battle, and this was missing a bit of the charm. Why was the centaur the subject? There were bigger moments. None as funny, though. And for the record, the man had kicked the centaur first.

Compared to the art, work was minimal. There were graphs and charts, but they were employee satisfaction numbers—trending down, and with an unhappy face drawn in red pen next to it—and a personality test—extroverted. Very.

"Do you want to take a seat?" Chloe asked.

Scarlett looked at Daza, and he gave an unsure shrug. Taking the clue, Scarlett sat in one of the seats, figuring there'd be more questions. I stood behind her, ready to defend her best I could.

"You oversee everyone?" Scarlett asked.

Chloe nodded. "Anyone else want some candy? Or water? I don't have much else to offer."

"A few answers are all we want," Scarlett said.

Reminded of the candy in my hand, I popped it in my mouth, the sweet melting as I chewed. It wasn't the same as the fresh fruit, but it was tasty. Nothing bad happened, and admittedly, I might have tried it because I wanted a sweet treat to calm my nerves instead of testing a theory.

"Where'd you get these?" I asked.

"The grocery on floor 3b," Chloe said. "They have all kinds of goodies."

"Those are not the kind of answers we're after," Amar said, as if it wasn't obvious. "Do you have the transaction records?"

Chloe smiled. "I don't keep the paperwork here, but I can tell you who to talk to."

This time, it was Daza who asked the question. "Your analysts take care of all that?"

Scarlett looked into Daza's eyes, as if hoping to see the reflection of what he saw.

"Yes," Chloe said. "I'm more a big picture person. They know what they're doing, otherwise they wouldn't be here."

The last phrase was a bit chilling, but it was said in such a happy way, it didn't sound as much as a threat as it might've been.

Daza bit his lip. "Can we talk to them?"

"Of course," Chloe said. "You are an odd-ball group of investigators."

"Do you have a list of employees?" Scarlett asked, ignoring the comment and focusing on what Daza meant—we might find our chaos god among the junior team members.

"I have a map of the floor." Chloe dug through her desk. She found the single sheet—there wasn't much to dig through—and handed it to Scarlett. "This is from when we moved offices."

Scarlett studied the paper. "Was that recently?"

"A few months ago. We're still adjusting."

Even Scarlett couldn't help but look at the employee satisfaction numbers. "I appreciate your help. We want to make sure everything is in order and nothing was lost in the move."

Chloe's cheer faded. "If you find the smiles, let me know."

"I think it'll improve," I said.

"Do you have any new employees?" Daza asked, looking towards the door like a bloodhound after a trail.

"Turnover has been low. But we recently lost a few. Haven't found anyone to replace them."

Scarlett got up, almost sorry she had spent the time to sit. "We'll come back after we talk to them."

"Wait a second," Chloe said. "You reminded me the map's out of date. Let me cross out the ones that left."

Scarlett hesitated, but handed over the paper. With a blue pen, Chloe crossed out a few offices and returned it. There was an awkward silence without a "There you go" or "Thanks".

Once we closed the door behind us and were a little down the hallway, Scarlett said, "X marks the spot."

"You think she crossed out the ones we want?" I asked.

"Those are where we'll find our clues." Scarlett crinkled the paper with a tense hand. "Daza, what did you see?"

"A strong aura. At least at first sight. But it's not entirely hers. She's not the chaos god, I think, but something's off. Weird. If she walked into the restaurant, I wouldn't say she was a regular mortal, I'd think she's a myth."

"The empty offices will give us a few clues," Scarlett said. "But I think we'll find our god among her employees."

"That's ridiculous," Amar said. "How would they have the power to control the markets as regular analysts?"

"Who do you think does most of the work?"

Following the map like a treasure trail, we looped around the office and reached the first empty cubicle. It had been recently vacated. Or, it was so dirty they hadn't bothered to clean. On the desks, there were still food stains. The monitors and work materials had been evacuated from the office, leaving only what was deemed nonessential. Scarlett opened a drawer, but there were no papers, only paper napkins. Taking only cursory looks, she flipped through whatever junk was inside the cabinets. Whatever chaos she made left them more organized than when we started.

"It's chaotic here," Daza said.

Scarlett shut a drawer hard. "You're telling me."

"I mean the aura. This whole area is."

A little perturbed, Scarlett brushed past us and headed to the next open cubicle.

There was less mess in this one, but plenty more work. Old papers filled drawers and cabinets. There was a standing desk, still stuck upright. A few cords were left behind, dangling. Still, too, there were some similarities with Chloe. A personality test. Social. Friendly. But, unlucky for me, there was no candy.

"This is the same," Daza said. "All kinds of colors."

"Do you have a purpose besides being vague?" Scarlett asked, getting annoyed.

I pulled her aside. "What's the matter?"

"I can see all he does, just in a different way," Scarlett said. "We're getting nowhere. The clues are here, but the god isn't."

"Patience," I said.

Scarlett crossed her arms. "As soon as the god knows we're here, we'll lose our advantage."

"You're underestimating the hubris of gods, even one as minor as me."

"Something's wrong."

"Besides my humility?" I tried to make a joke, but I sensed even this brief time here was affecting her, too. "Keep your head, the god will feed on that."

She shrugged me off. I understood her frustration and felt the influence of the chaos god in the air like a distorted hum.

It was stronger than I expected.

We went to the next cubicle, which was empty except for papers. Not only were there the drafts and graphs like the last one, but there was a volume that filled the office like the tide. Hurried notes. Variations. Reconciliations. Numbers were connected, checked, and rechecked. But, even to the untrained eye, there was something going on here. What numbers they represented was anyone's guess. Too chaotic. Too out of context.

Scarlett, though, followed the thoughts from one drawer to another as a detective following the strings between people in a murder investigation, except Scarlett was on the trail of numbers.

Amar, Daza, and I stood around, not knowing what to do—any time we went near, she shooed us away. For such comprehensive work, it was also speedy, and when she was done, she didn't even bother to ask Daza what the aura was here. She knew.

Scarlett said, "Daza, we're looking for extreme auras. No aura at all or more than you've ever seen."

"I'll let you know."

We went on to the first filled cubicle on the map. The analyst there had a cynical smile on his face before we arrived, and it only increased as he noticed us. It was basically tattooed on.

Even as we introduced ourselves, the man continued to sort pieces of paper, stacking them into a presentation. The smile was unwavering and his eyes had a faux brightness as he focused on the next step. We explained why we were here.

"I'm Bob."

"Scarlett," she said, buying a moment. "What do you do here?"

"I add and subtract. I'm an elementary school kid without recess."

"Does that mean you do arts and crafts?" I asked.

"Close. Staples and presentations," Bob said.

Scarlett mused, "Sounds boring, but it could be worse."

"It's wonderful, if you like being dead inside."

The analyst pressed down the stapler on his thumb. He didn't flinch. He didn't scream. No sound at all. Since he didn't make any response, none of us dared either.

He plucked the staple out, bloody and bent, and flicked it into the trash, where there was already a streak of dried blood on the plastic bag.

He noticed our look. "I had a paper cut earlier." He showed off the scab on the webbing of his forefinger and thumb.

The blood didn't bother me, but the stapling was still unsettling. "Didn't that hurt?"

"The staple is easier to get out of than my job."

Scarlett looked to Daza.

He shook his head and said, "Small wound. I think he'll be alright."

"As long as I finish this presentation, I will be."

"We'll leave you to it," Scarlett said. "By the way, that graph looks like it should be printed in color."

Bob cursed. "I have to be more careful."

Leaving the blunt man behind, we moved to the next cubicle. There, a woman was spinning in her seat, magnetized to us as soon as we arrived.

"Hi there, I'm Mary. Nice to meet you all."

After we explained what we were doing here, she only grew more intrigued, pulling us into her small cubicle and talking in hushed tones.

And, before we could ask a question, she asked one instead, "Who else have you talked to?"

"Is that important?" Scarlett asked.

"Oh, you talked to Bob?"

Scarlett nodded. "He was very cooperative."

"He usually isn't. Last month, he told Chloe that she was wrong in a monthly meeting with her boss. Chloe gave Bob quite the dressing-down afterwards."

"What did Bob say she was wrong about?"

"He said the numbers were wrong."

Scarlett said, "Were they?"

"I don't know, but it was the talk of the office for the next couple of weeks. We all thought Bob was going to be fired, but that's almost impossible with how few people we have."

I asked Daza, "Is there anything you want to ask her?"

The waiter said, "There's nothing here I can think of."

"Nothing?" Scarlett said, picking up on the hint. "Is that the only drama with Bob?"

"Yes," Mary said, deflating and reinflating to another subject. "But Oliver and John had a fight last week."

"Other coworkers? What about?"

"You didn't hear it from me, but John is being promoted." For something so secret, she was surprisingly loud. "Usually Oliver's quiet, but that got under his skin."

"Who told Oliver?"

Mary kept a tight-lipped smile. The lips loosened and as her mouth opened, there was blood between her teeth. She'd split her tongue with a bite, but didn't seem to notice. "There's always drama. That's no big deal. Ed had a heart attack last week and almost choked on his spoon."

Scarlett asked, "The messy cubicle?"

"It was very sad. I heard he's still in the hospital."

Daza whispered to Scarlett, "Do I have to tell you there is actually something here?"

"We'll go talk to Oliver and John," Scarlett said, inching out the cubicle. "You might want to drink some water or something. If we hear anything interesting, we'll let you know."

"Thank you," Mary said after us, teeth stained red.

For someone in the business of gossip, Scarlett was in no mood for it, and led us towards new pastures, hoping it'd have greener grass.

"How are you doing Oliver?" Scarlett asked the man in the next cubicle on the map.

He was sitting in his chair, hunched over and intent on the screen. He offered us a shy smile. "Good. How'd you know I was Oliver?"

"I guessed. We're here—"

"I heard," Oliver tapped his ears. "Mary thinks we're deaf or something."

"You got into a fight with John?" Scarlett asked.

"Yeah."

"Do you feel jaded by him getting the promotion?"

He continued typing. "I just have to work harder."

"We also heard that Ed had a heart attack."

"Yeah."

"Anything to add?" Scarlett's frustration was bubbling.

"It is what it is."

Scarlett took a deep breath. "Daza, do you have any questions here?"

"Besides what he's doing that's so interesting? Nothing."

Oliver didn't respond with what he was doing.

"I'm assuming nothing worth an explanation," Scarlett said into Oliver's silence.

Daza shrugged. "This is a normal amount of abnormality."

The four of us left the cubicle to the deserted hallway and an echo of nothing. I looked back. The man had stopped typing. Unlike his two coworkers, there was nothing wrong here. No staple. No bite. No blood. Nothing outwardly wrong. I thought to say something, but what was there to say?

What could I say about nothing? A feeling crept up on me that I couldn't catch.

Scarlett knocked on the cubicle wall of a man who had slicked back hair and a tall, expanded posture in his seat.

"How's it going?" Scarlett asked.

"Better now." The man got up and shook our hands. "I'm John."

"I hear you're getting promoted, congratulations," Scarlett said. Apparently, Scarlett had no intention of offering that information as to why we were here—and the man didn't seem to care.

"Thanks, I put in a lot of hard work," John said with a big, self-important brightness.

"Heard Oliver was not too happy about it."

He waved the comment away. "Yeah, but he's a paper pusher."

"What do you do here then?"

"I keep the place running. I keep the lights on. I make this a well-oiled machine. I do this and that and everything."

He bent under his desk, reaching for something. On the way up, he banged his head.

"This is my employee award," John said, showing us what looked like a cheap sports trophy for kids.

"You're bleeding," I said, watching a bit of blood mat in his hair—it almost fit in with the hair gel, except for the color.

"I'm fine," John said. "Did you see the trophy?"

Scarlett rolled her eyes. "Is it really a well-oiled machine? You all fighting and Bob calling Chloe out."

"Chloe is right. Bob is stupid, like he always is."

Scarlett said, "I looked at the reconciliations and I'm no expert, but something seems wrong."

John turned back to his screen. "You're right, you don't know what you're talking about either."

I had to pull Scarlett away before she caused any damage to John. The chaos god must've been affecting her, as she barely missed smacking him upside the head. She was surprisingly strong as she struggled, and it was only on our way back to the elevator that she finally calmed.

"Some interesting characters," Daza said.

"Did you see anything on the last one?" Scarlett's face flickered with anger at the mention of John.

"The aura is as big as his ego."

"The people who least deserve an ego are usually those who have the biggest," Scarlett said. "Do you think it's him?"

"I can't be sure—" Daza stopped and we all looked.

Oliver was leaning on the glass railing and looking into the gap between the Tree of Life and the floors below. There was nothing out of the ordinary except for a feeling. He was a little too intent on looking down. Our conversation fell into that gap.

Oliver straddled the glass.

The sense that something was wrong built to a crescendo. We held our breath as he held on to empty air, slipping over the barrier and into the void.

Oliver disappeared into the gap. Instinct almost kept me still, but I ignored it and ran. I had to save the mortal from himself.

I leapt over the railing. When you can fly, jumping with wings catching the wind is a joyful experience, without them, I flailed as I fell. There was nothing joyful about it. My whole being clenched, but that was good—I needed to pull. Shadow tendrils netted under the man like a net, tying to the tree on one side and approaching floor on the other, stringing tighter.

Oliver's body punched straight through it.

The Tree of Life devoured my tendrils and left me clinging to nothing. Air cut at me and this was far faster than the elevator. We didn't have much time. We came perilously close to sharp bark and floors flying by.

I dove headfirst like a peregrine falcon. There wasn't enough room for much else. As I caught up to Oliver, I tried something else.

Black tendrils clasped onto the siding of a floor further down and drew towards me. When the shadows met my hand, I grasped on as if it was a rope, falling past the attachment point and tightening to the right tautness. Like swinging on a vine, the snap pulled us towards a floor.

It must be said, I got the timing a bit wrong. Going back-first, I cushioned the squishy mortal.

I shattered through a glass half-wall, and rolled over an abrasive carpet at startling speeds and through a cubicle wall, bits of wood and fluff and glass cutting around and into me. An effective, if painful, stop.

I bled gold. Luckily, there was no one in the cubicle and the man probably wouldn't notice as I stitched my form, healing the cuts. The pain remained, even if the wounds did not.

Shock. Oliver's eyes were closed and he was unnaturally still. He didn't seem mortally injured, but by his lack of movement, if I wasn't the god of death, I might've thought him dead; instead, he was just unconscious.

That was the best result that could happen. I got up and dusted myself off, leaving him as a present for people to discover. As I walked out the destroyed cubicle, there was a voice that followed me.

It was coming from Oliver's mouth, who sat straight up and stared at me with deep brown eyes, but it wasn't the voice I'd heard before.

"Zarik. I thought you had enough clues to get to the root of this matter and figure out who I am. Your memory must've gotten worse with age. But then again, maybe you'd rather forget what caused our meeting. I'm looking forward to the next one with a more interesting face than this one."

Oliver fell to the ground, unaware he'd just been used by some manner of god. There was no point in responding in such cases; I'd heard enough to know what we needed to do. I had to find Scarlett and tell her.

Luckily, Scarlett found me while Amar went to check on the mortal and Daza meandered behind, never in any rush.

I said to Scarlett, "I think the god is already gone. Apparently, the chaos god and I have met before. We can beat Amar and find out what god we're dealing with first—but to move forward, we have to look back into my past."

TWENTY-ONE

I RELIVE MY PAST

Where had I met this god before? Somewhere in millennia of memories. The question now, was when? A smell of evergreens seemed to haunt me as Scarlett and I walked through a park.

We were headed to the logical place to revisit my memories—Belle's. There, we could use the VR beds to relive the past. The voice I heard in The Root twined through the web of my memories, tying into strands here and there. When you're as old as I am, recalling anything was a wonder. Eventually, life became a permanent state of déjà vu. That said, recently, it had been more novel. But I'd heard more gods over my years than raindrops in a storm.

A few gods stood out. And, if the chaos god was not leading me astray—a distinct possibility—since my revival, I had a few clues on where to start.

I figured the pieces around the ninth floor's offices might be clues. They had, after all, reminded me of old, chaotic times.

Belle opened her door with a bright smile, and after surprise faded, she kindly agreed to let us use the pods once

Scarlett convinced her of the importance to a case. They seemed on good terms, but I figured they must've talked more when Scarlett came to delete L.

Offering a few more pleasantries, Belle led us in. The pods were in the same place, and it was hard to tell whether they'd been used or if it hadn't been long enough to collect dust. At the very least, Steve wasn't around, and Romeo pretended not to pay much attention to us, only giving us a nod from a plushy dog bed.

Strapping into the VR beds, Scarlett instructed me on how to relive my memories. Memories didn't need programming; there was only one problem, they were only as accurate as the memory itself. With gods, though, memories were buried and never tarnished—just like us.

We began in a time before the route was called the Silk Road. A time when it was called the Persian Royal Road, and I was free to explore the world on a whim.

I warped into the new reality and felt desert sand shifting under my feet. I was overlooking a ridge and there was a vague feeling of being watched, which I knew was Scarlett. Unfortunately, I had to relive this embarrassment with her watching like a god above.

My muscles carried me along by programming, but I was familiar with being chained in this manner.

I was in the form of a bustard, and although it's close enough to another word that'd give the wrong impression, a bustard is a long-legged bird native to the Arabian desert that's one of the world's heaviest flying birds—if it can be called flying. I was younger then; I didn't know better.

Despite all that's happened since, some things didn't change. I saw a basket of apples. Although I always liked fruits, I was unsure whether my taste for apples was as keen as during my time with Scarlett. Still, I wouldn't turn them down.

Down in the valley below, a man and his mule cart were traveling along with various wares. Of these, there were beautiful pieces of Egyptian and Chinese porcelain like I'd seen in Adam's office. At the time of the memory, I didn't really think much of seeing these pieces in the dry lands I sometimes liked to roam. If it wasn't for the apples, I would've left him. I think the apples were for the mule—now they were for me.

As the man stopped and dug through his wares, I swooped down from my perch. Well, I fell. It was the only time I ever used the form, but luckily, I was graceful enough to float down on the winds rather ceremonious as I changed form. By the time my feet impressed into desert sand, I was a radiant man. When I say golden skin, I do mean it. The light off my form ate energy, but everyone in those days wanted to be a sun god.

"I am the great and mighty Zarik, what do *you* want here?" This whole experience was weird—this time, there was no wiggle room in my choices, as the voice came without thought, as if the mouth was not mine, even though I felt the vibration off my tongue and throat as I rumbled into sand.

I waited for surprise, awe, or worship. At the time, I was a household name.

"I've never heard of you," said the thick-bearded man as he spun around.

I didn't say which households. "Answer."

"I'm trading some goods."

"And you wish for safe passage?"

I did not say what I wanted in exchange. Always leave the first offer to them. You never know what they're willing to give up—gold, special skills, their souls—then I could negotiate for some apples.

"I already have safe passage," the trader said, spinning a gold bracelet on his wrist. A desert red trimmed both sides of the gold, and I sensed the heat radiating off it more than the spitting sand that kicked up at his touch.

"Is that so?" I asked, bluffing, but already knowing the answer.

Buoyed by the bangle and my hesitation, the man dared to turn his back on me, rummaging through his wares and leaving me and the mule staring at each other. The animal brayed and I thought about braying back louder.

"I've got a different wish," the trader said, not even bothering to look back at me. He pulled out an apple, which was not entirely ripe, transitioning like a color wheel from green to red. "I want a Roc feather. Consider this a small offering of good will, but my protector would be very pleased if you helped me." Holding the apple out, he touched the gold again, sending a wave of heat crashing upon me. More than an offer, it was a threat.

A Roc was an enormous mythical bird native to these lands, and smacking him with a big, fat "No" was the obvious response. Back then, though, I was no demon—I was a vanquisher, and facing a Roc was an enticing story. At best, it would sprinkle my myth to far reaches, and despite what a bad deal it seemed, at worst, I'd get an apple and do a courtesy to this man's protector god.

Thinking of what happened next, I wondered if the protector god was what I had heard in The Root. This had been such a minor incident; I couldn't be blamed for not remembering the god.

As I thought forward, the taste of apple teased me and I found the world changed. I had taken the form of a massive mistake—an elephant. The logic was solid. I planned on using my trunk to pluck a feather from the Roc as it tried to unsuccessfully carry me off.

The Roc was in a nest as tall as castle walls at the time, which was perched on a plateau overlooking the desert on one side and a verdant river valley on the other. I stomped along confidently, kicking dust with big, grey feet.

The bird was bigger than I imagined. I'd almost forgotten how massive. As I got closer, my steps lost confidence as I realized how outsized I was. White and copper feathers ruffled, and the bird of prey faced me with a sharp beak and eyes. When it unfurled from its nest and flew away with hefty wingbeats, the job seemed too easy. Some shed feathers must be in the nest, and there were no eggs yet. I figured the myth could sense what I was and gave me space.

Diving off the cliff, the bird flew out of sight, and I reached the nest without incident.

Probing my trunk over the lip, I searched with tensile touch for soft barbs.

A shadow fell over me. By the time I realized the Roc had merely looped around to grab me from behind, it was too late. Some mortals would be forced to do crazy things—there were no pigs around for the saying to be "When pigs fly", and no one thought they'd see a flying elephant. To be fair, I didn't expect to be one, either.

The talons dug into my tough skin. Flying, the city in the valley became a speck under me. Wings that blotted out the sun glided on the wind. Minus the flight, this was essentially my plan, and I managed to grab a leg feather with my trunk. The Roc gave such an earsplitting scream for a small pluck that I couldn't help but thinking it was being a little dramatic.

It was a few seconds later that I realized I was falling, and the couple tiny feathers I was holding wouldn't help me fly. My trunk flapped anyways.

The Roc had dropped me to make elephant soup. Hard earth flew towards me, but luckily, I was a god and not an elephant.

I clutched the feathers tight, and their warmth sent me forwards in my memories again. I returned, triumphant, with the feathers to the trader.

"I've got the Roc feathers," I said, arriving as a cloud of smoke and letting the feathers fall to the trader on wispy tendrils.

He took them and ran his finger on the bristle. "Did you get these from a golden eagle? They're really small."

"You didn't say what part of the Roc to get them from."

"I thought it was obvious I wanted the flight feathers." He paused a moment, thinking. "You're a bit tricky, aren't you?"

"The leg plumage makes for great quills. I'll have to get some kraken ink." I did save a feather specifically for that purpose. "Are you ungrateful?"

I transformed to a burly, bear-chested man—I would've had bear claws, too, but I settled with the right to bear arms. This bear-human hybrid form was meant to be intimidating. Today, as with many other days in my long life, was not going my way.

A golden lamp smacked me on the head.

Stunned more than hurt, I backed up. "What was that for?"

The man looked just as confused. "This was the lamp I touched when you appeared. Why didn't that work?"

"I'm not a genie. I'm a god."

"That's what a genie would say." He looked more concerned now. "You granted my wish and I'd heard you could be devious."

I was obviously annoyed by this. Anyone would be. Being thwacked on the head and insulted at the same time didn't happen that often.

Darkness followed in the desert.

The man panicked, spinning the gold bracelet. A desert wind cut through my frustration.

"What do you want?" said another god's voice.

The mortal said, "I want you to protect me like you promised."

I realized what the other presence was—one of those Egyptian gods. There'd been conflict between our pantheons in later memories, but I hadn't had much formal contact with them yet.

I said to the other presence, "This mortal has insulted me. I got him the Roc feathers he wanted and he's still not happy."

"The Roc and the elephant," the god said, almost chuckling. "You might not want to be associated with that story."

"You saw?" I paused. "Of course, the deserts."

"Yes," the god said. "But these lands are not mine. Do with the man what you will. I have no loyalty to this swindler, and no obligation to protect him from his lack of respect."

"You promised to protect me, Set," said the trader.

"That's no protector god." I laughed. "You should've respected age; it comes for all." That was a constant lesson I'd taught throughout the millennia.

But I left the rest of the story to where it lay, lost. The god, Set, was different from the one in The Root. The disorder and dualism were similar, but there was no heat or sand in The Root, and most importantly, the presence did not feel the same. I still had the inclination that the chaos god was merely misleading us into wasting time, but I'd be foolish not to try.

My grin faded with the memory, and in the space between memories, I heard Scarlett.

"So?" she asked.

"The clue wasn't the vases in Adam's office," I said. "I was hoping it was."

"You were different, then."

"Yes, wisdom comes with time."

"How much more time do you need until you're wise?" she joked.

I didn't take her seriously and ignored the slight. "I saw a rug in Rebecca's office that reminded me of a mis-weave in history I might've mentioned. Let's hope our god is there."

The simulation transitioned to a temple. Half the candles were lit and a table was laid with seven S's: sweet pudding, sumac, apples, garlic, vinegar, coins, and wheatgrass. Fine, it didn't make sense in some languages, but in other languages, this day was a different "S"—Spring.

When I mentioned a smell from the mythical restaurant's shakers to Amar, I was speaking of this memory.

This was the one of two days a year Amar and I spent together as friends, and in this truce, we did not fight for the temple that was dedicated to each of us for half the year. The bull and lion statue came later, after this last meeting as anything besides rivals.

We sat across from each other at the long-table, symbols of life dividing us. Amar was a dark-haired woman in plant-colored clothes. The smell of flowers remained a constant, as did the emerald-blue eyes that pulled on my heartstrings. I, too, had my similarities and differences. We had different names then, but I had the same eyes, same smile, but on a golden-haired woman in black mourning garb.

I ate a crisp apple, the crunch echoing. Between bites, I made small talk. "It's your time of year again."

"What are you going to do in your time off?" Amar asked, offering the ritual pleasantries we presented each other.

"What did you do during yours?" I was genuinely curious; the voice was completely different to the disdain I held in my heart now.

"I built a palace."

Wanting to frown, my body smiled instead, competitive but cordial. "I'll have to do something better, then."

"Would you like to see it?" Amar asked. "There's a new king who lives there."

The present me wanted to say no and leap across the table, but I rose calmly from my chair. "To outdo you, I'll have to see what low standard you left for me."

Together we went to this new place, dancing across my memory as a raven and bluebird spiraling around each other at immortal speed.

When we landed in front of the palace as humans, I was impressed then and remained so. The grand stairway was like two lightning bolts, and Amar and I took opposite ones. Meeting at the top, I was quieted by the scale. Hand-sculpted columns and artwork and bricks were placed and painted by steady hands. Sunshine warmed gold and blue skies matched turquoise paint. Bull statues stared down at us on either side of a god-sized crimson door, which were pulled open at our arrival.

Inside, the ceilings were expansive as outside and people flowed with food, while messages and gossip bounced like tweeting birds. The place was a reflection of Amar.

"Colorful," I said simply, not wanting to sound as impressed as I was.

"I only used the best materials and dyes."

Amar took credit, but I knew I could match the effort—if I found the mortals to sweat for it; gods provided ideas, inspiration, and motivation, not manual labor.

Amar led on. This was only a reception room, not the one for the king. Out a set of doors and into a courtyard, I found a sort of zoo. Of course, there were doves and cheetahs and other quiet and pleasant animals to keep around, but there were a louder group that made it more of a zoo. Royal guards grunted, pacing the ground, some leaning like statues and others actual statues—the façade of the temple was sculpted with guards and people bringing gifts to the king—a reflection of real life, which would remain long after the living.

A section of art before more steps made me smile.

"A picture of us, how sweet." I motioned to a plaque with a lion biting a bull on the backside. "Can't say you taste good, though."

"You are quite the pain." Amar smiled back and we walked together into the throne room.

Inside, the air was perfumed and cool. Rosewater and fruits and flowers were sprinkled through the hall, which was filled with more columns than people. Our steps echoed across marble, announcing our arrival to this king.

The king had a beard braided like curling waves and wore gold and turquoise clothes that matched the colors of the palace, which seemed a temple dedicated to this mortal. As mortals go, he was impressive by his aura rather than looks, holding a golden scepter with a turquoise bull and lion on the top.

"You brought a friend?" the king asked Amar.

Much to my surprise, and still to my disgust, Amar kneeled at the king's feet—something beneath any god. Sometimes, it was necessary to do so for a more powerful god, but never a mortal. There was nothing less godly. But Amar was already a laughingstock, so I wasn't surprised.

Amar rose. "A friend only today. The rest, he is a rival."

"Keeping enemies close is good, making them dead is better." The king examined me. "But that is not the business today. What brought you here?"

"To greet you and see this palace," I said.

"Persepolis," the king said, correcting me with the name. "And I'm not sure you've greeted me well enough."

I wouldn't kneel, but at the time, I had the ability to keep my rage under wraps. Under the mask of the past, I felt the poise unraveling.

Before I said something I meant, Amar intervened and said, "I brought an offering."

With Amar's finger-snap, two men came into the hall with a rug that barely fit through the door rolled up. They unfurled it as they went, rectangular and long enough to cover the fields of empty marble.

"This will help the echo," Amar said, and immediately it did, the sweet voice ringing like a clear bell through the hall, the rug deafening any impurity.

The rug was an imperious tapestry of life laced with intricate florals and symmetries. The colors put rainbows to shame. And it was so silky smooth, my eyes eased over the serene luxury, soothed by the sight as if I had touched the gentle fabric.

I had nothing similar to offer the king. And as much as the king was impressed by it, he waited to pass judgment until I presented him with a gift.

"You'll have to excuse me," I said. "I did not bring helpers. I did not weave; I am no spinster. I am a vanquisher, and I had to wait for the right moment, but I will return shortly with something much better."

Luckily, I had an idea where to get an appropriate gift. Or should I say, curse. Amar had betrayed me by forcing my hand into what happened next. It was not the first time, nor the last, but this was where it started to go downhill.

But I wasn't here to live painful embarrassments again. I was here to find a god.

The memory skipped ahead.

I'd appropriated an egg from a dragon's den in the mountains, and the only clue of what came later was the smell of burning hair that lingered on me, but that wasn't important.

The memory was in the same throne room. A turquoise stone-egg warmed my hands and glowed and sparkled like a bioluminescent bay.

I offered the king the dragon's egg, and I still had never forgiven myself for what happened next.

To really sell my gift, my knee touched the ground before the king, who smiled with pleasure.

I wasn't pleased, and someone else was less so.

As if my knee split the earth, I was pulled into the void by true, rage-filled power. Chief of chaos among daevas, Azi Dahaka had dragged me away. At the time, he was at the pinnacle of his powers, watching all daevas from the void.

After my insulting disappearance, the king heightened Amar and his compatriots, while my days of worship were numbered. Other daevas thrived as terrifying entities, but old age was less feared then—it was a blessing. Although I had other aspects like poison, I was ashamed of killing randomly, and few fear the hesitant.

Azi Dahaka and the other daevas underestimated that king. He would eventually take over most of the known world. For that simple act of respect, I'd been reprimanded. Azi Dahaka's laugh still shook my essence.

Despite being more powerful then, I was a rather limited god. Gods with true power lived on a different plane than Amar and I. Trying to explain what it was like to be in their presence is like trying to stuff a cow into a rabbit hole—it tends to get messy.

The simulation couldn't mimic the void, but the conversation remained.

"You dare kneel to a mortal?" Azi Dahaka asked, his booming chaos chomping at my essence. "Tell me why I should not devour you for your embarrassment."

"That was no gift, it was a curse so the dragon would destroy the palace, but I had to kneel to make my offering appear genuine rather than a trick."

This was all true; unfortunately, dragons were patient and sleepy and the king was long dead before Persepolis burned down and the egg was plundered. The dragon never got its egg back, and it ended up with some "Great" mortal. After that, I think the dragon baby hatched and might've destroyed the largest empire on earth with a single infected bite. At least, that's what an unreliable Greek god told me about Alexander's demise.

Other daevas chimed in.

"What an excuse."

"How weak."

"And he likes to call himself death."

"Yes, death kneels to a mortal." A few laughs.

"With such creaky knees, I'm surprised he could even get back up."

Azi Dahaka laughed, haunting me through the centuries.

I could not take the joys of a family reunion anymore. The memory melted, and I was left with Scarlett again.

"What happened?" Scarlett asked.

"I'd recognize if the voice was that of family." My voice was shaken, too.

Scarlett prodded with her words. "Why did we bother, then?"

"I'm being thorough."

"Thoroughly evasive."

"I'm good at that. Just like in this next memory. Being agile kept me alive. I hope you're enjoying my most painful memories."

"You know that's not what I meant."

I thought of the carving, a metope, I'd seen in Chloe's office with the centaur. This one might've been a stretch, but that's what art was—a reflection of reality. An inspiration. A mirror into one's soul.

There were a lot of souls in this memory.

The battle between gods was cataclysmic and chaotic. In this fight, I hated both sides. This was a battle between Egyptian, Persian, and Greek gods—I was on the selfish side. These were the places and times of stories and legends. I wouldn't have missed it for a million apples. With all the death, I couldn't. Yet, no one here died of old age.

Over bloody plains and seas, celestial gods fought. I messed with mortals and minor deities alike. Plunged into the memory, I found myself with a familiar item—an apple.

However, this was no ordinary apple, it was Eris' apple of discord. Gold and cold in my hands, I lobbed it into a fray, resulting in utter nonsense. The god, Pan, became a pan flute, if only temporarily. A man turned into a donkey and was ridden by a comrade. And if the soldier was just an ass at heart, that was the last of normality.

I left the rest to my imagination, as I was busy with the rest of the battle. I was, after all, seeking attention and heroics that would be told through the ages.

As my body sliced through the throngs like a scythe, I focused on the voices, hoping to hear the god we were searching for. Myths sprung up and died. Mortals minded their own business and were devoured like biscuits. There was no time for guilt in war. I embraced what mortals thought of me, and only later did the regret come.

The voice at The Root was not that of Eris, chasing me for stealing her apple. The voice was obviously not Zeus or Ra or Ahura Mazda booming above, nor of Poseidon or old sea gods that crashed from the depths, and it wasn't even a god that could be confused for chaos like Hades or the gods of death that gathered and worried about all the paperwork and judging they'd have to do. There were so many forces, and it was difficult to single out only the tricksters and chaos gods.

Before I could leap into the fight I had with Amar, Scarlett shattered the memory.

She knew me too well.

"Stop," she said.

We were back in darkness, leaving the battle behind.

"I was enjoying that," I said.

"It's not what we're looking for. You're vaguely proud of these memories, but the one we need, you want to forget."

I would take the beating Amar gave me any day. "As usual, you're right. I was hoping the god's wording wasn't intentional. There's only one memory I want to forget. But there's no way the god could know about that."

"What is it?"

"The grave."

"The grave?"

"The one we used to get to the restaurant," I said. "But how could any god know that? It was only Amar and I."

"I was at the restaurant, too."

"Not the restaurant—the memory in the shaker that knocked out Amar—a memory that smells evergreen...."

TWENTY-TWO

I WAS A DEMON

EVERGREENS overlooked the sea. On their mountaintop perch, the world was bright as the future. Skies were limitless, and the seas a mirror. Nature sang sweet smells. Birds darted along fresh winds. The world was pure and pristine.

Except for me.

I was thin as the air. My raven form was gliding rather than flying. The plague I'd caused brought more vengeance than fear. With my vision flickering in and out, so was the memory.

The winds stilled, and unable to keep aloft any longer, I'd have to rest and die and be forgotten.

If it wasn't for a single updraft, history might not've been different, but I would've.

Wind caught my wings, and I floated over tall spruces, buoyed by bouncing off a few dead branches and to a clearing, still barely aloft.

Through darkness, I saw a wood house. This time, the shadow was not my vision or even mine—clouds were coming over the mountain, and the sun was engulfed.

A storm? No. A god. Not the chaos god we were looking for, but a thunder god with a hurtful hammer.

Lost. Out of my element. I needed shelter. I struggled and fought for one more burst of flight to make it to the house.

Thud.

I misjudged where the curtains were and went face-first into the wood wall. If I wasn't a god, I'd be dead, but still, the neck-breaking impact stunned me. And as my vision faded with the memory, I remembered *her* face—a form I'd taken many times since—but this time, the woman was not washed clean by time. She was framed by her long raven-black hair, beautiful in her imperfection; there were no marks or scars, but the imperfection was the hope in her eyes. And that was something I could never replicate.

That memory washed away as I slipped into unconsciousness, but I was left with a lasting feeling—a happiness I'd forgotten.

She sheltered me and deceived the god. The gap between my injury and what came next was warm as the stew she hid me in.

Words embraced me from a memory—the time she realized what I was and did not recoil.

"I'm Zarik."

"Maja."

"Maja what?"

She paused. "Maja Ravn."

"Did you just make that up?"

"I'm as lost as you are," she said with a smile.

Flashes passed. As I watched over her, the house became a village. Maja found love besides me. A child played; I juggled apples for the child and there was laughter—the only thing sweeter than the fruit.

The hillsides grew proud trees and people. My strength returned. There were happy and sad moments. Harsh winters. Relieving rains. I leaned into what was overlooked about age. Wisdom. Growth. And Maja's family flourished.

I couldn't imagine being without her.

I remembered that thought, and the memory it was from, spurring me forward in the simulation and finding familiar eyes. Amar looked at me. I was weary from my long return to my original home, but purpose had driven me there.

"You're still around?" Amar asked, amused as if I were a frail pixie that the god had sent on an almost certainly fatal errand.

"I didn't come for small talk," I said.

"Then why are you here?"

"Something I never thought I'd ask for. Your help."

I couldn't remember how Amar reacted—I looked at the floor in the memory, not even to see my shameful reflection, which was dulled by a rug that burned my feet. But later, I'd come to realize that if anyone was the genie for granting wishes on wording, Amar was one.

"I want you to make a mortal, immortal," I said. "Her name is Maja, and I can't be without her."

Amar, at the time, was plump with belief from the king's descendants. Although such requests were commonplace, they could rarely be granted and were tied to the god. But since Amar and I were already connected, that was good enough.

"I'll do it," Amar said, the agreement possibly coming from remorse of what became of me.

I almost cried at the answer. Joy then. Regret now. How similar the feeling could be.

When I returned in time and memory to Maja, I got to watch her age again. I thought Amar lied to pacify me. But the life god didn't. Maja grew older, but she never died.

As long as I was around, she wrinkled and got sicker. Age makes children into adults and adults into children again. Maja's children took care of her as they grew, but the burden grew heavier than they could carry.

"I could leave," I said to her as she lay infirm. "You'll be better without me."

She smiled, and as often as I tried to replicate that light, there was nothing like it. No fire, no sun could come close; for the first, and maybe the last time, I didn't want to take the light, I wanted to see more of it.

"I must be pitiful if you're crying over me," she said.

I grasped her hand, tender, feeling her frailty. My touch aged her faster. She never pushed me away, only pulling me closer. Devotion echoed through the ages.

"Don't leave," Maja said. "You've been my friend and companion when I had nothing."

"And you were mine when I was nothing." My hand trembled with hers. I could not hold back tears then or now. Never was I happier, and never could I feel as guilty for feeling happy.

She sensed everything in me. "Don't cry. Age is a beautiful thing."

Her eyes shined into mine, filling me with energy. The feeling was more satisfying than the strength of being a great god. The love of one was more treasured than the belief of thousands.

What an odd realization for a god: the most powerful gods and mortals are not those that move mountains, they're the ones that move hearts.

As Maja offered me hope and love, she was left with pain—and sometimes, we have to do things that hurt ourselves for the benefit of those we love. As the memory faded, that thought brought me onwards.

Maja couldn't die of age, but she could die of other causes.

Woods sprouted around me like the memory—evergreen. Ancient and frail, Maja could've been blown away by the breeze, but I had her hand and we walked through familiar forests. No one else would take her out of bed; she outlived her husband, her children, even her grandchildren. All that time, her loyalty to me never faltered; gods rarely have such loyalty, but I learnt it from her.

I could feel the tension of what was coming. Even now, I couldn't bear what I set into motion.

My grief shattered the simulation into fragments. An evergreen was cut and cracked and fell. I choked and cried and yelled and felt blood on my hands. Then, there was grief and guilt—both lasted, indistinguishable.

As much as time should make pain fade, the feeling remained the same and only the interval between moments of grief grew longer, leaving more room to absorb it. Yet, I still wasn't prepared to absorb the pain from what I'd done.

"The god we're looking for isn't in this memory," Scarlett said, cutting the memory off. As if trying to comfort me, she brought the two of us into a VR copy of her apartment, cozy and familiar. Similarly, she kept her words careful, as if sensing I might be barbed and ready for a fight. "What else could the chaos god have meant?"

I didn't need to leave the simulation of Scarlett's apartment to know what the chaos god could've meant, I merely looked out the window at the street and prices on the screen outside.

"Maja and I met again in a different world—this one. I've always thought 'afterlife' was a misnomer. This is still life. An after-world, perhaps. Different groups of gods had their own ideas about what to do with mortals. The Tree of Life had many sprouts and as many factions back then. And despite the name, I started a small part of this grand city with the village of Paradaeza. It wasn't a place of reward or punishment, but one of second chances. I thought that by joining Maja and creating such a place, I could spend at least the rest of my godly life trying to make up for what I had done to her. Yet, the curses and gifts of the gods affect people in this new life."

"Iris' mother?" Scarlett asked, looking at me with softer eyes than the lounger she stood next to.

I nodded. "Her curse reminded me of Maja."

"Our wrongs can make us do right in the future."

"What is right?" I pounded my fist into the wood of my usual seat at the nook. "All I know is I can't change what I've done. I can't make up for what I am. In this life, most people stay in the form of their 'prime'—whatever they define that as—but my presence connected with something in Maja's soul and aged her anyways. I should've known better. I should've stayed away. Or I should've left earlier. But even when I distanced myself, Maja kept aging." I bit my lip, pain releasing sadness. "And when people die here, their souls are destroyed for good."

"The grave to the restaurant is hers, isn't it?" Scarlett said. "People don't bury bodies here anymore."

"It's hers, but I met no gods while Maja was in this world. Most gods were busy on earth still. It's strange that people don't believe in the gods that once walked among them. Yet, I guess when the gods used mortals and gave nothing in return, why bother?"

"Will you show me how it happened?"

I sighed. Despite her care, she wouldn't let me change the subject. Good.

As if going back in time from the world outside the simulation, the futuristic hub reverted to a village and I was at the root, but not The Root, of all the markets now. Shops and stalls. A white-haired Maja ahead of me, no longer smiling, but grimacing.

Her suffering was mine.

"What did you buy?" Scarlett asked, as if in my head.

"A few small things. I don't remember. You're looking too specific, what's important was the general fascination I still have with markets. I look at the prices because it reminds me of that day. I ignored her wishes, and I still don't know if I did the right thing."

"You killed her twice." Scarlett sounded nervous, as if I was different than she expected.

"I'm a daeva. But hurting the only mortal I loved was the only time I thought I was a demon. Maybe believing that opened the door to me becoming one. After this, I went back to the void and the Pull started."

I watched as Maja reached her frail, shaking hand out to pick up a rose. She smelt it and smiled. It was her final smile.

The memory broke and I was plunged into the void and then spat back out into the real world.

Scarlett yanked me out the pod and said, "Were you trying to prove a point? You might be fine ending the simulation that suddenly, but you could've killed me."

"I didn't do that." There was no point in trying to prove I was a demon—I was reminded that I was.

On the screen of the pod ahead of me, there was a phrase printed over a reflection of the living room we were in: "Hello, Scarlett."

If sound could escape the simulation, I thought I would hear a woman's laugh.

"Is that L?" Scarlett asked.

"Seems you didn't get rid of her well enough, you only made her angrier."

Scarlett huffed. "We can find another pod."

"No need. We've seen all we need."

"There was no god in any of those memories."

"And there won't be," I said. "It's a chaos god, why would it tell us how to find it? The god wanted to remind me of the last time I cared for a mortal; to look, to suffer, and cause as much chaos as possible. That's what they do."

Scarlett stood firm. "Everyone has a reason."

"And their reason is chaos. Try finding a pattern in that."

"Maybe we don't have the context yet. If it wants you to look back, that's where we'll go. We don't need a pod to retrace our steps."

"We've already wasted time," I said.

"You wouldn't want to relive every little detail, but this god knows you, not me." She paused, her eyebrow raised as she looked at me.

In the curved reflection of the glass, I saw Maja—without meaning to, I had changed into the younger version of her.

Maybe it wasn't perfect, but it was a tribute and I loved seeing her smile on my face because, even if it wasn't her looking back at me, I was only here because of her.

Scarlett laid a comforting hand on my shoulder. "Maja would forgive you."

I was silent, and as we left Belle's home, my mind was still stuck on the past.

Halfway across the city, I finally asked, "Where are we going?"

"To see what's left of Izak Cayne," Scarlett said. "You said it wasn't him or I that brought you back, but that's where you came back, and that's as good a place as any to start."

TWENTY-THREE

I MISS THE VOID

WE returned to a beginning, finding what seemed rather final. Neighboring apartments had been spared, or at least, repaired already. But past the boarded-up door and renovation notices, Izak's apartment was smolders and rubble. I'd returned to the scene of the crime.

Beams broke through piles of blackness. A life lost more than color, fire burning everything away. One of the few things left was the fireplace I'd formed from.

I coughed as I dug through rubble where the lounger used to be. Scarlett let me search, using her exacting eyes to try and pry something free from the mess.

Like a pig in mud, I felt quite at home in the cinders and charcoal. They were like me, dark and absorbent, merely ruins, relics, and remains. Soot-covered metal cut at my tender hands and I left a few sparkles of gold blood; yet, the pain was deserved.

Under a pile, I found a silver spoon and broken mug. They were clues, but not to what we were looking for—they were clues to what I had done, and I could feel Scarlett's eyes peering through me at the discovery. Obviously, she knew what had happened here with Izak, but seeing it first hand was always different than the idea of it.

"Where did you first arrive?" Scarlett asked.

"The fireplace. That was the light that sparked me."

I took her hint and crawled into the opening. There was even a log left, burnt white and it crumbled as I touched it. I swept away the charcoal to see if there was anything underneath. Covering my mouth, I looked up the chimney and sidings for any clues. Besides burn marks, there was nothing.

"Zarik," Scarlett hissed.

"What?" I spun and bumped my head on the brick.

Scarlett had gone to the apartment door and was peering out into the hallway.

"What?" I repeated.

"The man from The Root."

"Which one?"

"Arrogant. Unpleasant."

"John?"

Scarlett hid inside, while I peeked out, seeing the man strutting around the corner. Before he could see me, I pulled back and closed the door as slow and silent as I could. Footsteps stopped at the apartment next door, and then, I heard the lock click. The door shut behind him.

Scarlett said, "Imagine if I mistakenly knocked on that door instead of the other neighbor's."

"Daza did say John had the biggest aura."

"It seems too obvious."

"Even if he is the chaos god, what are we going to do about it?"

"Something." Scarlett walked into the hallway. "We're going to solve the mystery; whatever happens after that is up to you." She chuckled. "I guess we'll find out what happens if I knocked on that door, anyways."

She knocked on the door before I could stop her.

John opened the door, his slicked back hair straight as his tie.

The element of surprise was my only weapon, and I even surprised myself. I tackled John, bands of shadow restraining. It was pointless. Any formidable god would break free, but Scarlett was right, I had to do something.

Feigning weakness, John barely made a move, shocked.

My voice crackled like fire. "Who are you?"

"I'm John." He regained enough sense to try and wrestle free, but I had him tied down. "Wait, I recognize you."

Scarlett smiled. "Me? Didn't know you could even see beyond yourself."

I shook him. "What sort of god are you?"

"God?" John laughed. "I don't believe in gods."

I darkened the entranceway. "Don't play dumb."

"John," Scarlett said. "Do you really oversee all the trades and reconciliations?"

"Of course I do."

"Zarik, do you think gods are real?"

"Of course I do." My grin became tendrils of darkness, enveloping the room. My presence was louder than fireworks. I felt stronger than I had in a long time.

"Now that you see reality, John," Scarlett said. "Maybe you'll reconsider what your reality is."

"Stop." Panic distorted his over-confident face. "What trick is this?"

Scarlett's fists were clenched. "Tell the truth."

"No, I don't do all that. Oliver is the one who does the work and I just sign off on it. Knowing the right people and how to take credit gets you so much farther."

"You're so full of hot air, it's a wonder you haven't floated off." Scarlett left to the hallway.

I pushed off John and slammed the door behind me. He wasn't the chaos god.

"We need to find Oliver," Scarlett said, looking from the balcony, a complete opposite to the attention she'd paid to me when we'd first met on this walkway. "As much as you and I hate it, we have to call Amar for help. We beat him to the answer, though." She smiled. "Together, you may be able to take down the chaos god. We're close to the truth. You might've even had the chaos god in your hands. When he spoke to you in that voice, it was a trick."

"But how did he know me?" I asked.

"I don't know."

"And why would he let us get so close?"

"To gloat? I don't know." Her brief smile was weighted down by remaining questions, and she gripped hard on the railing. "How can I understand chaos?"

She wanted reassurance, but I had none to offer.

"We missed something," I said.

"It's too late now."

"Not yet—we might still get answers."

"Even with Amar, we don't know what we're walking into."

"We have to try." I laid an arm on her back, and she didn't pull away. "At least we figured it out."

"I'm not so certain we have," she said.

"Oliver is the best answer we have."

Scarlett sent a message to Amar. I looked at prices on my ring. Nothing seemed out of the ordinary.

As we arrived at The Root, everything was normal. The city ran like an unimpeded river. People balanced on the scales of happiness and despair, tilting towards laughter and smiles. The sun was out, and serene green parks offered comparisons and contrast to the dancing colors of markets and business.

Scarlett stopped in the middle of the sidewalk. "We were slow." Scarlett's disappointment made the sunny day seem dark as she read a message on her BioScreen. "Amar figured it out and is already questioning Oliver. Seems the chaos god wasn't a match for Amar."

I said nothing, my rage at being beaten dragging me along to see my defeat. Still, I held onto hope that the chaos god was only toying with Amar. We walked towards the building where Amar and I had questioned Belle. Someone we knew saw us on the street.

Daza ambled towards us through light crowds. "All the disguises and I can still see you a mile away."

"The chaos god has been apprehended," I said.

"You found it?" Daza glanced at The Root. "Did I help?"

"Amar found it. We thought it was John because of you." I softened my words. As much fire as I had, a chaos god was dangerous, and I was relieved the case had been solved. "But in the end, I guess that led us to the conclusion it was Oliver. Amar's questioning him now."

"I've got a break before I'm due at the restaurant. Can I take another look at the chaos god? I can't believe I missed it. I suppose with Amar's aura as dark as shadow and you as bright as a lit candle, gods are more subtle than I thought."

"Before you said I was a snuffed candle." I plumped up. "You're saying I'm brighter now."

"You couldn't have been much dimmer."

"You can come as long as you give Amar a hard time," I said.

Scarlett bit her lip. "If Amar's really stopped the chaos god, that might be hard to do."

"Over the years, I've realized there's an almost equal amount of success and failure. We'll beat Amar next time." My stride was determined; whether Amar bested us here, I was not hopeless.

"Will the next case be as big as a chaos god?" she asked.

She managed to take the shine off my face. "No."

"The two of you are raining on such a bright day," Daza said.

"Amar will have enough optimism for all of us," I said.

The three of us went into the station, where the detective who'd worked with Amar on Belle's case brought us into the fortress of rooms and to the investigation room where Oliver was being held. We watched from behind the one-way glass.

There were more precautions than with Belle. The room merely appeared bright, but it was filled with Amar's oppressive presence.

"We know what you're up to," Amar said.

"Fill me in," Oliver said with a smile reserved for confusion.

"You've been messing with the markets—there's no oversight, anyone who looked at the numbers is conveniently gone, and you're the only one who checks the reconciliations."

"Bob checked it."

"And he figured something was wrong. How long till he was gone?"

"We barely have enough people as is." Oliver shrugged. "If people don't want to listen to even the few words I say, I can't change that."

"You're trying to bring the whole system down. We know what you are."

"Which is?"

"You're a chaos god."

"I'm not."

"You still won't admit it?"

"It wouldn't make it true."

There was a lull. Amar's frustration bubbled, but he checked over his shoulder as if he could feel my presence and pushed the chair in before leaving the room

The life god was not surprised to see us. "Why won't he say it?" Amar asked us in the other room, the door closing behind him.

"If you were sure, you wouldn't be asking," I said.

"I went to capture him and he turned into a centaur to run away."

"You never know what a chaos god will do." I mused. "Maybe he turned into a myth because of the chaos god, or maybe it's trying to lull us into relaxing."

"Maybe it's only a trickster god."

"A trickster god could have this effect on people if they spent enough time in one place," I said. "But if I'm the clue— if what I fear is true and every memory of me was completely forgotten and I returned anyways—we're dealing with something much stronger. Azi Dahaka, Set, and Eris—all chaos gods, all with different levels of power. In the best case, they're not as strong as Zeus or Ra, but they'll still be unpredictable. But if it's something stronger, something from the stories…."

"Gods have myths?" Scarlett asked.

"The original chaos gods that came with creation were gone before I existed," I said. "They're real, we just don't know to what extent."

Amar's BioScreen pinged once, then again, cascading down like the start of a rainstorm on a metal roof.

Reading the messages, Amar's face lost its usual brightness at every passing notification. "I think the god's managed some sort of trick."

We headed for the front of the station. I turned my ring and searched asset prices. Once outside, The Root mirrored my ring—all the prices were red and falling with every ticking second. Then, it stopped. Prices went blank.

So too, did the full extent of The Root become apparent. Whatever technology let light pass through the branches failed, and the whole building above became visible, showing a mess of gardens and elevators and houses in the sky.

The Root left the whole city in its shadow.

Daza laughed, "That'll certainly cause some chaos."

"I don't understand," Amar said. "I removed all of Oliver's technology. Did everything I could to contain him. I suppose it doesn't matter after all; he was just toying with us."

"We've still got him," I said.

"If he was still in the room, this wouldn't be happening," Amar said, and his BioScreen went dark. "We've been tricked."

The Root was not withered, but the people coming from it were. Vacant stares were bigger shocks than the failed technology.

"Or maybe the trick hasn't happened yet," I said.

"I have to see what I can do to minimize the damage," Amar said.

"So you can take the credit, Detective A?"

"Better than the blame," Amar said. "Unless you know how to fix this?"

"No."

"It's settled then. I'll get the system going again."

Amar left.

"It's not settled," I said. "Scarlett?"

"We've all been blind." She was the quietest I'd heard her, and she held a hand on the silver chain around her neck—unlike normal, she didn't spin it, only her knuckles turning white around it.

She unclasped it and handed it to me. "Take care of this for me."

Now, I was worried.

I tried to subtly say I wanted her to stay. "We still have a chance to catch Oliver—or this chaos god. It could be a trick to escape."

"Zarik's right, better to be certain that he's gone," Daza said.

Scarlett frowned, but her eyes met mine with the glimmer that comes with a hopeful smile. "I won't be any help with that—you go. I have an idea."

Without enlightening us what it was, she strode off with purpose, not towards home, but towards the trunk of The Root.

I wanted to follow her, but she did not want me. Left with Daza, we walked back inside, and I asked, "What does a chaos god's aura look like?"

"At a glimpse, nothing special," Daza said with a shrug. "The better the look, the more it's like looking into the abyss. Not nothing—but not something either."

We returned to the interrogation room.

Sure enough, the door was open. I opened it just to check that Oliver was gone and Daza followed me in. There was no one.

"You know," Daza said. "Abyss isn't the right word—a chaos god's aura looks a lot like the void."

I examined the door handle and frame; everything looked normal. "Did someone leave the door open?"

"I did," Daza said. "Here, let me close it."

Without touching it, the metal door slammed shut with abnormal force, locking us in together.

When I first met him, I did say Daza looked *too* normal.

TWENTY-FOUR

I AM ZARIK

"YOU'RE the chaos god?" I asked.

Daza said, "Some call me Te Kore. Others, Ginnungagap—I think that's the most enjoyable to say. But you call me the void. In many mythologies, they say the universe was created from chaos. They are not wrong. From nothing—from me—gods appear and disappear. You know that well. You were lost, and I gave you another chance."

"You were a terrible waiter, but you might be even worse at choosing gods."

"Where's your usual ego?" Daza smiled, and his wrinkled white shirt turned black as space. Then, the wrinkles didn't show. "Collared shirts are the worst. They're the only thing more limiting than taking form."

"Everyone finds their limit eventually, like me and my ego." Even in the face of my doom, I had to keep a sense of humor. Especially then.

"We're kindred opposites. You funnel yourself into a neat container of what you are, and I go the other way." He laughed, changing form into a powerful python with a fox head, slithering around the floor without missing a beat. "The

350

truth is, I could've brought back a thousand more powerful gods. I could've made Thor quake the world to bits. I could've made Guanyin heal it. I could've brought back the victor of the gods to rule everything. But I choose a lost god to counter me, and I did not choose wrong."

"I didn't suspect you."

The snake-fox Daza wrapped around a table leg, weaving over himself like tangled yarn. "You hadn't figured it out yet, but I think Scarlett did. I could tell by the look in her eyes when she left." He completed a loop and tied into a knot. "I'm surprised she did not discover me earlier. I almost hoped for it; playing a set part is so tiring. Even when the end is constant, my path wanders and focusing in the moment is difficult. As Daza, I took a lot of breaks, and when working at The Root, I ate constantly. When you wanted my two disguises in the same place, it was too late. My analyst form already faked a heart attack because you were close. Then, after saving Oliver, I gave you the push I thought you needed. You were the first of your pantheon to embrace the void. I knew something made you want to be forgotten, and it could only be because of something you wanted to forget. I thought you would've realized I was the void, but you must've not taken my advice again."

"I saw Azi Dahaka in the void, but I didn't expect you to take form," I said. "If I knew, I'd be hiding in the desert as the world's smallest sand mite instead of being here. However, my trip through memory lane was interrupted, and I didn't get the misfortune of seeing what happened after Maja was gone or the time to connect it to what you said. Amar already found Oliver before we could retrace our steps any further."

There was a pop, as if the snake had been tied too tight, bursting into brief smoke that floated up and onto the table, reforming into a black jaguar with vulture wings folded on its sides.

Others might be taken aback, but to me, this was all normal. If I had the power to waste, I would've tried to outdo the forms—but I would need every ounce of power I had for what might come.

"I'd find you anyway." The lower canines grinned under a cavernous mouth. "There's no reason to hide."

"That depends on how powerful you are in this form. But you must not be very concerned if you told us about the ninth floor."

"It wouldn't be chaos if I had my way without any obstacles." The vulture wings flapped, the tips of the feathers scrapping the low ceiling. Despite powerful wingbeats, Daza did not fly. "Seems I've put on weight." The wings folded back down and the jaguar lay, paws crossed. But, as if proving a point that the god could fly like any good reality-bending power, the jaguar levitated an inch over the table. "Izak Cayne wanted a demon, and I gave him you. Scarlett thought she made you. Partially true. All I know is the chaos you brought into the equation was a better meal than the apple pie I baked."

I took a seat. So far, a very quaint chat. "How did you do it?"

"The pie?" Yellow cat eyes glared at me. Even Daza's eyes changed easily. There was nothing set about him, a true master of disguise.

"The pie was the best I've ever had," I said. "But I should've been more specific."

"Sorry to disappoint," Daza said. "But I never write down a recipe; otherwise, I would've brought you a final meal if you wanted it."

"That's too bad." I did not lean away or search for an exit; I always knew this day might come. Instead, my only way to survive a few more minutes was to look for an opportunity to keep Daza talking. "I meant, how did you do all of it—how did you bring me back, how did you mess with The Root, and how did you know Rodrigo would be arrested so you could come into the investigation?"

"Rodrigo is the easiest answer—that was your choice. If anything, that took me down a different path." Daza yawned. The jaguar laid its head down and like wax, began to melt. The liquid condensed and Daza became an octopus on the table, splayed out and squishy. "Too messy?"

I nodded.

"I suppose I owe you an explanation for waking you so rudely." Daza transformed into a huge black spider with a scorpion tail. "There had to be balance for me to take form and destabilize the world. With my return, opposite gods such as life and death, served as counterweights. Amar and you were the first, but time is a fickle thing, and we arrived offset. I already learned everything about Amar—rather straightforward—but you were harder to know. As you investigated me, I investigated you. With some digging, I found the restaurant and the chef, deciding to wait for you there. You walked in, and I was close to an answer—the shaker was the clue to the past that connected us. That memory led you to the void, and that's what's important."

"Actually, that memory saved me from the void for a while," I said.

"But it made you what you are."

As much as I wanted to ask why that was important, I found an opportunity to stall. "What about The Root?"

"The Root? I won't bore myself with answering that question. I am one of the oldest beings in the universe. I think I can learn finance." Daza's scorpion tail flicked back and forth, annoyed. "But still, you wouldn't believe all I had to go through as an analyst. I'm old. I forget things. Who remembers the butterfly bond strategy?"

"If it's anything like real butterflies, it would taste through its feet."

Daza the spider grew a cartoon mouth to grin. "I was good at what I did, though. It helps when you can get rid of any oversight." The spider scuttled around the table, growing an extra leg every time it paced back and forth. "Yet, I couldn't work at The Root and be involved in your investigation as Daza at the same time." The spider stopped and piercing eyes stared at me like orbs of deep-space. "You think these questions distracted me? No. They converge into a single answer. That small choice with Rodrigo defied my expectations and changed only the form of my ultimate purpose with you and The Root."

"Which is?"

"You're dim, but I only thought in the literal light sense."

"You want to absorb gods like Amar and I, then cause chaos," I said. "That's the only plan—well, I guess plan would be the wrong word—something like you can have. But in what form?"

"Exactly." The mess of legs tangled, and Daza tumbled like a wheel over the edge of the table and into the seat across from me. When Daza reappeared, he was dressed as Daza had been in his human form, except with a coyote head on his shoulders. "All my work was going to send the world to the stone age again. There might not be as much chaos then, but the path back would've been filled with it." An anteater tongue licked coyote lips. "This was only the first step to a world where nothing would've been traded except in sheep and salt. People would turn back to the gods and myths I brought back. What would come next, I don't know, and that would've been delightful."

"I didn't think chaos was supposed to be evil."

"Evil?" Daza's eyes dilated angry and then gentle. "No, not evil. A new beginning. We're in a cycle. It swings one way and another. Good would've done good, evil would've done evil. You know that well. Or, maybe, the only result of my work would've been to take down The Root for an afternoon and everyone would have a pleasant day off."

I couldn't tell whether the chaos god was serious.

Daza's hopeful coyote eyes glimmered as much as the smiling canines. "As much 'bad' as I could've created, there would be good, too. I sometimes make beautiful chaos."

The door handle jiggled, and Daza snarled at it. The noise stopped.

Unlike a calculated mastermind or an improviser that could adapt to anything, the chaos god adapted the world instead. What struck me most was how the god could snap from benevolent to malevolent, happy to angry, and still find a continuous, winding string in the chaos.

"Must be door mice," Daza said with a dry humor that was the only constant because it was unpredictable. "But we're talking so much about me. Let's talk about you. That's why we're here." Like wiping away a mask, Daza's coyote head vanished and he became human once more—the same Daza that seemed all too normal. "I brought back an unknown god. Yet, still, I choose one that was bound to specific purposes. Aren't you curious why?"

"Can I say no?"

"It'd be funny if you did." Daza smiled. "Without a purpose for the first time in so long, you'd have to discover one. And free will is chaos."

"When was I free? You've been pushing me the whole time."

"You had more freedom than I ever expected." Daza licked his lips. "You made your own choices. Life and death ones. Some might be considered good, like not killing at Rodrigo's request."

"That was because of Scarlett," I said. "She would've hated me."

In my hand, I still had Scarlett's pendant. The touch was reassuring, and like she did, I fiddled with it under the table.

"You still aren't sure you have choices?" Daza asked.

"I have some."

"You don't want to," Daza said in an unjudgmental tone.

I grimaced. "Maybe I don't have a choice about choices."

"You could've killed Lars, but you gave him the evidence."

Daza was the one offering me evidence, now. I shrugged. "He still died."

"You could've killed Steve, but you aged him instead," Daza said.

"I thought that was a fair punishment."

Daza slunk in the chair, and I expected him to melt, but he merely sat lazy, remaining human. "Maybe you made good choices, but you are a killer at heart, aren't you? You were planning on killing Lars?"

"I was."

"And you killed blindly with Gwen and Izak."

"I did."

"But those didn't make you a demon. What changed you was this Maja you mentioned. This was someone you loved and ended up destroying because of what you are, right? How could you ever make up for that?"

"You're right—I can't," I said. Without Daza's flashy transformations, the humanizing affect brought my focus back to myself. I would've preferred the octopus on the table. "Is curiosity the only reason I'm alive still?"

"You misunderstand." Daza met my eyes with comfort. "I'm offering you a chance to make a good choice before you harm the people you care about." The god's voice was serene. Welcoming, like the void itself was. "Wouldn't you like to have peace again? You can be back in the void, where you'll never have another reason to feel guilty."

I knew temptation when I heard it—but that didn't make it sound less appealing. I held Scarlett's pendant tighter in my right hand. Opposite to what she might've intended, it was the best argument to accept Daza's offer.

"You didn't just do harm," Scarlett yelled through the door.

"Scarlett?"

"You'll kill her eventually," Daza said, seemingly not surprised that Scarlett was back. "Would you prefer to dream of being a cat, sleeping in the nook? I could arrange that."

Scarlett yelled again, "I told you I wanted your help, and I still do. You can be a positive force."

"Look what you offered my mom—peace." The other voice was Iris.

That took me by surprise, but even more surprising, Iris spoke at a normal tone. I could hear her clearly through the door and whatever Daza was doing to keep them out.

Of course. Iris was at least somewhat immune to godly powers. I smiled. Maybe she could keep Scarlett safe.

Contrary to her calm voice, Iris pushed against the door, but her immunity did not mean strength. The door was still locked.

"We're talking." Daza waved at the door like saying goodbye to them, and no more sound came. "Don't worry, despite how rude they're being trying to interrupt our little chat, I don't intend on hurting them. I just want our conversation to be private. Yet, they're a good reminder. You're not Scarlett. Not Iris. And they don't know you."

From this side of the one-way mirror, I caught the reflection of myself. My own judgment stared back in the form of Maja. Even if Scarlett saw me from the other side, she had only seen the surface of my past. "Besides Maja, I've done more to deserve being called a demon, no matter how I dislike it."

There was a click from the door. The lock had come undone.

"What now?" Daza asked, annoyed.

"Apparently Scarlett was telling the truth," I said. "She can lockpick."

Iris pushed the door ajar.

"You found the weirdest companions," Daza said to me, forcing the door mostly shut with godly power, almost like suction.

"I know." A sad smile. "But despite my best intentions, eventually, all I bring is destruction. My very touch threatens to kill those I care about. This time, it'll be their souls that are gone for good and not just their bodies."

"An end is inevitable." Scarlett said through the gap. "I'm not scared."

Iris pushed again at the door, but it didn't budge past the small gap. She had hit the limit of her immunity.

Daza frowned, having drawn a line in how far he would let the door open. "What is it you want, Zarik? From what I've learned about you, the only thing you think can make up for your past is to save the world."

"You're not wrong."

"Opposing me might seem like that, but no one has ever saved the world," Daza said. "It will exist with or without us, without joy or happiness, sadness or pain. What does age and wisdom bring? Out of darkness, of fear, of blood, of oppression, of inequality, humanity pulls itself out of one sin and into another. Human history is not a march forward, but a winding path to nowhere. There is no end, except death, destruction, and chaos. A path you know well."

"Somehow mortals move forwards anyways," I said, offering what might be a final comfort for Scarlett. "There may be a long way to go, but from my first days, I've seen those who worked for the world to be fairer, happier, and better."

"It took great gods. Great heroes. Those who moved mountains out of the chaos. As much as you might want to be one, you are not."

"I'm not," I said. "But the world did not change solely at those hands. What seems like chaos is only what we can't understand. What we have now was molded by the hands of everyone that came before—Iris told me something like that—we all have our part, good or bad." I hoped she heard me. "The world doesn't require anyone, but making a small change in the world is the biggest step anyone can take. Infinitely more than doing nothing. I don't have to change the world. I want to change what I can—who I am."

"Sounds like you already have," Daza said.

"Daza?" There was another voice outside the door. This time, it was Amar. "I told you mortals with the sight are crazy."

"Daza, the chaos god," Scarlett answered.

"More company?" Daza frowned, but returned back to me. "But as you said, it will never be enough to make up for your past."

"All you say is sweet and sour half-truths." If I survived, I was going to steal Daza's form for temptation—no. That would be wrong. And fun. Maybe I could find a good use for it. "There's more than what you're saying, Daza. I may never move mountains, but I can move hearts. I can't make up for my past, but I can make my future. And you may be chaos, but you're not all of it."

Daza nodded. "I'm contained. If you join the void once more, I'll take Amar, too. Isn't that what you always wanted? Mutual destruction. One day, it will happen. Time will make me stronger. There will be other gods. But for now, I'm offering you the choice—that's what makes you more than a meaningless obstacle. Like your past with Maja, look at Scarlett and that pendant that haunts her. I can see it in her eyes. For a mortal, that made her quite the fun adversary. But we can only play for so long. As you have seen so many others at the end, I will see you. You can delay the inevitable. I won't mind. But you'll destroy those around you. Is that what you want?"

I was holding onto Scarlett's pendant so tight, it seemed to burn into my palm. But in the belief she had for me, there was strength. "It's a false choice."

"What is today or tomorrow to you or me?"

I stayed silent. My thoughts were empty, too. Instead, I felt something similar to the Pull tugging at me. But I was not a demon. Instead of letting it take me, I grabbed on and pulled back.

Daza motioned to the door. "Don't you care about them? You're a death god. You know what that means."

I did, but I also knew a god of life. Last time I asked Amar for help, it ended up destroying me. But that was the past, and this was an opportunity to move forward.

"Amar!" I called to the door. "I need you to push the door!"

My counterpart had changed, too, and had enough sense not to question me for once. Light pushed at the door in beams, and I pulled from this side, shadowy tendrils trying to pull the door open. Together, Amar and I's power was enough to edge the door open. A butterfly's wingspan. A raven's. Soon, it would be enough for us to join together to face Daza. Despite all the changes of forms and displays of power, I reasoned there was a motive for all the talk—the chaos god really was still weak.

"I think you solved Scarlett's mystery," Daza said, his face showing the slightest flicker of strain. "Gods can change."

"What happens now?" I asked between gritted teeth.

"I do think you make a good detective." Daza exhaled. "In the future, I won't underestimate Scarlett—she's clever and understands what seems like chaos."

"But not herself."

"See. Good detective." Daza poofed into smoke, his voice drifting down on me. "She must really care for you to give you that pendant. I hope you don't betray that."

The force on the door disappeared as the smoke snuck out the room through the tiniest of cracks in the ceiling.

I could stymy Daza's plans, even if I could not stop him entirely. That was better than nothing.

The door opened, and Scarlett was the first to venture inside.

I greeted her with an embrace. "Guess you'll have to keep me around a while longer."

"I'm glad you chose to stick around."

"Did you think I would?" I asked, releasing her.

She smiled. "Does it matter?"

"No." I offered the pendant, but I closed my palm before she could grab it. "I'll give it back if you tell me what it means."

For a second, I thought she wouldn't play my little game. Instead, she whispered an answer. "It's how I died."

"You died from an apple seed?" I asked.

"You make it sound so simple."

I handed it over. "With you, nothing is that simple."

Scarlett put the necklace back on and shyly went up to Iris, who stood awkwardly at the door. For a moment, I thought Scarlett might slip by to avoid her, but instead, Scarlett hugged Iris in the same way the necklace clasped around her neck. "Thank you. I owe you more than you know."

Iris was taken aback, her bangles jangling as she debated hugging Scarlett back. She did, for the record.

"You don't owe me anything," Iris said. "I wanted to help."

Amar interrupted my view of Scarlett and Iris. "That doesn't count as solving the mystery. Daza revealed himself to you."

"Don't be sore," I said. "Surely the time I bit you doesn't still hurt."

I twisted my ring and an alert popped up with the title: "The markets will be offline for the rest of the day. Trading will resume tomorrow at the normal time."

Amar said, "See. I told you I could take care of it."

"Thanks, but you didn't foil Daza completely. Everyone still got the day off."

"What?"

"You can take the credit, but I'll always know we didn't do too bad working together."

"Don't get used to it."

I laughed, and for the first time in ages, I was happy—enough to not care what Amar said. In every long-enough-lived life, there were one or two sweet moments that surpassed all others. Besides all the apples, I knew there would be more sweet moments to come. Despite my past, I am Zarik—death, daeva, and now, detective.

That was my choice.

Darius Ebrahimi is inspired by his Persian-American heritage, world travels, and love of mythology. A graduate of CU Boulder and UT Austin, with a BA in Economics and MS in Finance respectively, Darius decided to follow his heart and has been writing full-time since 2018. He is currently living in San Francisco with his calico cat, Ivy, and is working on his next book.

I hope you enjoyed the book as much as Ivy liked
sitting on it. If so, please leave a review and
expect more from Scarlett and Zarik.